Fletcher Moss

Folk-lore, Old Customs and Tales of my Neighbours

Fletcher Moss

Folk-lore, Old Customs and Tales of my Neighbours

ISBN/EAN: 9783744778954

Printed in Europe, USA, Canada, Australia, Japan

Cover: Foto ©Andreas Hilbeck / pixelio.de

More available books at **www.hansebooks.com**

FOLK-LORE

Old Customs and Tales of my Neighbours

By

FLETCHER MOSS

Of The Old Parsonage
Didsbury

Author of "A History of Didsbury," "Didisburye in the '45
and "The Chronicles of Cheadle."

Also Vice-Chairman of the Withington Urban District Council,
and Member of the Manchester City Council.

" A quaint and curious volume of forgotten lore"

Published by the Author from his home *The Old
Parsonage, Didsbury;* and from his room in *The
Spread Eagle Hotel, Hanging Ditch, Manchester.*
March 1898

Printed by BALLANTYNE, HANSON & Co.
At the Ballantyne Press

To

The good old folk,
whose lore with love I learnt,
and tales I heard with joy,
this book I fondly dedicate

Preface

HE greater part of the contents of this
book consists of a series of articles
that originally appeared in *The Manchester City News*, which were inspired by a pamphlet sent from the
Committee of the British Association for the Ad-
vancement of Science, appointed to organise an Ethnographical Survey of the United Kingdom, to the
Lancashire and Cheshire Antiquarian Society, with a
request for information and answers to several questions. Having some knowledge of the subject, with
unusual advantages for acquiring more, and a fondness
for the work, it was left with me to take up the subject, which I readily did, getting more and more
interested in it as it grew upon me. The articles
in the press, which I hoped would elicit information
as well as give it, caused a much wider interest in
the matter than I expected, though they did not
bring much information. That was mainly derived
from two sources—my father's kindred, especially the
branch still living at Standon Hall, the well-remem-
bered tales of childhood, and my father's childhood,

and the extraordinary local knowledge of Thomas Bailey of Gatley, who told me so many things relating to the history of Gatley and its neighbourhood. His knowledge was mainly derived from his grandfather, who must have been well acquainted with the tales and customs which were dying out from sixty to seventy years since in the district of Gatley, the extreme northern part of Cheshire. The halls of Mees, Walford, and Standon, where my father's ancestors lived, are in Staffordshire, near to the borders of Shropshire and Cheshire. Therefore the district of the following tales and folk-lore may be said to be that which has Didsbury on the Lancashire border for its extreme north, extending forty miles due south ; or, approximately, the county of Cheshire.

It is not nearly so easy to get authentic information as many people suppose. The great difficulty, as in so many other affairs, is to get at the truth. There are few who say they believe in ghosts, but we must needs beware how we write of haunted houses. A gentleman who gave me permission to write what I liked of his house, which was reputed to be haunted, sent a man-servant down in haste with a note, saying his wife would not allow such a thing to be mentioned on any account.

The two simple-looking questions, "When does the new year popularly begin?" and "What is the first food given to a new-born babe?" brought forth extraordinary answers. With regard to the latter I found that very few indeed were even the fathers of families who knew, and the mothers often objected to the question, or did not tell the truth. The doctors

did not always know, for they were deceived or misled in their turn, and the information I obtained and
published has been often commented upon, and has
been of use to Boards of Guardians and others.

The first seven chapters are much more discon-
nected and rambling than the others, for they are
composed of bits published separately, and replies
to querists or correspondents, which I have tried to
weave together.

To learn a tale it is often necessary to tell a tale.
People will tell things to those who have their confidence, which they will flatly deny to any one who
seems to them to be inquisitive, or to be a superior
person trying to get something from them.

The dialect should, on the whole, be considered
as the dialect of Cheshire. It may differ slightly
and be somewhat confused in my own mind if it
come from the Standon district, or the Gatley and
Didsbury district; but these places, if not actually in
Cheshire, are adjoining it, and have approximately
the same dialect and pronunciation. The natives of
Didsbury used to have Stockport in Cheshire for
their market town and court town, they knew little
or nothing of Manchester; now the old natives are
scarce, and Didsbury is a large suburb of Manchester.
The dialect of the old natives of the latter place and
Lancashire generally always seemed to me to be
much harder and harsher than that of the slower
and broader speech I had been accustomed to as a
child, with the farm - labourers, gamekeepers, and
country folk of Standon and Didsbury.

The tales of my neighbours in the latter part of

the book include some experiences of modern elec-
tioneering, for the man who goes canvassing falls
among thieves and good Samaritans, and has them
all for neighbours, as if he lived between Jerusalem
and Jericho. In the rural rides, or pilgrimages to
places of historic interest, we see our neighbours
under other guise. It has been a deep, unfeigned
pleasure to see our beautiful country, and to hear
the quaint tales and lore of our country folk. If
others may here share it, and this book be a memento
of it, I am content.

FLETCHER MOSS.

THE OLD PARSONAGE.
    DIDSBURY.

Contents

List of Illustrations

FULL-PAGE ILLUSTRATIONS

The Illustrations are mostly from photographs by the Author, reproduced by A. Brothers & Co., Ltd., *of Manchester.*

ILLUSTRATIONS IN TEXT

ILLUSTRATIONS xvii

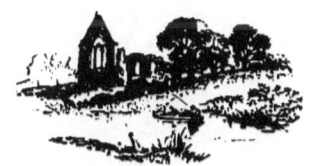

CHAPTER I

BIRTH

HAT is the first food given to a baby? Let us begin at the beginning of separate existence and inquire what is this most important first food with which we begin our life. Very few people know, and those who do know will not always tell, or tell the truth. Bachelors, in their bashful and blissful ignorance, and simple-minded persons of both sexes, would suppose that the natural food is the first food, but that is very seldom a fact. Doctors do not always know, for that important personage the monthly nurse, who rules the roost when an interesting event comes off, has what she calls thoughts of her own, and says, "Drat them doctors, what does men know?"

Leaving out of consideration the miserable things that are brought up "by a bottle," it appears to be a fact that even in the best regulated families the natural food is not generally available at first, and something else is substituted. What, then, is this important article, our first food? The commonest answer is,

A

"Butter and sugar," and very similar answers are,
"Sweetened cream," and "Butter and honey."

In fact these three answers may be taken as one,
for if we consider that sugar was formerly unknown or
very much dearer than it is now, and that honey was
cheaper, it is evident that sugar is only a makeshift for
the honey. In country places honey was formerly an
ordinary article of food, used to sweeten things, and
eaten with bread instead of toasted cheese and ale, the
common supper of our grandfathers. A well-known
passage in Isaiah says, "Butter and honey shall He
eat, that He may know to refuse the evil and choose
the good," and it also shows the great antiquity of
some of our common customs, customs that are passed
by unnoticed and unheeded even by those who observe
them. Other answers are, "Skimmed milk and water,"
evidently the answer of a "skinny scrat," or, in more
fashionable phrase, an ultra-economist. "Castor-
oil"!!! What horrible stuff to begin life on, surely
this is doctoring gone crazy. "Some warm water
with just a leetle drop of gin, and happen a lump o'
sugar." Oh yes! we know who wants the gin; but
there is no harm in asking innocent questions. "What
do we give 'em gin for? why, to wicken 'em, to be
sure; it takes th' 'umours out of their little in'ards, an'
mak's 'em as wick as wick. They soon gets to like a
drop o' gin; only just a drop, mind you." "Wouldn't
milk do better? not it, indeed; such stuff, it 'ud turn
to crud on its little stomach an' happen kill it, ask any
doctor."

Certainly many doctors have a great antipathy to
milk, for every doctor who has ever spoken to me on
the subject has told me that my practice of having a
basin of new milk every night and morning is exceedingly bad for me; fortunately I never heeded them,

and I have stuck to the new milk for more than fifty years. Some of them say milk should never be taken without whisky "to kill it," and one of our medical men of high standing took the trouble to explain to me, and give as his professional opinion, that if I took a basin of new milk at night it would form a compact mass of curd, a small cheese in fact, and keep me awake all night and be there next morning. To which I replied, "Then first thing in the morning I should have another, that would be cheese number two, and a third the next night, and so on." The subject was not discussed much further. I mention this to show that ignorant women, with their horror of milk and their fondness for gin, are backed by authority, and the majority of people neglect the best food on earth, or spoil it with stimulants. It used to be said that jockeys were reared on gin to make them little and sharp, and give them a short life and a merry one.

Here are the words of a great-grandmother, still hale and hearty, who likes her toasted cheese and swig for supper. "Well, old Betty Trickett was the most famous midiff in these parts. She brought all mine into the world, and the first thing she did was to bind their little heads with linen bandages as tight as she could bind them, with a bit of flannel on the top, and these bandages were kept on for six weeks; then she gave them rue tea. She was a grand midiff was Betty, but she's been dead fifty years. She died on her hands and knees on her cottage floor, poor old body, thrashing out her leaze corn that she had gleaned on Stawne flats." She evidently preferred the "straitened forehead of the fool" to the expansion of the intellect; and rue tea! rue, the bitterest herb in the garden, the type and emblem of sorrow, remorse, and regret.　She literally made the poor little beggars "rue the day they were born"; and yet the rue tea cannot have been injurious, like gin or castor-oil, for another aunt of mine, who has had some experience, says that she had Betty Trickett and her rue tea to the first seven of her children.　Then as Betty became older and somewhat drunken, she had another nurse, who gave castor-oil, and the next three children died very soon, so she made no account of the castor-oil and went back to the rue tea for the remainder of her family, and the net result showed ten children reared who were started on rue, and three killed with castor-oil.　Her mother also reared twelve out of thirteen on rue tea, and as they mostly lived to old age, and none of them, male or female, were under five feet six in height, the rue tea could not have given them a bad start.　It was said they all would have lived if one had not been called Anne, for no Anne or Hannah Moss had ever lived many days after being christened (but that is a tale for another chapter).

It is very natural that when any child first appears on the scene of life any little peculiarity about it should cause those who are interested in it to see omens, and from their wisdom and knowledge of mystical lore to form conclusions, and to make guesses or prophecies as to its future life.

I find there is a very unanimous belief that if a child is born with teeth it will be "a hard-bitten one," one that "will have hold somehow," and probably be unlucky; or, if apparently prosperous, its selfish and grasping life will end disastrously.　That is the belief of the common folk about us to-day, and it coincides exactly with the beliefs of the kings and queens of England four or five hundred years ago, for remembering that Shakspere wrote of King Richard the

Third as "the dog who had his teeth before his eyes,"
and "who munched a crust at two hours old," I again
read his noted tragedy, and found it to be full of
allusions to what is now called folk-lore—the birds
of ill-omen are continually croaking and chattering,
"the chattering pies in dismal discords sung," the
bewitched arm, the dead body of a murdered man
bleeding afresh on the approach of the murderer, the
haunting ghosts, and in the last scene of "King
Henry the Sixth" the reader will find another bit
of old folk-lore that is still believed in. It is just
before the following lines :—

> "The midwife wondered, and the women cried,
> 'Oh, Jesus bless us! he is born with teeth.'
> And so I was, which plainly signified
> That I should snarl, and bite, and play the dog."

Our people have only known one man "from start
to finish" who was born with teeth, and he certainly
was unlucky, for he died a bachelor. There are
others living, but on the principle of calling no man
happy till he's dead, it is better to say nothing about
them.

The popular opinion respecting any one who should
happen to be born with a caul is very favourable. It
is even said there is a distinct money value in a dried
caul, for sailors will give several pounds for them, as
they are believed to be an infallible safeguard from
drowning, and therefore most valuable in shipwreck.
Sir John Offley, one of the ancestors and endowers
of the Lords Crewe of Crewe, left the caul in which
he was born to his heirs male, with the pretty little
village of Madeley, near Crewe, strictly enjoining that
it should never be hidden or concealed.

The beliefs and omens about birth marks, mothers'

or longing marks, moles, and warts, are more numerous than it is well to express. It must suffice to say
that there is a firm belief, apparently backed by an
abundance of testimony, that children are marked and
influenced by some act or desire of their mothers
before they are born. This has given rise to a
common saying, "We must not have the child
marked." I will give one instance only, there being
many others more or less similar, and in some cases
a remark was made at the time (that is, before the
birth, not after it) that the child would be marked, and
it was marked. My father was born in the month of
June, when no one would think of partridge shooting,
and he had a very distinct mark of a partridge behind
his ear. The tale, well noticed at the time, is, that
some time before his birth his father was going out
with his gun, and his mother begged of him to shoot
her a partridge. This was not done, and the mother
in an irritated manner scratched behind her ear and
marked the child.

When I was writing some of these articles and
studying folk-lore, a curious popular superstition was
forced on my notice, and the truth of it in that case,
at least, was demonstrated. A man-servant who had
been with me some years, and whose wife was in the
family way, became strange in his conduct. He would
groom the horses and do his work before any one was
up in the morning, and then absent himself. He
went steadily worse, until the work was not done at
all, and I was gravely told that it was because he was
"breeding"; his wife was going to have a child. He
had two little girls, and had not been affected before;
but this time, I was told, it was different—the child
would be a boy. Shrewd, sensible men told me so,
and I watched the case. At the same time we had

an old cow that was behindhand with her calving, and knowing the farmers' experiences with cattle, I expected, and went so far as to offer to make a small wager with some neighbours, that when the cow calved the calf would be a bull, and also probably of a dark-red colour. The man went worse, until he was quite off his mind, and his wife had to have him taken care of. At last she got her trouble over—a boy who weighed eleven pounds—and the man returned to his work all right the next day. I watched the whole case most closely, and was much struck with it. The cow also did as I expected, bringing a big, rough, red bull calf.

Another curious fact regarding this man is, that his name is Crispin, and his occupation was a horse-soldier or trooper; he was born in barracks (and so was his wife), and his father's name and occupation were as his. When I was reading Freeman's "History of the Norman Conquest," I read that a certain mounted soldier named Crispin came over at the Conquest, and had lands granted him at Exeter and Daventry. I at once went to the stable to ask Crispin where his family came from; and after some little hesitation, saying they were always soldiers in the Fifth Dragoon Guards, he said the family came from Exeter, and he never saw the name but there and at Daventry or Oxford.

One of the questions asked by the folk-lorists is, "Does the father's position alter immediately after the birth of a son?" Judging from the answers I received from my friends who are fathers, to the simple question, "What is the first food given to a baby?" I should say their position does alter very considerably, for they know very little indeed about what is being done in their house at that time. They are

more or less politely informed that they must find
some money, and then go about their business, and
not bother.

There is also a curious piece of folk-lore—that it
is very unlucky to weigh babies. They are gifts from
the Lord, and are not to be weighed or measured,
though it is permissible to count them when they are
numerous, or they may get mixed with other people's.
Remembering that David got into trouble for number-
ing Israel, I have searched the Scriptures to find if
there was any reason given as to why it was wrong to
take a census. The old book merely says that the
Lord moved him to do so, and then punished him for
doing it; which seems rather hard on David. In
another place it says Satan provoked him to do it;
and as the accounts are rather contradictory, I had
better leave them to professors and divines learned
in inspiration and infallibility. Utterly reckless of all
consequences, the women weighed a baby that my
man-servant above-mentioned had born to him, and
it weighed eleven pounds. So, when they are proud
of something, they chance the future. It is said to be
very bad to rock an empty cradle. I asked if this
were true; the aunt mentioned above, who had reared
ten children, who were started in life with rue tea, and
lost the others, whose first food had been castor-oil,
said she always kept her cradle full, and lazy folk
ought to be unlucky. The answer is worthy of being
put on record. An old notion was that it was every
one's duty to rear soldiers for the king. We are
getting past that nowadays.

There appears to be an old custom with some
people to take a child upstairs (if possible) to the top
of the house before it is taken downstairs, this being
symbolical of its going to heaven. We were all taken,

dressed in our best bib and tucker, with bells and coral at our girdle, for our first visit to some one who was known to be "a good sort." The good Samaritan gave us bread and salt and silver. Sometimes an egg was added, and the whole was given in a small oval basket for good hansel. The silver might be anything from a bent sixpence or old coin to a silver mug, and the giver was henceforth supposed to be interested in the little darling who unconsciously received the gift. In my case, I was taken to a Mrs. Fielden, of the Todmorden family, who gave me a silver "bank token," marked "XXX Pence Irish," which token I still have.

There should always be butter and honey, or rum and honey, or rum in the tea, at a christening feast, or for the first callers. I should think this custom had its origin in every one being supposed to taste the butter and honey given to the child, and then rum would be provided for those who preferred it. The tea must be a modern invention.

Here is an old rhyme that should be comforting to some folks :—

"If there's a mole above your chin,
You need never be beholden
To any of your kin."

There are plenty of rhyming proverbs taught to children about trivial matters that are scarcely worth remembering. For instance, if a mark appears on a nail on the hand—

"A gift on the thumb
Is sure to come ;
A gift on the finger
Is likely to linger."

For small ailments children were bathed in water from a holy well or celebrated spring, of which there

were some in most districts, and it was often the last
thorough washing they ever got, even though they
lived to be old. A native of Didsbury told me that
he had not washed all over for more than sixty years,
"never sin he wur a chilt," and that he had done as
well as most folks. How infinitely better was this
bathing in pure spring water than the more modern
custom of giving the children some nauseous drug or

TALES OF EIGHTY YEARS.

doctor's physic, that might cure one thing and upset
everything else. Chamomile, dandelion, or tansy tea
were bitter enough, but there was very little harm in
them. There was also the split-tree cure. If a briar
bush could be found that had formed an arch and
rooted again, the sick child could be passed under the
arch a time or two, and that with a little patience
would cure some complaints, as whooping-cough, for
instance ; but for diseases such as measles or scarla-

tina the following recipe was once used : Take a piece of linen, home spun and home woven (if such there be), tear it in nine pieces, and spread powdered garlic from nine plants or bulbs on lard on each piece, wrap each piece separately round the child and nurse it for nine days, then take off the nine pieces, bury them in the garden, and the child will be cured. Letting nature heal itself was the best practice, good nursing sometimes came to its aid, and faith and patience were very useful if a sufferer had any.

CHAPTER II

WEDDINGS

" Money buys lands, wives are sold by fate."
—MERRY WIVES OF WINDSOR.

HE custom of throwing the shoe after a newly-wedded pair when they leave the bride's home has a symbolical meaning, and is of the very greatest antiquity. In one of the oldest and most beautiful tales in the world it is recorded that in a still earlier time men plucked off their shoes when they parted with their rights as to the marriage of a kinswoman, and when Boaz "purchased" Ruth to be his wife the ceremony was observed. In the laws of Moses, as stated in Deuteronomy, it is ordained that if a man would not marry his deceased brother's widow she was to take off his shoe and spit in his face—not a very ladylike proceeding, but one that the man might possibly prefer to the marriage.

The shoe, then, is the symbol of authority, and is given to or thrown after the bridegroom when he takes the bride from her home, signifying that he is to have the dominion over her. Cynical people are not to infer that he has a right to kick her with it, even though the provocation be very great; or to use it as mothers sometimes use it to their children when they persistently talk out of their turn. Even the great reformer Martin Luther, when "he shook the world," did not attempt to reform this old custom, for he expressly states, "Put the new husband's shoe at the head of the bed in token of his authority." In our Church of England wedding service the priest asks, "Who giveth this woman?" And he asks her, "Wilt thou obey him?" (the man). Therefore the Church upholds and confirms this most ancient custom of it being the duty of the woman to obey, though it is rather irritating to some of our modern ladies, especially when they find the money, for it is openly said they "instruct" the minister to omit the objectionable words. It is perhaps as well to observe that the term "shoe" does not mean a boot, and that in olden times shoes had no heels. Nowadays heels are generally worn, and the height of them is in inverse ratio to the height of the forehead of the wearer. In some cases where there is no forehead, or it is hidden by some frowsy hair, the heels are of great height, and those shoes are not proper to throw at a bridegroom unless it be as a warning to him to assert his authority and have none like them in his house.

The custom of strewing flowers in the path of the bridal party and offering them bunches of wild-flowers is old, is English, and is beautiful; why neglect it for the rubbishy foreign rice?

> "Of two such customs why forget
> The older and the prettier one?"

The custom of throwing rice about at weddings is merely a fashionable and foolish one of modern times, that in our country has not even the sanction of age.

When rice is thrown about, it may blind people, or cause the horses in the bride's carriage to run away, as lately happened. It is very little use even for the birds when it is raw, for I once killed a lot of chickens with feeding them on unboiled rice ; therefore the best thing to do with it is to use it for a pudding.

It is a well-proven piece of folk-lore that weddings are dreadfully infectious, for ladies of uncertain age who have been on the market for a score or so of years long to be chosen as bridesmaids so that they may rub up against the groom's men and the mysterious contagion may spread. They try to wear

"Something old and something new,
Something borrowed and something blue."

Some of them weep, whether it is for envy, or pity, or joy, or out of pure "cussedness," they do not tell. The bride's mother certainly ought to weep. If tears do not come freely, a bit of fresh raw onion has a good effect. The parson is in all his glory. He is more important than ever, and he claims to have the first kiss when he has completed the ceremony. In olden times the lord of the manor also claimed his dues.

The bridal party should be careful to leave the house and re-enter it by the same door, and to do the same at the church. When we have had servants married from our house, they have always used the front door, and returned by it to the wedding breakfast in the servants' hall. With the poorer people the fathers and mothers of the bridal pair do not usually leave their work to watch the ceremony. The bride-groom walks off with the bridesmaid, and his best friend or man sticks fast to the bride till the fatal knot is tied, then they change partners and return, and those are precious moments for the bridesmaid.

In Leap Year special facilities are allowed by custom to the weaker sex to assert their rights, and then it behoves eligible men to be cautious, or the banns may be "asked" before they fully know who¯ has taken advantage of their bashfulness and confusion.

It is important that none of the bridal party should trip, stumble, hesitate, or look back when on their way to the church. "Remember Lot's wife." All women wearing widow's weeds should keep out of their way, and all women who "sken" should certainly not come near or else they should wear blue spectacles. To meet a funeral is considered dreadfully unlucky, and if there should be an open grave in the church-yard it should be covered over or concealed. It is a remarkable fact that at Didsbury and at other places bridal parties usually enter at one gate into the church-yard and burial parties at another. There is no law or rule on the matter, they seem to be guided by natural instinct : the lych-gate is for the funerals, and the wedding guests with the bride and bridegroom run joyfully up and down the steps at the smaller wicket opposite to our gate, quite reckless as to what the future has in store for them.

> "They frolic too and fro
> As free and blithe as if on earth
> Were no such thing as woe."

Millions of times have the old proverbial lines been muttered, said, or sung—

> "Happy is the bride that the sun shines on,
> And blessed is the corpse that the rain rains on."

The folk-lore as to the all-important wedding-ring is like the ring itself, very plain and very binding. Numberless instances could be given where marriages have turned out unfortunately when there has been, or because there has been, neglect, carelessness, or heedlessness about the ring. There should be no trifling with the golden circle ; when it is put on the woman's finger it should never, never, in life or death, be taken off. One happy instance is well known to me where the ring has never once, from any cause whatever, and not for one instant of time, been off the finger for more than sixty-two years, and is not yet worn out.

When travelling was more difficult and honey-moons were not so common, it was the custom for the wedding guests to escort the bridal pair to bed, and having tucked them in and blessed them, they left them to blissful repose while they went on with festivities and copiously drank the health of the happy pair.

There is an old local saying very expressive of the holy state of matrimony when a woman has married three men in succession : she is then said to be wearing her third husband, the inference of course being that she has worn the other poor fellows com-pletely out, although she may speak of them as "dear departeds."

It is to be hoped that some readers may profit by this accumulated lore of ages, but "experience is a bitter school, though fools will learn in no other." To be blessed with a numerous family has in all ages been looked upon as one of the crowns of earthly bliss. It is expected that in the words of an old song

> " The boys have all their father's sense,
> The girls have all their mother's beauty ; "

and though each individual's share of the beauty and of the sense may be very small, it will suffice for all practical purposes where a contented mind is a continual feast :

> " The dear delight
> Of hearts that know no guile.
> That all around see all things bright
> With their own magic smile."

For a well-worn old proverb tells us—

> " There's never a fow face but there's a fow fancy."

OFF TO THE WEDDING.

CHAPTER III

BURIALS

*" Is she to be buried in Christian burial, who
wilfully seeks her own salvation?"*—HAMLET.

HE word burial is derived from bury-
ale, the ale or feast that was given to
the kindred and neighbours who were
bidden to the burying of any one ; as
bridal is derived from the bride-ale, or
feast given at the making of a bride.
The custom of neighbours assisting one another in
their turns, at the last sad rites on the burial of the
dead, is doubtless one of the oldest of all customs,
and the giving of meat and drink to those who come,
whether they were "bidden" or not, is very natural ;
yet, as Hamlet said—

"It is a custom
More honoured in the breach than the observance."

The waste and revelry at the "wake" of a corpse
has in our land and time nearly disappeared. The
simple burial-cakes and harmless sprigs of rosemary
are no longer given. The rubbishy crape scarves
and hat-bands are not fashionable, and I have even
followed a life-long friend to the furnace in the crema-

torium that has been set up in the parish. The custom of the friends and relatives attending the morning service at the church on the Sunday morning after the burial is not now observed in these parts, for so many funerals are in cemeteries. In my memory it was considered heathenish to put flowers on graves or in them, and I believe that it was on my father's grave, in December 1867, the Rector of Didsbury first gave his consent to having plants or flowers planted on a grave.

In all ages, savage and civilised, it has not been uncommon for treasures, weapons, ornaments, and other things to be buried with a corpse. This may have given rise to a saying among the worshippers of Mammon when some one has died and is said to have "left a deal of brass," there comes the ready reply, " Will he tak' it with him." It was said to be a custom to put a coin in the mouth of the deceased, and I have been told of a plate of salt being put on the breast prior to burial. I have known men ask that they should not have their legs tied, or be put in brick graves, or have any post-mortem examination ; and, on the contrary, I have known men insist on being promised that a doctor should make a post-mortem and instrumentally ensure death. These rather gruesome details lead us to an article that I wrote on resurrectionists, or the once common custom of "body snatching" or rifling graves. It was written in 1895, when the organ chamber and south transept were added to Didsbury church, and is as follows :—

"As my thoughts and writings centre round ' the home I love,' I cannot do better than begin again at Didsbury. The old church there is again being enlarged, and another piece of the old churchyard is being built over. I have been rather surprised to hear from the workmen what a large and general demand there is from the public for skulls and teeth. Common skulls are worth five shillings each. Men like playing Hamlet, and say, 'That skull had a tongue in it and could sing." A very old charm against toothache is to wear a sound tooth found in a churchyard, having it tied by string and worn round the neck. If the toothache continues obstinate, an infallible cure is to have the bad tooth taken out and the sound one put in its place. Modern artificial teeth are of very recent invention. It was formerly the custom for wealthy people who wanted new teeth to buy them from some one who would sell theirs, and the change was made direct from one to the other, just as a poor girl may now sell her long and beautiful hair to some wealthy withered woman. Others had to be content with sound old teeth, and they were preferred if found in a churchyard, for they would be deemed better as charms, and there seems to be a very general opinion that teeth centuries old are better than our modern ones. A man showed me a newly disinterred skull that he said had thirty-four sound teeth, and as he calmly threw some of them back in the grave he very truly said, 'There wanner as much tea drunk when them teeth were grown.'

"The monks of old generally kept skulls in their cells to remind them of what they must become, and the custom still lingers in many of our old country halls. I have been told that when the railway was being made by Coombs Moss, near Buxton, some of the navvies took an old skull that had been in a farmhouse there for many generations. Bad luck overwhelmed them and their work at once, acres of land slipped on to their line, their ground gave way, the men got ill, and dreadfully mysterious noises were

DISELEY CHURCH FROM THE OLD PARSONAGE.

continually being heard, until the master was told the
reason, whereupon he ordered the men to restore the
skull at once to the old house, and even offered to
give its ghost a free pass on the line for ever. As
soon as the skull was replaced the difficulties ceased,
though the hillsides still show the landslips. The
Lancashire and Cheshire Antiquarian Society lately
visited Browsholme Hall, in Bowland. The house is
full of the most beautiful old oak furniture, with all
sorts of curiosities, and amongst them is a skull that
is supposed to bring terrible bad luck to any one who
meddles with it. One of the party was a Holy Father
of the Society of Jesus, so it could not possibly hurt
him, and he boldly grasped it and showed its beauties.
It was then said to be the skull of a female, and the
lower jaw was missing; and therefore, as the power
of mischief probably lay in the lady's jaw, that particular skull may henceforth be harmless. By far the
most interesting skull in this county is that of Colonel
Townley, of the Manchester regiment, in 1745. It is
kept at the altar of the chapel of Townley Hall. I as
a pilgrim went to see it, and, like Thomas a Didymus,
to use my finger to strengthen my faith. It has evidently been jammed on the top of a spike, and the
teeth are still as good as when they ate their last
breakfast on Wednesday, July 30, 1746, and were
then clenched in the torture on the scaffold. Hogarth's
picture of Temple Bar, with the heads of Colonel
Townley and Captain Fletcher and somebody's leg,
is copied in my ' Didisburye in the '45,' with the last
speeches of Fletcher and others.

"The horrible custom of ' body-lifting,' or selling
bodies that had been buried to doctors and others,
was very common in our district in the early years
of this century. It was so common that it also became

usual for funeral parties to take bundles of straw and
sticks to put in layers over the graves, so that digging
was made very difficult; and the rich had their relatives buried in the churches, or they put up tremendous
tombs over them, as we see in the ponderous prison-
like structures so common in our old churchyards.
There is one at Didsbury with stone-work from two
feet to six feet high, and an iron railing five feet nine
inches on the top of that, enclosing a large stone with
two weeping willow trees and four bushes round it—
rather a formidable fortress to put on the top of any
one. In some cases the bodies were stolen before
the funeral, in rare cases before they were dead, and
very often they were watched and wanted before they
were dead. As an instance of the first-named, there
was an Irish harvestman in our neighbourhood who
was badly injured in the harvest. He was taken to
the Stockport Infirmary, and there he died. His
comrades intended to give him a respectable burial,
but when they were carrying the coffin to the grave,
sand was running out of it all the time, until at last
it got quite light, and in their perplexity they lifted
the coffin lid and found it to be empty. The body
had been used for dissecting, and the coffin had been
filled with sand. His comrades were naturally very
wroth, for the man having been an Irishman and a
Roman Catholic, the crime seemed to be much worse
than if he had been merely an ordinary pauper of no
specific denomination.

    "Northen was the worst place for the resurrec-
tionists. A public-house there had a very bad name,
as also had a house on the site of Rosehill, half-way
between the churchyard and the wild country called
Gatley Carrs; it was inhabited by a family with the
euphonious name of Badcock, and its site gave special

facilities for eluding pursuit across the river or into
the swampy carrs. It has been said that nearly every
grave in Northen had been ransacked. I am not referring to anything having been done in the lifetime of
any one living excepting very old people. There was
a crippled youth there who had long been 'wanted,'
and his mother knew it, and when he was buried she
set a man named Vaudrey to watch the grave, and at
the same time there were two doctors of that name in
Cheadle. One dark night the watcher became aware
of some one groping about the grave, so he called out,
'Who's yon?' 'I'm fro Vaudreys,' said the new-
comer, thinking he was answering a helper. 'I'm
Vaudrey hissel,' replied the watcher, as he lit up.
'The devil, the devil,' was the only answer as the
other fellow bolted. Downes, a well-known resurrec-
tionist of Cheadle, sold his own body for £5 to Dr.
Solomon Vaudrey, to be delivered when he died.
Downes got the money and drank it, or what it
bought, and went on living until long after the doctor,
for he probably only drank home-brewed ale, while
the doctor may have taken his own physic. Then
Downes's family buried him in quicklime at Wilmslow,
and had to pay their own funeral expenses. Perhaps
they had no need for the quicklime, for one Sunday
evening years ago, I heard the sound of a grave being
dug, so I went to ask the sexton the reason for his
untimely working, when he said, 'It's for ode R——
as keeps th' ale 'ouse on Barley More, he deed to
morn, an' he's nobbut so much sour beer, th' weather's
'ot an' he wunner keep.'

    "There is one more moral to be drawn from this
very grave subject, and that is, never buy old oak
furniture from near a churchyard (at least in country
places), for the coffins were largely used for the manu-

facture of oak furniture, especially grandfather's clocks,
as the venerable tints of age that connoisseurs admire
so much in dark oak are acquired much quicker when
the wood is buried under ground than when it is exposed to the air.   A good coffin would sometimes be
more valuable than its contents.

   " There is an old saying that may still be heard in
country places, ' We shall live till we die, if th' pigs
don't eat us ' ; it may be a relic of metempsychosis, or
a belief that our spirits shall in some future state in-
habit other bodies or animals.   I have several times
heard the saying, but those who said it could not give
its meaning, they merely remarked the oft-quoted 'the
old folks said it.'   It might also indicate a survival of
fatalism.

   " In our old churchyards the priests were buried
with their heads to the east, and the common folk
with their heads to the west, so that when all rise
together at the proper resurrection the priests would
face their flocks.   This is a very nice arrangement if
we could be sure it would work properly ; it is evidently a very old one, much older and much better
than the piling of tons of stone or iron railings on the
top of one, for surely it is simpler and pleasanter to
have the green grass growing over our commingled
dust.

   " As an instance of those living being ' wanted,' as
it was termed, there is now a man whose head was
indented very much when he was young, by a brick
falling on it, and the indent has grown and solidified ;
he has been several times told that his head is worth
more dead than alive, and it is wanted as soon as he
has done with it."

   The above article brought several rejoinders in
the following week's paper.   Mrs. Linnaeus Banks,

the novelist, referring to the skull near Coombs Moss,
said it was also mentioned by Croston, and from
being then called Dickey it was perhaps the skull
of a trooper named Ned Dickson, who was strangled
at Tunstead by his kinsman for his inheritance. This
may or may not be true; her information about the
Wardley skull was all wrong. There is at Wardley
Hall, near Manchester, a skull which raises storms
if it be removed from its time-honoured niche in the
house, and this can be testified to any time by several
business men of my acquaintance who have tested
the matter. This skull is of Father Ambrose, O.S.B.,
a Romish priest who suffered martyrdom with all the
horrible cruelties of the English Church and Government of the day. He was one of the Barlows of
Barlow Hall, his mother having been Mary Brereton,
daughter of Sir Urian Brereton, the rebuilder of Hon-
ford Hall in Cheadle parish. He was baptized at Didsbury church, November 30, 1585, the church register
stating, "Edwarde, ye sonne of Alex. Barlowe,
gent."

As I was lately inquiring about marling, I came
across a good tale about the last lord of the marlers.
It comes from a bit beyond Gatley, a likely place for
the fraternity. It appears the last lord was a man
called Legh, who lived at Heyhead. I don't know
whether his name was spelt Legh, Leigh, Lee, Lea,
Ley, or Leghe—it is immaterial, and therefore I have
taken the oldest and most proper spelling. He was a
very tall man, as all lords or leaders of men should
be, and he was generally known as Lord Legh. In
due course of time he died, and had to be buried, and
a neighbouring coffin-maker got the order for his
coffin. This man's name was Bailey, or Bayley, or
Bealey, a member of another large clan or family, for

in our part the Saxons left many descendants named Legh, or with "ley" for the end of their name. I mention this more particularly in order that if any one thinks I am referring to their grandfathers they will understand that I am not doing so. The reference is to another man's grandfather of the same name.

Bailey made the required coffin with the longest boards he had, and took it to fit Legh into it, but it was too short. Legh was very long, and had been a stiff-backed man in his life, and death had not made him any suppler. His head, or his knees, or his feet would stick up. Bailey tugged, and shoved, and thrutched, and squoze, as he began to think he would have to bear the expense of another coffin as well as the derision of his neighbours, but it would not fit, and he would have sworn if he had not been alone in the presence of the dead. Now, the Baileys are men who are not easily beaten, and who do not stick at trifles. This one sat down to think, for the credit of the family was at stake. A bright idea soon came to his troubled brain. He had cut up a few pigs in his time, as had most of his neighbours, and he suddenly opened his big knife, cut off the dead man's head, placed it between his legs, and fastened up the coffin. Nothing else happened, and Legh was solemnly buried in Northen churchyard ; but as "murders will out" when men "get in their cups," or swagger, or think they are going to die, this tale also got out, and it is as well to publish it, for some day there will be alterations in Northen churchyard, as there are in all our churchyards, and a coffin with a strange skeleton may be found, and men will say, "Here is another man been buried alive. How the poor fellow must have struggled to get his head in that uncomfortable

position between his legs!" and others may now
say that that is the last of the last "lord of the
marlers."

There is a very old church at a place called Giggles-
wick, about fifty or sixty miles north of here, on the
border of Yorkshire, and tradition said that in the
Stainford chantry there had been buried a Sir Richard
Tempest with his "horse and all," the date being
some time after the battle of Wakefield, 1460. At
the rebuilding or restoration of this church a few years
since, the churchwarden, a good antiquary, found the
bones of the horse in the grave, and showed me a
horse's tooth that he had kept. Another well-authen-
ticated case of a horse being buried with its master,
and about the same date as the preceding, or four
hundred years ago, was that of Lord Ranulph Dacre,
who was shot by a boy in an elder bush when he was
drinking at a brook after Towton fight; he being
buried at Saxton churchyard. A man at Madeley,
a few years since, had a very large tooth which he
kept as a charm, and which he swore he found in the
churchyard at the digging of a grave, with some large
bones; the tooth being certainly a horse's, though he
thought it was a man's. I knew a Manchester merchant lately who had his carriage horses killed when
his wife died. He was a very kind-hearted gentleman, and could not bear any one else to have them.
I certainly left word that my favourite horses (when I
kept horses) should be buried if I went suddenly.
The last I had is buried in the garden, as are the
dogs also.

To return to the burial-cakes that my mother
says were quite common when she was young. When
her parents went to a burial (that was the old word
for funeral), the children always expected some burial-

cakes, exactly as nowadays old children and young
look for bride-cake from a wedding. Genteel people
now provide what they call funeral biscuits. The
working classes generally have currant bread. I
lately heard a plain-spoken man say some one was
"too slow to go to a burial and eat currant dough."

The "bride-cake" or "bridal-cake" is the great
cake at the bride-ale or feast given at the making
of a bride, and the burial-cakes are the cakes given at
the bury-ale. A still older name was heir-ale, cor-
rupted to aral, from the ale or feast given by the
heirs. I lately called at the good old-fashioned shop,
so long kept by Mrs. Mary Scholes in Hilton Street,
to ask about burial-cakes, and was told it was twenty
years since they made any, and then the real old burial-
cakes were specially made for the burial of some old
lady at Bolton, who left strict instructions in her will
that these cakes were to be supplied to any one and
every one at her funeral. Burial-cakes were small
rich sponge-cakes, with a smell of ammonia. They
were wrapped in tissue paper, then in black-edged
note-paper, and addressed to those who were bidden
to the burial, or sent away to others who could not
come. If the master or the mistress of the house
were dead, and bees were kept, some cake and wine
were given to the bees, who were told of the sad
event, or they would not stop. Sprigs of rosemary
were also given to every one at the burial, and they
might be used in three ways—to cast in the grave
at the words "ashes to ashes," thereby signifying that
the deceased was done with and the remembrance
of them would soon be forgotten—for, as readers of
Shakspere well know, "Rosemary is for remembrance; I pray you, love, remember"; or the sprig
might be kept as a sweet-smelling savour; or it might

be planted as a cutting to grow again, and then one of the older generations might show it in after years to the younger, and say, "That is the rosemary bush from the slip when your Uncle John was buried, and that is your Aunt Mary, and, perhaps, some day you will plant one for me."

IN THE CARRS, DIDSBURY.

CHAPTER IV

FESTIVALS

*" Dost thou think, because thou art virtuous, there
shall be no more cakes and ale?
Yes, by Saint Anne! and ginger shall be hot i'
th' mouth too."* --TWELFTH NIGHT.

The New Year.

HEN does the New Year popularly begin?" is a question that is not nearly so simple as it looks, and is one that seems to broaden out indefinitely. Any ordinary person would promptly answer, "On 1st January," for that is the official date for our nation at the present time; but it was not always so, and it is only partly true now. It is impossible to say when Nature begins her new year, but it would apparently coincide much nearer with Lady Day on 25th March, which was our official time up to 1752, than it would with 1st January. The treasurer of the nation, that is, the Chancellor of the Exchequer, still makes up his yearly balance-sheet to 5th April, that is, the same day as the 25th of March according to the old style of reckoning the calendar. The Christian churches begin their new year at Easter, though they do not agree exactly when Easter is or should be. The great army of farmers mostly take their land, or, in other words, begin their year, from Candlemas Day, 2nd February ; in some cases they change houses on Lady Day or on May Day. They are the most conservative, or, in other words, the least given to change, of all men, and their customs are generally very ancient. Their cattle are still sent to ley, or turned into the fields to sleep out at nights, on old May Day, and the leys or parks owned by the large land-owners are on that day opened to receive them. In many districts in the north the terms of service of the farm-servants are reckoned as from old May Day and Martinmas, or, in other words, 12th May and 11th November. My friend the local wise man tells me that when "my grandfeyther wur a lad th' King an' Lords awtered th' kalendar, an' tuk eleven days off poor folk, which they ne'er got back. Th' yeer used to begin March quatter, when th' bumble bees come out, an' grass an' things grow gradely, an' yon's propperest time."

Beginning at 1st January according to the modern fashion, and taking the festivals somewhat in order, after having the year "let in" by a dark person, we come to the Epiphany or Twelfth Night, when the orthodox supper with old-fashioned people is lobscouse and lamb's wool, the latter being another name for mulled ale with roasted apples ; and on that night (6th January) my late uncle at Standon Hall "blazed his wheat" to scare the witches, a custom to which I must refer again.

Then cometh Candlemas, and though there are thousands of townsfolk who do not know when it is, and probably never heard it named, most country folk know it by many old proverbs, for

> "On Candlemas Day
> Good geese should lay,"

and the evergreens that decked the house should be given to the cattle for them to eat.

Farmers give or take possession of the land on that day (when there is a change of tenancy), an old custom that has lately been legalised in the Agricultural Holdings Act. As they would not have much time for eating if they were flitting, the many good proverbs relating to that once important day refer to the weather or other matters :

> "A farmer should, on Candlemas Day,
> Have half his corn and half his hay."

> "If Candlemas Day be fair and bright,
> Winter will have another flight ;
> But if it be dark, with clouds and rain,
> Winter is gone and will not come again."—

referring to a well-known fact that February is sometimes the coldest month of the year, as it was in 1895, for in some years—

> "As the day lengthens,
> So the cold strengthens."

Then, as the days lengthen, we come to the Lengthen or Lenten fast and the world-famous Shrove Tuesday, or Guttit or Gutsing Tuesday, when is the time to be shriven of our sins, to toss and eat pancakes, and see the time-honoured sport of cock-fighting. Long ago a Frenchman wrote that on Shrove Tuesday the English eat a certain indigestible cake, whereupon

they go mad and kill their cocks. This referred to
the barbarous custom of throwing at cocks and killing
them in cruel manner, instead of letting them have
the fun of a fight. Nowadays the main observance
of Shrove Tuesday is the eating of pancakes, and this
should be preceded on the previous day, or Collop
Monday, by the eating of collops of fat bacon, so as
to lubricate the inside as a preparation for the pancakes, for it used to be considered that the more
pancakes any one ate, the more it was accounted
unto him for righteousness, was evidence of zeal in
the cause of religion ; in fact, a big subscription.
There was a youth at Cheltenham College, about
forty years since, who held the record for eating pancakes, and although that record may be surpassed in
these days of improvement, it was a substantial feat
conscientiously accomplished. His name was Hughes,
and he came from Wales, or that way on. He was
long and lean and hungry, dressed in black, and very
solemn ; therefore he was supposed to be a Calvinistic
Methodist when he was at home ; but having to con-
form to High Church doctrines when he was at college,
he loyally did his best at the Church feasts, and on
one Shrove Tuesday he was credited with having
eaten at his boarding-house and "tuck-shop" no
fewer than thirty-six pancakes. He was consequently an object of envy and admiration for a time ;
but he must have "put his meat in a bad skin," or
been troubled with worms, for he was as hungry as
ever before the end of the week. The eaters of
pancakes should have to cook them or toss them in
the pan, and if any one tosses them into the fire,
then the tosser should be carried out and thrown on
to the dunghill. One of my earliest recollections is
that of seeing a gentleman, who subsequently became

C

sheriff of a county, carried out of our house and put on the heap in the stable-yard.

If plenty of pancakes is one of the advantages of a High Church and Tory education, there is the corresponding disadvantage in the hasty pudding of Ash Wednesday. The custom of putting ashes on our heads went out of fashion before my time, but we went to church like good Christians and cursed our neighbours—cursed them all, or very nearly all, most impartially, solemnly, and religiously—ten separate and most comprehensive curses ; very few could escape them or some part of them. Cursed are the covetous. How all the good folk of Manchester, with their eye on their neighbour, would heartily respond Amen. Cursed is he who removeth his neighbour's landmark. As it is only the very rich who remove their neighbour's landmark, this curse is not likely to be fulfilled. There are in Didsbury ancient highways repairable by the inhabitants at large, where the landmark or fence has been moved two and three yards into the road, in one case right up to the old wheel-ruts. If the people love to have it so, what are ye to do ?

> " The law will send the thief to prison
> Who steals the goose from off the common,
> But lets the greater villain loose
> Who steals the common from the goose."

When the law and the prophets and the cursings are of no avail, we can try patience and hope, and go home to our dinner of hasty pudding, the orthodox dish for the fast of Ash Wednesday. This was made of flour and milk, and probably derived its name from the haste with which it was made and the haste with which all the effects of it disappeared. It was helped with treacle black as ebony, that was believed to have derived its colouring matter from the feet of the niggers who trod the sugar canes in Barbadoes. To any one who has seen a black pig scalded and scraped into being white, this theory of the colouring matter seems not improbable.

Simnel Sunday.

The long Lenten fast was partly broken by Mid Lent or Mothering Sunday, the remembrance of which is perpetuated by the well-known simnel cakes. "Simblins" or simnels derive their name from the Latin word for fine flour (hence semolina), and are said to be mentioned in the Chronicles of Winchester in 1042, "conventus centum simnellos," or "the convent a hundred simnels." This is a long history for the old-fashioned cakes. In those days currants would probably be unknown, and a pinch of spice worth an acre of land. Bury and Shrewsbury would be merely wattle and daub huts in some Anglo-Saxon burh (that is borough, bury, or stockaded hill fort) in a swampy wilderness, with no dreams of the fame that was to come upon them by reason of their simnels, though they may have known of the bragot or hot ale that seems to have been one of the most cherished possessions of the Anglo-Saxon race.

Mothering Sunday is said to have derived its name from a Roman Catholic custom of making offerings at the mother-church of any district on that day, and it is also said that this custom only supplanted the still older heathen custom of making an offering to the mother of the gods on the Ides of March in Rome. Let us take the simplest explanation and believe it to be a custom to take an offering to our mothers, and we can still observe the day as the anniversary of the return of the Prodigal Son, and we can say, "I will arise and go to my Father," and we will all commemorate the killing of the fatted calf and have veal for dinner, with perhaps a bit of simnel, repeating the lines a century old :—

> " I'll to thee a simnel bring
> 'Gainst thou go'st a mothering,
> So that when she blesseth thee,
> Half that blessing thou'lt give me."

The eating of carlins or carling peas is still observed by some old-fashioned people in what may be termed the more Catholic parts of Lancashire, that is, about Ormskirk and Preston ; in Manchester and Cheshire the custom seems to be unknown. I have taken some trouble to ferret out all that is left of this old custom, not from books, but from living folk, and with a re-membrance that when we were doing a large corn-trade business we sold carling peas. Few corn-dealers nowadays know what carling peas are. They say it takes them all their time to make their own living, therefore they cannot bother with anything else, and their heads are full of corn. When Adam Smith wrote his "Wealth of Nations" he said the corn trade was "abandoned to an inferior set of dealers, millers, bakers, meal men, and meal factors, together with a number of wretched hucksters." Perhaps the great author was bilious when he wrote that, for the trade is respectable, although long struggles with poverty make it rather melancholy.

There is a sort of pea grown in the Eastern Counties variously called maple, partridge, or grey peas, and at the end of Lent these are called carling peas, and are sold to people, who boil them first, and then fry them

with butter in a pan, and make them savoury. If the
old corn-dealer can get an extra price for his wares by
giving them a religious name, there is no great harm
done ; any trader would do that. Carling seems an
interesting old custom in various ways. Firstly, what
does the name mean? I do not think it is derived
from care—the vulgar pronunciation of the word is
different—it is more probably from carl or churl, meaning rough or common, for the peas are certainly tough
and rough, peas that will stand boiling first and frying
afterwards. The proper time for eating them seems
to be doubtful, although it is certainly at the end of
Lent. Carling Sunday is the fifth Sunday in Lent ;
that is, the next one after Simnel or Mothering Sunday.
An old rhyme is—

"Carl Sunday, carl away,
Palm Sunday, Easter day ;"

and "carl away" was said to mean, you should eat the
carled peas all the week up to the next, or Palm Sunday.
Then as to the origin of the custom, a dreadful thought
has occurred to me. It is an old tale that before the
decay of faith and the belief in the efficacy of punish-
ments, our superiors in religion ordained penance or
punishment for their inferiors, and a common form of
penance was to go on a pilgrimage with peas in the
shoes. Then as men became more deceitful and
desperately wicked, Satan prompted them to boil the
peas, as that would make them easier for their corns,
and afford them sustenance by the way, with a chance
of pea soup for supper. When the long Lenten fast
was coming to an end the proper thing to do would
undoubtedly be to consume the remnant of your sins :
and in remembrance of the penitential peas that once
did duty in a double way, succeeding generations

refrained from part of the penance, though they ate tough peas that took two good cookings, with plenty of butter and pepper and salt to make them " savvory," and they were called the carl's or carlin peas. There were some dry biscuits called cracklings or cracknels that were also eaten at the end of Lent.

The hot cross buns of Good Friday are too well known to need any description. They are said to be prehistoric or heathenish cakes that were signed with the sign of the cross to make them holy, and the sternest Protestants do not protest against the cross on their cakes on that day ; and if there be any remnant of the older superstitions in any of the newest sects or schisms of the present time, they may keep a " cross bun " until the next Good Friday, and it may be unto them as a charm against vague maladies and as a medicine for some, for it will keep free from mould and must and moths until Good Friday comes again, if only the maker of it have clean hands and a pure heart.

For those who do not strictly observe the fast of Good Friday the orthodox dinner is fish—turbot and lobster sauce with the wealthy, codfish for the poor, or perch, carp, or tench, in inland places. At many country houses there are still the pools of various sizes for the keeping of the fish.

Easter.

The proper food for the great feast of Easter is, of course, eggs for the breakfast, or furmety with the poorer people, they being typical of the Resurrection. Furmety is wheat stewed in the oven until the kernel of the wheat swells and bursts its outer bran. It was a common dish until recently, but nowadays both the growers and the sellers of wheat are scarce in our country. Easter eggs or "pace eggs" appear to be used all over the world by both Jews and Christians, and their name, pace eggs, seems to be very similar in the various languages, for older than any is the Hebrew word *pessach*, which, I am told, is pronounced *pasach* (with the *a* long, as in pace), and means Passover. Most country children in England know that to go pace-egging means to beg eggs for Easter Day, the only day in the year they ever taste them, unless they find a nest for themselves and suck them on the sly. The orthodox dinner for Easter is the well-known roast lamb and mint sauce, the paschal lamb and the bitter herbs. If lamb be too dear at that season for the majority of people, they substitute veal, there being an enormous number of calves sent from Cheshire to the Lancashire towns in Passion Week ; in fact, many dairy-farmers then send off all their calves, and begin another season's cheese-making. The old-fashioned pudding for the day is tansy pudding, tansy being another of the bitter herbs. Its name is derived from St. Athanasius, there being some old connection between the saint and the herb. With many other religious plants it grows wild in parts of our old garden.

The well-known custom of having new clothes at Easter is another sign that Easter was regarded as the beginning of another year. Until quite recently very few people had new clothes oftener or as often as once a year.

Easter Monday and Tuesday were called heaving or lifting days, from an old custom of raising or lifting one another on those days, it being another custom that has survived in a wonderful manner. It doubtless commemorates the raising of Christ. On Monday the men lifted the women, and on Tuesday the women

lifted the men. Formerly the person operated upon
lay down, but in modern times they sat on a chair and
were raised up with the chair. There was a well-
known character in the corn trade named John Old-
ham, from Carlton-on-Trent, who was a very big man,
his weight being over three hundred pounds. He was
too much for the combined strength of all the barmaids
in the Spread Eagle Hotel, who made desperate efforts
to lift him one Easter Tuesday. When he went to
live at Withington he took up more than his share of
the omnibus, and one day he partly sat upon a small
man, who objected to being sat upon, and remarked
that passengers should be charged by weight. "Then
they'd never stop to pick thee up," said the big man,
and the discussion ended. Some of our fathers who
were always travelling about the country on horseback
grew into very big men, and I have heard my father
say of the original Cobbett (the grandfather of the
present generation) that when he was speaking at a
farmer's "market ordinary" he said something that
roused the wrath of the farmers, who cried, "Turn
him out, turn the —— out." Cobbett, waiting for the
storm to subside, spoke again and quietly said, "When
you talk of turning me out, bear in mind that I weigh
more than a four-bushel sack of wheat." The bushel
being a measure of capacity, its weight varies, but old
Cobbett's weight may be taken to have been above
two hundred and fifty pounds, and the farmers would
appreciate the difficulty of carrying a sack of wheat
that had ways of its own and would struggle strongly.

At pace-egging time the youth of the villages
round about our district dressed themselves up with
tinsel and finery, and went morris-dancing and partly
acting, in the old farm-houses, or on the lawns, or in
the servants' halls of the gentlemen's houses, the old

mummers' play of St. George and the Dragon. A real horse's head was got from the neighbouring tan-yard, that snapped its jaws (worked by strings) at the legs of the girls, who would scream and want to be taken care of; or a sham horse would be made round a youth who was apparently riding, curveting about, banging others with a bladder, and sometimes called "Tosspot." The horse was called Old Hob or Old Ball, the name Hob being common to hobgoblin and hobby-horse, and a bit of well-known old folk-lore says it is well for any one to have "a hobby."

May Day.

Between Eastertide and Whitsuntide there comes the great festival of flowers. Poets and authors have raved and written so much about the merry month of May, May songs, Maypoles, and other delights, that a bare mention of some of them is all that is here attempted. The seasons in their course would natu-rally bring before the pagans and heathen— that is, the dwellers in country places and on the heaths—the beauties of spring, and they would gladly welcome the lengthening days and increasing warmth, with all their promise of another harvest and time of plenty. The Christian Church was not able to entirely appropriate the worship of the goddess Flora, for the dates of the Church's anniversaries are movable, being ruled by the full moon of the Passover or Easter; and then comes a time of rest from religious anniversaries, and the flowers that are welcome in May come regardless of Easter or full moons, for they worship the sun.

The eve of May is still observed as a Wakes in many country villages, for then the Mayers sing their songs and prepare their garlands of flowers, or make ready the Maypole with the Lord and Lady, or Queen of the May, as it is now called. In an account of what is, perhaps, the best-known of the old May ballads I find a version given as being peculiar to Didsbury and the neighbourhood. It begins :—

> " Rise up the master of this house and take his plow in hand,
> For the summer springs so fresh and green and gay."

As soon as day dawns on the first of May the face or head should be bathed in May dew, and the wild flowers' first-fruits be gathered for the decking of the houses and cattle. The specific name of Mayflower is given to many flowers, the hawthorn, the marsh marigold, the lady's smock, and others. I should judge the hawthorn to have the best claim to the name May, and it was probably after that flower the pilgrim Puritans called their famous ship. In our northern district it is very seldom that the hawthorn is in flower by the first of the month, though it some-times is by Old May Day, or the twelfth of May.

The flower I have seen most used for decking the portals of farm-houses on May Day is the marsh marigold, or meadow bout, as it is locally termed. The name "bout" is probably "bolt" in the vulgar tongue, and the flower may be supposed to act as a charm against lightning ; hence its name—meadow bolt or light bolt that has fallen in the meadow. There was an old farmer who was afraid of thunder and light-ning, and when he was being comforted during a great storm by being told that God sent the thunder and lightning, and He knew where the lightning would strike, he replied, " Aye, aye, I know as how God shoots th' bout, but yo canner mak me bleeve as how He knows weer it'll leet."

My grandmother Moss used to go in the cellar and cover her head with a silk kerchief if there was a thunderstorm. She thought there was great virtue in the silk, the light bolt would respect it, and "silk was silk in those days."

The meadow bout is hung in bunches, with the stalks uppermost, round and over the doors of houses and shippons, to bring good luck and to ward off the light bolt. If the hawthorn is in flower it also is used, and mischievous lads and lasses hang other flowers or branches of trees at their neighbours' door. There is a symbolical meaning to many of the common plants that are used, and much ill-feeling has been caused thereby. For instance, a bunch of nettles is understood to mean that the women of the house are singing kettles, otherwise tattlers and slanderers. A birchen bough is the offering to a pretty lass. A nut shows a slut; an owler (or alder) a scowler; a bramble, one given to ramble; a wicken, a dear chicken; an oak, a joke; a gorse in bloom signifies a lady who would kiss any one even at noon, there being an old country proverb that says, " Kissing's out of fashion when the gorse is out of bloom." As the gorse or furze is seldom or never out of bloom except in prolonged winters, the proverb is not so dreadful as it appears, for in very hard frosts it is too cold for that interesting occupation.

Another survival of the once common Maypole lingers in the term as applied in country places to a girl who is unusually tall, and perhaps bedecked with ribbons and finery : she would be termed "a perfect Maypole." And another old proverb says—

" Married in May
Will soon decay."

This also is older than Christianity. It was mentioned

by Ovid; it was written on the gate of Holyrood
Palace when Mary Queen of Scots married Bothwell,
and even her sanctimonious character and strong self-
will could not avert the evil or break the spell. It is
current now, and although the banns of five couples
were asked on one Sunday in this last May (1896) at
Didsbury church, it only shows that the happy couples,
when thinking more of Whit-week than of May, are
running great risks, and ought to have known better.
One of these brides, I hear, died in November. I
have not asked about the others, and, indeed, do not
know who they are. Some folks say it is unlucky
even to go courting in May; others abstain from it
on Fridays or fast days; and there are some people,
pure-minded though perverse, who object to it at all
times, quite regardless of the fact that if every one
did as they told them to do we should soon become
scarce.

It is strange there should be so much ill-luck
attending so many things in this "merry month of
May." It is said to be trying to old people when the
sap is rising and the trees are coming into leaf again.
A May baby is said to be sickly and hard to rear, and
all kittens born in May should certainly be drowned
at once. The law prohibits the drowning of babies,
but it does seem a pity that some of them should be
reared. Fanciful mothers bathe their babies in May
dew, and that is believed to be very beneficial, especially to the skin.

May is the month to gather yarbs. The amount
of herb tea our grandmothers used to make when tea
was a pound a pound was prodigious. Mint, nettles,
wormwood, chamomile, dandelion, hop, and rue were
all appreciated and extolled, for they did far less harm

than the doctors' and brewers' stuff that is so largely
taken now.

> " Ne'er cast a clout
> Until May be out "

is good advice based on the experience of the treacherous weather of the month. A finer May than this one,
1896, could not be, and there has been no snow and
very little frost all through the winter. The most
disastrous frost, perhaps, ever known occurred on
May 21, 1894, the night after the Queen opened
the Manchester Ship Canal. On that night almost
every fruit and every green thing in this country was
blackened and killed by ten degrees of frost after
heavy rain and cold winds from the east.

> " A wet and windy May
> Fills the barns with corn and hay "

is another good proverb, if by corn we understand
straw, that being the basis of a good harvest, for rain
in May certainly helps the growth of vegetation.

In my boyhood's days it was considered wicked
not to have a bit of oak in one's cap on Royal Oak
Day, and the neglect of it rendered one liable to
be pinched, or nettled, or sodded. The horses were
decorated with it, and even the church towers all
sported their big bough of oak. Every child knew
that it was worn to show that the oak was in full leaf
on that day, so as to hide the king from the wicked
men who wished to kill him. Then it happened that
one of the first things to shake my belief and faith
came from a tutor who might have known better than
teach the truth in such a reckless manner. He asked
when the battle of Worcester was fought, thereby
showing the absurdity of the oak apple anniversary,
and then lectured on the enormity of commemorating

"the worst king that ever disgraced the English throne." We had thought until then that kings were always "paragons of perfection," but this anointed of the Lord got such a blackguarding that I am afraid it was scarcely fit for print. This is an instance of the difficulty of defining a sound religious education, for among the High Church and Tory instructors of Cheltenham College was one who not only taught as above, but explained the meaning of absolution as follows : "If one of you steals a leg of mutton, cuts it in half, and gives half to a priest, and he gives you absolution, it's all right." Many years afterwards I thought of this, and personally applied it as recorded in my book on Didsbury ; for when churchwarden and on duty at the church, the Bishop being the preacher that evening (Easter 1871), I sold to a stranger ten eggs from my game fowls, and told the rector of the transaction. He was shocked at Sunday trading, and was much against any profanation of the Sabbath ; but when I suggested the putting of the five shillings as so much extra into the collection, he was very pleased, and I got absolution with a little more experience, though I lost all the eggs and the money.

Whitsuntide.

The name Whitsuntide is probably derived from the Anglo - Saxon word "witton," to have wit or knowledge, alluding to the miraculous gift or knowledge of tongues and speech that is commemorated on Whitsun Day. Whitsunday is said to be a corruption of White Sunday, so called from the white clothes of the communicants or others who attended church ; but that derivation could not possibly account for the old terms Whitsun ales, Whitsun hirings, Whitsun holidays, Whitsuntide, Whitsun week, or Wissun wik as we sometimes hear it called.

It was customary in former times to have tame or captive pigeons made to fly down from the roofs of churches in imitation of the descent of the dove. The orthodox dinner for Whitsun Day, for those who could not afford the paschal lamb so early as Easter, is lamb, and many people then have their first gooseberry pie. In Chester it has always been considered necessary to have the first gooseberries for the race week, that is, the beginning of May, when the apple-trees are in blossom, but they are only for the favoured few. It was customary in Manchester, even in my remembrance, for nearly every house, public or private, to have practically "open house" for friends during the races in Whitsun week, especially on the Cup Day. Even the hotels did not charge their customers for their dinners. As this old custom of hospitality was sometimes abused, it was avoided by leaving home for a few days, and hence has arisen the great Whitsuntide migration that is greater from Manchester than elsewhere.

To see "th' childer walk" is the great sight for Whitsun Monday. Twenty-four thousand pledges of love parade the streets in their best bibs and tuckers, and show their new clothes to one another and their proud and happy mothers, while the poor men things, their male relations, have to take a back place and do as they are told. It is truly a great time for "th' childer." If, in the words of the old song,

"The boys have all their fathers' sense,
The girls have all their mothers' beauty,"

it must not be inferred that the respective parents are left without any of those desirable qualities. The

Saturday in Whitsun week is called Gorping Saturday, from the crowds of country folk who go gorping
or gaping about like geese on that day.

The beating of bounds or parading round the
boundaries of the parish, that was once common in
England at Rogation-tide, does not seem to have been
practised in our neighbourhood. It would, in fact,
have been almost impossible to have done it, for townships and parishes are involved and detached in a
wonderful manner. This jumble probably arose from
there being so much waste land that was either swampy
marsh, or barren moor, land that was held in common
with manorial rights and claims, if any, very vague
and lax, and from the fact that the rivers many times
shifted their courses after the boundaries were fixed.

The last of the Church festivals that I propose to
mention is Ascension-tide. The House of Commons
has lately debated whether to get on with its work on
Ascension Day, or go to church or play ; and there
are people who religiously or superstitiously believe
that if it should rain on that day, the water is particularly precious, having some specially holy or beneficial
properties.

"The Wakes"

certainly was originally the name of a festival of the
Church, though now it is used in some of our Lancashire towns as the name of the annual autumnal trip
from home, when all the mills close for " Wakes week."
In some places it is simply a time for dissipation, a
sort of low fair, with mild attempts at *rouge-et-noir*
at stands in the street, and, of course, drunkenness,
though the people are decidedly improving as regards
the last vice. In my books on Didsbury I have

written so fully about the wakes that here I will
merely give an historical sketch of them.

When Christianity was being established in England, Pope Gregory the Great decreed that all churches
should have a feast or festival on the anniversary of
the dedication of the Church, and that booths should
be erected near to them for the accommodation of the
people attending the festival, in order to gradually wean
the pagans from their heathenish feasts. For many
centuries the direct successors of these primitive booths
have been annually erected near to Didsbury church
on every 5th of August until within the last twenty or
thirty years, and in them and round about the people
kept their vigils or wakes all night, and kept others
awake also, and consequently the annual feast of
the anniversary of the dedication of the Church was
familiarly called " The Wakes." The rush-cart was
made up at Withington, the part of the parish where,
as the name shows, the withies or rushes were most
plentiful, and it was drawn in triumphal procession
from the house of the lord (the old Hall or the Hough)
to the church, where the rushes were strewn on the
floor, and the garlands and other decorations were
hung over the altar in the chancel. Before the new
rushes were strewn on the floor the old ones were
taken away and the church cleaned. The parish meeting was held, and the year's accounts of the church
were rendered, and the cess or ley made for the
following year. Then followed the jollification.

The garlands and flags were survivals of the old
custom of making offerings at the shrine of the local
saint, and they were annually offered at Didsbury on
the 5th of August, that day being the anniversary of
the death of Oswald, King of Northumbria, who was
killed near Winwick, about twenty miles west of Dids-

bury, in 642. Many years after his death Oswald was canonised and enrolled in the martyrology of the Church, but when the great Defender of the Faith was regularly and systematically breaking every one of the Ten Commandments, and establishing the Church of England, with himself as its "only Supreme Head on earth," he reformed the list of saints and struck off those who were not Jews. Therefore Oswald, our oldest local Christian martyr, is not recognised by the Church of England, although many of our oldest local churches are still called after him— for instance, Malpas, Brereton, Backford, and Nether Peover, in Cheshire; Marton and Grasmere, in Lancashire: these have their wakes on August the 5th ; and the original Abbey of Chester was dedicated to St. Oswald and St. Werburgh. The foundation-stone of the last enlargement of the old church at Didsbury has recently been laid by Sir Oswald Mosley, whose Christian name, like that of so many of his ancestors who were lords of the district and patrons of the church, is the same as that of the man who, I believe, was formerly considered to be the local saint and martyr, namely, Oswald. It may seem hardly credible in these days, that within thirty years the 5th of August was really a great festival, and that men of all ages actually danced on the high-road before the ark of rushes the whole of the two miles of journey, just as David and others danced before the ark in the Israelitish processions. After several intervals, the last rush-cart was made in Jubilee year (1887), but the wakes were not religiously supported, and the time-honoured festival has quietly slipped into being merely a thing of the past. The next Bank holiday is on St. Oswald's Day, and the new order of things is again engrafted on the old, and the new holidays supplant the Christian's holy days as they supplanted the pagan's feast. Complaints were lately made to our local council of the nuisance caused by the wakes or the survival of the remnant of them, and when I said it was a religious or Church festival, and the complainants should see the parsons, for the council had no power, I seemed "as one that mocked."

Close to Northenden church, by the side of the lane to the ford, there were formerly some pits called the ducking-pits, where women who persistently talked out of their turn were publicly ducked; and there were old pits that had probably been used for the same purpose by the green at Didsbury. The large sycamores just outside the college wall still mark the site. These ducking-pits were considered to be excellent institutions, for when women were imperfectly educated they sometimes wrangled, nagged, and scolded their poor men things into early graves; whereas, nowadays, if some lady talks too fast, the local medicine-man inserts a thermometer in her mouth and notes her temperature, a most interesting performance that enables some one else to get a word in.

Harvest Home.

Those who have studied folk-lore say that the best of all places for learning the customs and the wisdom of our forefathers is some solitary country house that has been inhabited by the same family for generations. Such an ideal house, and one that has always been a second home to me, is Standon Hall. It is forty miles due south of Didsbury, and near to the main line to London, and yet it is nine miles from any town. I now record the great festival of harvest as it was there kept up, until in our latter days there has ceased to be any wheat harvest to celebrate and rejoice over.

In the early years of this century there were tremendous efforts to prove that wheat could not be grown in England to pay the farmer under 80s. a quarter. Then down to the time of the Irish famine the corn laws were fixed, so that wheat came to the country free of duty at 72s. At the time of the repeal of the corn laws it was accepted that wheat must be grown to pay at about 50s. Soon after I knew the business it was vehemently urged that the farmers must all be ruined with wheat at 40s. Then it settled to 30s. Now, in 1895, it is 20s. Still the farmers are not all ruined. But there has not been a grain of wheat or barley grown at Standon Hall for three years. The land has (to use a much misunderstood term) gone out of cultivation. It is now under turf, and worth far more than being under plough, and the great labour difficulty is not with harvestmen, but to get milkmen or milkmaids. As I could not get a good photograph of the former I give one of the latter. There should have been three boys in the picture, but as it is almost impossible to get two "country wenches," three boys, and a dog all still for one second, the boys were left out, and then the others kept quiet.

From an old book of my late uncle's, I was surprised to find what quantities of wheat he sold from the farm forty to fifty years ago. He always treated his men (and every one else) well, and the harvest supper was literally a great feast.

The wheat was then sown in autumn, before the full of the moon, and on January 6, as soon as it was dark, all the household, servants, and visitors, took bundles of straw, tied tight like torches, lighted them in the wheat fields, and ran shouting over every bit

GONE A-MILKIN'...

of ground that had been sown with wheat. This was done to scare the witches from the corn, for, as Shakspere knew, the witches mildew the young wheat and strike dead the lambs. I believe it was done on that night as being the anniversary of old Christmas, not because it was the Epiphany or Twelfth Day, and it was possibly a survival of the Saturnalia, or festival of Saturn. The Church has always been appropriating the heathen's festivals, for even now there are harvest festivals at every church, though we never heard of them thirty years since, and they have become fashionable as the farmers' harvest homes have gone out. It is very right and proper to have them, and to decorate the churches with corn and fruit from all over the earth, for there are always harvests somewhere; but the Church festivals in their decorous respectability are as like or as unlike to the wild revelry of the harvest home, where the men and women were gorged with beef and goose and ale, as the early Church festivals were to the riotous feasts of our Anglo-Saxon forefathers twelve centuries ago.

When the harvest was being reaped, if a stranger came into the field he was expected to pay his foot ale, and it is said this term is the origin of the word fuddle. If a waggoner upset a load or a gatepost he was said to "loose the goose," meaning he was not to have any of the Michaelmas or stubble goose; but I think the meaning is obscure, if not altogether lost. There was always a little corn left standing for luck, or for the birds, and the rakings that some people took were by others left for the gleaners or leazers, as in the days of Ruth. In the last few years the custom of gleaning, a custom almost as old as the human race, has entirely ceased. The country woman would not take the corn home and use it if it were given to her.

She would say the grocer's cart brings the bread—
with the pickles and the gin. When the last load was
being carted, a great shout of triumph went up for all
the neighbours to hear. There are several versions
of what was shouted, though I believe the following
to be the most proper one : " We'n sheared and shorn,
we'n sent the hare to So-and-So's corn "—mentioning
some neighbour who had not finished his harvest.
The hare is doubtless the old symbol for the witch, as
witches always took the form of hares, or, failing them,
of cats and reptiles. Shouting of " Sickery, sickery
shorn, hip, hip hooray," was loud and continuous as
the last load was being carted, and in some districts the
last sheaf was dressed up and held in special honour.

Then came the great supper—the feast that was
greater even than the Wakes or Christmas. The hall
or house-place of Standon Hall is the size of a
Cheshire rod—that is, eight yards on every side. At
one end of the table were two or three geese, with
plenty of sage and onion stuffing ; at another, a huge
round of beef, from which could be cut "slices that
wouldner bend " ; and there were gallons of nut-brown
home-brewed ale. Grace was reverently said, and
then there was a worrying and gulping of flesh as when
a pack of hounds or wolves seize their prey. Then there
was plum-pudding and ale, apples and pears and ale,
nuts and ale, tobacco and ale, songs and ale, plenty of
ale. One man would boast he could teem it down his
throat without swallowing ; another, that he would take
two dozen glasses right off the reel. Then came the
songs, and of these I must only give the first verses :—

> " Nimble Ned comes dancing in,
> 　With a jug of ale so brown and prim ;
> 　Come, fill your glasses to the brim,
> 　To welcome harvest home, home, home,
> 　To welcome harvest home."

STANTON HALL FROM THE FOLD.

There was always the well-known John Barley-
corn, and as the ale was known to have been made
from barley grown and malted in the parish, and the
mash or worts duly signed with the sign of the cross,
the enthusiasm was prodigious; in fact some of the singing resembled bellowing. The master's song was—

> " Did you ever see the devil,
>   With his wooden spade and shovel,
>   Digging 'taties by the bushel,
>   With his teil cocked up?"

There is a common belief in most countries that a
goblin does supernatural work on a farm if well treated
and not disturbed. Shakspere and Milton refer to it.
Note also that the spade is wooden. Iron is not liked
by demons, it gets too hot.

Another verse of my uncle's song was—

> " He was dressed in jacket red,
>   With his breeches of sky blue,
>   And they had a little hole
>   Where his teil came through."

There was a ditty which my father used to sing, of
which I only remember one verse—

> " The miller was drowned in his dam,
>   The weaver was hung by his yarn,
>   The devil took off the tailor
>   With the broadcloth under his arm "

I am afraid the third line is wrong, but no one ever saw
these old songs in print. Other snatches of songs were—

> " Sing old rose and burn the bellows,
>   Let us do as wise men tell us :
>   Now we're met as jovial fellows,
>   Sing old rose and burn the bellows."

A great song of my father's, if he were present on
these festive occasions, was—

> " A bumper of burgundy fill, fill for me."

Others were "The Love of Alice Grey," and "The Soldier's Tear"; but the one that "brought down the house" was when the missus came in to sing

"She wore a wreath of roses."

That had to be repeated two or three times, till the women mingled their drink with their weeping, for their tears ran down into their ale, and they enjoyed it immensely. Then the women-servants would sing in their turn, generally in a high-pitched quivering falsetto voice—

"Mark yonder turtle-dove that sits on yonder tree,
He sits and he sings to his favourite she;
Then grant what I ask and believe what I swear,
That a kiss from a maiden's the 'batchelder's' fare";

or "Gorby Glum"—

"My name is Gorby Glum,
I'm just turned one-and-twenty,
My face, I think, by gum,
Will get me sweethearts plenty."

Another song was "Sweet William a-mourning amid the green rush." I could only get one entire verse and the chorus, which I wrote down "phonetically." We used to think this chorus was only nonsense, but my recent studies in folk-lore have taught me to find all sorts of meanings in old words and customs, and this also turned out to be an interesting case. The verse was—

"I'll sell my locks, I'll sell my reel,
I'll sell my mother's spinning-wheel,
To buy my love a sword and shiel.
Shule, shule, shule aroon,
Shule gang shoch a locher,
Shog a mocher lu."
(Chorus repeated.)

The word "shule" sounded Irish, and as I know several

Irish gentlemen about Hanging Ditch, who sell eggs
and bacon and butter, I called on them to ask them
about it. They are all Home Rulers, bursting with
patriotism and eloquence, but there is not one of them
who knows his own language. They say their parents
knew it "elegantly," but from centuries of oppression
they have not learnt it. Then, like the Israelite of
old, I drew a bow at a venture, and writing to a man
who never lived, I directed the letter to the Professor
of Gaelic or Celtic at Owens College. This brought
a reply from the Rev. Father Henebry, who sent me
a most learned epistle, part of it being in Irish words
and letters. He says the original song was probably
Irish, translated into English nearly two centuries
since, and as the refrain or chorus would lose its
timbre in English it was kept Irish. This is very
probable, for the word "shule" may be a wailing lament
or a stern shout, very much more romantic than the
English word "come." He gives the proper chorus
to be—

> "Shule, shule, shule, a roon,
> Shule gü sucker oggiss shule gü cyüne,
> Shule gü thee in dhorrus oggiss aleig lum,
> Iss gü dhay thoo mü voorneen slawn ";

and the translation of it—

> "Come, come, come, oh my secret love,
> Come quietly, and come silently,
> Come quickly and elope with me,
> And mayst thou fare unscathed, my love."

" Fare " is here used in its old sense of travelling ; and
in the following verse, also supplied by Father Henebry,
red is taken as the typical English colour. Mr. Crofton,
of Didsbury, has also hunted up and given me another
version of the song. It is evidently the passionate
lament of an Irish girl for her lover who has emigrated,

perhaps to England as a harvester, and the chorus is
his call to her to come after him, and the Irish have
sung it at our harvest homes until it has been learnt,
parrot-like, and the meaning forgotten : —

> "I'll dye my clothes, I'll dye them red,
> Around the world I'll beg my bread,
> Till I find my lover, living or dead.
> Shule, shule, shule," &c.

Imagine these songs being sung with all the wind
of men and women who were used to shouting to one
another across a forty-acre field ; they would have
blown the windows out or the roof off a flimsy-built
house. After hours of feasting and revelry, the highest
happiness of which these peasants could conceive, they
would become noisier or drowsier. Some would want
to climb the cupboards, a row of old oaken cupboards
on one side of the room (Darwinites would say they
wanted to climb as their reason got weaker). That
was a sign that they were to be got to bed, if possible.
Others would keep up all night till the broad daylight, and it was time to fetch up the cows and go
a-milking.

The picture of the interior of Standon Hall is
from a photograph that I took in the summer of 1896.
After many attempts which were not satisfactory, for
the windows are very low, with diamond-shaped panes,
and the whole interior is therefore very dark, I persuaded the ladies to sit still for four minutes, which is
really a long time. The south window is to the left
of the picture, the weather-glass being alongside it.
The lantern, dog-whip, and almanack are shown. The
lady with her back to the light is my mother, then
in her eighty-eighth year ; the next is my father's
youngest sister, Mrs. Aston, then in her seventy-fifth
year ; and the other one, Mrs. Woolf, who was in her

STANTON HALL.

eighty-fifth year.   The door of one of the oaken cupboards is thrown back, to give more light at the right
of the picture.   Overhead is the old-fashioned rack
for walking-sticks, tools, rods, guns, &c.

Many and many a time it has seemed to me like
leaving one world for another to leave the hurry and
bustle of Manchester, where every one is talking of
money or of some new thing, and in two hours to be
in the calm solitude of a country place, where money
is seldom seen, where they want no new thing, for
they say the old is better; where there is no noise
and no hurry, and where the talk is of cows and crops
and country pursuits, as it was with the patriarchs of
centuries ago.

STANDON HALL FROM THE SOUTH.

Souling

is another old custom that is not yet extinct. It is used as an excuse for the poorest class to beg soul cakes or anything else on All Souls' Day. Soul cakes were plain, flat, round cakes, seasoned with spice. If they could not be got, fruit was asked for.

The custom of Souling seems to be another of the very old or pre-Reformation customs, for it evidently originated when we were all Roman Catholics and the Requiem Mass for the repose of "All Souls" was attended by all on the second of November. It is difficult to see the precise connection between the soul mass cake, as it was formerly termed, and the mass for the souls, but the poorer people may have virtually said to their richer neighbours, "Give us cakes that we may feast to-day and fast to-morrow, and pray for the repose of the souls of your forefathers and ours." Souling was certainly a regular custom in my time; it is still observed by boys, who are more or less dressed up for the occasion, and quite ready to stow away any amount of apples or pears, or cakes.

> "A soul cake, a soul cake.
> I prithee, good missus, a soul cake,
> One for Peter, two for Paul,
> And three for Him who made us all.
> A soul cake, a soul cake."

That is one version of the Souler's song, and another verse that is also used by the Easter Pace-eggers or the Christmas Carollers is—

> "An apple, or pear, or cherry,
>   Or aught as'll mak us all merry;
> Up wi' th' kettle an' down wi' th' pon,
>   Gi' us good ale an' we'll be gone."

The variations of these verses are almost endless. The word "ale" in the last line should be "handsel," but that word has one syllable too many, and the beggars preferred the ale for other reasons. An old toper said he never knew any bad ale; he knew some sorts were better than others, but as long as he could drink it, it could not be bad. In the longest printed version of the song that I can find, the lines are altogether different from the above, with continual repetitions of "souling for apples and strong beer." The word "beer" sounds modern, and is suggestive of the chemical decoction sold at a "tied house." It was always ale with the old folks, in the old records, and in the old inns or ale-houses.

If their songs or eloquence still failed to bring out the soul cakes or other good things, the soulers would get lower and beg for money, coming down in price a halfpenny at a time, like our merchant princes on the Royal Exchange when the bargaining is hard and they haggle for ha'porths.

> "If you ha'ner a penny a hawpenny 'll do;
> Gi' us a soul cake or an apple or two."

A few years since there was some excitement in Cheshire about the Master of the Hounds shooting some Soulers who begged and sang outside his window when he was having his dinner. The name Sowler has probably been Souler originally. Shakspere mentioned the custom (as he mentioned all things), "puling like a beggar at Hallowmas"; All Hallows or All Saints' Day being November the first, and therefore the eve of All Souls' Day, that being the day for praying for the repose of those souls who had not been exactly saints. In late years the number of souls is considerably greater than the number of saints.

There is a good old-fashioned sweet pear called Brown Beurre, or Toad Back, from its rough leathery skin, that is ripe at Hallowe'en or All Souls', and it is then largely consumed. Any one is welcome to those we have left, for fruit is often so plentiful that quantities are left on the ground uncared for.

There are some old verses of perhaps similar age to the Soulers' song that are sometimes used as prayers, sometimes as children's songs, and often with considerable variations. As they pray for the intercession of saints and are used by children of all religions, they also have probably descended from pre-Reformation times. The first couplet is well known :—

> " Matthew, Mark, Luke, and John,
> Bless the bed that I lie on."

Then come endless variations, for instance :—

> " There are four corners to my bed,
> And four angels o'er me spread,
> One to watch and one to pray,
> And two to guard me through the day."

The parody I heard the oftenist is—

> " Matthew, Mark, Luke, and John
> Went to bed with their breeches on."

As breeches have long since been discarded by all but horsemen, the word itself shows antiquity.

The custom of going a-Tummusing shortly before Christmas is nearly forgotten. It was on St. Thomas's Day that poor folk went round to the farms or elsewhere begging wheat, or in later days anything they could get. It was probably in anticipation of Christmas.

Christmastide.

"God rest you, merry gentlemen,
Let nothing you dismay,
For Jesus Christ, our Saviour,
Was born on Christmas Day,
And 'tis tidings of comfort and joy."

Another old carol that has many versions was a great favourite when we were young, but never until lately did I notice that it began with exorcising the demon or spirit of evil as personified in the old folk tales in a magpie :—

" The magpie sat on the pear-tree top,
The pear-tree top, the pear-tree top,
The magpie sat on the pear-tree top,
On Christmas Day in the morning.

I'll lay her a crown, I'll fetch her down,
I'll fetch her down, I'll fetch her down," &c.

Pear-trees are often the tallest trees near to country houses, and I have a distinct recollection of seeing on a Christmas morning long ago a magpie on the very top of the lofty "Timothy Moss" pear-tree that still stands near to our lodge. We all defied her, and spat, and carolled, and fetched her down quickly.

What lines can be more enlivening for boys to whistle and girls to sing than the concluding ones of this old carol about Joseph and his Lady –

" He did whistle, and she did sing,
And all the bells on earth did ring,
For joy our Saviour, He was born
On Christmas Day in the morning."

The well-known tale of the shepherds watching their flocks by night comes home to our country folk more than to the dwellers in towns. The lambing season is at hand, with the time for the calving of cows and the farrowing of sows, and as men sit up in expectation through the night they wonder how it is the animals know it is Christmas. They say that at midnight on Christmas Eve all the beasts go on their knees in silent adoration ; certainly some go on their knees for a short time, for I have seen them, and we could scarcely expect them to be praying all night. If any one goes through a sheep-fold at that hour, or even on a hillside where there are sheep, they may be heard calling to one another "Baa lamb," "Bethlehem." "Bethlehem" may be heard being bleated forth on all sides in various tones, and in the voices of the sheep the children hear the name of the favoured birthplace. It is well known that ghosts start and vanish when a cock crows, and that cocks crow all night at Christmas to scare the ghosts away. Some people say the cocks are kept awake then by the unusual stir of carollers and revellers, but some people will say anything sooner than their prayers. Mine are the proper orthodox gamecocks, and they certainly crow very often on a Christmastide night. There is a most beautiful allusion to this old belief in the first scene in " Hamlet "—Marcellus is the speaker :—

> " Some say that ever 'gainst that season comes,
> Wherein our Saviour's birth is celebrate,
> The bird of dawning singeth all night long :
> And then they say no spirit stirs abroad,
> The nights are wholesome, then no planet strikes,
> No fairy takes, nor witch hath power to harm,
> So hallow'd and so gracious is the time."

To which Horatio replies

> " So have I heard, and do in part believe ; "

and so say all of us.

Fifteen years ago my poultry were being looked after by Michael Macnamara, the man who cleft the Russian general's head at Balaklava. It was Mac's fate that his bones were not left to bleach on some foreign shore, for when his stormy life was done he was quietly laid to rest in the shadow of the old church at Didsbury, and in the dust that had already held so many that had fought in England's battles. On Christmas Day Mac said, " Plaze, yer honour, what'll I give the burruds for their Christmas dinner ? " When I replied, "Their usual food," he looked very disconsolate, and said, "Oh! sorr, plaze God, the pore craturs is hoping for a trate." So he got the remains of the plum-pudding, mixed with meal, and plenty of pepper from the old mill that has ground our pepper since before I was born, and gave them "a trate." Some people say pepper warms the fowls' gizzards and makes them lay. There is also an ancient belief that bees, although torpid at Christmas, hum a drowsy echo of the angels' song. Their humming appears to me to be more like the familiar tune of "Christians awake," but we now get so saturated with that tune at the time, that it may have got into our heads or gone humming round the hives on its own account.

The great festival of Christmas was decreed by the Roman Catholic Church to be held at the time of the midwinter feasts of the older religions, and traces of the older forms of worship still exist in some customs respecting our fires and the decorating of our houses with evergreens. There are people still living who well remember the time when there were no matches, and then it was usual never to let the fires out, nor to kindle fresh fires, nor to give fire or light to another household, or to a stranger, during Christmastide, that is, during the twelve days ending with

Twelfth Night or the Epiphany. It is still usual to
have an extra big fire, a yule log, or big brand, and
to watch the sparks go up the chimney, saying, "There
goes the parson and there goes the clerk." The fire
is religiously kept up all through Christmas Day and
on New Year's Eve for the New Year. This is
almost certainly a survival of the fire or sun worship
of the ancient Eastern nations ; and the decking of our
houses and churches with holly and ivy is a survival
of Druidism, for most people know that the mistletoe,
the sacred plant of the Druids, is still in the greatest
request at a family gathering, while it would be awfully
wicked to take it into a church. Any orthodox bishop,
dean, priest, or curate would be shocked at the mere
mention of mistletoe in a church. It was probably
one of the clergy when rather far gone who wrote the
following verse that was recited at Christmas :—

> "The holly bears a berry red,
> The ivy bears a black 'un,
> To show that Christ His blood did shed,
> To save our souls from Sattan."

Every one knows the virtues of mistletoe. I dare not
say more about the sacred plant than this, that at
Didsbury I cannot get it to grow on the oak-tree,
although we have sixty bushes of it, many of them
self-sown on our apple-trees.

A most important old custom still in force at all
the farm-houses in Cheshire, and for fifty miles south
of Manchester, is for all the servants to go home and
leave their work during Christmas week. Everything is well cleaned, and stores of food made as
ready as possible before Christmas Day, and then all
work that can be stopped, is stopped, until the second
of January. Quantities of mince-pies should be made

beforehand of the shape of a manger or broad cradle, and filled with Eastern products symbolical of the offerings of the Magi. It is vainly supposed that every mince-pie eaten in a friend's house during the twelve days of Christmastide ensures a happy month in the coming year, the days and the months to be of corresponding numbers.

The time-honoured custom of mumming or acting plays in our country houses must be referred to, as well as the waits and carol singers, for it is probably the original of our Christmas pantomimes. The mummers, masquers, or guisers go from house to house, demanding admission, and acting a rude play in which St. George fights with the Dragon, *alias* the Slasher, who is slain and brought to life again by the elixir of life. The most sensible man of the party, who is generally called the fool, goes round with a ladle for a collection, and if contributions are not forthcoming, he gets a broom to sweep the floor and make a dust, saying—

> "It's money I want, and money I crave,
> Give me some money, or I'll sweep you to your grave."

He then sweeps towards the fire, and sometimes scatters the ashes as if he were making a raid upon the house fire, perhaps a survival of some long-forgotten attack on the household gods. A witty actor could make many personal and political allusions that were entertaining to the company. Their politics were inspired by the local Tory newspaper published once a week in a remote country district, and as saints and kings were considered to be very much alike, St. George became King George of glorious memory. The Slasher did duty for Buonaparte, or old Boney, as he was familiarly called. There was some friction between England and France just before the Crimean War, and I remember distinctly how an old uncle, who had volunteered against the First Napoleon, frightened us almost into fits with news about Napoleon the Third and some fancied invasion of England. He said, "Boney's coming," and didn't we practise the Slasher.

A verse of the old Wassail Hymn, that is, or was, perhaps, oftenest used as a short carol by the children in this neighbourhood, may be taken to conclude this chapter :—

> ' God bless the master of this house,
>   God bless the mistress too,
> And all the little children
>   That round the table goo."

HAY HARVEST, DIDSBURY.

CHAPTER V

THE WEATHER AND FLOWERS

" Winter's not gone yet, if the wild geese fly that way."—AUTOLYCUS.

" There's rosemary, that's for remembrance—pray you, love, remember ; and there's pansies, that's for thoughts."—OPHELIA.

HERE is a vast amount of folk-lore respecting the weather, but unfortunately a great deal of it is like the weather itself, and cannot be depended on, therefore I will only mention the more trustworthy proverbs and sayings, leaving the great multitude severely alone. There are many versions of the following lines ; they are undoubtedly true in the great majority of cases :—

"The evening red, the morning grey,
Are certain signs of a fine day."

"A red sky at night
Is the shepherd's delight,
A red sky at morning
Is the shepherd's warning."

"A dripping June
Sets things in tune."

"Drought ne'er breeds dearth in England."

This last is a proverb I wrote about in the *City*

News some years ago, when there were so many complaints about the hot dry summer. It has been proved over and over again by practical farmers that in the fine hot years they do the best. If the grass is short it is good, and the hay and corn are good, and cost little to get ; the cattle and all live stock do well, and the fruit is good. In many places the fruit is an important crop, and the following lines are more of a prayer than a proverb :—

> "September blow soft
> Till the fruit's in the loft."

The weather depends more on the wind than on anything else. The wind has also great effect on the cattle, for farmers know that "wind drives away milk."

> "No weather is ill
> If the wind be still."

A peck of March dust may be worth a king's ransom, for kings have come down in value since so many were made in Germany. The March winds certainly do good in drying the land at a time when the live stock should be under shelter. The proverb—

> "If it rains when the wind is in the east,
> It will rain for twenty-fours at least"—

is not contradicted by the old question, "What's the use of praying for rain when the wind is in the east."

Another of my churchwardenship experiences that has escaped publication is as follows :—During a time of prolonged wet weather our late rector thought it was time for him to interfere with special prayers for fine weather. When he consulted his wardens, I said I had heard that our neighbours the Methodists had been trying their best for three weeks, but no notice seemed to have been taken of them. He appeared slightly shocked at the comparison, for surely he, with all the authority of the Established Church and the weight of the apostolic succession, would have more influence than they, and it was evidently a case where the prayers were sure to be answered—if they were continued long enough. A Cheshire farmer was once "leading hay in a catchy time," on a Sunday morning, when he had the misfortune to upset his load. A perfervid parishioner, who had been watching him through the church windows instead of getting on with his own devotions, was so rejoiced at this manifestation of the vengeance of the Lord on the ungodly, that he startled the congregation by crying out to them, "'Er's warted, 'er's warted."

Those who are used to country life can foretell the weather by noticing the animals, for they are more susceptible to its influences than we are, and their movements show what they expect. Any old cow or sow that is loose on a farm is a more trustworthy weather prophet than all the meteorological reports in the newspapers. It is said that certain learned members of the British Association at one of its annual gatherings ascended a high hill to make some observations, and congratulated themselves upon the fine weather and the prospect of its continuance; but one of them condescended to ask a simple shepherd what he thought about the weather. The shepherd said it would be wet, that was certain. The collected wisdom and science of the age totally differed from the simple boor, and further inquired if he had any reasons for the faith that was in him. The reply came at once, simple enough but weighty, "If yon owd tup turns its rump to th' wind an' that uns, it'n be wet, I tells ye, chus 'ow ony on yo say." And it was so. Some years since I was witness of a strongly-marked case of cattle foretelling the weather.

The day was August Bank Holiday, the weather had been wet, the morning was very dull and heavy, and we were anxious that it should be fine, as some elderly ladies wished to go a long drive in a pony carriage. The reports were bad, there was little or no consolation to be got from the barometer; but my late uncle, to whom we are indebted for much of this folk-lore, was certain the day would be fine, and as I had the greatest respect for his judgment I asked him for his reasons. From the windows or garden of Standon Hall we could see the country for miles round, and pointing to the various herds and flocks of live stock, he said, "See how the cattle all over the country are spreading themselves out and grazing up bank; the day will be fine and hot, that's certain." He was right, for the cattle grazed up bank, until towards noon they were all resting on the tops of the hills, or on the highest places in the fields to get as much fresh air as possible, for the day was very sultry. Pigs are said to see the wind, because they run about with straw in their mouths to make a bed long before the storm comes; but if it is going to be hot they lie in the mud and wallow. Swallows fly low before rain comes, because the insects on which they feed seek the protection of the grass and herbage; if they fly very high and circle round in the air, that is a very good sign for fine weather.

It would be impossible to mention all the cases in which the movements of animals may be relied on as foretelling the weather. Here are some instances of the more fanciful side of the folk-lore respecting our good friends the pigs. If pigs are not killed before the moon is at the full, the bacon will "front" and not set properly. If there is much talk and little work at a place, the country folk say it's like shearing a pig—

BETTY AND HER DOZEN PORKERS.

much cry and little wool. When we were young we each had our own little pig; they were called children's pigs but daddy's bacon; but when we ate as much of the fat bacon as we could, we levelled things up again and made it as broad as long.

Writing of pigs reminds me of another curious bit of folk-lore or fact respecting them. A sow has only twelve paps, and if she produces more than twelve young ones at a time, the little ones have to settle which are the "ricklings" that have to go without suck and die. Sometimes the mother will eat the supernumeraries, and let the others have them at secondhand. The accompanying illustration is from a lucky snapshot showing old Betty and her dozen porkers going foraging for pannage and unconsidered trifles. Pannage is an old term for gathering acorns. It may be noted that the young ones wear their tails curled, while the old one is careless, or anxiety has taken all the curl out of her tail.

Here followeth another very short and fragmentary notice of a large subject, one that would take a volume to do justice to. I never more fully realised the truth of Darwin's saying that we are like children on the sea-shore picking up a few grains of the sand of knowledge, while all around us stretch the countless miles of sand that we cannot grasp, than I did when attempting to set down some of the folk-lore concerning flowers and herbs. Their really useful, edible, and medicinal qualities I must leave altogether alone, and merely mention some of the more ancient and fanciful associations.

There were certain flowers associated with some of the holy days of the year by the monks and nuns of old, who tended their gardens with such loving care, and their rhymes and records still linger in our country places, and are well worth handing down to those who are to come after us, for it is written, "God Almighty first planted a garden, and indeed it is the purest of human pleasures and the greatest refreshment to the spirits of man ;" and "the wisest actors in human affairs and the best benefactors to mankind have in the ending of life sought gardening as a solace."

The snowdrop comes in flower for Candlemas. It is the emblem of the purification, and was once called Fair Maid of February. Why it should be said to be unlucky to bring it into the house, and fatal to chickens, I do not know. The yellow crocus flowers for the once famous day of St. Valentine ; the daisy or marguerite, once called Herb Margaret, for St. Margaret's Day, February 22. Love-lorn damsels seek to learn their fate by plucking off one of its petals, saying, " He loves me ;" then off goes another, " He loves me not ;" and so on to the end. The Lenten lilies or daffodils come in Lent :—

> " Then comes the daffodil beside
> Our Lady's smock at our Ladyetyde."

The French call the ladysmock Chemise de Notre Dame. How much more elegant and ladylike the word chemise sounds than our old-fashioned vulgar smock?

Then for St. George's Day, at the end of April, comes his flower, the hyacinth or bluebell, that carpets the woods and hills with such a beautiful blue. The snapdragon ought to have been dedicated to him, but it is not in flower early enough. St. John's wort blooms at midsummer, and is another of the plants so anxiously inquired of by the maidens who seek to anticipate the great question of their life. They will visit the churchyard at midnight ; they will sow hemp-seed ; they will practise wiles and divinations without

number ; and they will consult either priest or gipsy
with the same burning question, " Who's to wed me ? "

> " Oh, silver glowworm, lend me thy light,
> I must gather the mystic St. John's wort to-night,
> The wonderful herb whose leaf will decide
> If the coming year shall make me a bride."

The Madonna lily comes for the anniversary of
the Visitation, on July 2 ; and when the year is ending
and most of our flowers are faded and gone, we have
for consolation—

> " The Michaelmas daisy, among dead weeds,
> Blooms for St. Michael's valorous deeds."

It was the custom in olden time to cherish certain
flowers in commemoration of Christian saints ; nowadays it is fashionable to destroy and waste flowers
in commemoration of those who were neither saints
nor Christians.   The great party whose proud boast
it was that they were " *semper eadem*," " *stare antiquas
vias*," and that they meddled not with them who were
given to change, have spoiled nearly all our beautiful
old churches, and have now spoiled hundreds of miles
of flowers.   There were miles of banks in this neighbourhood lately covered with bluebells and primroses
that are now desolate and waste.   The sacrifice is an
offering to an idol neither saint nor Christian.   This last
spring I saw one solitary wild primrose in Didsbury, and
I covered it with grass for fear some rampant modern
Tory should pounce on it and tear it up by the roots
to deck the mixture of builders' refuse and rubbish called
the garden of some genteel semi-detached modern
villa, where it would inevitably pine away and perish.

It may be all a dream, but to me it is possible, if
not probable, that the numerous old-fashioned plants
with religious names that spring up in out-of-the-way
places, and even in the walks of this old garden, were

originally planted and cared for by the priests or monks of old. There is no doubt that this house stands on the site, and was partly built from the remains, of a still earlier one. The mud-built thatched cottage that stood in Cheadle churchyard until about twenty years since, and of which I fortunately had a photograph, and was able to rescue the name, was once known as the Priest's House, and was at least three hundred years old, as is shown by the parish registers.

Antiquaries know that nothing lasts longer than names, and the names of the flowers that grow wild in this garden are curious and remarkable. Here are some of them—monkshood, madonna lily, marigold, ladysmock, Star of Bethlehem (comes up all over the place), Solomon's seal, Aaron's rod, Aaron's beard, balm, herb of grace or rue, Lenten lilies, Canterbury bells (Canterbury was the great place of pilgrimage in England), golden rod (this was dedicated to St. Augustine, whose "sublime genius and sincere piety" earned him the name of Tormentum Infantium, for he was the first great Christian who taught that children dying unbaptized went to hell, and his golden rod was for them ; it flowers on his day, and he is a saint of the Church), St. John's wort, Turk's head or stinking lily (the Turk's head became a fashionable sign after the Crusades), fleur de lys or flower of St. Louis, or iris, Lammas damsons, Jacob plums, St. Martin's plums (they hang on the tree to Martinmas), Michael-mas daisies, with many herbs called after saints, and the mystic mistletoe that has certainly reproduced itself. There are others that I cannot say are wild, though they flourish, namely, the hollyhock, Veronica (the saint of the handkerchief), the passion flower, the rose of Sharon, our Lady's mantle, and others named after our Lady, also the peony, dedicated to St. Boniface

(another good dedication). These plants have probably reproduced themselves in continued succession
for centuries, and their names lead me to believe that
they were originally planted and cared for by the
priests or others connected with Didsbury church
before the great change of faith. The flowers come
up in their season, and bloom in their beauty, and
fade away irrespective of our little creeds, and we may
rest assured that "even Solomon in all his glory was
not arrayed like one of these."

THE OLD PARSONAGE GARDEN.

CHAPTER VI

ANIMALS

" The cock, that is the trumpet to the morn,
Doth with his lofty and shrill-sounding throat
Awake the God of Day."—H**AMLET**.

HERE is much quaint folk-lore about animals, and many worthy and religious people are very superstitious about meeting them or even seeing them.

A magpie is always the symbol of bad luck. As children, if we saw a magpie, we were taught to say, "Devil, I defy thee!" then to spit out, thereby exorcising the devil, and then to whistle. Two might be an omen of good luck, three of a wedding, and four of a death, but a single chattering pye forebodes evil continually. It is also considered by some people to be unlucky to meet a hare, or a strange cat, but worst of all is a "skenning" woman. We were taught to get over any fence or run round any way, sooner than meet a skenning woman, especially in a morning; and my paternal instructions even went so far as to tell me never to trust a man who squinted. More than twenty years ago, I, who wished to be guided by pure reason and laughed at old superstitions, disregarded this paternal advice and trusted a man who squinted,

and thereby lost £1000. That loss would certainly
have been saved if I had obeyed the precepts and
folk-lore of my father. The cuckoo will bring good
luck if, when you first hear it, you at once turn your
money over. If you unfortunately have no money
that you can turn over, then you do not comply with
the rule, and of course it does not apply to you—
more's the pity.

Cocks and magpies have drawn the attention of
the credulous and superstitious oftener than any other
birds. There is, or lately was, for
I have known it done, a strange
custom of placing hens' eggs in a
magpie's nest, so that the devil's
own bird could hatch a chicken
that might grow into a gamecock
which would be endowed from its
birth with some of the supernatural
sharpness of the devil's own. On
the other hand, the dust has been
swept off the church altar, and preserved to strew over the cock-pit,
to give better luck or supernatural
strength to the fighting cock, and even the consecrated bread is said to have been secreted to be given
to some favourite bird.

GAMECOCK CROWING.

In the present day it is seldom realised that, for
thousands of years previous to the last fifty years,
cock-fighting was one of the chief pleasures of our
forefathers.

From the far-off day when the fighting cocks in
the agora of Athens inspired the eloquence of Themis-
tocles and aroused the armies of the Athenians to one
more stubborn and determined defence of their homes,
the gamecock has played a not unimportant part in

the social life of the nations who have ruled the world. He has inspired them in war, he has solaced them in peace, and he has provided them with some of the best sustenance that carnivorous man could desire. Countless generations of our forefathers found their chief pleasure in cock-fighting, and many sayings in connection with the sport have passed into proverbs : " A cock fights best on his own bonk ; " " A good cock may come out of a bad bag "—one interpretation being, that a good or clever person may be shabbily dressed ; " To live like a fighting-cock " meant to live like a lord, not to be "as drunk as a lord "; " That cock won't fight " and " Nowt beats cock-faytin' " were common expressions. I have heard of a country gentleman going to the Italian opera to hear Mario and Grisi, and when the Queen and Prince Albert entered the house the whole audience rose to sing the National Anthem, and for one unguarded moment our friend sighed, " This beats cock-fighting," but presently he grew tired and sleepy and longed for a bit of real fighting again.

Orthodox Christians know that for ages it was the custom to have a day of feasting and revelry before entering on the long Lenten fast, and therefore Shrove Tuesday was specially devoted to pancakes and cock-fighting. Large masses of pancakes were eaten by all sorts of folks, so that they might have something solid on their stomach for the forty days of abstinence and fasting ; and cock-fighting was indulged in, for the cocks and their masters were to be denied the pleasure of fighting until the great festival of Easter, when they might go at it again. And here comes in a curious old custom that I have never seen recorded in any " quaint and curious volume of forgotten lore." My aunt, who still lives at Standon Hall, and is long past

the fourscore years, has all her long life religiously
taken the first pancake on Shrove Tuesday and given
it to the gamecocks. It is said to make them lay—
not the cocks, for if they laid, their eggs would only
produce serpents or askers, which would have to be
burnt; but the cocks should share the pancakes with
the hens, and talk to them about laying more eggs,
which will be wanted for pancakes and other things.
Some cocks gobble up the pancake in a hurry, and
won't give their wives a bit; others call the hens to them
and share it amongst them; and others cackle and cluck
and make a tremendous
fuss, but keep gobbling it
up as fast as they can, for
there is a deal of human
nature among cocks and
hens, and cocks are like
Christians in more things
than their fondness for fighting. The old-fashioned
game fowl, locally known

REAL OLD DERBY GAME.

as the Lord Derby, after
the celebrated cock-fighting earl, is now almost
extinct, and the loss of it is a great loss, for none of
the wonderful and horrible breeds of poultry that are
now the fashion of fanciers are fit to compare to it for
the general purposes of a country gentleman, and I
am rather proud to state that we still keep the old
breed with an unbroken pedigree of at least a
hundred years.

It is said that if a cock crows toward the house-
door it heralds the approach of a stranger, and certainly
many cocks, especially pugnacious ones, do always
crow their challenge when they see a strange man or
animal. Sometimes they get savage, and have been

F

known to kill children, the chief weapon of offence
being the spur, which is aided by the driving power
of the wing when they strike.

There is an old saying relative to the days increasing in length with the new year: "The day is longer
by a cock's stride." This has evidently come to us
from the time when sundials were used for telling the
time, and cocks perched on the dials to say they were
cocks of the walk. Our present mode of telling the
time by clocks is not always correct, for many years
since I noticed the sun did not always rise and set
at the times stated in the almanacks, and lately I have
had an interesting explanation. For instance, on the
first days of the year the sun is generally stated to
rise about eight minutes past eight, but I have been
certain it has not risen until after half-past eight, that
being my usual time of going to town. If I asked
any one whether they could explain the discrepancy,
they would say no, or there was none, or I should get
up earlier, or they perhaps asked if I set myself up in
opposition to the almanack. Mr. Alfred Brothers was
the only man who appeared to think it was a sensible
question, and he and Mr. Broughton worked out the
following answer for me:—The sun should rise at
Didsbury nine minutes later than at Greenwich, because Didsbury is farther west. There would be one
minute for equation of time and two for refraction.
There would also be fourteen minutes to be reckoned
at midwinter and also at midsummer for the different
altitude of the sun ; or, in other words, because Didsbury is so much north of Greenwich, and therefore so
much nearer the land of the midnight sun. It was
this last item I had been wanting to learn for many
years, for our days are certainly shorter at Christmas
and longer at midsummer than they are in London ;

and adding all these items together, with omitted fractions, I now understand the sun should rise at Didsbury on New Year's Day at 8.35, not at 8.8 as given in the almanacks.

To return to our cocks and hens. If cocks lay eggs, the eggs are said to produce serpents ; therefore it is not well to encourage such bad practices, and the cock should be burnt with the egg. If hens crow, their necks should be screwed at once.

> " A whistling woman and a crowing hen
> Are neither fit for God nor men."

I well remember the first time I saw a hen crow, for on running into the house to tell about it I was told to catch the hen at once, there and then, and screw her neck. Boys like prompt justice if they do not suffer themselves, so that poor hen fell a victim to folk-lore for appearing masculine.

The merrythought of chickens is used for divination. If a youth and maid, holding a merrythought by their little fingers, split it up the middle, they will almost certainly be married. This is a very cheap and harmless mode of divination. The interested parties try for themselves, and there is no ambiguity in the answer as there often is with fortune-tellers or prophets. Even a celebrated Roman oracle, when consulted by a man as to what he was to do with a bad-tempered wife, replied, " Dust her daily." The feathers of hens or of pigeons should never be used for feather-beds or pillows. They are said to be uncomfortable when any one is dying, though I should have thought the wings of doves would have helped the spirit on its flight.

There are many proverbs and old sayings relating to eggs. An unlucky venture is said to be a bad egg,

or eggs taken to a bad market, and it is not prudent
to put all your eggs in one basket. Anything very
full is as full as an egg is full of meat. Anything very
dear was said to be as dear as eggs at a penny each ;
nowadays three times that price is sometimes paid
for eggs for eating in the winter. It was also customary to break up the shells of eggs after the contents
had been eaten, for fear the fairies should use them.
Some economical persons who keep fowls give them
the empty shells and ask them to fill them again.
This is strict economy, and is all right if the shells
are smashed up. Otherwise they may tempt the hens
to eat their own eggs as soon as they have laid them,
and that is another bad practice. Some folk ask which
came first, the hen or the egg? The answer seems
obvious if incubators were not provided.

That wonderfully wise bird the goose must come
in for its share of folk-lore. What is sauce for the
goose is sauce for the gander. To play at fox-and-
geese is everywhere synonymous with the attempt
of craft and cunning to circumvent others as wary
as themselves. To go a wild-goose chase is well
known to mean an arduous chase or pursuit that will
probably end with nothing ; for the wild goose is
one of the wariest and fastest fliers of any birds,
although they are very tame when well treated. I
have some at Didsbury now, and it is a beautiful sight
to see the terrific pace they can go when on the wing.
Ordinary tame geese never forget their wild instincts
altogether, for they go into the middle of a field to
rest, and have sentries to stand and watch. An old
Roman legend relates how the watchfulness and cries
of geese saved the city of Rome.

Shakspere quotes an old proverb, "Winter's not
gone yet if the wild geese fly that way." It happens

sometimes in the spring migrations that there is a return of very cold weather, and the wild geese fly back again. Their fast-decreasing numbers now make their great flight north-east to the Siberian tundras or into Arctic regions. A few are seen passing over us about April, often at an immense height. When many geese are all talking together the sound of their voices reminds some people of the silvery tones of women's voices blending harmoniously together. If a child does not thrive, it is said to pine like a midsummer gosling, for late-hatched goslings generally die, as they cannot stand very hot weather, their natural time for breeding being in early spring, unless they are in very cold countries. Some of our farmers still quote the old proverbs—

> "On Candlemas Day
> Good geese should lay ;
> But on St. Chad [i.e March 2]
> Both good and bad."

These proverbs are probably older than the reformation or the alteration of the calendar. We had an old goose that always laid her first egg on or about the 26th of February. She never varied more than a day or two, and that variation was probably because she observed leap-year at the proper goose time, irrespective of our almanacks. When she was eighteen years old we killed her and ate her, and she was very good. This seems very shocking, but it is only another survival of our savage nature. Cannibals kill their best friends, or even their parents when they get very old, and eat them out of pure kindness. Some years since there were some geese stolen from the Peel, in Northen Etchells, and the thieves sent word saying if the geese were not younger and better fed another Christmas they would not fetch them. A neighbour

of my grandfather's had his geese not exactly stolen,
but bought cheap. The gander, who was known to
be about thirty years old, was left with the following
message, containing a sixpence, round his neck :—

> " Mr. Wood, your geese are good,
> You live here and we live yonder ;
> Here's pence a piece for your six geese,
> And the money by the gonder."

For the elucidation of the following old customs, it
should be stated that they are kept up at Standon
Hall, where there is only one cellar, a deep hole in the
ground, that may have been the dungeon of the old
hall. In this cellar are often found askers and toads,
and it was the custom to take these reptiles by the
tongs and then cast them alive in the big fire. I have
lately discovered the origin of that cruel custom, for
any one may read in the trials of the Lancashire witches
that it was formerly a common belief that if witches
could not get access to a house, they would assume the
disguise of toads and crawl in to listen to the talk of
the household, and therefore the reptile in the house
was to be burnt alive. The custom survives long
after the belief, or even the knowledge of why it is a
custom. When children we asked to save them alive,
and made little carts and harnessed the toads to them.
Toads make very solemn and sedate cart-horses, and
can draw surprisingly big loads ; but askers are too
skittish, they wriggle about, flap their tails vigorously,
and damage the harness.

Being in the midst of "a hunting country," the
doors of the stables and hen-cotes are adorned with
the pads of the fox, and this also is probably the
survival of another very old custom, for I lately read
in the *Field* an officer's account of the shooting of a

tiger in India, and the demand of his *shikaris* and the natives for a goat to be killed, so that its feet (instead of the tiger's) should be hung up as a sacrifice or propitiation to the gods of the jungle. The teeth and claws of tigers, bears, or other savage beasts are regularly used in wild countries as amulets, and here the grooms sport breast - pins made of the canine teeth of the fox. On the wall of the cowhouse was recently hanging in chains a "picked" calf, most certainly a survival of propitiation or sacrifice to the evil spirit of pestilence, for they who hanged it there avow that it was done that the cows might look upon it and that the plague might be stayed.

Here is another little superstition in the natural history line. I distinctly remember, above forty years since, one of the milkers showing me a gawn partly full of bloody milk fresh drawn from a cow named Beeston, one of the white cows with reddish necks and heads. The man said the milk was bloody because some one had taken a swallow's nest, for, he said, cows always gave bloody milk if the swallows' nests were "ragt" (*i.e.* taken); and on the beam above the cow there was found the ruined swallow's nest, and there was the milk all clotted with blood, and the mischief was laid to my charge, and I felt sorrowful and guilty although I was innocent, for there was the accusation and the silent evidence against me, and many a man and woman has been done to death in due process of law with no more proof of guilt ; for as the cow had undoubtedly given bloody milk she was evidently bewitched or some one had done something. False accusations are dreadful things, but when any one has stood a few contested elections they get used to them.

Cattle-drovers say it is very unlucky to hit a cow

with a withy stick.   A good ash plant, they say, will
wrap round their ribs just as well ; and they certainly
would not desist from using anything out of any regard
to the feelings of the cow ; in fact, they would probably prefer that which would give most pain with least
damage to the market value of the hide of the poor
beast.   The objection seems to be in a survival of the
belief that the withy or willow is unlucky, and an
emblem of mourning or lamentation, as shown by the
old term "wearing the willow."   "Every one to his
taste, as the man said when he kissed his cow," is
another old expression.   And if cows break into a
garden, they not only do damage, but forebode further
disaster.

After magpies and cocks, the best known birds in
folk-lore are owls and ravens.   The screech of the owl
is still regarded as the harbinger of death and woe,
but as the birds become scarcer they are seldom seen
or heard.   There are too many of what our county
councillor calls "fools with guns" after them.   Still
there are a few owls, not only in Didsbury, but in the
midst of Manchester city.   Shakspere's allusions to
the common folk-lore concerning them are very fine :—

> " It was the owl that shrieked, the fatal bellman
> Which bids the stern'st good night."

> " The raven himself is hoarse
> That croaks the fatal entrance of Duncan
> Under my battlements."

All the Corvidæ or crow family, which, of course,
includes ravens, jackdaws, and magpies, are well known
in folk-lore, though the ordinary mortal seldom knows
the difference between rooks and crows.   The superstitions regarding the raven may be as old as the time
of Noah.   In all Christian countries, and for many

ages, the clergy have always been associated with the crows, that term being inclusive of crows, rooks, and jackdaws. A Russian peasant would shrink with horror from killing a crow, for he believes in some vague way that the soul of some predeceased priest inhabits it ; and in our own village at the present day, when the students at the Wesleyan College, Didsbury, are trooping off together on the road, irreverent youngsters may be heard to ask one another, " What's aw them crows arter ? " History tells us that when the Reign of Terror was at its height in England, and our great King Henry the Eighth was regularly and systematically breaking every one of the Ten Commandments, and earning for himself the titles of Defender of the Faith and Supreme Head on Earth of the Church of England, it was a common cry to raise when the stately abbeys that are still venerable and beautiful in their ruin and decay were being spoiled, " Down with the nests and the rooks will fly."

Rooks are intensely conservative. They all hold together, and build their houses as near as they can to the house of the richest man in the parish. There are cases on record where the lord or squire of some country mansion has turned Radical, or openly changed his religion, and the rooks have promptly deserted his ancestral rookery. The man may change his party or the faith of his fathers through pique, " temporary aberration of intellect," or strong religious fervour, but the rooks look with suspicion on all changes, and meddle not with them that are given to change. They have also been known to hold a solemn conclave over some offending member of their flock, and then kill him at once. This extreme penalty is not inflicted for theft, for thefts are as common with

them as with us, as may be seen any time when they
are building their nests.   The crime must have been
a more serious one.   Perhaps the erring brother had
voted against his party, for that would be a great
shock to their conservative instincts.

> " Let laws, religion, learning die,
> But leave us still our old nobility."

Rooks are said to observe the Church festivals,
building their nests in Lent, and ceasing to build on
Good Friday.   There is ample proof that on Easter
Sunday they show their contempt for Christians who
do not then wear new clothes by spoiling the old
clothes in the most barbarous manner.

On the south side of Manchester rooks have increased very much in the last thirty years, although
the suburban population has increased enormously.
I can remember when there were very few of these
black and hungry birds, and now at times they cover
the fields "thick as autumnal leaves that strow the
brooks in Vallombrosa" ; or, as Milton would have
written if he had lived in our times—

> " Thick as the letters H
> That strew the floor of Council chamber."

Rooks are said never to complain without cause.
This may be only a pun, for if it were strictly true it
would not be another point of resemblance between
them and their clerical prototypes.   The babel of their
voices comes on the breeze even while I write, and
seems an endless repetition of the proud old Norman's
motto—

> " Ung foy, ung roy, ung loy."
> [One faith, one king, one law.]

" Night brings home crows " is said to young folks
who do not come home to tea, and " As the crow

flies " is another well-known expression. An old folk-lore proverb was once common in that oldest and most respectable of all occupations, namely, farming, that rooks, rabbits, and rats were the three pests of the farm. Nowadays farmers say that servants and land agents are worse than any of them, but a great capacity for grumbling is part of the heritage farmers have received from ancestors whose lives have been one long struggle with poverty.

The robin, one of the most friendly of all our English birds, owes much of the respect and sanctity in which it is held to two old legends. One of them is that when the Christ was crowned with thorns a robin tried to pull the thorns from off the bleeding brow, and His blood stained its breast ; and hence the blood-stained breast is the badge of the robins for ever, and gives them confidence that no true Christian will kill or harm them. It is a beautiful old legend, that has done no harm to any one, and immense good to the robins, for country lads are still told that if they kill a robin they will go to the gallows, and that terrible threat has doubtless protected many a robin, as the bloody milk theory has protected many a swallow's nest, and the mischievous lad has turned his energies against the mischievous sparrow. In my young days elderly folk often assured us we should go to the gallows, and called us "gallus lads" or "gallus birds"; but some of those meddling reformers got hanging for petty thefts abolished, thereby taking away the pleasure that many people had in seeing one another hanged, and although many things went wrong through lack of punishment, and prophecies were not fulfilled, we have so far escaped the extreme penalty.

The other of the well-known old tales is that about

the babes in the wood and the covering of them with leaves. It also must have been an old tale in Shakspere's time, for in that beautiful passage where he writes of sweetening the sad grave with fairest flowers, "the azured hairbell like thy veins," the ruddock (that is the robin)

> "Would bring thee all this,
> Yea, and furred moss besides when flowers are none,
> To wither round thy corse."

A little doggerel rhyme by some author less known to fame says—

> "A robin and a wren
> Are God's cock and hen ;
> A spink and a sparrow
> Are God's bow and arrow."

The spink is probably the chaffinch. The swallow is often introduced into the many variations of this couplet, and it may save the time of correspondents by saying, as the showman said to the child who asked which was Wellington and which was Napoleon, that they can take their choice. Cock Robin and Jenny Wren are often coupled in ballads and tales for children; and in some districts the pretty little wren, with its tiny cocked-up tail and sharp movements, is specially hunted and stoned by lads on St. Stephen's Day; but this, I am glad to say, is not a local custom, it comes from Ireland, and seems a very curious way of commemorating the stoning of the first Christian martyr.

One of the wonders of the world has always been the half-yearly migration of birds, and no more is known about it now than was known thousands of years ago. Lighthouses have thrown some little light on the matter, but none of the discoveries of science tell us anything as to how birds know the time and the direction for their flight. It has been said and written over and over again that the old birds know the way and fly by sight and teach the young ones. The contradiction to that statement is that in many cases the young birds migrate by themselves, or go first, and the great masses of migrants go at night, very often on pitch dark nights, when the only guides they can possibly have are the stars, if they are visible. Years before I read Gatke's book on the birds of Heligoland (that great observatory for bird life, where the natives seem to live out of the migrating birds), I had noticed that the first broods of young starlings which were reared in our garden all flew away and left the old ones to hatch another lot. Now Gatke states that the autumnal migration begins in July, with vast flocks of young starlings passing over or resting on the island. The young birds are easily distinguished from the old ones by their dull, sooty colouring. With cuckoos the case is reversed : the old ones go long before the young ones ; and how do the poor orphan cuckoos, without a friend or relation in the world, find their way to Africa and back ?

There is no doubt whatever that the great mass of migrants fly at night, for in some places they can be heard incessantly, and at immense heights. The light from lighthouses perplexes and dazzles them, for they rush into the light and are killed against the lantern in myriads. Fifteen thousand larks were killed at Heligoland lighthouse in one night. It is evident they do not fly by sight. Then how do they know their direction, and, assuming they know it, how do they keep to it ? They fly north to north-east in spring, and south to south-west in autumn. The south-westerly course explains the fact of there being so very many more migrating birds on the east coast of England than on the west coast, and the light from the lighthouses shows millions of birds flying in the dark in one direction as steadily and correctly as if they were all guided by the mariner's compass.

Then, as to the time for migration. Birds do not go according to the weather, as many people suppose : they go at a certain time of the year whether the weather be good or bad, unless it be extraordinarily bad. A large flock, or gaggle, as the wild-fowlers call it, of the pink-footed wild goose comes every year, on the twenty-fifth of September, to a certain place in Norfolk, where they are not molested, and there many hundreds, if not thousands, stay for the winter.

When Seebohm wintered at the mouths of the Petchora and Yenesay rivers to observe the life and migration of birds, the first signs of spring were always the wild geese, strong, hardy birds of immense powers of flight, that sometimes overshot the advancing spring and had to return to open water and rest awhile. These wild geese breed on the Siberian tundras or bogs, on the extreme northern parts of Russia, and they fly south-west to the east coasts or fen districts in England, because that suits them better than if they went due south, and their time of arrival may be predicted to a day. How do they manage this? There is no accounting for it, and we know no more than was known thousands of years ago, when it was written that "the swallow knoweth her appointed time."

I have long since observed that April 25 is about the time for swallows to come to Didsbury, and as I had nothing particular to do on that day this year, and the day was fine, I had a long walk through the fields to see what bird life there was to be seen. Going by the river to Northen, there were no swal-

lows to be found flitting over the water. Then by
the footpath round the churchyard and across the
high-road at Sharston I wended my way towards
Cross Acres and Brownley Green, where the nightin-
gale once came. In those secluded fields it was evident that the spring migration of birds was on, and the
corncrakes had probably come over on the previous
night, for their hoarse "croak, crake," resounded on
all sides. The cuckoo's well-known voice was heard
again, and I had to try to find a bit of money to turn
over. The peewits and the songsters were very busy ;
but there were no swallows, and the most likely place
to find them, namely, Castle Mill, that picturesque
pass of the Bollin, which was a castle or camp in the
Roman's days, and a mill in the days of Elizabeth, was
rather too far. Then I bethought me of the moat at
the Peel, and turning to the left I was soon there, and
there were the swallows skimming over the water and
flitting under the old stone arches of the bridge, just
as their ancestors had done for the last five hundred
years.

The mystery of nest-building and the hatching
of the eggs is as great a mystery as the migration.
Young birds will build a complicated and good nest
without being taught. Missel thrushes build early in
the spring, before the leaves are opened, and often in
a conspicuous place. I watched a pair that built on an
apple-tree near to our windows, and found them very
interesting, for the wife was a lazy one, and the husband had to pluck feathers from her and thrash her to
make her work, for we know some wives are troublesome, and require a little judicious chastisement. This
one took it all in a truly Christian spirit, for she never
rebelled or told tales of her husband, and was not at
all like the poor man's wife who, when the parson

was enlarging on the beauties of religion, and explaining the amiable qualities of the devil by quoting, " Resist the devil and he will flee from you," provoked her poor husband to reply, " Nay, nay ; my wife's a reg'lar devil, but if tha resists 'er 'erll flee at thee damned sharp." So we may learn lessons even of the birds. And here I should like to correct a popular error that seems to be copied from book to book. Missel thrushes do not eat mistletoe berries, and therefore I think they are not called after them. We have quantities of mistletoe berries in our garden, and they are never eaten by any birds, not in the very hardest frosts. The berries of the Cotoneaster microphylla are much liked by all the tribe of thrushes, who will take them even from the glass of the window.

It is good folk-lore to regard the building of birds' nests on, in, or against a house as a sign of good luck, especially if the nest be at the front door, and the young become "fletcht and flown." I knew a man who shot the blackbirds in his garden, even off their nests when they had young, because they took his fruit ; and when he was complaining of everything going wrong with him, I asked him what he could expect when he had treated the birds as he had done. He stared at me in wonder and amazement. So I asked him if he had never read an old tale that had been put into undying verse, about an ancient mariner who shot an albatross. "What nonsense ! Is it true ? " was his reply ; and mine to him was, " I don't know. What is truth ? "

This is the second winter that the remains of a blackbird's nest have clung to the roses and honeysuckle over the porch of our front door. The young were safely hatched and reared, undiscovered by boys or cats, and when fully fledged they left the nest.

One at least of them flew into the house and into the pantry, where it opened its beak, which was equivalent to opening all its body, for it seemed to be all mouth, as noisy, hungry, empty, and hollow as a windbag politician—

"A merciful Providence fashioned us hollow
That we could more easy our principles swallow."

It may or may not be that the bird's nest at the door, or other birds' nests against the walls of the house, were the outward and visible signs of good luck, that is, of peace and happiness within the house. The agnosticism engendered by a busy, varied life prevents one from being too superstitious, but I may thankfully say that with the years as they have been I have been content, and for any better I never wish nor hope.

One of the best known bits of old folk-lore is that the howling of a dog forebodes disaster, and that, when that weird sound is heard, the angel of death is hovering over the neighbourhood. Many an invalid has heard a dog howl at night, and has wondered if the warning was meant for them. In several cases they have told the doctor of it, and he, to comfort them, has said it was nothing—the dogs were often howling when he went his rounds at night. Instead of being comforted, the family have only reproached themselves for not having got some other doctor who was not so well known to the dogs.

Church bells were instituted, not only to call believers to prayer, but also to frighten away evil spirits, and the dogs know this as well as Christians, for at the first sound of the church bells, toll or chime, any well-disposed dog whose natural instincts have not been blunted by too much education or restraint will

G

become uneasy and begin to howl, plainly showing that they know there are evil spirits abroad. Many a time I have heard the "passing bell" tolled at Didsbury, and at the sound of its first note all our dogs have sat down to howl.

"The wolf's long howl
On Oonalaska's shore"

is not more melancholy. One of them used to sing "The Last Rose of Summer" with variations of her own, for the word "rose" was always highly pitched and long drawn out.

The "passing bell" was tolled, not only to let the neighbours know that some soul was taking its flight to the unknown country, but also to scare away the evil spirits in the air, so that the soul should have a fair start of them in its great race. At Didsbury there was a pause after the tolling, and then sixteen, or twelve, or eight tolls were rapidly given to denote that the passing spirit was either a man, or woman, or child. It is another old custom that has endured for centuries, and in our own day is being rapidly forgotten ; there is not a ringer at Didsbury now who could tell me the proper number of tolls to give. They smile at these superstitious beliefs, and yet they ring the bells. In some places they ring the church bells after a violent thunderstorm to clear the air and frighten away the evil. We have long since got past that, although bells are rung to commemorate some foolish political event. It is said that a very enthusiastic and religiously-disposed person remarked to another who was tending his garden by the church in the midst of the deafening clang of the bells, "How pleasant it must be for you in this sweet garden and in the sound of those heavenly bells." "Aye, what?"

said the gardener. "How pleasant it must be—"
was repeated rather louder than before; and then the
gardener replied, "Shout louder, man; I canna hear
a word you say for them beastly bells." The word
he really used was not exactly "beastly," but a cor-
rupt form of the old oath, "By our Lady."

My old dog Gomer got so used to howling at the
church bells, that he would begin at five minutes to

GOMER'S DAUGHTER MEG, THE DAM OF TARTAR AND TOSSPOT.

eight on Sunday mornings (that being the old customary time for the first ringing) whether they were
being rung or not. It has always been a mystery as
to how he knew the day and the hour, but he certainly did know them; and the very first time he was
ever taken outside the garden he got frightened at an
omnibus, and ran off home, not by the road or by the
way he had been taken, but straight across gardens
and fields as a bird would fly, and where he had cer-

tainly never been before. Volumes and articles without end have been written to prove that there is no such thing as "homing instinct"; but I saw the dog do it. I know every yard of the district, and know it was a fact.

Another strange piece of folk-lore about dogs is that black dogs are more likely to go mad than others, and statistics prove that black retrievers are the most subject to rabies of any breed. To eat a hair of the dog that bit you is an old preventative against hydrophobia. Perhaps it is as good as most others.

To have a black dog on one's back is an old term for being in a very bad temper. It is probably another survival of some ancient belief that is otherwise forgotten. "As thrunk," *i.e.* as thronged or busy, "as a dog in dough" is another old saying evidently come down to us from the times when dogs were used to knead the dough and turn the spit. The turnspit dogs are as extinct in Manchester as roast beef. I can just remember seeing dogs drawing carts in the streets, and have a lively recollection of having once been able to get good roast meat at most houses or inns. There is no roast beef nowadays, or hardly any: it is baked, or fried, or stewed, or messed. This is not the wailing lament of an antiquated, benighted Tory, or the superstitious belief of a religious fanatic; it is sober, simple fact. Almost every one bakes their meat in ovens, sometimes in ovens heated by gas, and they tell you the baked meat is as good as the roast, thereby showing their incapacity to discern the difference, or verifying the old adage, "There are none so blind as those who won't see."

An ignorant dictionary-maker described the dog as

an animal that lives in a kennel and is fed on bones.
A poet's rather mournful description is—

> " The rich man's guardian and the poor man's friend,
> The only creature faithful to the end."

When a lady is seen nursing a dog, especially if she
be riding in a carriage with one, it is a well-known
sign that she lacks children. If a dog for reasons of
his own leans his head against the wall to bark, he is
said to be an idle dog, for any stick is good enough to
beat a dog with, and you may give him a bad name
and hang him. Every dog has his day, and the difficulty of getting butter out of a dog's throat is often
commented on. For instance, if any one finds a valuable article in Manchester and leaves it with the
police for them to find the loser or real owner of it,
and they cannot trace anything, they may say they
will return it to the finder, but to get it will be like
the getting of butter out of a dog's throat when the
dog has swallowed the butter. They will wriggle and
twist and snarl and bite before they part with it, as if
they were parting with their front teeth.

When people live what is termed a dog and cat
life, it is understood that their domestic bliss is spoilt
with continuous jars, as when a dog looks at a cat
and the cat sets up its back and spits. Then, if the
dog wags his tail, the cat scratches his nose and
swears. The folk-lore respecting cats is correct as
usual. They are looked on as being uncanny and
treacherous, the companions of the witches. The
ordinary boy detests cats, and if girls are fond of them
it is a sign they will probably be old maids, and, as
some people would say, the worst sort of old maids.
Any mother knows that kittens and babies should not
be in the same house together, and that the cat might

suck the baby's breath or smother it. Black cats are
especially unlucky ; and if the cat has a cold, every one
in the house catches it. It is also bad to let cats die
in the house, and their fleas are objectionable, whereas
the fleas from dogs never molest human beings.

Altogether it is wonderful how many cats survive
when they are a nuisance to so many people. Out of
six gentlemen who were lately travelling together in a
railway carriage, there were five who owned to keeping traps for the destruction of cats. The treacherous,
deceitful beasts, who prowl about in the dusk with
their green eyes and electrical fur, seeking robins
and cream, or whatever else they can find to devour,
appear to be properly associated with the malevolent
witches, and the devout peasant in country places when
he sees a black cat in his path involuntarily shudders,
or crosses himself, or wishes to kill the evil beast.

Since writing the above a very strange thing
happened among our poultry. A one-year-old game
hen of the old fighting sort had some ducklings in
a wire enclosure, and a black cat jumped the wire,
having probably an eye to the little ducks ; but the
hen was a termagant, and although she had only one
eye, she killed the cat dead, and served it "jolly well
right."

"'Osses is grand beeasts, but they're ticklish to
deal wi', and like women it does no' do to have 'em
too thick on th' bonk." Bonk or bank in this wise
remark is a country expression for homestead or farm.
The former part of the sentence may be otherwise expressed as follows : The horse is a noble animal, but
it has a most pernicious influence upon every one
connected with it. There are thousands of men in
England now, and wherever the English tongue is
spoken, whose talk from the cradle to the grave is

mainly of horses. In childhood their wish is for a
gee-gee and whip, especially a whip; in youth and
manhood their chief thoughts, energies, and intellect
are spent on the horse they worship, and in their
dotage they tell again of the wonderful cattle there
were when they were young. From the rich noble
who lives to hunt and race, to the driver of a hearse,
the talk is of horses, and a good horse will even now

THOROUGHBRED.

excite more enthusiasm than any member of the
House of Lords.

It is generally believed by our country folk that
horses can see spirits or "boggarts" better than men
can see them. I do not think a horse's power of
sight is better than a man's, but his hearing and
smelling are more acute, and his memory is very
wonderful; he also has the homing instinct. In the
thousands of miles of solitary rides along our Cheshire

lanes that I have enjoyed, I have noticed that horses
are most frightened by a rustling sound behind them
or by a strange animal smell. This is a fear of wolves
inherited from a remote past. Horses never forget
any place where they have been frightened, or, generally, where they have ever been. Several times I
have ridden horses of my own breeding to Buxton or
Knutsford, for instance, and years after they have
known directly they have got on to any road on which
they have once been. The last mare I rode once
"got the wind" of a billygoat with which some lads
were struggling in an orchard, and ever since she
almost trembled as she looked for "boggarts" when
nearing that place. Thrashing a horse for shying is
simply folly and cruelty.

It is said that one of our local colonels of volunteers hired a horse from the Carriage Company for
his charger on parade. As the gallant colonel was
proudly riding at the head of his men up Market
Street, the guard of a passing tram rang his bell, and
the colonel's charger suddenly stopped. "Come hup,
you hugly brute," said the gallant colonel, and even
threatened to use his ornamental spurs, but the noble
charger stayed. The serried ranks of the British
army went marching into the colonel, and there was
confusion even as if the Boers were in laager with the
Ship Canal waggons. Then the tramcar guard providentially rang his bell, and immediately the charger
resumed his stately march, and the colonel's dignity
was saved. All this was highly creditable to the
horse's memory.

Years ago the black horses of a hearse were white
with foam at a certain funeral, and being always
anxious to know the reason of things, I learnt from
the old coachman that "if 'earse 'osses were in a

muck sweat as if pumpt on, it showed th' corpse 'ad
'ad too much brass or done summut wrong." There
is a general belief that if a man is "thrutcht out wi'
brass" he has been a little unscrupulous, to use a mild
term ; and if he has not left a right will, or if he has
done something very wrong, it raises a doubt as to
whether he is worthy of Christian burial in the churchyard, and the horses in the hearse find this out as soon
as any one, in the difficulty they have in dragging him
to the church. When they know what the crema-
torium is for we must expect they will go there at a
gallop when they get a dragging load, for they will
naturally think that is the proper place for the disposal
of bodies of doubtful character.

When writing my "History of Cheadle" I learnt
the pathetic tale of the bringing home of the body of
the last Chedle witch from Chester. The poor horse
had had many a sore struggle, and when crossing the
Forest "th' 'ess dur fell off an' Bella fell oot. . . . It
wur neet, snowin' 'ard, an' 'er wur in 'er shroud. . . .
They was awfu' feart, for they tho't owd Nick 'ad ta'en
'er. Sammy fun th' owd witch rollt i' th' dytche stiff
an' stark, aw i' th' snow, an' they reart 'er up an'
loaded 'er agen ;" and she got Christian burial in
Cheadle at last. Very different was the ending of
another bit of local history. One morning I spent in
the vestry of the church, extracting the tales of long
ago from some old natives. When I asked where the
once notorious chief-constable was buried, there was a
deep silence among the white-headed old men ; and
then one, named Gill, who looked very like the Iron
Duke in his old age, solemnly said, "He ne'er was
buried. No 'osses would drag him to th' church.
There was a big storm, and some said the devil fetcht
him, but others said th' devil wouldner have him, and

we dunner know what became of him." I thought
better of the horses when I heard that, for they
appeared to have known the great constable, the man
whose paltry salary never exceeded £350 a year, but
who accumulated, by his industry and ability, a
fortune estimated by his neighbours to be at least
£100,000, and whose executors sold "pecks of
watches" and "bushels of pistols," those being the
commoner perquisites of the profession.

Since writing the above, and in consequence of it,
I learnt by the merest chance that a friend had
helped some of this head-constable's family to find his
grave—the place of it had probably been kept secret
for good reason—and they inspected the coffin in the
vault. The coffin was very large, and of peculiar
deep shape ; as one of them got on it to decipher the
inscription, he fell in, and the shock made him ill for
months.

Some people think that horse-dealers are bigger
rogues than gentlemen in other professions. This is
not strictly correct.

> "The sight of means to do ill deeds
> Makes ill deeds done."

And when some one wise in their own conceit, and
relying on the inalienable privilege of every English-
man to be a judge in horseflesh, though he may hardly
know a horse from a cow, treats the seller as a rogue,
then it may be as well to remember some folk-lore as
old as the Latin's *caveat emptor*—"Hawks dunner
pick out hawks' een," at least not often. When
Murray, the great horse-dealer of Manchester, was
at the height of his fame, he badly wanted a splendid
black charger for the Emperor Louis Napoleon, and
knowing where there was such an one, in order to get

it he bought the entire stud of a wealthy gentleman in the Midlands, who had died, and owned this horse. Having paid for them, the horses were to be sent on at once. There was delay, and then came word that the grand charger was ill. Murray wired, "Send the horse at once." Reply came that the horse was too ill to travel. Murray wired, "Send the horse at once by train, alive or dead." The reply came, "The horse is dead; sending his hide and hoofs by train to-night." Murray had to make the best of a bad job, and seek comfort in another direction. Some months afterwards he was in Hyde Park with a "horsey pal," watching the constant marvellous procession, when again he saw a magnificent black charger, and asked who was on it, saying he would give any money for it. His friend said, "Well, now, that's the very 'oss you bought a bit since, and got 'is 'ide an' 'oofs by train."

It is said to be lucky to meet a man riding a piebald or skewbald horse. Therefore if you meet one you should wish for something, and if you have any money there is no harm in turning it over. Farming folk sometimes say, "It's desperate odd where all the scolding wives and grey mares come from. You never see an ill-tempered lass or a grey foal." Townfolk may need the explanation that the foals or fillies that grow into grey horses or mares are born dark-coloured, nearly black sometimes, with merely a very few grey hairs round the eye or the nostril. Another old country saying, referring to wives who are better managers or farmers than their husbands, is, "The grey mare's the best horse."

There are not many asses in our locality (I am alluding to the four-legged variety), and perhaps still fewer with the mark of the cross on their shoulders.

Children should have their first ride on a donkey, and they are sometimes passed round their neck or round their belly as a charm. Those that have the cross are considered to be much better to use, being luckier for the children. The cross is in some cases well defined. It consists of a black mark down the spine to the tail, and black marks on the shoulders, and is traditionally said to be shown only on those asses which are directly descended from the one on which our Saviour made His triumphal entry into Jerusalem. The shadow of the cross clung to it and to its descendants for ever, and some folk consider the hairs on the cross to be sacred. Old tales record they have even been eaten.

CHAPTER VII

ODDITIES

*" Then it was not for nothing that my nose fell
a-bleeding on Black Monday last at six o'clock
i' th' morning."*—MERCHANT OF VENICE.

HE "odds and ends" in this chapter
are really the originals out of which the
series of articles preceding this book
and this book itself grew. I began
by answering the numbered questions
on folk-lore and old customs in the
schedule of the committee of the British Association
for organising an ethnographical survey of the United
Kingdom. As explained in the preface to this
book, Didsbury is really in Lancashire, though it
joins Cheshire, and should be considered part of
that county ; almost everything related appertains to
Cheshire, or the neighbourhood of Standon in the
Staffordshire border.

Question No. 25 has reference to wells, and at
Didsbury there is a noted well or fountain of water
that I have referred to elsewhere as probably being
the fountain and origin of Didsbury, the place the
Saxon settlers would choose first for their church
and community. This fountain has still some reputation for curing diseases. It was said "to be holy in

papist times." Only last summer I several times saw
three young ladies who came every morning to bathe
their eyes and faces in it, saying, "It was good for
sore eyes." I could not see anything the matter with
their eyes, but that may have been my ignorance, or
that they were already getting better. In the spring
time or early in May the well has often been nearly
choked with wild flowers, and pins have been put in
for luck. If rags or crutches were ever left there,
it was when the water bubbled up in the roadway on
the hillside. The flow of it is lessened by drains or
sewers, and now it is taken down in pipes. The lane
is enclosed with brick walls, and all the romance is
gone ; but in the longest drought or severest frost the
water from the holy well has never failed, and though
it may come from the churchyard, we and many others
drink no other.

No. 39 asks for customs or traditions respecting
the site or erection of buildings, and I find there is a
strong belief among our oldest natives that if any one
could build a house on the waste strips by the road, or
on any waste land, between sunset and sunrise, and
have the smoke coming out by daylight, then they
were entitled to do so ; and if they held adverse possession for twenty years, it became their own property.
A man named "Croodle" Barrett built one on Lindow
Moss in a night within living memory. The wooden
framework for the house was made ready, a cartload
of bricks was sufficient for the chimney, and the walls
were formed of clods or turves. Previous to this
century there was an abundance of open waste land,
and scores of these squatters' houses are still standing,
but the lords of the manors have generally managed
to get "a hold" or some acknowledgment that may be
used some day. Lindow Moss is the only large space

that is still unenclosed. Kitts Moss, Shadow Moss,
Handford Moss, Outwood, and Baguley Moor have
been enclosed within the memory of the old natives.

No. 43. "Does the building of a house cause the
death of the builder?" Yes. I have heard that expressed very often, and I know of many cases in our
immediate neighbourhood where the proverb has been
verified. Unfortunately it does not apply to jerry-
builders who build for sale. In olden times they
would have been considered to have made a compact
or contract with a certain party, and therefore to be
exempt.

No. 90. "Are split trees used in divination or
for the cure of disease?" I have heard of a noted
witch, to be mentioned hereafter, who cured a boy
of one of the Baileys of Etchells of a diseased hip by
passing him with certain charms through a split rowan-
tree.

No. 210. Witchcraft is still believed in in our district, though the believers will only admit it or talk of it
to those who have their confidence. My elder relatives
regularly say of anything that is troublesome, "It
might be bewitched." Hear what my old friend
says: "Dunner be fradgin' about witches. You've
heerd th' seed, breed, and generation of 'em, wheer
they lived, an' aw about 'em, and yo' known theer's
witches still. What wur owd Betty—near yo',—or
owd Becky o' Whaley Bridge, or Bella Mottram o'
th' War Broo, Chedle? Why th' men as fot 'er from
Chester Castle when th' passon or lawyers 'ad done
'er ta death, an' then lost 'er i' th' snaw i' th' forest,
they 'anner bin long dead. An' what wur Betty
Piers as lived at th' last little 'ouse as yo' go doon
th' broo to Castle Mill? As fow an untoothed hag
as e'er brewt mischief. Theer's witches still, an' folk

an' things is bewitched yet. Doesn't th' Bible tell
yo', 'Thou shalt not suffer a witch to live.' Read
thy Bible an' dunner read it back'ards."

I have already published several tales about Betty
Piers; the name Piers or Pears or Pearson is a
common one. On Castle Mill itself is the name
Pierson, and the date 1810, so I have adopted the
older spelling. Betty was effectually quietened by
having her image, with nine pins through it, and the
nail out of a horse-shoe, also a toad, all put in a bottle
and buried by John, the wizard of Hale Barns.

No. 295. "Are amulets, talismans, gestures, used
to avert evil spirits or to ensure good? If so, how,
when, where?" If a person sneezes, it is usual and
polite to say, "Bless you." That averts the evil
spirit that caused the sneeze. If any one's nose bleeds,
the front-door key should be put down the back; and
a raw potato or a lucky stone carried in the pocket is
a preventive of rheumatism. There are innumerable
charms for all sorts of purposes, and crossing one's self
is simply a gesture to avert evil. The horse-shoe is a
well-known charm, though it is nearly always placed
the wrong way. It has been supposed to be a survival of the emblem of Astarte.

No. 297. As to animals or parts of them being
hung up to avert the evil eye, old farmers in Cheshire,
when troubled with the mysterious visitation known
as "picked calves," bury a picked calf at the threshold
of the shippon for the cows to walk over, and hang
another in chains on the outer wall.

No. 298. When John o' th' Hill, a famous wizard
at Hale Barns, died, he left instructions for his heart
(or a piece of beef similar to it) to be left in a tree
near to his house-door, and a watch to be kept. If a
magpie came first and pecked at it, that showed he

had gone wrong; but if a crow came first, then he was all right.

No. 432. "Are bones, nails, hair, the subject of particular customs and superstitions?" Certainly; when done with they should be cremated. An old tooth should have a pinch of salt on it, and then be put in the fire. Sometimes it is thrown over the left shoulder backwards into the fire. The nails or hair should not be cut on Sundays or holy days :—

"Sunday shorn
Had better ne'er been born."

If the skin at the root of a nail becomes torn and painful, that is called a stepmother's blessing, a mild form of being bewitched.

It is very natural that there should be many strange beliefs and much lore about the human hair, the omens that may be drawn from it and the customs regarding it. In this matter also, our local folk-lore is very similar to the customary beliefs and teachings of all ages, and therefore it must have a considerable element of truth and experience for its basis.

If a child is hairy, our wise women say it will be strong, and maybe it will be wild. An observant old farmer (anticipating Darwin) will say, "Aye, it's bred back a bit to'rds the beeasts." The old Biblical tales of Esau, the wild, hairy man, and Jacob, the smooth, cunning man, or Samson, who had more strength than sense, and whose strength lay in his hair, are counterparts of the folk-lore of those living to-day who never read their Bible. In the droves of lunatics and their keepers who parade the country beyond Cheadle, the readiest way of telling which are the lunatics is by observing the exuberance and roughness of their hair. If the hair is coarse and

H

rough, unkempt and unshorn, instead of being fine
or silky, and neat, it is a bad sign in man or woman.
It is said about Cheadle that bald-headed lunatics
are scarce, and that if the doctors, keepers, and other
attendants at the asylum do not keep their hair and
beard trimmed, they will go as mad as those they
take care of. Even with the ordinary public, if any
woman has a lot of rough towzly hair over what
should be her forehead (hair that looks like old hay
that a hen has been scratching in), she might be considered fashionable, but she would not be considered
sensible ; and there would probably be skins of dead
birds stuck about her hair or hat, another indication
of a lapse towards the ancestral savages.

It may seem almost incredible to this generation
that forty years ago there was scarcely a beard or
moustache in Manchester, because it had always been
the custom to shave. Shaving was the badge of
servitude, and we had all been servants of the King
or of somebody. A moustache was the badge of a
cavalry man, and the disgust of the cavalry was said
to be very great when the infantry were allowed to
grow moustaches after the horrors of the winter in
the Crimea. Then the volunteers thought they had
the right to grow moustaches, and when that was
allowed, thousands on thousands joined the ranks to
gain the coveted privilege. In many cases it cost
them dear, for their masters were tyrannical Tories,
who hated new-fangled ways, and would insist upon
their men shaving. Still the movement grew, until
a noted Manchester banker gave his clerks leave to
have moustaches outside his bank, but they were not
to be worn on the premises. This was rather hard
on the budding bankers, and the deprivation was
not sufficiently considered in the paltry amount they

accepted as remuneration for their services, for it was said they could have more salary as well as a moustache in the new joint-stock banks.

The first man I remember seeing with a moustache was a refugee from the second French Empire, who taught us French. We lads thought it showed our patriotism to shout after him (when at a safe distance), "Who's got a scrubbing brush under his nose?" The first ordinary citizen that I remember who grew his beard was Mr. Thomas Bright, the brother of the orator, who was then our friend and neighbour. Gradually the movement spread, the police soon thought it added to their importance and adornment, and slowly and timidly parsons grew beards. It was often remarked that with them the new hair came grey or white, while the hair on their head was black, and unkind people said that was evidence they had used their jaws more than their brains. As beards became more common, they were said to be the distinguishing marks of Radicals or field-naturalists, and then gardeners grew them, and very likely places they seemed for robins to nest in. Horsey men still inflict upon themselves the penance of shaving ; and gentlemen's servants, valets, butlers, grooms, footmen, look very unorthodox when unshaven. Even now in the cavalry regiments the men who wait at the officers' mess have to shave off the cherished moustaches, although as cavalry it was customary to wear them when ordinary citizens here would have been stared at, and possibly hooted, if they had not shaved.

Good orthodox people still consider it very wicked or unlucky to be "Sunday shorn." It is said a local man who had been very wicked or "nowt" turned Methody, and was then extra good. One Saturday he forgot to shave, and as he was not going to be so wicked as to shave on a Sunday after his conversion, and he could not go to prayer-meeting unshaven and unshorn, he lay in bed all day on the Sunday, and thereby eased his conscience.

Omens as to recovery from sickness are drawn from the state of the hair, for it is well known the hair hangs limp and lifeless in bad cases, and if the hair is "wick" it will frizzle or burn brightly in the fire. In my "History of Didsbury" I gave an account of old Billy Wood testing his hair; but as many have unfortunately never seen that interesting book, I may be excused from telling the tale again. Pages 34 and 35 have some account of the Woods, who were clerks of Didsbury for 250 years, and possibly much longer, as the parish records only begin in the first year of the reign of Queen Bess. Rather more than twenty years since old Billy Wood lived in the next house but one to our gate. He had lived in that house for over eighty years. I have a great respect for any one who lives in one house for eighty years. It shows that neither the man nor the house has been the work of a jerry-builder. He was not the clerk or the parson, though he was somewhat in the same line of business, for he had been a bellringer for sixty-five years, as is recorded on his gravestone. He sometimes dug graves. When he was getting on for ninety, and very feeble, he asked me if he could be buried in his cellar, for he had begun to dig, and it was beautiful gravel, as is all that part of Didsbury. I had no objection, but others had. The old rector was shocked. He said he should not perform the service in a cellar, and the ground was not consecrated. Old Billy cared nothing for the ground being consecrated, and not much for the burial service. He

said he "wur welly shrivellt up ; he should ne'er 'urt
none, an' it wer'ner likely he should walk or come
again." The rector had lately been much perturbed,
and had legal opinion on the advisability or otherwise of a re-interment with another burial service of
a body from the unconsecrated chapel-yard of Cross
Street Unitarian Chapel to the consecrated churchyard of Didsbury. The burial ground being consecrated is of enormous importance to some people,
though the great forces of nature do not alter their
course on its account in the very slightest degree ;
and even the authorities do not say how far down
the virtues of consecration go, for it is said there are
coalpits under some of our local churchyards. Old
Billy never troubled himself about such matters, and
they buried him as they liked, not as he liked.
When old and feeble he told me he "wur badly last
neet, an' our Bet said 'er mun send for th' passon ;
but I pluckt a yair out 'o my yed an' held it to th'
candle leet, an' it frizzlet gayly, so says I, Nay, nay,
there's no need o' sendin' for th' passon yet if one's
yair frizzles an' that uns." So the moral of this tale
is that you need never send for the doctor or the
parson so long as your hair frizzles.

I should like to remark here that the house in
which old Billy lived and died has had only two
tenants in the last hundred years. Sanitary authorities and scientific gentlemen have said, and do say,
that it and the adjoining houses must be very un-
healthy, for noxious gases must be continually escap-
ing from the churchyard, and there are not modern
closets, and some of the dwellers will drink the water
from the "holy well." Old Billy never liked the
nasty pipe water, though it was put in mainly on his
account, for a certain wealthy gentleman said he would

give the four sovereigns that he was using as counters
for whist to put the town's water in the houses, and
when it was put in he forgot to pay, and the tenants
would not drink the water.

There are many instances recorded where the hair
has turned grey or white in a few hours with much
sorrow or fright.

Some people still have vague ideas as to its being
better to have the hair cut when the moon is new,
and that any loose hairs should be burnt; they
should never be left flying about, or others might
swallow them, or mice would take them to use for
their nests. We always consider the outward and
visible sign that a youth is becoming a man is the
growth of the hair on his face, and we note the pride
and delight with which a young man is always twirling
his moustache. Conversely the outward and visible
sign that a girl is becoming a woman is that she " does
up " her back hair.

Having asked an old man one of the folk-lore
questions as to there being any custom at the cutting
down of trees, I could get no information, until he
suddenly looked like a terrier who smells a rat, and
said, " There's a mug o' ale o' course." " Is that all ? "
was my inquiry. " Well, if it's a toughish job, there'd
be a sup or two more wanted, o' course." I tried to
explain there might be some other old custom or
religious ceremony, and then came the further information, " We could allus get another sup o' drink
for th' chips, mind yo'."

For some romantic or poetical reasons that I could
never learn, young ladies sometimes curtsey to the
full moon ;. and if we wished to divine our fate or
luck, we sometimes tried to do so by means of snails.
If, when you take your walks abroad, you meet a

snail with its horns out, you should stand opposite
to it and tell it or recite what you want; then taking
hold of the left horn of the snail (not touching any
other part of its body), throw it over your left shoulder,
wishing for what you want as you do so. To make
the charm perfect, this should be done as the church
clock strikes twelve on the night of the full moon,
and any one who does it then is sharp enough and
clever enough to get wealth beyond the dreams of
avarice, with dozens of children and aught else that
men crave for.

Some of the beliefs and customs of our local folk
are remarkable from their very oddity; and their history or genesis being doubtful, they can only be described in general terms as survivals of some religious
or superstitious observances. For instance, every one
knows that it is considered to be unlucky to walk under
a ladder; comparatively few know that the anticipated
evil may be averted by spitting through the rungs
of the ladder. In the interior of Africa there are
now tribes of savages who place boughs or young
trees round about and leaning against their huts;
then, at their religious festivals, they walk between
the hut and the trees and spit at the evil spirits to
defy them. This performance of the savages is very
similar to, and perhaps the origin of, ours with a
ladder. There are many persons who consider it to
be very unlucky to meet another on the stairs, especially for the one who is ascending. This belief is
probably a faint survival of a notion that their ascent
to heaven is being hindered. Some say it is unlucky
for servants to go to a new place on Fridays or
Saturdays, or to have a wet job first, or to carry a
broom or any other utensil over the shoulder when
in the house. There is a widespread belief against

the giving of a knife or scissors, for the gift is said to entail the severing of friendship, and therefore even a pocket-knife should be bought, or something given in exchange for it. If a boy is too sharp, he is very likely to cut himself.

There is a strange superstition when any one is suddenly seized with an involuntary shiver, that it is caused by some one walking over the future grave of the shiverer. If any one's ear burns, some one is said to be talking of them. If the right ear burns, they are speaking well; if the left ear, it is evil; or *vice versa*, according as the feminine mind wishes. There are plenty of jingling lines on this and similar subjects :—

> " Left or right is good at night,
> But neither's good in the morning."

> " Then rub it on wood
> And 'twill come to good ;
> Or rub it on steel,
> 'Twill very soon heal."

> " If your hand itches
> You will have riches."

It was long since written that Cassius hath an itching palm, and the experience of ages has only confirmed the belief that it is necessary to grease the palms of some people, not only to allay itching or irritation, but also to smooth away other difficulties. " Palm oil " is now considered necessary to facilitate business, not only with constables and the buyers for co-operative societies, but with gentlemen of high standing, for it is known that honours and even peerages can be bought, or, in diplomatic phrase, conferred on those who know how to distribute their " palm oil " judiciously.

"Palm oil" is not much used in the corn trade, for very good reasons : the trade is too poor for adequate returns, and honest millers were always known to have a tuft of hair on the palms of their hands. On market days at the Corn Exchange any one may see hundreds of men closely examining the palms of their hands on which are spread a few grains of corn. It is difficult to see in the dim light of Manchester whether the hair is growing on their palms or not ; and the atmosphere is rather against its growth. Some millers stoutly maintain they have it, but only an honest man can see it ; and although rewards have been offered for good specimens, they have not been forthcoming. The customary way to making it known that "palm oil" is wanted is by rubbing the palm of one hand with the finger of the other.

It is also generally believed that when any one bites their tongue they have been telling—what is not strictly accurate. There are some semi-religious people, mostly females, who practise divination with the Bible and the front-door key. I know a man who is now going about, and looks most respectable, with a long beard, who showed his family Bible to a meeting of his creditors to prove that he was a minor when he was defrauding them.

The innumerable superstitions about Friday and their origin are too well known to need any comment ; also about the spilling of salt. It may be as well to state that the most plausible explanation of the belief about the salt is, that salt was considered by the ancients to be incorruptible, and the symbol of friendship. An apparent contradiction to this explanation is in another old superstition that it is unlucky to help any one to salt ; but this may only mean that it is not well to thrust friendship upon any one. Salt and bread are sometimes put upon the body of any one who has lately died, and any looking-glass in the room in which the corpse remains prior to burial is turned to the wall and draped in black. At any time it is ominous to break a looking-glass.

There is good luck in odd numbers—three, five, seven, nine, and eleven—but thirteen is the unluckiest of any. This idea is generally said to have arisen from the number of the apostles, although there never were more than twelve of them at any one time. Another tradition in reference to them is that Judas Iscariot was carroty or red; hence the origin of the dislike to red hair. But independently of Mr. Judas, there is a widespread belief that people with red hair are not gifted with much sense or luck. In reference to the number thirteen, I should remark that it was always considered the proper number of eggs to give to a broody hen.

I now mention the old agricultural custom of marling, a custom that is now quite extinct in our locality. When mossy or poor land was being brought under cultivation, it was usual for gangs of men in their spare time to dig marl out of pits and spread it on any one's land who would pay them for so doing. Several dressings with marl added to the soil and to the productiveness of a field. Nowadays it is seldom required. These men were called marlers, and their foreman or leader the lord of the marlers. They gradually degenerated into loafers or sturdy beggars, who cadged for odd jobs or drinks, and it was their custom to join in a long loud shout or howl when any one treated them. It was said that these howls could be heard a mile off, the burden or chorus of them was, Oh yes! oh yes! oh yes! a corruption of the Norman Oyez or Hear.

There is an almost universal belief among our country folk that stones grow, and as this belief is at variance with the teachings of professors of geology, I will shortly state both sides of the case, and leave readers to please themselves as to the side they may take.

I have known several farmers, who were very shrewd, sensible men, who have farmed the same lands and ploughed the same fields all their lives, in some cases for sixty years, and they have said that every year they have had all the loose stones picked by hand off the fields when they have been ploughed and harrowed, and they have been carted away to mend the roads, yet every year there are fresh stones. The depth of the ploughing has never varied ; nothing but farmyard manure has been put on the land ; it has never rained anything but rain, hail, or snow ; from whence then have come the successive crops of stones?

Adjoining the stackyard at Standon Hall there is a field called the Blakeyard, that has been ploughed every year of this century, and from which hundreds of cartloads of stones have been taken away, and yet it is littered over with stones of every shape and colour, although it has produced a very good crop of oats this last season. We lately searched, and found what the natives call " breeding-stones," some of which I brought away. They appear to be a rotten or friable granite ; and a theory about them is that, being easily broken, they fall into many pieces, and these bits, being left in the soil and turned about by the plough, receive fresh deposits or accretions of mineral matter, and become larger, or, in other words, they grow. Many farmers will swear that particular stones they have noticed (especially when in water-courses) have grown larger in their recollection.

Geologists say stones do not grow in size, that they have been brought by glacial action and deposited in the fields ages ago, and by the look of the stone they profess to tell you whether it has come from Scotland, Cumberland, Wales, Norway, and goodness knows where. I was once talking to a man who is a member of most of the learned societies in Manchester, about some new member, and he said, "Oh! he is a geologist; don't have any of them." I innocently asked why not, and he replied, "Geologists are the most quarrelsome beggars on earth. Whatever one says, another contradicts; then a third contradicts them both; and a fourth says they are atheists, and what they say is against the Bible. If you want any peace don't have anything to do with geologists." I know one of them, who is awfully clever, told me that a large boulder stone at our front gate had been polished by glacial action. The little bare-legged children from the neighbouring cottages sit straddle-legged on this stone and "slur" down it continually, and that polishes it beautifully. The geologist said, "The most callous part of the epidermis of a child could not possibly excoriate those striated lines; they must have been caused by ponderous masses of superimposed rocks being slowly ground along by the vast powers of glacial action. The stone is a syenite or porphyry of plutonic origin." Then, having choked me with fine words and vast knowledge, he smiles at my ignorance, and, looking as wise as any owl, he thinks—

> "How blest are we who are not simple men;
>   Yet nature might have made me as these are,
>   Therefore I'll not disdain."

There is a very old proverb, "He who is born to

be hanged will never be drowned," and although Didsbury cannot compete with Gatley in the number of its natives who have been hanged professionally— that is, done to death by due process of law—I can from my own memory give two local and noteworthy incidents that show the truth of this old proverb. Rather more than thirty years since there was an elderly man, who had been gardener at Scotscroft, and who did odd jobs; it was generally supposed that one of his jobs had been that he had done a murder. There was a poor half-witted youth, with the aristocratic name of Howard, who had lived with him, and who had died under suspicious circumstances. Howard was what the country folk call "moonstruck," and people with a slightly classical education call "a lunar," it being a common belief that if any one goes to sleep with the moon shining on them, their wits will be affected, and they will be worse at the full of the moon. I well remember Howard telling me his wage. He said his "wage wur a shillin' a wik an' meat, an' no meat but on a Sunday."

It was rather a curious statement, for in his limited vocabulary the word meat had two meanings. He meant to say, "A shilling a week and his food, with flesh meat only on Sundays." Howard died and got buried somehow, and as he was worth very little more than his keep, and not even that when the moon was full, his neighbours cared very little about him, and the parish jogged on as formerly. But not many years after, some men were working at the river banks, when they saw something like a good topcoat come floating down the stream. They pulled it out, and inside was found the withered body of the above-mentioned old man, who had tried to drown himself higher up the river, and had been floated down by his clothes. The

almost lifeless body was laid on the grass, and from it
came sighs and gasps, as the rescuers stood round
making remarks in their primitive and unconventional
manner : " Rum fish this."   " I thowt I'd gotten some
new clooas."   " Woy, it's him as smothert th' softy ;
let's chuck 'im in again."   " Nay, nay, lad, we mit get
i' trouble ; let's tak' 'im whom."   " Let him bide a bit,
and th' watter 'll dreen off an' then he'll be leeter." So
when the water had drained off and he got lighter they
took him home and left him, with the parting injunction
that it was no use " him trying to drown hissel' ; next
time he were a bit tired like he should try hanging."

The other case may be said to be somewhat similar,
and yet very different.   A big rough chap, of a tribe
of the same name as one of the tribes of Israel, lived
to a great extent on the earnings of his wife, and if
she would not find him beer money he would threaten
to drown himself, and even come home again all wet
and dirty, with some wonderful tale as to how he had
been rescued, or could not sink, or something.   Then,
as these tales lost their effect, he would go in for
hanging himself.   Before his poor wife's eyes he would
put a cord round his neck and hitch himself over a
hook, and wait to be cut down.   But in time they got
used even to that, and the neighbours began to think
it would be better to leave him alone to get on with
his dying.   So they did not take him down one day
as quickly as he expected, when lo ! and behold ! they
were all too late, for, as it was elegantly expressed,
" he was as numb as th' dour."   It was quite a mistake, of course, and a great pity, and very shocking,
and so on, but it was a fact, and they had to make the
best of it.   The man had fulfilled his destiny, and the
bereaved widow could marry again.   If he had lived
he might have given the hangman a job ; or if he had

provided himself with a pencil and paper and written down his impressions when he found they were leaving him hanging too long, he might have left us some very interesting notes on various subjects, but especially on the good old proverb, " He who is born to be hanged will never be drowned."

Folk-lore similar to this must have been current in Malta when St. Paul was shipwrecked there, to judge by the remarks of the natives when the snake fastened on his hand. There is even a lingering belief in some places that it is unlucky or unwise to rescue any one from drowning, and it may be the original reason for this belief was that it was saving the persons for some worse fate. If any one be drowned in our district, the body is taken to an inn-yard, and the women and children crowd to see it, and most of them touch it. They say they touch it so that they shall not dream about it ; but that is another custom that almost certainly refers to one much older, and the original meaning of which they have forgotten. In olden times every one in the locality was required to touch the body of any one who was found dead, or had suddenly died, to show they had no malice or had done no harm to the deceased. If any one who had murdered the dead person touched the body, the wounds were believed to bleed afresh at once ; and even if those who laid their hand on it had seriously injured the dead, some manifestations of displeasure would be shown. Not many years since a maid-servant at Tong Castle was found drowned in the ornamental water, and the old-fashioned squire, anticipating the law, summoned all his vassals and retainers to look upon the corpse, and lay their hands on it in his presence. It was then found that a young gamekeeper had absented himself, and suspicion accordingly fell upon him.

Our coroners at their inquests (called in old terms
crowner's quests) still require the jury to view the
body, and a barbarous practice it is. The custom of
touching it has lapsed, if ever it was required by the
law. The belief in the consequent immunity from
dreaming about the dead is most certainly a relic of
the belief that the ghost of the dead would haunt those
who had injured it. Children generally go to see the
dead because their foolish nurses or mothers take
them. One of my mother's earliest recollections, one
that is fresh in her memory after more than eighty
years, is that of being taken by her nurse to see a
drowned man, and told to touch the body.

A HEN WITH CHICKENS, GUINEA CHICKS, SEVEN YOUNG
TURKEYS, AND A DUCKLING.

CHAPTER VIII

GHOSTS

" It is an honest ghost—that let me tell you.

.   .   .   .

There are more things in heaven and earth
Than are dreamt of in your philosophy." HAMLET.

HOUGH no respectable ghost stirs abroad in the Holy Week, or until Twelfth Night is past, yet the festivities of Christmastide bring round again the old familiar tales of spirits who uneasy rest, and in the witching hour of moonlight flit across our path or hover round our bed, the dim, shadowy ghosts of the departed. It would be imprudent of me to tell of all the haunted houses that I know, for I should render myself liable to that most unghostly action, an action at law for damages or losses incurred by depreciation of property through my reckless statements. Many there are who scorn the very idea of a belief in ghosts, but they would not take a haunted house on any account, and they dare not sit alone in a churchyard at twelve o'clock at night to save their souls. When houses are haunted the usual cure for the annoyance is to have them at least partly rebuilt and rechristened. In olden times priests or parsons would have been called in to

lay the ghosts. Nowadays people are losing faith in the powers of the priesthood; they want the drains inspected and the rent reduced. That is the chief requisite; a good reduction will cover a multitude of sins.

Of course it is only old houses that are haunted, although the flimsy walls and doors of the genteel modern villas would seem to be eminently adapted for ghosts or any one else to glide through. There is a house in a country lane about two miles from here that I have seldom known to be inhabited. The front windows are all broken, and if they are mended they are soon broken again. There is a melancholy pit in the orchard, and the whole place looks lost and lonesome. No one will stay in the house, for they say a man named Aaron Warburton, who lived there sixty years ago, "comes again," and will persist in showing new tenants how he did that deed that ends all other deeds.

There is a house at Didsbury that was once called the Swivel House, where a fine lady "walked." I wrote about it in one of my books on Didsbury; but as every one has not read the tale, here is an extended version. Once upon a time there was an old bachelor named Sam Dean, who lived at the Swivel House. He had made lots of money out of swivels—they were little hand-looms for making tapes or smallwares —and when he died the money was missing, and the house changed hands. Every night there passed through the house a beautiful, fine lady, dressed in the fashion of our grandmothers, all frills and furbelows, powder and patches. She wore a rich silken gown of green flowered brocade, that stood out stiff, and rustled as she walked. Her shoon were of brocade to match, with high wooden heels covered with red

leather; and her hair was dressed high off her face,
done up with bows of fine ribbons, and pouthered
beautifully. On her face were little patches of black
to make the skin look whiter, and round her neck she
wore a snowy kerchief with the ends tucked in her
bosom. She merely glided through the rooms, looking everywhere with a stony stare, but never speaking
to any one; and she would quietly vanish away, while
her silken gown rustled as the dry leaves rustle in the
winds of autumn. No one ever knew who she was, or
whence she came, or whither she went, for old Sammy
had kept himself to himself. But some feared she
was an old sweetheart or light-o'-love who had gotten
more from old Sammy than he had ever bargained for.

It is very probable the late Mr. Dean, like many
other men who spend their lives in making money, had
not had time to study Shakspere, or he might have
profited by some of his worldly wisdom. " Let not
the creaking of shoes nor the rustling of silks betray
thy poor heart to women." Or, as an old picture
that has hung in our office from time long before I
was born, says—

> " Silks and satins, scarlets and velvets,
> Put out the kitchen fire."

The lady in the high-heeled shoes has probably purged
her sins in purgatorial fires or gained rest for her perturbed spirit in some other way, for I do not hear that
she has been seen for many years. It is about seventy
or eighty years since a new housekeeper, when going
to the house, was told she could have any one she
liked to sleep with her if she was afraid of the ghost.
The house has been rebuilt and enlarged until there is
very little or any left of the old building; and since
writing the above, and in consequence of writing it,

I have heard from the daughter of the man who rebuilt it, that when they were pulling down the old house they found in the chimney-stack a small secret chamber, with some mouldering remains of a chair and table and some fowl bones. It is very singular there should have been this "priest's hole" unknown to any one, and yet to some extent confirmatory of the old legends. Since the rebuilding, the house has been rechristened twice, and has now a very aristocratic name, so there is little inducement for the lady to revisit her old haunts. I did intend to give the present name of the house, but thought it better to ascertain whether the owner or tenant had any objections to my doing so. So I wrote to ask, and received a reply saying that I was perfectly at liberty to mention anything and everything, and my article was anticipated with pleasure ; but a postscript was added saying the wife had been consulted, and she would not allow it on any account, for several of her friends and relatives would never sleep in the house again if they knew ; therefore the dread secret must not be publicly divulged.

The Deans were a very old and respectable family in the neighbourhood. About a hundred years since one of them was hanged in chains on Stockport Moor for having murdered his wife at the instigation of one Sal Fogg, a lady of easy virtue who lived at Cheadle. An old man says that his grandfather often told him how he, when a boy, had gone to see the murderer's body on the gibbet and thrown a stone at it. The results of the stone-throwing were rather startling, plainly showing that flies were no respecters of persons.

The Gatley Shouter was a much better known and more vulgar bogie. He was an uneasy spirit who came out of his grave in Northen churchyard, and

squeaked and gibbered about the Carr Lane to Gatley.
There is no evidence to show that he did anything
more than adulterate the goods he sold, and that has
been described as only another form of competition;
but he did it rather unmercifully, or his conscience was
tenderer than it is convenient for the conscience of
a tradesman to be. It is said he even whined about
the water he put in the milk, though it is a very
common failing to water milk. Indeed, some doctors
recommend it, saying that even the milk of commerce
is too strong for the stomachs of some people. The
Gatley Shouter sang a verse of an old song, sang it
often in Gatley Carrs when the moon was at full :—

> " Milk and water sold I ever,
> Weight or measure gave I never."

This spirit's vagaries became a nuisance and a dis-
credit to the good folks of Northen, and it was resolved
to lay him, for the resurrectionists would not fetch him
although they often paid Northen churchyard a visit
in those days. The *modus operandi* of laying a ghost
was to wait until it was on the prowl, and then a
parson, or priest as they are still called in some country
places, got on the grave with a Bible and a lighted
candle, thereby cutting off its retreat, just as the earth-
stopper goes round at night to stop up the foxes' earths
or holes when the hunt is expected to be on the
following day.

If the laying is to be done regardless of expense,
there should be seven or even more parsons, all with
Bibles and lighted candles, for there is great virtue
in the light, and the belief in it probably shows a survival of the ancient sun or fire worship. Candles are
still put on the altars of churches, and about a corpse
that is being " waked," and if something comes in the

wick of a candle it is called the winding-sheet, and
forebodes a funeral. If Holy Church excommunicates
any one with bell, book, and candle, I am told the
candle is put out when that soul is put out of the
Church. Now in laying a ghost the great thing is to
corner it, keep your candles burning, and pray like
fury. It will sweal away under the prayers, and if
you have a holy circle round it that it cannot pass
until daylight doth appear, it will be done for, or laid ;
or, in other words, the devil will be cast out.

The rest of the tale, of which there are several
versions, had perhaps better be given somewhat as it
was told to me years ago by an old man who was
then over eighty. I am not sure whether he said he
was present at the great hunt or only remembered it.
"Aye, sure, th' Gatley Shouter wur Jim Barrow's
ghost. 'E cum fro' Cross Acres, t'other side o' Gatley.
Them Gatley folk wur allus a gallus lot. Owd Jim
wur desprit fond o' brass, an' 'e stuck to aw as 'e could
lay ode on. 'E'd a fleyed two fleas for one 'ide, 'e
wud, an' when 'e deed Owd Scrat got 'im an' 'e warmt
'im, 'e did so, an' Jim mi't a bin 'eard a neets moaning, 'Oh dear, oh dear, wa-a-tered milk, wa-a-tered
milk,' till folks got plaguey feart a goin' yon road arter
dark. Now there come a new passon to Northen, a
scholar fresh from Oxford or Rome or someweers,
chok'-fu' o' book-larnin', an' 'e played th' hangment wi'
aw th' ghoses i' these parts, an' 'e said 'e'd tackle 'im.
So 'e got aw th' parish as could read or pray a bit to
cum wi' their Bibles, an' one neet when th' moon wur
out Owd Scrat mun a bin firin' up, for th' Shouter
wur bein' rarely fettled by th' way as 'e moaned. An'
aw th' folk got round 'im, an' they drew toart one
another in a ring like, an' kept cumin' closer till at last
they'd gotten 'im in a corner i' th' churchyard by th'

yew tree, an' th' passon was on th' grave, an' 'e whips
a bit o' chalk out o' 'is pocket an' draws a holy ring
round 'em aw, an' aw th' folk join 'ands and pray
desprit loike, an' th' passon 'ops about an' shouts an'
bangs th' book till 'e's aw o' a muck sweat. An' 'e
prayed at 'im i' Latin too, mind yo', as weel as English, an' th' poor ghost moans an' chunners an' gets
littler an' littler till 'e fair sweals away like a sneel
that's sawted. An' at last th' devil wur druv out o'
'im, an' 'e lets 'im abide as quiet as a mouse. 'E's
now under yon big stone near by th' passon's gate.
Yo' may see it for yosen. It's theer now."

The name hob for hobgoblin appears several
times in the names of fields or places, there being
Hob Lane, Hob Croft, and Hob Bridge at Gatley,
near to where the Black Pit Boggart resided. At
Didsbury we had Boggart Lane until the Methodist
Church was built in it, and since then the bogies have
not been seen, and the lane is called Didsbury Park.

In the fields near Adswood Hall, where Fanny
Fowden was murdered on her way from church one
Sunday afternoon, her ghost appears at times to
naughty boys who are after mushrooms or mischief.
She merely glides harmlessly about in the mist or
gloom.

Jinny Chorlton, of Gatley, used " to come again,"
until they pulled her old house down. There was
supposed to be a ghost at the Old Parsonage, Hand-
forth, of a woman who was frightened to death
when Prince Charles visited Handford Hall on his
celebrated march in 1745 ; and a gamekeeper at
"Authorley used to 'walk' wi' a black dog till th'
passon laid him ; but th' passon's yure wur as black
as a crow th' day afore, an' in th' morn it wur as
grey as a badger ; so he mun a bin rarely feart."

Combermere Abbey.

Combermere Abbey is the most famous haunted house in Cheshire. Having known the place fairly well some twenty or thirty years since, I give its history in rather interesting detail.

When the Normans overran this fair realm of England, they had many high dignitaries of the Church, who went with them into battle and helped them in all things. These men, it is recorded, would not shed Christian blood, but carried maces or croziers that would break the thickest head that could be found among the Anglo-Saxons. They were stern upholders of the Scriptural injunction, "If thine eye offend thee, pluck it out," and "If thy hand or foot offend thee, cut them off," but they departed slightly from the original meaning of the text in interpreting it as against their enemies, not against themselves. So many of the poor natives were robbed, not only of their lands, but of their eyes and hands also, that at last the Normans, being satiated with success, began to think of the repose of their souls, and founded churches or monasteries, just as in our time brewers build churches when they wish to "hedge a bit."

One of the barons who divided the county palatine of Chester under the Norman Earl who there had regal jurisdiction was William Malbedeng, or Malbanck, Lord of Wich Malbanck. The name was spelt in various ways, and gradually came to be Malbon, pronounced Morbon by the country folk, who generally retain the old pronunciation. In this case the name is pure Norman. Some of the last generations whom I have known spell their name

Melbourne, ignorantly thinking that form to be more aristocratic. Nearly eight hundred years since, the second baron, Hugh de Malbanc, signed a deed which is still extant, which explains itself, and of which the following are translated extracts :—

" In the name of the holy and indivisible Trinity, Father, Son, and Holy Ghost, I, Hugo Malbank, of the one part, applauding the promise of the Lord by which He saith to His elect : ' What thou hast done unto one of the least of Mine thou hast done unto Me.' . . . Therefore I oftentimes revolving in my mind this and other precepts of the Lord . . . give and grant to those who have given themselves wholly to Divine services this donation. With the consent of the Earl, the Bishop, my son and heir, wife, children, and friends, I give humbly and devoutly to our Lord God Omnipotent . . . the place and site which is called Combermere for the founding and erecting an abbey for the monks of the order of St. Benedict, with everything in it above the earth and under the earth for ever."

Then follows a long list of the bounds of the estate, which he says he and his wife and son and many others have perambulated ;—other manors and towns and gifts, including free pasture in all his woods and pastures in Cheshire, the fourth part of the town of Wich Malbanc (that is Nantwich, " wich " being an old term for salt works), tithe of the salt and of the lord's money, free salt for themselves, Acton Church, and the chapel of Wich Malbanc, with all their appurtenances, with many other most valuable gifts ; and he reiterates they are all given in free, pure, and perpetual alms, or charity to the monks and their successors for the services of God. The charter is signed, sealed, witnessed, or heard by the Earl, the

Bishop, the Abbot, the family, and friends, and concludes as follows: "And as to this same charity, whoever shall in any way violate the gift and grant, or diminish it, or knowingly impede it, the curse of God, and the Blessed Virgin, and Saint Michael the archangel, to whom all these things are given, shall be on him, and mine own also, unless he make full restitution. FIAT: FIAT: AMEN."

This great charity was added to by many subsequent donors, and its charters confirmed by the local Earls and the Kings of England until its title must have been as good as it was possible for any title to be, and so it continued for over four hundred years. Then there arose in England a great King who wished to change his wife, and as he could not do that without changing his religion also, he changed them both and quarrelled with both, and went on quarrelling until the great wealth of the religious houses excited his avariciousness, and he robbed them of everything they possessed, and did not scruple to hang those who refused to give up the trust committed to them.

Combermere Abbey was given to a young courtier named Cotton, and his wife Mary. The gift of the voluptuous King to the wife is noteworthy. The Cottons took and kept possession. But let us look back a bit. There were doubtless children who saw the sack of the monasteries, and who lived to see the end of the great King, his six wives, all their children, and all the Bloody House. The strong expression is not mine; it has long been commonly used by the different denominations as they persecuted one another in their turn. In folk-lore terms, "the seed, breed, and generation" were rooted up, and the long-suffering English had to send to Scotland for a makeshift King until Mr. Cromwell showed them that kings could be done away with, and punished like common men, if they would not behave themselves properly --a lesson we are all benefiting by.

History has shown how the curse on the spoiler was fulfilled, and fulfilled speedily. How have the receivers of the spoils and the public fared? Every man or woman in Cheshire who pays poor-rates or subscribes to hospitals is a loser through the aliena- tion of this charity. At the beginning of Hugh Mauban's charter he quotes a passage from Holy Writ, which doubtless ˙he considered (as he says) with the passages immediately preceding it (I give the words of our authorised version): "For I was an hungred and ye gave Me meat; I was thirsty and ye gave Me drink; I was a stranger and ye took Me in; naked and ye clothed Me; I was sick and ye visited Me; I was in prison and ye came unto Me." Then he makes the gift to those who will do those things, to those who have given themselves to divine service, and he names the monks of the order of the Benedic- tines as the most likely men living to carry out his wishes. The Cistercians, a reformed branch of that order, whose rules were work and study with sim- plicity, or work sanctified by prayer, took possession of Combermere, and for more than four hundred years they did feed the hungry and visit the sick; they were guardians of the poor, who maintained hospitals and dispensed hospitality to all comers freely. If, as they got wealthier, they waxed fat, idle, and dirty, well, the same charges have been brought against poor-law guardians in our day, and even against their autocratic and well-paid officials. Most of us who tinker at public work have many faults laid to our charge.

The land and wealth bestowed on Combermere

Abbey is enough to keep all the poor and all the
hospitals in Cheshire to-day. That favoured county
had many other abbeys also, for the Church always
knew where the loaves and fishes, or the corn and
wine, were most plentiful. There were the abbeys of
St. Werburgh, Chester, Vale Royal, Stanlaw, Pulton,
and the priories of Norton, Warburton, and Birkenhead.
The priory of Birkenhead owned the town to Bidston,
with several other manors and the rectory of Bowdon,
also the right of ferrying across the river to Liverpool ;
a superabundance of riches. The great county families
of Cheshire. mostly got the lands, and if some scion
of a noble house subscribes to church or hospital
the one ten-thousandth part of what his ancestor got
from them, he is belauded and honoured as if he were
half divine. Some of us may live to see a Socialistic
Government reasserting the rights of the hospitals and
the poor to some of these alienated charities. Many of
them have never been sold since the great spoliation.

To go back to my tale. The Cottons got Combermere, and soon began to make alterations. The
King gave the belfry, bells, and burial-ground, with
other things specially mentioned. The bells were
being taken across the mere when a great storm
arose, the grey mists took human shape, and bells,
boat, and boatmen were dragged under the water and
never seen again. The King gave the burial-ground.
"Oh, ho!" say legions of dead monks, who for centuries past had been quietly laid in their narrow,
nameless graves under the green sod, under the
spreading oaks, and by the garden side that stretches
down to the waters of the beautiful mere ; "Oh, ho!
he has given us, has he? Whence came his right
or power to give? Has he given body and soul
also? Our finger is in the pie yet."

COMBERMERE ABBEY.

As Longfellow wrote on the other side of the
Atlantic—

> " Owners and occupiers of earlier dates
>   From graves forgotten stretch their dusty hands,
>   And hold in mortmain still their old estates."

This gift by the King of that which was not his to
give, was enough to make the monks turn in their
graves and become uneasy and restless, especially as
the Cottons began to convert their hospital and alms-
house into the house of a country gentleman. The
Cotton family benefited more than any other family
from the robbery of the charities and religious houses.
They were foremost in the alienation of the lands that
were given to the Dean and Chapter of Chester, and
that were lost through the omission of one word in
the charter. That was in the reign of Elizabeth, when
Sir Thomas Egerton came into power.

The wealth of the Cottons must then have been
enormous, but it took to itself wings and flew away,
and the heirs took to marrying heiresses. One was a
Miss Hester Salusbury of the blood royal, who had
immense estates in Denbighshire and the district.
In three generations those estates had slipped away ;
and another heir married an heiress aged thirteen,
who was said to have owned a large part of Jamaica,
her guardian getting a good sop as his commission in
the transaction. It had always been the custom in
England for guardians to more or less sell their wards ;
even kings and noblemen were not above making
honest pennies in that manner, and therefore it must
have been fashionable, proper, and respectable. One
of the family became famous as the dashing cavalry
officer, the hero of Salamanca. He went through
the Peninsular War, and some smaller wars in India,

receiving £60,000 for his share of the sack of Bhurt-pore. The wealth came now from the sack of a town, not a monastery, and from the Indies, east as well as west. But it all went, and Parliament granted him a pension of £2000 a year for two lives. For an additional crest he was granted a mounted dragoon charging, and the motto "Salamanca." Full of years and honours, for he attained the great age of ninety-one, Field-Marshal Viscount Combermere was gathered to his fathers in Wrenbury Church, and over his monument, with a long list of his battles and another long list of his titles, with nearly half the letters of the alphabet after his name, is the mournful line from Gray's elegy—

> "The paths of glory lead but to the grave."

Combermere Abbey has now been on sale or to let for many years. Successful men of business from Manchester and the district go to inspect it (I have known some of them), and their thoughts may be taken to be somewhat as follows :—" What a lovely spot in which to end one's days. What fools we are to stop in Manchester with such a country as this so near. Here I might found a county family with a long line of statesmen, perhaps noblemen (who knows?), to come after me. A gallery of ancestors could soon be bought. Who wants sixteen quarterings? How can they have sixteen quarters on one piece? Their arithmetic is all wrong; but I've brass enough to buy up the blooming lot." Then he goes home and tells his wife what a beautiful place Combermere is ; that the mere is the finest natural water in any park in England, the fishing is excellent, the hunting and shooting first-rate, the society most select, lords and esquires being plentiful in the neighbourhood ; and

he tells again interesting tales about the Abbey and
the monks till he comes to the fatal word "ghosts."
Then his wife starts and says : "Ghosts, my love—
you know very well I can't bear them ; I shall never
go, I am sure of that." Then he replies, "What
nonsense, my dear ; ghosts are only tales for girls and
curates. Business men know there are no such things.
Run of bad luck ? Yes, I know what bad luck is, but
my own indomitable energy and perseverance have
always overcome it ; though I don't like it, as you say,
and it is bad business to throw a chance away." With
his wife's last words, "I don't care what you say, my
love, I tell you I shan't go," ringing in his ears, he
goes back to piling up the money, and the day-dreams
or castles in the air are put off and put off, until the
long line of statesmen and capitalists who were to
have come after him, and the ancestral warriors and
priests who were to have gone before him, all vanish—
vanish into air as impalpable and unsubstantial as the
ghosts which scattered them.

Combermere is, as its name implies, the mere in
the wooded hills, or the crooked, that is, the winding
mere. The Abbey was built close to the water on a
strip of land that was once nearly an island, so that
the place should be safe from the marauding Welsh,
for Taffy and the Cheshire men had centuries of
quarrels. The green sward of the surrounding park,
with the cattle, the water-fowl, and the gigantic trees
reflected in the water, make Combermere one of the
fairest scenes on this fair earth. I once saw an almost
miraculous draught of fishes taken out of the mere by
a large drag-net. There were hundreds of bream
weighing two and three pounds apiece ; there was, in
fact, a cart sent to carry them away. There was also
a corner of the mere noted for the big pike that were

taken there ; and some one wondered why the biggest pike came there, and they dragged that corner, and brought up the remains of a footman from the Abbey who had drowned himself for the love of woman. The pike ate the man, and men ate the pike, and neither of them disagreed the one with the other.

The old abbey or convent was a timber-framed black-and-white building in proper Cheshire style. Very little of it is left, and that is sadly marred and spoilt, being plastered into a ghastly sham. If you ask why the place does not sell or let, the natives only shake their heads and sigh. If you gain their confidence they are more communicative, and croak like ravens, "'Cause it's haunted"; and if you get still more into their confidence, and something is given to loosen their tongues and cause their ideas to circulate, they may tell you, with bated breath, that the curse of the monks of old is on it, that ill-luck comes to all who meddle with it, that rest and sleep flee away, for the monks "come again" even to the bedside. There is a deeply-rooted tradition in the neighbourhood, that the Cottons only hold Combermere so long as they dispense hospitality to all comers, and although they have been hospitable in the past, it is not right to shut up the house and leave it. This is one of those interesting traditions that abound in our country places, and are well worth recording. Like most of them, it is undoubtedly founded on fact. The monks relieved and gave free hospitality to all comers, and probably did their duties as well, or better, than hired officials do the same duties now. When they were turned adrift, and the Cottons came into immense wealth, it would be only natural that they (the possessors) would do something like the same, if only to keep their neighbours quiet, instead of from a higher motive.

In all country places hospitality is given in a manner that is utterly impossible in a suburban district or in a town. Perhaps some one will ere long make some restitution according to the last clause in the original charter of Hugh de Mauban, and avert what remains of that curse that was written down nearly eight centuries ago, and which writ may still be seen. It was on the spoiler certainly, and on him and his house it has been fulfilled, but some remnants of it seem to cling to the place and on those who participated in the spoils.

I have supped and chatted with lord, and steward, and tenant, and serf, and heard the romantic tales and legends of centuries. In that grand old refectory, panelled with oak and ceiled with walnut, the grisly spectres of cowled monks are still said to rise unbidden at the midnight revelries. Their ghastly phantoms gaze with lack-lustre eyes on the intruders who are in their places. Their moans and sighs mingle with the moaning of the wind, and their shadowy forms mingle with the mists off the mere, and float over their long-forgotten graves in the garden, and where the convent cloisters stood. Sooner or later the stranger shudders as if some one were walking o'er his grave, and as his flesh grows more creepy he says, " Let us go hence."

Cheadle Bulkeley Hall.

There are only two houses in this neighbourhood that I can publicly allude to as being haunted : the owners or occupiers of others strongly object to the term "haunted" being applied to their premises. One house is my own, the Old Parsonage, Didsbury, and the other one is commonly known as Cheadle Hall, its proper name being Cheadle Bulkeley Hall.

The owner of it is my friend Mr. James Watts, who traces his pedigree back to the original Chedles of Chedle, who owned the manor before its partition between the heiresses, and as he is a teetotaller he is not frightened of ghosts. In fact, he rather likes them, for they confer an air and flavour of antique respectability, family heirlooms to be proud of, and to a good conscience nothing to fear. It is only when people have done some wrong or taken too much spirits that they are afraid of the other spirits ; for when they take nips in the morning and all through the day, the other spirits become objectionable, as they become bluer in colour, with a slight smell of brimstone or sulphur.

The present Cheadle Bulkeley Hall stands at the end of the village street by the village green ; and a little behind it, nearer to Stockport, is the Hall of Cheadle Moseley. The original Hall of Cheadle Bulkeley stood where Mascie Street now is, being one of the old-fashioned timber-framed houses. That name of Massey, I find, is variously spelt. A family pedigree gives it Massey, Massye, Massy, Massie, Mascie, Mascye, Mascy, and Massi. Its derivation may have been from the Mass or Masses. The present Cheadle Bulkeley Hall was built by Rector Egerton about 1760. Whether he ever lived in it, or died before it was finished, is doubtful. As before mentioned, it is known in folk-lore that the builders of houses generally die as soon as the house is finished. This does not apply to the modern jerry-builders ; they are reserved for judgment in the future. It is another lamentable instance of the degeneracy of these times, that some builders who do not die naturally, should not be put to death or kept in confinement to prevent them building any more.

Rector Egerton was a scion of that numerous family who, taking their name from the little township of Egerton, in the parish of Malpas, gradually spread over Cheshire and a good share of England. The one who laid the foundations of their vast wealth was an illegitimate lad who rose to be Chancellor of England. He was educated for a lawyer, and made chapter clerk to the Dean and Canons of Chester. At the great robbery of the religious houses most of the lands of the Abbey of St. Werburgh, at Chester, were given to the new diocese of Chester, but, whether by accident or design, the word Cestriae (of Chester) was omitted from their charter ; and here was a nice flaw in the title, and a chance for the lawyers. Some of the neighbouring noblemen and gentlemen grabbed the lands, just as some grab land now if they get the chance ; but it was necessary to get the law or the makers of the law on their side, and therefore the lands in dispute were surrendered to the Earl of Leicester, Queen Elizabeth's man, until the case could be tried. It seems a similar case to that of the jury who acquitted the man for stealing a ham when the jury had eaten most of the ham. The landlords got the lands by paying a small chief rent as acknowledgment. The chapter clerk, Thomas Egerton, went over to help them. He knew the case for the other side, and used his great abilities against that Church of which he was a member. Steadily stifling all scruples of conscience or remorse, he helped to wrest acre after acre and manor after manor of the fair rich lands of Cheshire from their rightful owners, and investing all he could in cheap land, he built up the vast wealth of the family. As a large landowner and able man he was chosen to be Knight of the Shire, and worked his way to the House of Lords and to be Keeper of the Great Seal. He is the ancestor of the Dukes of Bridgwater, Earls of Ellesmere, and Lords of Tatton, the Earls of Wilton and Egertons of Oulton being other branches of the family.

Thomas Egerton, rector of Cheadle, had a full share of the hereditary greediness of his race. He fattened on the Church in what was then a perfectly legitimate and respectable manner, for he held the rich livings of Sephton, Warrington, and Cheadle. Sephton alone was worth thousands a year when money was infinitely scarcer than it is at the present day. He looked after the loaves and fishes, and half-starved curates had to do the work or leave it undone. At his death Cheadle Bulkeley Hall was sold, and passed through many strange vicissitudes. About sixty years since a girls' school was established there. It was probably a continuation of the one that was once held at what should have been Didsbury Hall, and is now the Wesleyan College. It was called a seminary for young ladies, but our country folk were not very highly educated, and, becoming confused with fine words, they called it a cemetery for young ladies. After a long and desperate struggle with age, poverty, ghosts, girls, governesses, bad debts, and all sorts of trials, the school had to be given up, and a hospital was the next scene in its strange eventful history. It is only fair to the Infirmary authorities to say that the house was haunted and stained with blood long before they took it. Then Mr. Watts bought it and lived there, and when he succeeded his father, Sir James Watts, as lord of the manor, its ancient glories were revived, the manorial court being held at the George and Dragon, where the feudal retainers called ale-tasters, with other varieties of beef-eaters and constables, are annually appointed,

and where some of the tenants of the manor pay their
fines or amercements, and do suit and service for their
tenures. When Mr. Watts went back to Abney the
place was let to a gentleman from Stockport, but he
soon died, and now the old house is empty again.

It is an exceedingly comfortable and convenient
house, but there can be no doubt it is haunted, and
there seems to be not even a legend as to who it is
that haunts it. There are stains of blood on a bedroom floor that nothing will efface, but no one knows
whose was the blood. There was an elopement from
the school fifty years ago, a most romantic affair, just
the sort for school-girls to rave after—a lover with a
carriage and pair in the Stockport Road, and an un-
fastened window where the girl elopes down a ladder
of ropes. All very nice and interesting, though there
is no connecting the ghost with the elopement or the
much older stains of blood. When Mr. Watts went
to live at the house he had not heard of the ghost, or
he took no notice of it, but very soon he had a house
full of company, and a lady from London, who certainly had never heard a word about the place being
haunted, was visited in the night, and described the
lady spirit and her mob cap exactly as the school-girls
knew it.

Since I wrote the "History of Cheadle" I have
been told by a lady who was once governess at the
house, that another ghost was nearly being made
there. It seems a "Ma'mselle" was imported from
Paris to teach the true Parisian pronunciation, and
she being used to living on butterflies and wafers, as
they do in parts of France, was too delicate for the
resurrection pie and barm dumplings of Miss Hunter's
select seminary. The village doctor was sent for, and
his practice was simplicity itself, for he had one ques-

tion and one cure for all cases. He asked his question,
which sounded like " Howsthbowls?" and the new
governess did not understand a word of English,
though it might not have made any difference if she
had understood him, for she got the universal cure,
the calomel pill, locally called a white bulldog. The
next day she was worse, and could only feebly moan,
" Non, m'sieur, non," but she had to take another
white bulldog. The third day she was *in extremis*,
and it was thought better, with the help of a French
dictionary, to get the doctor's idioms translated into
Cheadle French, so that some one else might turn
them into French French. This was done, partly
by my informant, and only just in time to save the
poor girl's life, or there would have been another
ghost (a French one) flitting about Cheadle Hall.

The popular belief is that it is the spirits of those
who have been suddenly or unfairly put to death, or
who have committed some great crime, that cannot
rest : " Sent to their account with all their imper-
fections on their head." There is plenty of good
evidence about this ghost, for many will swear they
have seen it. Others who have not seen it are not
justified in simply contradicting them. The sceptic
may say, Why don't they catch it ? The answer to
that is, Can any one catch the breath as it leaves the
body ? Termagants may say they will sit up for it
all night with a big thick stick, and in that case the
ghost would probably not appear at all. If it prefers
to look at young ladies in bed instead of a crusty old
curmudgeon with a thick stick, that is only evidence
of good taste and good sense. The ghost seems to
be a very quiet, inoffensive, ladylike ghost, a desirable
addition to any family or historical house, and I hope
it may long continue in good spirit.

The Old Parsonage, Didsbury.

Perhaps it is fitting that these writings on the folk-lore, old customs, and superstitions of the district, should give an account of the house from which they have been dated, for to some extent the place may have inspired the work that has been done in it.

Haunted houses must, of course, have a history, although it may or may not be known, and the ghosts which haunt them may or may not be the ghosts of any one whose history or life is written. Whatever little is known should be set down for the instruction, not of this generation only, but for those who are to come after us, for as the history mellows with age the interest in it increases. The unknown correspondents scattered over the earth who write to me for their family pedigrees, and address letters to the Rev. Fletcher Moss, sometimes beginning them " Reverend Father," may now learn how it happens that I write from an old parsonage.

In the time of the Commonwealth the parishioners of the then large parish of Didsbury (a parish or parochial chapelry containing four townships) chose their own minister, and put into writing the terms on which he was engaged. Here is one clause : "That the messuage and tenement assigned to the use of the ministers of the said church for the tyme beinge shall bee valued and acompted at the rate of tenne pounds per annum towards the said XL^{li} ffortye pounds per annum considringe the tymes, and that Mr. Clayton is a single man and soe cannot husband it to advantage." From this document it appears there was a special house for the parson, who was then called the

minister; in other times he would have been called
the priest, and the congregation or parishioners would
have had no voice in his selection, but would have had
to accept him from the higher powers with more or
less thankfulness. Any antiquary with the least knowledge of our pre-Reformation churches would say if
he visited Didsbury, and was told how the old black
and white cottages formerly stood round the church,
that the centre part of the house now called the Old
Parsonage was almost certainly the priest's house.
The assessment or "cess" of the house seems to have
been lowered to suit Mr. Clayton, who, though

> " Passing rich on forty pounds a year,"

was yet poor, for he had no wife to "husband it to
advantage," or to darn his stockings for him if he had
any. The priests of old well knew the best sites for
their houses, and this one stands on a gravel bank,
in what was doubtless the original Saxon burgh or
borough, facing south south-west, a warmer aspect
even than south, with every room overlooking the
church and miles of open country beyond it, in the
midst of a good garden still overrun with flowers,
more or less wild, as described on page 76 of this
book.

Passing over nearly two centuries we come to a
time within "living memory," when the parochial
quarrels were more than usually virulent. The Rev.
John Gatliff held among other offices the living of
Didsbury; but the parish had become too hot for
him, or he for the parish. The Bishop of Chester
thundered forth that the dead (parishioners and non-
parishioners) were being buried in unconsecrated
ground, that he absolutely forbade such things to be
done, and threatened the terrors of the law and his

THE OLD CARSON AGE GATEWAY.

displeasure. The reply he got was that there was
nowhere else to bury them, the old churchyard was
full and swollen, and the squire owned all the land
round the church, and would not sell any at any price
until his costs were paid. The garden of this house
was not his, and it was considered by the vestry
whether or not to add that to the churchyard and
divert Stenner Lane. The squire's hand was against
every man, and every man's hand against him, for he
was serving writs on the parishioners for £1464 law
costs in the Spiritual Courts, that he was out of pocket
in defending the rights of the parish to levy its own
church rates. The vestry had laid a cess (or "cessed
a ley") of one shilling and threepence in the pound
for expenses ; but few would pay it, for they said the
squire had gone to law to please himself, that he had
had all the fun, and should pay the costs. Mottram,
the tanner, of Burnage, and sidesman for that township, had gone to prison sooner than serve as sidesman, and all was in uproar, though they are quiet
enough now. The squire's white marble tablet in the
church, under his shield of arms, impaling Mosley
jure uxoris, says he was an active magistrate for the
counties of Lancaster and Chester. Even his activity
is now at rest ; and when the seething cauldron of
strife had simmered down, the advowson of the living
was bought by one Newall, a grocer at the bottom
of Market Stead Lane, whose premises became noted
in after years as Newall's Buildings, the office of the
Anti-Corn Law League. Newall bought the cure of
souls of Didsbury just as he traded in pickles, mus-
tard, pepper, or other fiery goods, and also bought
the house of which I write, and it was settled on his
son Samuel for his life.

The Rev. Sam Newall was licensed minister of

Didsbury in May 1832, though the other reverend gentleman still held the living, and would neither resign it, do his duty, nor die. Newall lived at the parsonage, and greatly enlarged it. He was a diligent young man, who worked hard and visited all over his large parish, being well respected by all classes ; but calumny began again, and in 1840 he left the parish, selling the advowson, but not the house. The fact was that the house being settled on him for his life, he could not very well sell it, though it was easy enough to sell the people, or the care of them. The new parson lived at the parsonage for ten years, though he complained greatly about it, and the new and the old seem to have hated one another with a truly religious hatred. The greater part of the church was twice rebuilt, and the parson and wardens were getting to law with one another when Didsbury parish was included to a greater extent than it formerly was in Manchester parish, and a new rectory was provided out of sight and sound of the church, where no clang of bells could mar the calm repose requisite for the composition of sermons, and where no supervision could be kept over what might be done in church or churchyard, for it was becoming fashionable for the shopkeeper to live away from his shop, and the shepherd from his fold.

In 1851 the Old Parsonage was again left forlorn, desolate, and deserted, abandoned to ghosts, who had to be restrained by more constant and vigorous clanging of the bells, as the priestly influence lessened. The house was let to common ordinary laymen, even a brewer being a tenant. We entered it on March 8, 1865, and in 1884 I bought it from the executors of the Rev. S. Newall, who had held it and been a priest of the Church of England for over fifty years. Here

my happiest hours have been spent, and here I hope
my days may end. The house had a terrible reputation for being haunted when we took it. It was said
that no servant would stop in the place, for the bells
were often rung in the middle of the night when
every one was asleep, and this we soon found was
quite true. It was also said that the ghosts came out
of the graves in the churchyard, and sat up in the
trees in the garden airing themselves on fine evenings,
but I never believed that tale. We were living near
by, and when the furniture was partly moved, a young
gardener named Billy Bonks, a big, strong young
man, was to sleep in the house by himself for one
night. He flatly refused, saying he would throw up
his place first; so I had to take the job, and some
very lively nights I experienced, one being a regular
blood-curdler.

A slight description of the house is as follows :—
The middle part of it is certainly older than one
hundred years. The room in which we live has been
two rooms. It is crossed in opposite directions with
beams that I can touch from the floor, and that shows
the room is low. There are no ventilators or ventilating shafts to it, no cellars, no drains, no damp
courses, no anything that is required by the modern
surveyor or scientific sanitary specialist. If I had not
been on the Local Board it is probable the whole
place would have been condemned as insanitary long
ago. The inspectors are like the priest and Levite
who pass by on the other side ; and as no doctor visits
us professionally, we have enjoyed good health. In
fact, I am thankful to say that no one has ever spent
a single day in bed in the house for thirty years.

We have a few old lead-light windows and a
round-headed doorway with Jacobean mouldings that

once gave access to the Cock Inn yard, but the latter
has long since been walled up. There is, unfortunately, communication between the adjoining stables
and our roof, whereby the rats invade us, and are
responsible for some of the mysterious noises. There
are also gravestones, or pieces of them, inscribed,
" Beneath this stone are deposited the mortal remains
of ——," or " Here lies the body of ——." Then
follows a name of one of the forefathers of the parish,
and perhaps a more or less imperfect list of his
virtues.   Pedigree hunters may like to know that
the commonest names in the parish centuries ago
were Blomeley, ffletcher, Chorlton, Rudd, Barlow,
Langford, Garner, Bancroft, and others.   There has
evidently been some mistake about these gravestones,
for the bodies were not beneath them, and Didsbury
never had the evil reputation for resurrectionists that
Northen had.   It is probable some parson or clerk,
for economical reasons, took the pieces of stone to
flag their pig-sties or yards with, thereby encouraging
ghosts, who would be justified in looking after these
irregularities.   If the ghosts became a nuisance it was
the duty of the parson to lay them.   If he did not or
could not do so, whose fault was it?   It would be
presumptuous for me to express an opinion, but old
records show that in similar circumstances elsewhere
the aid was invoked of seven priests with lighted
candles, or even his holiness a bishop, and it seems
needless to add that the Church would be triumphant
at last.   But in our case the ghosts won, and the
parson fled.

Some people complain that I do not give particulars, names, and addresses of the ghosts of which
I write.   How is it possible to do so?   They are
merely spirits that appear and vanish.   There are

(Wilfrid Johnson) 1870.

THE OLD PARSONAGE, DIDSBURY.

some bones in the remains of the clerk's house. I do not know whose they were, and was rather shocked at a nephew of mine, who is a medical student, saying they were the bones of a nigger, for I never heard of a nigger being buried at Didsbury. A human jaw turned up in the garden only last summer. It might have been a local female's, for it was rather worn about the hinges.

When we first went to the house the noises in the night were certainly extraordinary. They were mostly made by rats, who took refuge under the roof from the adjoining stables. One of them might jump on the ceiling, and in the room below it would sound like a body falling. Then there would be squeals and moans, followed by a rush like the sound of a troop of cavalry. In my bedroom are bell wires that are admirably adapted for the gymnastic exercises of the rats. They use them as parallel bars, and if some fat fellow tumbles off he probably rings the bells and frightens the maids. There is a hole in the ceiling where these bell wires go through, and in the early morning I used to see the rats come to this hole and peep down on me when in bed. It reminded me of a magic lantern scene for amusing children, where a man slept with his mouth open, and between every snore a mouse ran down his throat. My boyish experiences had taught me that no rat or mouse could bite or do anything if it were caught by the tail and held aloft, so long as the tail did not skin off. Therefore I waited till their tails came through the hole into the room and tried to grab them, but with no good result. Feeding them on phosphorous paste proved the surest way of quieting them.

One night there were extraordinary noises at the window, and I saw the figure of a man in the bushes.

I rushed out and collared him, finding, to our mutual surprise, that it was the local "bobby." He explained that he was on duty, trying if the windows were all securely fastened, and he had also a message for the cook. We had probably killed a pig, and, with the fine instinct of a detective, the active and intelligent officer was at once upon the track, and wished to interview the cook as to the disposal of the body, but he had unfortunately got to the wrong window.

Another night my mother awoke me to say there was something in her bedroom that every now and then gave a piercing scream. Hastily putting on some clothes, I followed her, and sat down by the bedside to await results, for I was certain she would not imagine anything. It was a very dark night, wild and windy. I must have dozed off in the chair, when there suddenly came a most horrible shriek, a regular blood-curdler that would make any one's hair stand on end. It gradually died away in jerks, as though some one were having his throat cut slowly and the life-blood ebbing away, until all was as quiet as the grave again. After a thorough search through the room I could find nothing whatever, and had to sit still again to wait, wide awake that time, and the gas lit. Before very long that piercing scream came again ringing through the room, and again I could find nothing, though I thought it came from the window. If it were anything earthly it must be a maniac outside, for it certainly was not an owl. Then I got behind the window curtain to wait for ghost or devil, or worse than either, some madman. At last it came suddenly, like a shot, and close to my ear, a wild, wailing, ear-splitting scream, that certainly stopped my heart and breath ; but I faced it as well as I could, and found it. There was a fractured pane of glass, the cracked piece

being of the shape of an isosceles triangle, with the
equal sides about nine inches long and the base one
inch. A strong gust of wind blew open this fracture
with a sound like an Æolian harp would make if it
had an epileptic fit. A bit of paper in the crack soon
stopped the noise, and with a new pane of glass that
boggart was laid, though it was very terrifying for a
time.

As for the real ghosts, the reader may be im-
patient to hear about them, but I feel I cannot
describe them. There is nothing real, and yet there
is something. Probably hundreds of times I have
been awakened out of sleep and heard some one
coming upstairs, stealthily and quietly, step by step ;
heard the doors open and shut ; have gone after them
and found nothing. There may be something light,
there may be a waft of chilled air, but there is nothing
tangible. I may state the case fairly by saying, that
in my younger days I have often distinctly heard
some one, have rushed after them, and found nothing,
although conscious of something. I have been wide
awake with a very matter-of-fact mind, and a body
trained in all athletic exercises from my youth, but I
could catch nothing. Nowadays I never trouble about
the ghosts. They may roam about as they like, for I
never heed them. Three months since (December
1896) there was an earthquake and the bed shook
under me, wakening me up. I merely muttered to
myself, " Well, I wonder whether that is a bogie or an
earthquake," and instantly went to sleep again, for-
getting all about it until the next morning, when, in
the train going to town, the passengers were all talking of the earthquake. That reminded me of what I
had felt in the night.

The dogs know when the ghosts are about, for we

used to have them in the house until they became a greater nuisance than the ghosts themselves. They would see, hear, or feel them when we could not, and that multiplied the disturbance. My dogs are of the old English bristle-haired, rat-catching terrier kind, with a dash of badger and beefsteak in them. The old dog, Gomer, would lie dozing by the fire, and suddenly jump up, and go on tiptoe across the room to stop and scratch at the carpet; that might mean there was a rat under the floor, or the ghost from some prehistoric burial; or he would bark at apparently nothing, and it would be supposed there was something outside; or he would growl, and follow something with his eyes fixed when we could see nothing. That showed his senses were keener than ours, and we might say with Hamlet's mother—

> " How is't with you,
> That you do bend your eye on vacancy?
> Your bedded hair starts up and stands on end."

When we were young we were taken to hear sermons, and were not allowed to go to sleep during the tedious infliction, one consequence being that I can retail parts of these sermons for the edification of this generation. Our spiritual adviser was mighty in the Scriptures, but if a text did not suit him he would alter it to what he said was the correct translation. Although he deemed the Scriptures infallible, he did not think the same of their translators, and he knew as much or as little of the original Greek as he did of the Aramaic. There was a sermon came in its turn, from the tub or box in which he kept them, upon the text, " The devils believe and tremble." This text he said would be more correctly rendered by " The devils believe and bristle up with terror "; that is, their bristles stand on end with fright and fury. When old Gomer's bristles stood up, and his tail curled at the invisible spirits, I naturally thought of those poor devils our parson was interested in, and wondered whether their tails would pop between their legs, and their bristles go flat as they suddenly shrunk into half their size at the sound of something holy. Gomer hated ghosts worse than cats, for he never could fasten the former as he sometimes did the latter deceitful, uncanny beasts. Hedgehogs were a puzzle that required patience. He nearly lost his life at a wasp's nest. The long warfare with the rats was the chief joy of his life; and he hated the sound of the church bells, for they too were connected in some mysterious way with the ghosts and the invisible world. His grandchildren now take his place, and the crocuses are blooming on his

GOMER.

grave under the weeping ash-tree. In the witching hour of night the ghosts still come and go. I know nothing about them as to whose they are, what they want, or whither they go. They will not hurt us, and we never heed them.

> " We meet them at the doorway, on the stair,
>   Along the passages they come and go,
>   Impalpable impressions on the air.
>   A sense of something moving to and fro."

L.

CHAPTER IX

LAWYERS, DOCTORS, AND PARSONS

" The first thing we do, let us kill all the lawyers."
—KING HENRY VI.

HEN some happy student of nature goes wandering through the copses and by the tangled hedgerows of our country lanes, noting the beauties there so lavishly displayed—the tiny dormouse with its beady black eyes and silky fur, the Peggy Whitethroat scolding and chattering at all who venture past its grey nest in the brambles, and the Red Admiral that flits around and flaunts its beauty over all—his delicious reverie may be suddenly and painfully interrupted by the long curved thorns of the wild rose or the briar, and the bronzed "hedger and ditcher" near by may say, "What's the matter, mester? Has a laryer gotten thi? We ca' them sharp hooks, laryers, for if they clip thi by th' leg an' tha tumbles among 'em, it's God help thi." The antipathies of our country labourers to lawyers, doctors, and parsons are rather interesting. Are they the product of inherited instinct, or of sad experience? They never mention dentists or gentlemen of other professions, as they are probably lacking in experience of them.

It would seem difficult for the sharpest lawyer that ever came out of London to wax fat on country folk, who do well and bring up large families on twelve or fifteen shillings a week, and yet these same innocent rustics will tell you that one lawyer in a parish will starve, whereas two or more get fat, "'cos they set neighbours by th' ears." In some respects they differ from magpies, for it is a universal superstition that a solitary magpie is a symbol of bad luck or the devil, though there is no harm in several magpies. Whereas with lawyers, they say there is no harm in one ; but if there are several, " an' tha tumbles among 'em, it's God help thi."

Another country superstition is that lawyers don't die ; they are "fetched." There is much meaning in that word " fetched." On the other side of Manchester they pronounce it " fot," and would say, " T' owd 'un has fot 'un." There is also a good old tale as to how lawyers got their patron saint. It is worth dishing up again for those who have not heard it. Once upon a time there was an honest lawyer. It was ages ago, and it was in a far country where people were scarce. The name was Evona. It sounds like a woman's name, but he was believed to be really a man. Evona went to see the Pope, to kiss his toe, and ask his blessing. He said he had always been honest, an honest lawyer and a religious man too, and he prayed the Pope would let the lawyers have a patron saint to bless and protect them. The Pope told him patron saints were scarce—things generally are scarce when you want them—and he temporised and delayed, just as his inferior clergy do when it suits them. But Evona was persistent, and worried at him like any common lawyer. So the Pope granted that he should choose a patron saint when blindfolded. Therefore

Evona was blindfolded in a church that was thronged with statues of the saints. He was then told to patter so many "paters," turned round three times, and left to grope for a saint. As he got warm, he hugged one, and cried, "This shall be our saint; we lawyers take him." Then the bandages were removed, and Evona found he had got the devil by the neck, for he had groped his way to the big statue of St. Michael trampling on the devil, and had clasped the latter gentleman round the neck. Then he cried, and was very sorrowful, and said, "What is the good of being honest?" A certain Scotchman passing by remonstrated with him in the manner of the clan, and told him that honesty certainly was the best policy, for he had tried both, but that if he (the lawyer) when he was blindfolded had loosened one eye, so that he could see a wee bit without any one knowing, he might have done better.

The unwritten lore or beliefs of our common folk with regard to "doctoring" are altering or being lost more rapidly than on most other subjects. There are some who still discriminate between charms and cures and "doctors' physic"; but with the greatly increased numbers who live in towns, and who consequently cannot get herbs and other old-fashioned potions, there is a very great increase in the number of properly qualified medical men, whose treatment is not so destructive as it formerly was. There are kindred of my own now living who have been bled, literally, even for indigestion, and who remember that the first act of a doctor was to bleed his patient, that being considered the highest and most scientific practice, as drawing all the humours out of the blood. Then medical science advanced, and mercury pills came into fashion. There are many living who remember the

"Cheadle bulldogs." They were white pills about the size of a pin's head, that made the patient think the pill when swallowed turned into a live bulldog. The survivors of them erected a beautiful fountain in Cheadle in grateful remembrance. It is no wonder that old-fashioned folk preferred their dandelion or rue or camomile tea to all the "doctors' rubbitsh" which was then said to be the perfection of medical science. It has really been said (of course I am writing of the past) that the doctors killed more than they cured, and when a doctor passing the churchyard asked the sexton who was about to dig a grave what he was doing, he rather rudely replied, "Finishing your work."

It would take volumes to give the wonderful lotions and potions that were formerly used to cure disease. Faith was the chief factor, as it is now, for the servant of an old friend of mine went one night to see a doctor, and came back with a big bottle of medicine, saying, "The doctor was as drunk as a lord; he couldn't see a hole i' th' ladder, an' could hardly talk, but he's given me a rare big bottle o' stuff to tak.' It should do me good, for it smells nasty." They always want "a bottle," and a big one for choice. I have read somewhere that a famous physician— perhaps Sir Astley Cooper— divided a lot of hospital patients into three classes, and doctored the first class with the strongest drugs, the second class with nothing, and the third class with bread pills and water made offensive. Nearly all the patients in the first class died off quickly, and many in the second, but those in the third did well, for their faith saved them.

A few of the old folks' remedies are as follows : Wine from the sacrament was a specific for many complaints. Silver from the sacrament offertory was also good for many things, either when worn round the neck or made into a ring. Silver begged from unmarried people of the opposite sex and made into a ring was also good for fits. Charming was very regularly performed. The charmer, in secret, prayed, or recited a verse or some gibberish, and the charmed gave nothing, not even thanks, and was made whole. There are wonderful accounts of the miraculous cures wrought by charmers. The late Charles Bradbury, the collector of curiosities (who was a connection of our family), had hundreds of people who went to him to have their jaundice charmed away. Perhaps the commonest medicine of all was rue. It was the herb of grace, bitter enough to keep the fairies away. It was often the first food given to babies; it was used up to old age; and it was given to all the cattle and fowls. I have always been an enthusiastic breeder of poultry, and at the old thatched farm that is still by our garden I learnt, when a boy, from old Jimmy and Mary Aldred, to give rue pills to any poultry or pigeons that we thought were ill, and if that did not mend them we gave them a spider in butter. A fine, fat spider, all alive and kicking, was considered by many wise men and women to be a grand cure for ague and all sorts of things. If people are at all nervous as to what might happen if the spider came out of the butter when they had swallowed it, I can assure them it was not as bad as a Cheadle bulldog pill, and it was always said he was a bold man who first swallowed an oyster. Spiders' webs are still used to stop bleeding. Snails are good for consumptive patients, who also take young frogs. Woodlice were frequently taken as pills, and the great cure for worms was alegar or sour ale, a practitioner remarking, " If thou'lt only tak' enoo' on it, if it doesn't kill th' wurrums it'll kill thee."

Country people so often see horses and dogs pass-ing worms that they ascribe all sorts of pains to a worm gnawing at the heart, or a worm at the liver, and then they recommend all sorts of "yarb tay." Rheumatism, the great torment of the country folk, is cured or eased by galvanic or charmed rings, by carrying the forefoot of a hare or a raw potato in the pocket; and a grand specific for it or lumbago, sciatica, or kindred pains, is to be "bishoped" at a confirmation. The laying on of the bishop's hands seems to be as efficacious as the old remedy of the king's touch. Powdered cockroaches are known to be a grand thing for the dropsy. For cuts, anoint the wound and the knife with lard or fat bacon, taking care to treat the cutting instrument the same as the wound. For ear-ache, roast an onion, and put it when hot with the stalk up the ear, keeping it there for some time. The cures for warts and corns would take a column; so we must leave them and many other com-plaints, merely mentioning a strange charm that is still in use.

If young persons misbehave themselves when asleep, they should eat roasted mice or mouse pie, that being an infallible cure. This is very interesting, for wealthy people still try it (though probably un-known to their professional doctors). It seems to me that people seeing mice run over sleeping children, attribute the disturbance to them, and suppose that by feeding the children on mice the other mice will soon be aware of the fact, and keep far away from the sleeping ogres. This is another harmless charm, for the mice are as good to eat as rabbits, and they cer-tainly are attracted by oiled or greasy hair, and nibble it while the owner's head is peacefully slumbering on the pillow.

After the paragraph above had appeared in the paper, a doctor told me that he and a noted physician had unsuccessfully tried to cure a son of one of the leading citizens of Manchester, when the family cook, on the advice of her sister in the country and with her master's sanction, served up a nice mouse pie, which cured the lad completely. This is a Manchester case, happening now, with well-known people. The doctor, who has been paid for not doing it, says it is merely a coincidence—"the medicine is not recognised by the faculty." Perhaps it's too cheap.

Some of the old-fashioned cures for the old-fashioned ailments known as coughs and colds are as follows: white wine whey; rum and honey; black currant tea; horehound tea; linseed tea and honey; ale porridge. This last was oatmeal boiled in ale and sweetened, and taken hot before going to bed. It was a grand thing with country lads; they would take it by "the peilful."

When searching into the customs of our fore-fathers, it is extraordinary how ale was used at every meal, on every day, with special quantities at all feasts or "ales." It must be remembered it was home-brewed, not the modern chemical decoction. The cheapest quality was then made largely from mow burnt hay from the middle of an over-sweated stack, that had plenty of dark colour and flavour without being injurious. It has been said the Danes originally came to England in quest of the good ale flavoured with heather-blossom instead of hops. Now the Germans come and bring their lager beer with them.

There are some extraordinary superstitions respecting charms still lingering among us, for I hear there is a woman at Moss Nook with a goitred throat who wants a dead man's hand to rub it with. Father Arrowsmith's hand is a relic of a local saint that is reputed to have worked many wonders. He was a Jesuit, who was born at Winwick, and who was hanged, drawn, and quartered after the manner of the Christians in 1628 at Lancaster.

There is a lady in Bowdon who brought the hand of a mummy from Egypt, and kept it under glass in her drawing-room as a curiosity, but the original owner of the hand found her out, and troubled her when she ought to have been sleeping the sleep of the just. Therefore, after several struggles with her conscience, she determined to make what reparation she could, and try her hand at amateur grave-digging in Bowdon churchyard when she thought she was unobserved. So with a spoon she dug a grave, and left the mummy's hand in peace, not knowing that naughty boys were watching, as dogs watch other dogs burying bones, and then scratch them up when the other dogs are gone. It is doubtful if the lady will have rest even now, for the hand should have been sent back to Egypt carriage paid. The antediluvian Egyptian who originally owned it would not be satisfied with burial here, even if it was in what we call consecrated ground, for her religion would not be exactly the same as the religion of Bowdon at the present day.

There is or was a belief that a man could gain the affections of a woman almost against her will by burying a placenta at the threshold of her house. This was actually done within "living memory" at Gatley by a man named Gatley, he having procured one for two guineas. The charm failed in this instance, the woman being very self-willed.

During one of the delightful little excursions taken by our local antiquarian society in quest of stately church, moated grange, or timbered hall, it chanced that four members were driving in a rickety shandry-dan along the Cheshire lanes one summer evening. They were far from home, and, in spite of the beautiful scenery and objects of interest, they wondered when they would get their supper. One of them, who was a doctor and a magistrate, said suppers were bad things; they produced indigestion, sleeplessness, and other evils. Then another, who was a town-clerk, said that he always had sausages for supper—Congleton sausages hot, with strong tea—and he was over fourscore years old, for he remembered men who had been "out in the '45." The third was a bee-master—a very hale old man—who said he always had a thick paste made, on which he spread strawberry jam about an inch thick, and ate that before going to bed. The fourth was a poor author, who said that he could not afford such dainties and delicacies, but he expected to have a gooseberry pie and about a quart of new milk when he got home. As he was a long way off being eighty, his evidence was not of much value; but he assured the others he had lately supped with his uncle and aunt, who were that age, and their supper was cheese and ale with raw onions. Then those three antiquated antiquaries mocked that vain doctor's new-fangled notions about going supperless to bed, and they bade him tell his tales to the women, for they were hungered, and their experience or lore is here recorded for the benefit of those who would live wisely and well and see many days.

My notes on the superstitions respecting the oldest and chief of the great professions must, for many and various reasons, be very brief. In all ages and in all

countries it has been the ambition of devout women to
have sons or grandsons in the priesthood of their religion,
and to give the best that they have unto their Lord.
The lads themselves may have other views, especially
if they have much energy or love of adventure.   But if
the hope and pride of the family is merely a big fine
sleepy lad, without much desire for work, he is educated for a parson ; and if he cannot be educated, and
keeps middling honest, he will do for a " bobby."

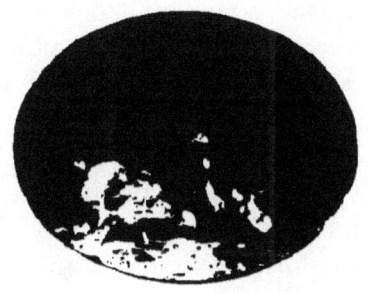

GUINEA-FOWLS.

CHAPTER X

SCHOOLMASTERS

" The schoolmaster is exceeding fantastical."
—Love's Labour's Lost.

CHOOLMASTERS have multiplied so exceedingly in late years, and have varied so much from the type of fifty years ago, that I am induced to put on record what I remember of one of the old-fashioned sort.

When I was a child I was often sent for change of air to a lonely house high among the pine woods, eight or nine hundred feet above the sea, whence is one of the most glorious views in any country. The house had been built for a private madhouse, where the owner or some members of the family were kept chained to the floor in the garret, and were said to be overgrown with long matted hair, and to howl horribly. The place naturally became haunted, so that no man durst pass that way after dark, for amid the soughing of the fir-trees they heard the clanking of the chains and the howls of the madmen. Being haunted, it became empty, and cheap, and the situation being wonderfully fine, my father took it on a long lease, to help his eldest sister, who had married a schoolmaster.

This man, who was my uncle by marriage, was born in 1792. He had been a volunteer when the great Napoleon threatened an invasion of England. He had struggled with poverty and kept a school. There are now two or three well-to-do men in Manchester whom he bottomed in education. He was painstaking with his pupils, for if he could not get the learning into them at one end he would try the other, being a believer in the motto of the psalmist—

"'Tis education forms the common mind,
And with the birch we drive it in behind."

Birch-trees were very common about the place when he went there ; but as they got all used up he had a much worse weapon than they, that was his hand. Rheumatism and bad temper had cramped his fingers and stiffened his joints, so that his fourth or little finger would not open. The third finger opened a little, and the second a little more, but they were all at various angles, and when he gave a lad a box on the ear it was like hitting him with a board from which large nails projected at various angles. One finger would strike into the ear, and another into the eye. He was reputed to be learnèd (please put the accent on the latter syllable), he was fairly honest, and good-tempered sometimes. He was an awful Tory, and swore like one—oaths and curses enough to blister the paper, if they were printed, and make it curl up. Of course he was churchwarden, almost an ideal churchwarden, for when he wore his company manners one would have thought butter could hardly melt in his mouth, and in the church, as in the police, size and dignity are of more account than mere goodness. He was six feet high, with white hair, looked very solemn, very severe, and wiser than any ordinary owl. His

hero or model was the great Duke, who, he would
remind us, was to have been a schoolmaster if he had
not got into the army. His reading was chiefly con-
fined to the county newspaper, which was published
once a week in the interest of the landed aristocracy,
and whose motto may be taken as——

> " For what are all the country patriots born?
> To hunt, and vote, and raise the price of corn."

It should be remembered that in those days the
line of respectability was drawn at £50 rental. The
common beggars who only paid £30 or £40 rental
were not allowed to vote. Their attention was drawn
to impending calamities and the ruin of the country if
the aristocracy had not all the power. At one time
we were continually frightened by the expected invasion of the French under Napoleon the Third, and
then the old man was in his glory. Another time it
was the Roman Catholics who were coming to burn
us all up. Then it was to be the end of the world.
Those blessed Tories were the only ones who could
save us, otherwise we should all be burnt or frightened
to death. That end-of-the-world scare was about 1856,
I think. Dr. Cummings had fixed the day of judgment and been making all preparations, even to taking
his coals in weekly so as to save his money and be
ready for any emergency. There was a blood-red
sunset and heavy storm one evening, and some of the
females fainted, for the archangel's trump was expected
every minute, and it was just then the old man seemed
happiest, being conscious of his own importance, for
he had foretold it all along, and if any one had had
the courage and forethought to ask for a holiday I
believe he would have got it.
        The only books of mere worldly wisdom that I

remember my uncle reading were Cobbett's "Two-penny Trash" and " Rural Rides." I could read them again now if life were not too short. This generation, who only hear the eloquence of the Cobbetts in the dreary, dismal drip of the police courts, have little notion of the storms that raged in many a country market-place and at many a farmer's dinners when the founder of the family spoke of the wrongs and follies and crimes of the England of his day. Another man, with whose name I unwittingly aroused my uncle's wrath, was about that time another centre of storm and bitterest calumny. To test my schooling, for I was only a small boy, who spent some time with his aunt in the holidays, the old man once asked me, " How many coombs make a strike?" I replied there were no coombs or strikes in Colenso; but I soon found there was a strike elsewhere, for the withering scorn with which he said, "Colenso! that condemned old infidel! Sent out to convert the niggers, and they converted him. The world is coming to something if he is to teach children. I'd have him and his books burnt, blow him!" could not fail to impress me as much as the strike. It may be news to some to know that Colenso was a celebrated divine, who took to arithmetic and wrote a book, it being highly dangerous to mix inspired records with arithmetic. He measured the capacity of the Ark according to Genesis, and found all the animals could not be got in it, so he wrote a book and got into trouble. I well remember asking at Mudie's for "Colenso on the Pentateuch" and being told it was "withdrawn."

There has long been a superstition that servants should work for less money for professional men than for others, because of the superior training and education they would receive. One of my aunt's servants

got married they had such nice names, and the giddy
things would get married if they could. It was certainly better for all parties that they should be what
was called "churched," for they punctually obeyed the
first great commandment. Myra was left alone, for
Lydia had gone, and Wilhelmina was to take her
place; but she wanted £5 a year for wages, and this
shocked the household. Even in that remote district
they had to go with the times and give increased
wages; but my uncle's patience and temper were not
improved. Shortly after the new girl came he saw
her take a lighted candle into one of the deep cupboards made in the thick walls of the house and leave
it there. The hurricane of oaths and curses that fell
on that poor girl's eyes and limbs dazed her. It was
her first taste of the sound religious training, and if she
had been reared on bread and butter and tea, as they
rear them nowadays, instead of on the oatmeal and milk
which had made her flesh somewhat of the colour and
consistency of a brick, she might have shrivelled up.
I heard it, and remember every word of the opening,
but not of the end, for I ran away and hid myself.

Those servants at £5 (or less) wages a year
walked once a week five miles to the market town
with baskets on each arm, containing twenty or thirty
pounds weight of butter and eggs, and walked back
with the groceries. The groceries were mostly candles,
"farthing dips"; they were precious articles then, and
my aunt would complain if there were three burning
at once. There was a saying from the time when
spinning-wheels were used—

> "Three candles burning
> And no wheel turning."

There was always tobacco and perhaps some church-

warden pipes for the master, and a little sugar—such
sugar, nearly black ; in fact it was said to be coloured
with the feet of the blacks in Barbadoes, and not to
be good or strong unless it was dark.   The price of
it was about five times its present price.   It was said
the servants had sometimes a third basket on their
head ; that I never saw ; but I have seen them often
with one or two, and walked with them.

The churchwarden forgot himself sadly one sacrament Sunday.   There were only three or four in a
year then, and my father, with several of his children,
was starting for church when the clock struck, and
the old man exploded.   He banged the clothes-brush
down, swearing at large, cursing everybody and everything, for he said he should be late for church, and
had to get the sacrament things ready and "take it."
The clocks were then made to vary, as they are now
in some country places.   There is the church time ;
that is official, and supposed to be infallible, although
the birds will perch on the clock fingers and alter
them.   Then there is the clock in the hall or house-
place, which is generally twenty minutes before the
church, and the clock on the stairs, which is nearly an
hour fast—that is the one to get out of bed by.   The
parish bell-ringers also ruffled the warden's temper.
If there were only five bells ringing instead of six on
a Sunday, he would mutter and swear, and swear and
mutter, perhaps making a note to remind him at the
Christmas doles.   He thought they should work for
nothing, as he did, and never be sick or sorry.   The
parishioners assembled outside the church on Sunday
mornings, and when the rector came the men took off
their caps and the women ducked their curtsies, for
they knew he was a near relative of the lord of the
manor, and they believed he was some relative of the

M

Lord Almighty. He had written a book, a wonderful fact then when the majority could not even read, and a good book too it is on local history, not one of those collections of sermons that are so often used for wrapping up groceries. During the church service we knelt for a long time in the high-backed square pew; and then I built houses with the books, and listened to the duet between the rector and the clerk. The latter I could not understand, for he spake in the vulgar tongue. He kept repeating something that seemed to begin with "why" and end with "good lard." When I asked my cousins what that meant, they replied, "We must all join in and say, 'We be sheep-shearers, good Lord.' The explanation being that if the Lord only knew we were merely shearers of sheep (that is, of four-legged sheep) He would know that we must be so jolly innocent that He would forgive us any ordinary or convenient sins at once.

Then came a hymn, when we all turned round "to face the music," and it was followed by a long time of sitting, when the rector waxed eloquent, for he was a beautiful preacher, and the congregation went fast asleep. From the neighbouring farms came the bleating of calves and the gaggling of geese. The swallows twittered from their nests in the eaves, and flew about the church. Wasps came sailing in, and moths of heavenly blue, while the gorgeous peacock butterflies opened and closed their glories where the chequered sunlight fell on the black oak of the pews. At times there seemed to be more wasps than men in the church, and I wondered whether there were many in that hell of which I heard so much. When the rector descended from the pulpit to preside at the distribution, not the collection, for theirs was a more primitive Christianity, the congregation stood up again, and the

women ducked their curtsies as to the chosen of the
Lord. Then came the happy walk home through the
ferns and gorse, with dozens of birds' nests and bilberries innumerable. Oh, that wondrous purple juice
from the bilberry pudding with the thick country cream!
Fifty years have not dimmed the remembrance of that.
The rector and the schoolmaster have long since passed
away and are almost forgotten, their sermons and
teaching are in oblivion, but memory brings back to
me most vividly those happy scenes with the gorgeous
butterflies, the singing birds, the dangerous wasps, the
luscious bilberries, and the old clerk's long monotonous
drone—

"Wey be sheep-shee-a-rers, gud Laard!
We beseech Thee t' 'ear us, good Lord!"

THE CHURCH WITH ADJOINING COTTAGE AS THEY WERE
BEFORE THE "RESTORATION."

CHAPTER XI

CHURCHWARDENS

" You are to call at all the alehouses."
—MUCH ADO ABOUT NOTHING.

LL sorts and conditions of men are liable to be churchwardens, and all sorts and conditions of men have been churchwardens. There have in our time been contested elections for the office, and law-suits about it, struggles to get in and struggles to get out. Most good Churchmen aspire to the office at some period of their lives, and few are disappointed. There is no pay, no profit, no power, and little dignity. The wardens "strut and fret their hour upon the stage," but they must do as their parson tells them. If there is no rector or vicar, resident and practising, but only a *locum tenens*, or "warming-pan," as the country people irreverently term it, then the churchwardens are in all their glory. They consider that in some respects they take the place of the successors of the Apostles, and in grand fashion they manage the charities of the parish.

The old parish of Didsbury included places that are now in the boroughs of Manchester and Stock-

port, and the parochial affairs were managed by two
wardens and four sidesmen for the townships of
Didsbury, Withington, Heaton, and Burnage. The
ley was cessed or the rate was laid and the parochial
affairs discussed at the vestry meeting that was held
on St. Oswald's Day, or, in later years, in Easter
week. In the early years of this century Robert
Feilden, Esquire, Justice of the Peace for the
counties of Lancashire and Cheshire, churchwarden
and lawyer, went to law to uphold the rights of the
parish, and perhaps to enjoy himself. He spent
thousands of pounds in law and won his case, and
wanted to be repaid by enlarging the churchyard
and selling graves. The parishioners said he ought
to pay his own costs, for he had had the fun of the
law. Thomas Mottram, tanner, of Burnage, still
refused to serve as sidesman for Burnage, and went
to prison to be a martyr. The office of priest of
Didsbury was continually being hawked about to the
highest bidder, and the parish appears to have been
tacked on to Manchester to get some of the spare
loaves and fishes, as the tithes had already gone
there. Then the glory of the wardens was departing,
but still they, and the four sidesmen, and the parish
constable patrolled the roads and visited the ale-
houses on the Sabbath to exhort wayfarers to go
to church or bed, for old law, which is a species of
folk-lore, decreed that every one who was able to
go about should be at church on Sunday mornings.
That is another old custom that is becoming somewhat neglected; for if the wardens fail in their duties
and do not reprove or admonish idlers, there will be
more idling and backsliding, and if they are over-
zealous, there will be obstructions and clamour.

An old warden once gave me instructions as to

the acts and duties of wardens, to guide me when
I undertook the office. They appear rather antiquated now, but they refer to "times back," and
were somewhat as follows : " You should mak' yoursel'
as big as you can ; blow yoursel' out, 'ode your 'ed
up, and spit ; put your thumbs i' your weskit armholes
and nod to folk ; tell 'em it's th' finest morning i' th'
parish, and you're proud to see 'em. We used allays
to go out when sarvice were hafe gone, wardens wi'
stauves, sidesmen, and constables, into th' High
Street (that's Wilmslow Road now) and round about ;
then we called at th' inns to see aw was reet. Some
one knowed weer th' best tap was. Nancy Twyford
kept th' Cock then, and wur noted for brewin' her
own. We knockt at th' dur, an' she'd squeak out
from th' inside, 'Go away, we cannot open now ; it's
church time.' Then we would say gruffly, 'We are
the wardens. Who have you got on the premises?'
Then there'd be a fine scuttering o' folk out at th'
back dur into th' brewhouse or stable, we could hear.
An' she'd bang about a bit, an' then oppen th' dur,
sayin', 'Oh, I beg your pardon, gentlemen. I didn't
know it was you. Come in and see for yourselves.
We are only just tidyin' up a bit.' Then we'd look
round and find all as quiet as mice ; an' some one
would joke 'er about th' brew, and say if it were ner
Sunday he'd be dree. She'd poor out a glass from
a brown jug (no pumps in them days), and hold it
up to th' leet as innocent as need be, an' as she
warved it by 'im he'd catch th' smell and snifft like
a tarrier at a rot, an' he'd say, 'Here goes,' an' keck
it up an' teem it doon his throoat afore ye could wink.
Then we'd all laugh, an' th' constable 'ud say, 'It's
werry 'ot,' or 'It's werry code,' or 'It's werry sum'ut.'
It allus is werry 'ot, or werry code, or werry sum'ut

wi' constables; an' some one would stand glasses round, an' if we 'ad ner bin used to carryin' a drop we mi't a had a job to walk street back to th' church. But we'd get in in time for th' blessin'.''

Some of the above-named customs and duties were rather neglected in my time, though I was one of the last wardens who ever patrolled the district with the long silver-headed staves or maces. We acted on the Shaksperian injunction, and if we met a man we knew to be a thief we bade him stand, and if he did not stand we let him go, and thanked God we were rid of a knave. We rather exceeded our duties in some things, for if we wandered too far we missed most of the sermon, though, as we had probably heard it before, that did not much matter. Folk-lore differs from book-lore in the matter of sermons. The latter often mentions the necessity and advisability of hearing them. Perhaps the difference in opinion arises from the difference in the sermons. Having never missed attending public divine service on a Sunday morning for over thirty years, my experience of sermons increases. The great majority of them have gone through my head as water goes through a sieve, leaving "not a wrack behind." A few there are, when once heard, are remembered; others were heard many times, for they came in their turn from the bottom of the tub where they were kept, and did duty over and over again, with slight variations.

Forty years have not dimmed the memory of some of these sermons, and as the wardens were to go in quest of Sabbath-breakers, and exhort way-farers to hear sermons, here is a sample of them: Text, 1 Corinthians xiii. 13, "And now abideth faith, hope, charity, these three: but the greatest of these is charity." Then the preacher would say,

"This word charity, my dear brethren, should be love;" and then suddenly striking out his arm and shaking his half-closed fist at us, he would sternly say, "I don't mean the passion of the sexes;" and after glaring at us for a while in deep silence the sermon would be resumed with the usual accompaniments. The young girls, whose eyes had brightened at the magic word love, would look abashed, and the old ones would hope there would be nothing indecent. The farmers would go on thinking of their crops, and the boys of their pigeons and marbles. All things come to an end, and even these sermons came to an end. It is rather melancholy to think that, though it is only twenty-five years since I was warden, every one excepting myself who was then officially connected with the church is now under the sod. Therefore what I write does not apply to any one living.

In those days it was the custom to have a distribution, not a collection, after the service. We gave out loaves of bread to the poor. As many as fifteen have been given at once, the funds to buy them having been left for the purpose by pious donors as charges on certain estates in the parish. Old men and women came, with snuffy-coloured cotton handkerchiefs, and bobbed their thanks as they took their dole. Or children came and said, "Please, granddad's back's bad," or "Granddam's cough was plaguey, and could they have their dole?" In older times it was said that money as well as bread was given from the altar, and the neighbours saw what was done. The old-fashioned distribution seems more apostolic than the modern collection. The bread, at least, was visible, tangible, and picturesque, and some there are who regret its disappearance.

Custom hath ordained that churchwardens may be
Pharisees, but they must not be publicans. The
Church and the public-house never fraternise except
in a contested Parliamentary election. Then their
agreement and brotherly love for one another is touching and wonderful. At other times the parson, and
consequently his satellite the churchwarden, shun the
publican, and say the most unchristian-like things of
him. Some of them even say he sells liquid hell-fire,
and the publican retorts in language more forcible than
polite. Therefore they never visit one another's
houses, and are at enmity until the next contested
Parliamentary election.

I once had a customer who had struggled desperately to make a living at a provision shop, and who
had been churchwarden for about twenty years. His
family were growing up, and to get his daughters
married he did as many others have done—he took a
public-house. Then his rector in sorrow told him that
he really could not be allowed to continue churchwarden ; that would be little short of a scandal to the
Church. So he resigned his office, and survived the
resignation. It was some time before I saw him again,
and asked as to his welfare. He said he was doing
well, and had very little trouble but with drunken folk
and police. "Surely you can manage them when you
have been churchwarden so long," I said to him, for
the wardens are a sort of glorified beadles. "Well,"
he said, "they're ticklish to work. Drunken folk are
always a nuisance to everybody, and young bobbies
reckon no small beer of themselves. By the time they
are sergeants they get harder faced, and can sup more.
Some of 'em will sup as much as would scald a pig,
and they aren't fond of parting ; they want a deal for
nowt. Oh, if the superintendent or inspector comes,

they are shown into the private room at once. Then, when you are looking for any papers, you leave out a bottle of John Jameson's ten-year-old over-proof, with the cork loose. There should be a glass handy, of course ; but it doesn't matter about any water. Then, as you come in again, you rattle th' door handle, and you'll find th' big man passing his hand over his mouth as he sighs deeply, and he'll say he's sorry to give you so much trouble, but no doubt it'll be all right, and he wishes you good morning."

Since the modern custom of collections in church became fashionable, the poorer classes have come to an unfounded conclusion that the wardens get something from the collection. I was solemnly assured once that a man I knew must be very rich because he had been warden so long. The man had been in the corn trade all his life, and I knew he was poor, for in that trade their wealth does not consist in their riches. But his neighbour stuck to his opinion, and laughed at my innocence. When some people see the warden bearing aloft the spoils, *alias* the collection, as the procession marches into the vestry, they wonder whatever becomes of all that "ready money," and they envy those who have the fingering of it.

In addition to the dole of bread that was given out on Sundays, there were other charities in aid of "the industrious poor of Didsbury who were not receiving parochial relief," and these charities were administered by the churchwardens, who made notes, and left an account of their work. These notes may not be exactly folk-lore, but they are interesting memorials of the times of our grandfathers. The churchwardens appear to have looked after their friends and supporters first, and the "ringers and singers" got their full share of the good things, while their poorer neigh-

hours got less, although all who were not in receipt of
parish relief appear to have had rights, and to have
claimed them. Here is an entry: " Thomas Blomi-
ley, *alias* Webb, *alias* Prod, *alias* Bonk ; " then comes
a big black mark and a note at the bottom of the page :
" This is a most impudent undeserving fellow, and a
Powcher of notorious character." So all he got was a
pair of black-ribbed stockings costing two and seven-
pence. Yes, he was a poacher ; what they wrote to
his shame I endorse to his credit, and his name may
endure, perhaps, for centuries after they are forgotten,
for he poached the last big salmon that was taken out
of the river, a fish that weighed eighteen pounds, and
this I write to be his memorial as long as Didsbury
lasts. This is he of whom his son told me with the
greatest pride, " Yo' should a known me fayther when
'e lickt Bill Downes, th' champion o' Chedle, on Chedle
Green at th' wakes – 'e wur thirteen stun strippt, an'
hard ; but 'e didner live long, 'e used hissel' badly.
He'd go a fishin' an' get drunk an' lay aw neet i' th'
wet grass, an' it told on 'im. 'E wur but seventy-
seven when 'e deed. I'm a wicker mon at eighty-six
than he wur at seventy-six, an' a can do a day's work
yet."

The warders got even with our old friend once, for
they took him in a wheelbarrow to " Justice" Phillips
at Bank Hall, and he got "six months," while his
"childer 'ad to fend for theirsel'." But, as the son
told me himself, and he is now aged ninety-three, he
appears to have survived that early trouble.

Another of the duties of churchwardens was to
" fetch " people who had illegitimate children, or " base-
born " as they were then called, and make them do
penance in the church. These " light-o'-loves " were
wrapped in a sheet – that is, a sheet to each person—

and made to stand facing the congregation during service in the church. The being taken in adultery is one of the oldest and most respectable of sins, and the duty of the wardens to hale the offenders before a righteous congregation has not been long lapsed, for I understand from an elderly man that his grandfather had often told him that he well remembered seeing a case of this penance being done in Northen church. The man's name was Shawcross, and the woman's name was Gatley, and the time would be little more than a hundred years since, though it appears more like the times of the Inquisition or of the "virtuous" Tudor queens. What large congregations they would have at Northen and in the neighbourhood generally in the summer-time if these interesting old customs were observed now!

There are many quaint old beliefs that I have not thought worthy of notice, simply because there seems to be "no sense in them," and yet some of them have an extraordinary knack of thrusting themselves on our notice at times. For instance, it used to be said by them of old that if the church clock tolled twelve when the parson was giving out his text, or even when he was preaching, it was a sign of a death in the parish. On last Easter morning there was a muffled peal rung on the bells of Didsbury church instead of the usual joyous Easter peal. In the midst of his sermon the rector alluded to it, and in the hush that generally falls on a congregation when something more than usually interesting is expected, the cessation of coughing, or the shuffling of feet, or the rustling of finery, the church clock slowly and solemnly tolled twelve. My thoughts at once went wandering off as to whether that toll was for the old ringer who had died that morning, or for some one else that even then might be passing away, and later in the day we heard of the body of a woman having been taken from the river.

It is said to be recorded on parchment in the archives of Chester Cathedral, and therefore it may be said to have to some extent the prestige of episcopal sanction, that the duties of a sidesman are to—

> " Hear all, see all, say nought ;
> Eat all, drink all, pay nought ;
> And when your wardens drunken roam,
> Your duty is to see them home."

I have heard the duties of wardens described in similar terms by the following alteration of the last two lines—

> " And if your parson drunken prove,
> Tell nought."

These old maxims of our grandfathers show in what interesting ways the customs of their day varied from the customs of ours. I lately read in some one's reminiscences that the greeting of a noble lord to an eminent divine generally was, " Well, John, which is it to be, cockpit or pulpit ? "

The wardens of Didsbury who made the unkind remarks about the " impudent Powcher " who poached the eighteen-pound salmon from the river, made some notes about old Mother Bancroft, " *alias* old Wanton," as they called her, for there were always many of the name in Didsbury ; they would originally have been called Barncroft. In the list of applicants for the charitable bequests to the industrious poor of Didsbury, there was a column stating the number of children of each applicant, and in this column, opposite to old Wanton's name, they wrote " numerous," thereby inferring that her children could not be counted. Now, Didsbury and the neighbourhood always was a healthy and prolific place. Any one may see on a gravestone in Cheadle churchyard, near to the high-road, that old Randy Allcock owned to being grand-father to ninety-one, and "great-grandfather to thirty-five known—unknown cannot say." If old Wanton's children were so numerous that they could not be counted, it proved she was industrious, and her right to an extra share of the parish dole; but those hard-hearted wardens only gave her one blanket that cost seven and ninepence, two pairs of hosen, and one "small girl's shift made from the residue of the petty-coat bindings." And she had to make shift with them, though what were they among so many? O ye scribes and Pharisees, ye do indeed write down your own condemnation. Ye enter five shillings each for your own dinners, and ye give to old Wanton one small shift made from "bits of linnen" (as described in another year) for her numerous children. Ye debit the church accounts with "drink when we was swore," and ye dine with the parson and the squire, and sup red wine and white wine and sack, and the shot is scored up on the shutter for liquidation another day, while the little Wantons have to cower under one blanket, and take their turns at the hosen and the one small shift.

Perhaps the reader does not know what a shift is, or whence its name. In olden times common people had only two garments or clothes. The outer one was a smock or frock that was to last for years, and perhaps be handed down as a family heirloom; and the inner one was a shift, so called because it was shifted or changed at the annual spring cleaning, or with extravagant people at the monthly wash. I remember asking a Didsbury man, who was working on his plot of ground with his shirt all in rags, and his hairy skin

showing through the holes, how he got in and out of
the shirt when it seemed so tender, and he told me,
" I ne'er osses to get out. When it's once put on it
stays theer as long as it 'ull howd thegither ; " and as
he is still living, a very old man, who never misses a
chance of getting drunk, and has probably not been
washed for seventy years, he sets at naught the teachings of doctors ; and when the local medicine men
see him they shake their heads sadly and smile a
melancholy smile, for according to their dogmas he
ought to have died long ago, and yet his life is a
mockery of them, for he has outlived generations of
their predecessors.

That amusing folk-lorist, Autolycus, said, " Every
lane's end ; every shop, church, session, hanging,
affords a careful man work ; " and if he had lived nowadays he would certainly have added an election to
his list. Very soon after I got to my temporary office
at our late election, an old native put his head in,
saying, " You've not told them in th' *City News* what
Cris Dean said when they put him in th' stocks."
Then another put in, " You've not told 'em what
happened when the wardens brought that woman and
child to th' church. Why, that was your own fayther.
See here, I've known Didsbury church eighty yeer,
an' your fayther was the finest, handsomest mon as
ever attended it. But there's none o' his childer as
favvers him." Then he voted right, so that was
something. This is the eldest of the three brothers
Hampson who were up a tree on Sunday, June 14,
1828, for twelve hours, before they could be rescued
by a Stockport boat from a flood that swept away
large parts of the river banks.

As the power of churchwardens has been declining
all through this century, their activity has grown in

another form, and they have assisted their parsons to
spoil their churches—beautiful old churches, quaint
and hoary, hallowed with the associations of centuries,
built when men counted not the cost, but worked for
a bare living, and found their reward in the work—
work that lasted through the ages and had to be blown
up by gunpowder, as that at Stockport had when they
put an ugly new gimcrack thing on the old foundations.
No devastating hordes of Huns, Goths, or Vandals
ever wrought a tithe of the havoc among our lovely
ancient churches that has been wrought by a number
of ignorant, self-satisfied parsons and wardens. In
one man's ministry at Didsbury there were five "restorations." A local historian, who has drawn largely
on imagination for his facts, has lately written a small
history of Didsbury for bazaar work, and says that
"the final restoration of Didsbury church was in
1855." Since that date every pew in the church has
been renewed twice over, and there have been several
considerable "restorations." The big oaken pulpit
has been sold to Methodists, who doubtless hope to
make a better use of it. The old oak has been sold
for lumber, and there is none left now, not even to
whitewash. "Churchwardens' Gothic" rules supreme,
and in the greater part of Didsbury church not one
stone has been left upon another. And yet, I believe,
on the authority of skilled antiquaries, there are still
some remnants of Norman and possibly of Saxon
work.

Churchwardens have given their name, not only to
a style of architecture, but to the long clay pipes that
add so much to their dignity when they are discussing
the affairs of the parish. The importance they assume
is out of all proportion to the work they do, or the
powers they have, and with our simple rustic folk to

be "as conceited as a churchwarden" has passed into
a proverb.

N.B.—In the local pronunciation of "as consated
as a churchwarden," the letter *a* in consated should be
pronounced as the *a* in fate; the *a* in warden as the
a in far.

CHAPTER XII

FAMILY LEGENDS

"One of his father's moods."—CORIOLANUS.

CATTERED up and down my folk-lore notes were so many legends and tales about my father's family, that I deemed it better to collect most of them into one chapter, and then any reader may skip the lot if he be so disposed.

There is one very remarkable fact and legend that only came to my knowledge after I had written most of the articles on folk-lore, they having produced or dragged forth other information. The fact is that no child has lived who has been christened Anne or Hannah Moss for many generations, I might even write centuries. To thoroughly elucidate the case I must go into minute particulars. My father was born at Mees Hall, which is in Eccleshall parish, on the Staffordshire border, near to Standon church and parish. The family appear to have lived in the neighbourhood, and to have been yeomen or large farmers for many generations. They were big, strong, healthy, active men and women, with more than the usual intellect, some of them having the vices of their time and class, and some of them being good lovers and good

haters. Their religion was Church of England; but
some of their customs showed plainly that they had
been Roman Catholics not many generations ago (for
the Reformation spread very slowly among the intensely
conservative farmers in country districts), and some
of their customs showed a decided survival of their
remoter forefathers' heathenish customs. From this
stock my father came to Manchester through a cheese
factor, John Fletcher, who was travelling the country
buying Cheshire cheese for his father. There he
married my mother, who was the youngest child of
her father, and sister to the above-named John
Fletcher. My mother's bringing up by her mother
was decidedly of the Puritan type, though they were
"Church folk." Her mother's maiden name was Mary
Barrett, whose father, James Barrett, although he was
married at Wilmslow Church in 1771, was living at
Oversley Ford or Hale, and was connected with the
Society of Friends, who worshipped at the little meeting-house on Lindow Moss. The usual Quaker names
were retained in the family of eight, and my mother's
favourite sister's name was Hannah. She married
Charles Bradbury, the once well-known collector of
antiquities. My mother was determined that her
first daughter's name should be Hannah, but it was
strongly urged by my father's sisters that the name
would be fatal to the child. They said that no Anne,
Anna, or Hannah Moss had ever been known to survive christening many days, and it would be the death-
knell of the child to give it the name. My mother
disbelieved and disregarded them. It was her first
daughter and second child, and perfectly healthy. She
was christened Hannah, and before many days was
buried. It is sixty years ago. There are three living
who remember it well, and though time has effaced

the keen regret of the untimely loss, it is one of those
private affairs that would not be made public except
to record the mystery, and ask for its solution.

I never heard of the tradition myself until lately,
when studying our local and family folk-lore. I wish
to emphasise that the protests were made before the
christening, as was admitted by my mother when my
father's two remaining sisters told me of the case. I
knew that in my grandfather's family of thirteen there
was only one who died young, her name being Anne.
I was then told that my great-grandfather had had
three daughters, one after the other, called Anne, and
they had all died when infants ; that he then believed
the tradition, and called his next daughters by other
names. It is difficult to substantiate any pedigree or
family affairs, especially as to young children, when a
century or more has elapsed, but there being a good
history of Standon parish by the Rev. E. Salt, the
present rector, with copies of the earliest registers,
and knowing the family had generally lived in the
locality, I searched and found that in 1591, John
Mosse, of Weston, married Anne Wetwood, thereby
bringing the name of Anne into the family. They
appear to have had five daughters very quickly, Mary,
Alice, Anne, Elizabeth, and Ellen. The marriages
of most of these are registered ; but Anne was christened on July 9, and buried on October 10 of the same
year, 1594. Therefore these dim and faded old registers of Standon, written more than three hundred
years ago, give some confirmation of the tradition
as to the doom of any of the race who are called
by the unlucky name. Internal evidence shows that
the tradition must have originated since it became
common to have two names and to have infants
christened ; and assuming it to have been in force in

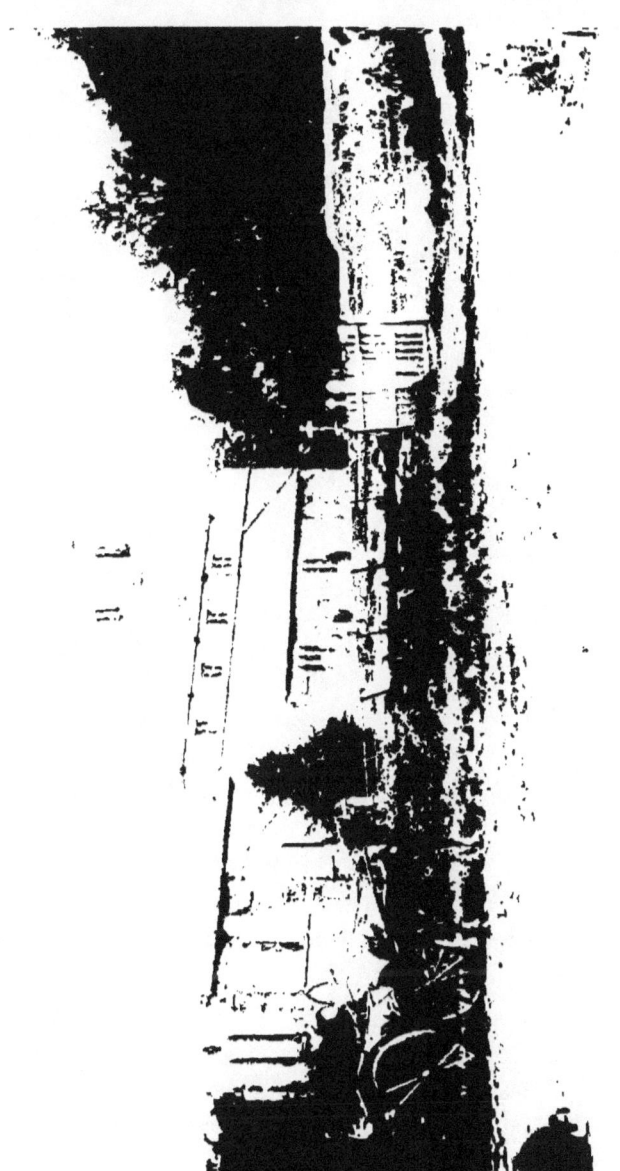

STANDON CHURCH.

1594, it must have originated in the century or two
previous to that date. The tradition itself gives no
reason for its origin. Was there once some noted
witch named Anne of the Moss, who was solemnly
cursed by Holy Church with bell, book, and candle—

> "Cursed in sitting, in standing, in lying,
> Cursed in walking, in riding, in flying,
> Cursed in living, cursed in dying,"

with remainder to namesakes as residuary legatees?
Then, when some little innocent namesake was received into the Church at baptism, duly crossed and
sprinkled, the blessing and the curse would be in con-
flict, and the way of least resistance would be speedy
extinction. This is merely idle surmise. Can any one
explain away the facts as recorded in the Church
registers for centuries? The different opinions about
the same events seem a revival of differences that
caused members of a family to take opposite sides in
the Civil War, the strong plain common-sense of the
Puritan as opposed to superstition or power of tradition in the High Churchman or Catholic.

I was also surprised to learn that my aunts still
"cross the leaven"—*i.e.* when the barm or leaven is
added to the flour for making the dough to be baked
into bread, it is signed with the sign of the cross; and
the mash for brewing is also crossed when the boiling
water is put to the malt, for in these parts ale is still
brewed from malted barley. The reader must not
suppose we are a Roman Catholic family; ours is
simply the ordinary respectable Christianity as by law
established; but the crossing of the leaven is indis-
putably a custom that has survived from the time
when we and all our neighbours and the country
generally were Roman Catholics; and it is most

interesting to note how the customs overlap one
another, and how they all are overlapped by the far
older customs of our heathen forefathers, which were
probably in the land when we were all pagans, before
the Pope sent missionaries for the conversion of England. In the old book called the "Vale Royall of
England," it was noted that the Cheshire folk baked
their own bread and brewed their own drink two
hundred and fifty years ago . . . and that they were
healthy though superstitious, tall, stout of stomach,
bold, and hardy ; it would be better for a many of them
to-day if they did bake their own bread and brew their
own drink, even if they "crossed the leaven."

Another old custom that I had almost forgotten has
also become of interest to me. When a youth I went
to my father and uncles for a day's shooting, and at
some cottages where water seemed scarce we rested
and washed our hands. I was then taught that if any
one washed in water that some one else had previously
washed in he must first of all say, "Ods bods, devil, I
defy thee," spit on the ground, and sign the water with
the sign of the cross. Then all evil would be averted,
and no skin or other disease contracted. The origin
of this custom or charm is very interesting, for "Ods
bods" is undoubtedly a contraction of the words "God's
body," *i.e.* the host in the Mass, though they who used
it did not know it. That is the beginning of the charm
to drive away the evil spirits whom you defy ; then to
spit like a cat at them is to do as savages do at the
present day to exorcise demons, and is a remnant of
our Anglo-Saxon heathendom : then the sign of the
cross completes the charm, and the user is cleansed
and purified.

An old aunt of an old aunt, that is to say, one who
would be well on in years a century ago, is said to

have been continually using the expression, " By th' godlint." It has lately been another interesting puzzle to find the original meaning of those words. I have no doubt whatever they formed an old oath, " By the Godling," or little God, probably referring to the large host at the Mass. The old lady was of the reigning religion as by law established, and would probably have shuddered, or even gasped, if her words had been explained to her.

Has it ever occurred to the reader as he passed a lot of roughs, and every other word he heard was " God " or " Christ," or " bloody," to wonder whether those who used the words knew the meaning of them ? I have passed through the meadows at Didsbury on many fine Sunday evenings when the birds were singing sweetly in the pleasant air, and the smell of the clover or the new-mown hay was sweeter than any of the fabled perfumes of Araby the blest, and on all sides there was heard the word " bloody " in what Shakspere calls " damnable iteration." The religion and politics of those who use it are evident ; they are of the " beer and the Bible " class, for they smell of the one and sound of the other. They do not and cannot use the word in its literal sense. It is another " swear word," or oath, passed on from generation to generation in unorthodox succession, with the meaning of it forgotten. It is derived from " By our Lady," hence " by-laddy," " bloody " ; or it may be the first part of the old oath, " By the blood of Christ." It is now a coarse oath to strengthen any assertion or " argument." " Becripes," and perhaps " crikey," are derived from the word Christ, and the Irishman's " begor " or " bejabers " is his mode of pronouncing " By God " or " By Jesus." Perhaps some day the common-sense of people may teach them to use only those words of which they know the meaning, but that day seems very far away.

The heathenish customs that had such a striking survival at Standon Hall were the raising aloft of the picked calf and the blazing of the wheat. The former seems to be an exact survival of the belief of the Israelites that if they looked on the brazen serpent which Moses lifted up in the wilderness they would be saved. The picked calf was hung in chains on the wall (I have seen it there), that the cows might look on it and the plague might be stayed, so that the cows should not prematurely cast their calves. The growing wheat was blazed on old Christmas Day, January the sixth being "blaze night," to scare the witches from the young corn, and ensure good crops for the coming harvest. Men and lads ran all over the wheat with lighted torches of straw, crying out to frighten away all harmful things. Any thinking person must admit that these curious old customs were in the land before Christianity was, and had so far survived it, being simply carried on because our fathers carried them on. In "King Lear" there is mentioned the foul fiend Flibbertigibbet, who mildews the wheat.

Considerably more than a century ago my great-grandfather, Moss of Mees, or Meece, as it was variously written, was riding home late one night through a ford, when he found the drowned body of a neighbour, who was known as Wood of Coates. In country districts it is still common to speak of men as "of" the place where they live. Their surnames were originally taken from their occupation, or from some peculiarity in their person, or from the place where they lived. Consequently, any one named John might become John the smith, or John Brown, or John of the wood, and therefore Smith, Brown,

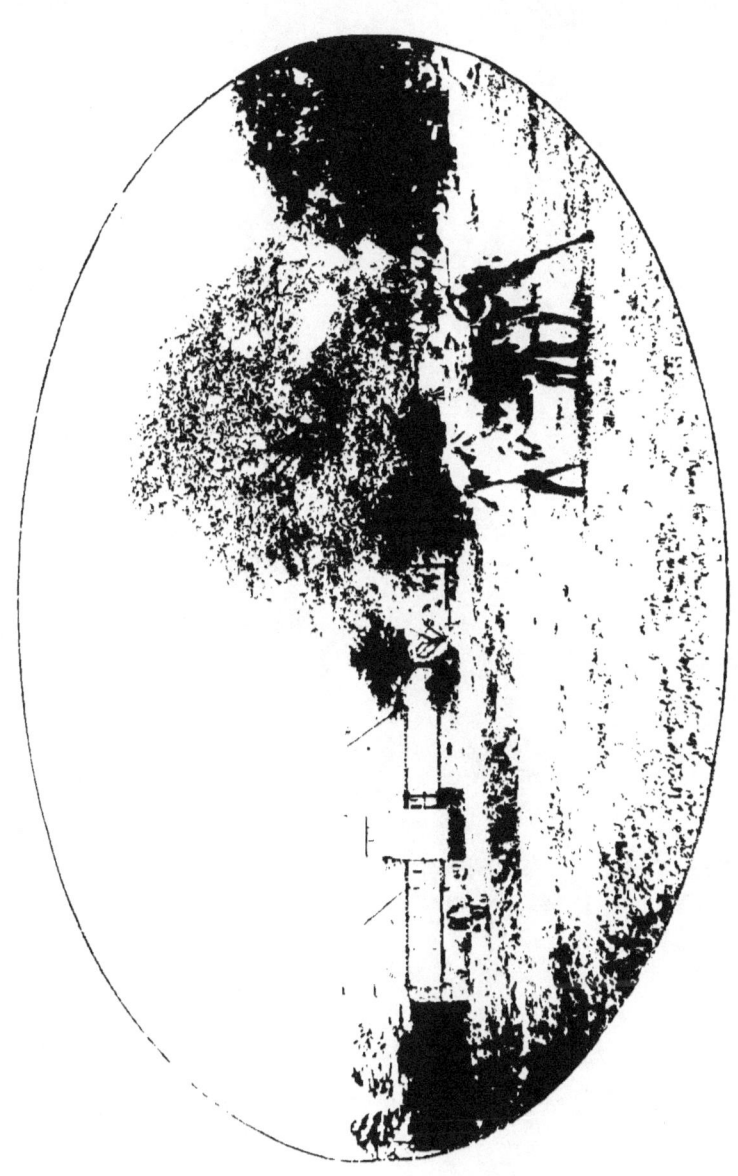

STANDON HALL FROM THE SOUTH-EAST.

and Wood, for instance, are such common names. I often wondered why the name of Moss was not much more common than it is, as there are so many tracts of land in this part of the country called Moss ; and the name of Wood is very common, although the woods have long been cleared, and the name as applied to places is rare. The reason would be that no one would live on a moss if there was land to be

A GABLE AT THE BACK OF MEES HALL.

got elsewhere. It would be in comparatively recent years, say three or four centuries since, that the name would be given to some John or Thomas who had taken to farming, cattle or horse breeding, and built himself a house on some lonely moss. The word moss, though very short, was spelt in many different ways—for instance, Moss, Mosse, Mus, or Mees—and it signified a very wet boggy tract of land. There-

fore Moss of Mees Hall was probably only another
form of Moss of the moss. The situation of the place
is low, it lying by the little river Sow, one of the
sources of the Trent. The Hall has for many years
been in a ruinous state, as may be seen by the accompanying photographs. My father was born in
the room to the right on the first floor, the one with
the window open.

Since writing the above I find from Rolls of
Edward I., i.e. *circa* 1300, that the name of the place
and of men is spelt Mes; and William del Mos or
Mes is several times mentioned, as is also a mill,
doubtless the predecessor of the present one.

My great-grandfather, Moss of Mees or Meece,
lifted the body of Wood on to the pommel of his
saddle. They were both very big, heavy men, and
the horse objected to the extra load. In those
days it was rather dangerous having anything to
do with a dead body, for the country terms were,
"A short shrift and a long rope." There, in a
district that even to-day is very sparsely popu-
lated—for I know the small river, now bridged over,
and Wood's house at Coates, and the roadside inn—
was the solitary horseman with the drowned man
across the saddle in front of him. It was late at
night, and no one would take the body from him, and
he had to ride with it for about three miles. Even
at the inn, where both men were known, and at
Wood's own house (he was a well-to-do yeoman who
farmed his own land), they would not open their
doors to the mysterious and untimely visitor. Then
Moss, who was doubtless thoroughly wearied of his
job, cried out to them in the vulgar tongue, or, as
it would now be called, the dialect of the district,
"If you doner tak' him I'll swot him;" and as no one

came, he swot him, that is, tumbled the drowned
man off the horse on to the ground, and left him.
The word swot or slat means to let fall heavily, to
dump down. It is now obsolete; but it was well
known to us when children, for my father often used

MEES HALL.

the term "swot it down," sometimes adding the words
"as my grandfather did old Wood of Coates."

After the above little tale had appeared in the
paper, I had a letter from the rector of Standon
corroborating the main fact from some record in his
possession; the date of it was 1772.

A quaint and comfortable, but not a beautiful old custom was to have the pews of our churches large and roomy, with high backs, and green curtains on brass rods along the top, so that no cold draughts or prying eyes could invade their sacred precincts. Then the tired worshipper could curl himself up and slumber peacefully through the dreary drip of the most dismal sermon. But as all men do not snore in the same tune it became necessary to have an official who was variously called a verger, a sacristan or sexton, an apparitor, or parroter, for the common folk thought his utterances were somewhat parrot-like, and this official had a long staff or wand with which he poked the ribs of those who slumbered too noisily, just as any one pokes up the sleeping sheep or the fat pigs in the pens of a fat-stock show.

One of the many tales my father told his children tales that are now being retailed, for their flavour ripens as the years roll on and the customs pass away which gave them birth—was about the verger of the church coming for his Christmas box. Gossiping about the affairs of the parish as he partook of the bread and cheese and ale that were then given to all comers, the old man waxed wroth at the treatment he had received at a neighbour's. This neighbour was one of the last men who wore a big old-fashioned wig. He appears to have been both careful and cross, "more for having than giving," as the country folk say, and to have vexed the verger, who spoke somewhat as follows: "There's owd Dicky yonder, as big an owd skinflint as e'er walked on two legs. 'E tells me to mind my work and not come a Chresmassing 'im. An' see how he snores i' th' church! 'E thinks cos 'e's rich 'e can do as 'e likes, 'e does. But th' very next toime as oi 'ear 'im snore, oi'll fetch

'im such a yatty yatty as'll mak' 'is owd wig floy, oi
will so, sure as my name's Tezzy Birchill. Mark
my words, both Mester and Messus Moss, he'd fley
two fleas for one hide, but oi'll fley 'im, an' oi'll
mak' 'is owd wig flee sure as oi sits on this 'ere
settle."

On the next Sunday morning my grandparents
went to church with about a dozen of their children
walking two and two, like the animals going into the
Ark to get out of the rain, and when the parson and
the clerk had done their duet, and the monotonous
sermon was being read, the heavy breathing of the
rustic congregation was heard on all sides, mingled
with curious low sounds, like the grunting of distant
pigs; and then amid the titters of naughty boys and
girls the anxiously expected snores from the old
gentleman in the wig grew stronger. Swiftly and
silently old Tezzy went up the aisle. His thoughts
were on the Christmas box he did not get, and the
insult he did get; his staff was in his hand, and he
was fully determined justice should be done alike to
rich and poor, and perhaps he thought there were
some arrears of justice that should have been due
before Christmas. With his staff or wand of office
"he fetched owd Dicky a pretty yatty yatty as made
his owd wig floy and welly killt 'im too," for he smote
him on the head, and then he walked back down the
aisle aglow with satisfaction and triumph, feeling like
a judge in Israel who had been specially raised up by
the Lord to execute His vengeance on the ungodly.

There were sundry boys in the congregation who
watched the proceedings with the keenest interest.
They stood on tiptoe and watched old Dicky tumble
off the seat and his wig fly as was promised. They
felt that justice was sometimes done; they had really

seen it done this time, not merely heard about it, for they were fully persuaded they generally came in for injustice, and for once they really enjoyed the service, and some of them never forgot it for the rest of their lives. I never heard what the parson did. Would he stop in his discourse to see the fun, or would he go maundering on, confuting in his muddled manner some old heresy of which his audience never heard, and for which they never cared, for their thoughts were on their treasures, on the price of eggs, or the price of bacon, or on country sports and pleasures?

Writing of eggs and bacon reminds me they were referred to in an old country saying descriptive of any one who looked sleek and dosome; and very recently I heard it said of the head of one of our large banks, that he looked as if he always had eggs and bacon to breakfast. Certainly the gentleman does look exceedingly sanctimonious, oily, and rich, and the description is good; his colleague is only inferior to him by "a short neck," as another old phrase has it. One of my grandfather's men at Mees Hall rejoiced in the beautifully euphonious name of Billy Onion. He had been promised an extra good breakfast for some night work he had done, and he asked for "a peilful of buttermilk well stodged wi' 'tatoes, and then a good rasher o' bacon, and a jorum o' black puddings, with a quart o' strong ale on th' top." (The *ar* in the word quart should be pronounced as in the word far.) Billy Onion's was a good breakfast; the pure air gave him a healthy appetite, and he was well reared. Buttermilk and potatoes is the breakfast of many a Cheshire farm-labourer at the present day. Milk and porridge is for those who can better afford it; but best of all is new milk and fat bacon. That I have always had,

as my fathers had before me, and can strongly recommend it. It must be better sustenance for "life's
endless toil and endeavour" than the common modern
breakfast of bread and butter and tea.

Another quaint old custom that comes back to my
mind as I have pondered over the days of my youth
and the folk-lore of them is from the time when wigs
were worn, not the little flimsy things we sometimes
see on old fogies or bank managers at the present
time, but the good old-fashioned ones like John Gilpin
wore, or that Tezzy Birchill made to flee. They had
some substance in them, some weft, as our websters or
weavers called it, and would last as a nest for the cat
or some equally useful purpose long after they looked
too rusty or moth-eaten for the owner to wear. A
parson's wig was naturally considered to be extra holy
as long as it would hang together, and was in great
request with really good old Tories as a charm against
witches.

I remember one that hung in the large old fireplace of Standon Hall. It was made of little curls
like those on a retriever's back, of a rusty brown
colour, and was said to be an old wig of Parson
Walker's. There were several Walkers who were
rectors of Standon. The one referred to had probably been the one who married my grandparents in
1800. As the house was partly rebuilt in 1850, and
as shortly afterwards the old fireplace was done away
with, and a Leamington range substituted, it is obvious
the wig would not be required afterwards, for no respectable fairy or witch would think of coming down
a chimney into a Leamington range. In the good old
days, if no amount of churning of cream would make
the butter come, it was evidently bewitched, and if the
groats swelled and burst the black puddings, it was

evident they were bewitched. There was the same excuse for any mishap in the cooking, or when the milk or porridge was "bishoped," the term "bishoped" being synonymous with burnt in the days when the bishops of different denominations burnt each other's lambs if they refused to pretend to believe what they were ordered to believe.

The witches of those days rode straddle-legged on their broomsticks, as modern ladies do on their bicycles, and when all was quiet at night, and the doors fast, bolted, and guarded with inverted horseshoes, they were said to come down the large chimneys in search of good fare, frolic, and revelry. They may have come to the scores of revels there were in the old Hall before the fireplace was altered, when we as children sat on the old oak settle "with our heart full of love and our mouth full of pie." The days of wigs were the days of snuff, and he who snuffed snoze, and the sneezer should always be blessed; then if some one gave an extra big sneeze, the parson would say, "God bless us and save us," and the mention of the holy name was terrible to any witches or fairies that might be about the house. Therefore on another night they may have looked down the chimney, and seeing the parson's wig, they would know His Holiness was not far off, and then these fly-by-nights would sail away to call again some other day.

The parson's wig, that redolent relic of antiquity, has long since gone, but I am assured this day that if black puddings are being boiled, it is necessary or prudent to think of certain things or say certain things to yourself, which, whatever the sayer or doer may think, are undoubtedly an exorcism against witchcraft.

A grand old custom that still survives, though it could not be observed at the present day except in

FOURSCORE YEARS AND THE GOLDEN WEDDING.

remote country districts, is free hospitality. As long as memory goeth back, and doubtless far beyond, no wayfarer, tramp, or beggar, however mean, has ever been sent empty away. It may have been only a bit of bread and cheese and a sup of whey or buttermilk that has been given to them ; but all through the long ceaseless struggle that the farmers of England have always had to make all ends meet, there has in this solitary old hall at Standon been always practised the grand old custom of universal hospitality.

Amongst the many who are still living, and who have been partakers of that hospitality, there are none more thankful than I. It has often in late years been a regret to me that I had not probed and learnt this folk-lore in my uncle's lifetime, for he had a wonderful knowledge of many things, and was a great stickler for doing exactly as his mother taught him ; but, at the same time, I am unfeignedly thankful that others were left, and on the spot I could learn more of the lore and take the pictures that in this book I hope will show to generations who are yet unborn one of the fine old English homes of a fine old English gentleman.

It was in January 1892 that death came to the old man. The winter was exceptionally severe, and the new influenza had seized the household, most of whom were very ill. He had passed his fourscore years and his golden wedding-day. He had been master of the farm for over sixty years, and churchwarden for fifty of them. He retained his faculties to the last, though even his great strength became labour as the big limbs moved wearily. In his prime he stood six feet three in height, with immense reach in his arms, a quick grey eye, resolute mouth, with teeth that cracked nuts when he was on the verge of eighty, and a nose that

stood out from his face like a ploughshare. He had
literally imbibed his mother's milk until he was nine
years old, and could take it when standing up, and he
had done well on it, he himself being a grand example
of the virtues of mother's milk. In the bitter cold of
continued snow-storms he refused to have a fire in his
bedroom, for, as he said, he had done without all his
life, and if he could not, it was time to go. He always
called his wife dame, and as she also was ill, he asked

MEES HALL FROM THE LITTLE RIVER MEES OR SOW.

her which was to go first. She quietly answered,
" You'd better go first, grandpa, and then I'll come."
They did what they could, but they could not save
him, and in the midst of the fiercest snow-storm that
had ever raged round the old house the spirit quietly
ebbed away. There was a great gathering of the
clan, and in the red earth of Standon we laid him to
rest, where the grass and the wild-flowers are growing
o'er his grave.

To this old house I have loved to get away from

the hurry and fuss of modern life, from the weary,
wearing talk of money where money seems the chief
or only god, to where the chief sounds are the sounds
of the wind or of the birds or the cattle.   The doors
jammed or slammed, and the windows objected to
shut, just as they had done for generations.   We sat
on the same old seats as some of us had done for fifty
or eighty years.   We ate what seemed the same food,
and we talked the same talk ; for in the midst of the
most delightful Toryism we learned again that education had ruined the country, that the good old days
were better than these, and that the mere book-
learning of a field full of professors and doctors and
bishops was as nothing to the concentrated wisdom
and traditional lore of our fathers.

CHAPTER XIII

CHESHIRE CHEESE

" Art thou come ?   Oh my cheese, my digestion."
            *--*TROILUS AND CRESSIDA.

HIS short chapter is a reprint of an
article I wrote on the history and folk-
lore of Cheshire cheese.   The latter
part of it would more appropriately
belong to the preceding chapter, but
as this was so short, I thought it better
to reproduce it entire.

The query by "C. Y." as to the proverb "Cheat
and the cheese will show," induces me to write a paper
on the folk-lore about cheese ; for I had already made
sundry notes on the subject, and then discarded them,
as I feared the refined literary tastes of the readers of
the *City News* would not care for such common vulgar
stuff as cheese.

From time immemorial, long before the coming
of the Normans or the Domesday survey, the great
products of Cheshire were salt and cheese.   On its
fertile fields are some of the richest pastures on this
earth, and one of the oldest manufactures known to
man must have been practised there ages ago.   A
chance note in history tells us that when a certain

212

archbishop came preaching the Crusades he was re-
galed by the Countess of Chester with cheese made
from the milk of deer. As a county palatine, where
the Earl had regal jurisdiction, and where the Earl was
often King also, the feudal tenures lasted long, and
some remnants of them exist even now. There are
to-day, or have been in my knowledge, lands or farms
let with the stipulation that the tenant serves in his
lord's troop of yeomanry, that the tenant does for his
lord so many days' team work a year, ploughing, har-
vesting, or carting, and, among the more fancy services,
that he walks a hound puppy, a game-cock or two, and
sends his lord, or squire, or steward, a good cheese in
convenient season.

It is generally considered that the money received
by the sale of cheese should pay the rent of the farm,
that the housewife should have the butter and egg
money for household expenses, and the sale of cattle,
corn, and other articles should meet other demands.
Now, if the wife be too free with the skimming dish,
so as to get more butter money for finery, the cheese
is made poorer, and its poverty is shown some day
when the factor or buyer bores it, for he may say,
" Where's the butter ? This wouldn't grease a gimlet.
You had better make this cheese into boot-laces, for
if any one eats it, it will last on his stomach a week."
Then the wife declares she has never taken out a
penn'orth of butter, and perhaps she cries, and the
old folks say, " Aye, aye, cheat and the cheese will
show." Or, it may be, the cattle are poor with being
clemmed or having had bad food. Then there is no
richness in the milk to begin with, and the cheating
of the cattle shows in the cheese. Or there may be
cheating in the work, slovenliness and dirt, the whey
not gotten out, or other things, all or any of which

will show in the cheese. There are other proverbs
about cheating never prospers, but the Cheshire
farmer's experience is well expressed in "Cheat and
the cheese will show."

It is said you might as well try to choose a wife
for a man as choose his cheese. A remarkable thing
in the appearance of dairies or lots of whole cheese
is that there is a strong family likeness descending
on the female side; that is to say, the cheese made
by a daughter looks like that made by her mother,
and the likeness may descend through generations.
If fifty farmers pitched cheese at a fair, a factor well
up in his business could tell from looking and feeling
at them who had made every lot. When the orthodox
supper of all good Church and State farmers was
bread and cheese and ale, the characters of the young
were divined from the manner in which they ate
their cheese. If they ate the rind, they would be
considered greedy and rather dirty; to throw it away
was wasteful; but to scrape it first and eat it after was
the perfection of gentility :—

> " Martha, cumbered with much caring,
> Ate the cheese and ate the paring.
> Betsy showed her careless mind,
> She cut and threw away the rind.
> But fair Nancy, sure to please,
> Like a clean maiden, scraped the cheese."

There are hundreds of ways of spoiling this good
food in its manufacture. The salt may have lost its
savour, and that cheat will soon show. They may be
oversalted, and become as hard as boulders. No
knife or axe will cut them, and farmers have been
known to put them in a pit to soak. It was said my
grandfather had some that he could neither sell nor

give away, so they were left outside the warehouse
door at night in the hope that some one would steal
them.   They were stolen, but unfortunately the
thieves brought them back again.   These would
have rivalled the famous Dutch cheeses that were
used as ammunition against the French.   There is
a poem somewhere, probably dating from the
Peninsular War, where the Spaniards show and boast
of their fruits and wine.   The Cheshireman replies
with a cheese :—

> " Look here, you Spanish dog,
>   Such fruits as these our fields yield twice a day."

No greater insult could be put on a Cheshire farmer
than to call his cheese American.   I remember a
wealthy man from this district buying a country hall
and hunting in scarlet.   I heard an old farmer say,
" He tries to be a gentleman, but it wunner do ; he's
like a bit o' Yankee cheese, you may tooast it, an'
tooast it, an' tooast it, but there's a hard leathery
loomp at th' end that you canner tooast."   He had
probably carried his commercial instincts into the life
of a country gentleman, and the farmer expressed his
contempt for the sham by the simile of the Yankee
cheese.   The ever-increasing demand for milk
steadily lessens the make of cheese in Cheshire.
The County Council teaches, and factories are established, but the good old blue mould sort gets rarer
and rarer, and by some not far-distant day will be
extinct.   It is as unlike the dirt which comes from
Gorgonzola as old English oaken furniture is unlike
the blackened shams of Shadrach, Meshach, and
Abednego.
    There are many other farmers' proverbs that are

seldom or never seen in print, and may therefore
be considered folk-lore. Here are a few of them :
" Breed is stronger than pasture ;" " Cursing the
weather is bad farming ;" " Muck's the mother o'
money ;" " There's more ways than one of killing a
pig ;" " A little horse is soon wispt, and a pretty
girl is soon kist ;" " Better wed o'er th' mixen than
o'er the moor ;" " It's as easy to wed a widow
as to catch a dead horse."

> " Man to the plow,
> Wife to the cow,
> Girl to the pail,
> Boy to the flail,
> And your incomes are netted ;
> But man ' Tally-ho !'
> Miss to piano,
> Boy Greek and Latin,
> Wife silk and satin,
> And you'll soon be gazetted."

In the year 1824 a provision merchant in Manchester, whose business included that of a cheese
factor, was journeying in what was then the distant
and wild district where the counties of Cheshire,
Staffordshire, and Shropshire join. His name was
Fletcher, and he called on a man named Moss, who
had a house crammed with children and cheese. He
bargained for the surplus stock of both, and one of
the many unforeseen results of that transaction is he
who now writes this. One who was present and
remembers it still consigns cheese for me to sell in
Manchester ; and in more than one instance the same
person has handled the goods for more than fifty
years. Another old custom was observed when my
father was married, for an oak-tree was felled, and
out of it the village carpenter made a plain panelled

oaken chest, a wedding chest of home-grown, winter-felled oak.   It is gradually darkening, and in another sixty or a hundred years it will acquire the dark-brown tint beloved by connoisseurs, which nought but age can give.

AN OLD-FASHIONED DAIRYMAID,
WITH CHESPIT.

CHAPTER XIV

GATLEY FOLK

" Pray you sit by us and tell's a tale.
Merry or sad shall't be?
As merry as you will."
—WINTER'S TALE.

HE following short addition to what I had written about Gatley appeared in the *Manchester City News*, January 1895:—

In your kind review of my " History of Cheadle and Gatley" you allude to an omission on my part in not recording more of the notable men of Gatley. If I were to give a full account of these worthies it would require another volume or long chapter, for the conditions under which they lived developed them into a hardy, self-reliant, and rather lawless community, and these qualities are to some extent inherited even by the latest generation, for only on Saturday last, as I was crossing Gatley Green, a well-dressed, nice-looking lad, about seven years old, said to his younger brother who was playing football with him, " Now, Tommy, it's time to go home." Tommy looked like a cherub, and replied, " Nay, I'm not going to the old devil yet, am I heck!" Wondering what was the derivation of

the word heck, and what was the relationship between the devil and the cherub, I left them to their
play.

Sixty years ago the Gatleyites were weavers,
squatters, tinkers, makers of platters and noggins,
fishermen, herbalists, besom merchants, poachers,
naturalists, Chartists, and red-hot Radicals. In this
century cavalry were twice sent against them. There
were more men hanged from Gatley than anywhere
else in the neighbourhood. If a Gatley man was
seen in Knutsford he would be run into gaol first
(if he could be caught) and tried after, on some
account or other. The locality favoured the de-
velopment of the species. Gatley is in two counties
and in three parishes, Stockport, Northen, and Didsbury. Within the lifetime of living men there was
much country about the Carrs, practically wild, and
the salmon-fishing and wild-fowling were good. The
rector of Stockport, who should have looked after
the spiritual wants of the greater part of the place,
was seldom seen excepting when he was looking
after his tithes, and then his reception might have
been like that recorded in the "Chronicles of Cheadle."

Your late contributor, Randle Alcock, F.L.S.,
was probably akin to the Randle Allcock whose
epitaph is quoted on page 114 of the book, as stating
that he did not know how many descendants he had.
These Allcocks came from Clembeggar Hall, and
"that way on." It is said that old Daddy Allcock
had a pear-tree with extra fine fruit, and as he went
under the tree a pear dropped on his head and
smashed. The old man sat down and cried, not
on account of the hurt to his head, but on account
of the loss of the pear, and that it should behave
so rudely to him. The man Brandrith you mention

seems to be Brundrit spelt classically. He was a noted fisherman, who always carried an eel spear to job eels in the ditches. He is reported to have caught twenty pounds of eels in a night.

Like some of the above-mentioned gentlemen, old Sly Parker was very appropriately named, for he was "as fause as a fitch," and "got his living mostly by thayvin'." Having kept ducks all my life, I thought I knew a thing or two about them, but old Sly's dodge for taking them was a revelation that it would not do to publish if your readers were not mostly town-bred folks, unconscious of the joys and troubles of a country life. Where water was three or four feet deep, Sly would fix a stake with its top about six inches below the surface of the water. On this was balanced a brick, and round the brick some fish-hooks baited with cows' "leets" were tied. When the pretty little duck swallowed the bait it soon dislodged the brick, which sank to the bottom, taking the poor duck with it. Then, when the rightful owner was comfortable in bed, Sly would fish up the duck and begin again. He was very good at wiring hares (the town-bred reader must not think this means telegraphing to hares), and was seen by Tatton's keepers to take one. They gave chase, and Sly made for home, and, rushing into his house at Gatley, said to his wife, "Now, Al, into bed wi' thee; ne'er mind thi cloas nor thi clogs, but get in bed and lay atop o' this old 'ar; let thi yure down and be main bad." No sooner said than done, and Sly was lighting a fire and very indignant with the keepers when they came. He'd no hare; they might search the place; he "couldner a hetten it in that time, an' th' missus bad too." The search was made even to under the bed, but no hare was found, and

the Tattonites retreated sorely discomfited, for had
they not seen it snared with their own eyes? After
the keepers had gone, and "soon as the evening
shades prevailed," the Gatleyites supped on jugged
hare, and triumphed gloriously.

Another noted Gatleyite was George Pownall,
who was very learned, and taught his dogs and pigs
to read and tell fortunes. His famous dog Charlie
may have been called after the Bonny Prince; at any
rate, he was very wise, like my old Gomer, who used
to howl when it was time for the church bells to ring.
Charlie was spotted all over like plum-pudding or
currant tommy, and would examine the lasses that
came to have their fortunes told, and give them the
most suitable cards. Not being more than human,
he might err sometimes, for a female Gatleyite, named
Matty, once kicked him on the head when he was
telling her fortune, and said, "Thou'rt a liar, tha brute!"
Charlie was sold for £20 to go to London, and he
found his way back to Gatley. Then he was sold
to America and could not get home again. Pownall
went to Liverpool to buy monkeys, and got one with
an extra long tail, and also a crocodile. He shortened
the monkey's tail by degrees until it fled one day,
leaving its master the bits of its tail, and then it lived
in the Carrs with the Gatley Shouter, the famous
ghost that the parson at Northen laid so cleverly.
The crocodile was also a bad spec, for the folk would
not let their dogs bait it; it was like going to law
with a lawyer. So it was clemmed and then stuffed,
with its mouth open, and put in a glass case in a
public-house to show people what they might expect
when they had the blues. Bears and bulls, badgers
and otters, were then kept for baiting, until the trade
languished away.

Finally Pownall "turned Methody," got his living by shaving, taught in a Sunday school, and died at Stockport "in all the odour of sanctity." He evidently thought Methodism to be inconsistent with bull and bear baiting or badger drawing, just as a devout Methodist of the present day would deem it inconsistent to be a member of the modern bear-pit or Stock Exchange. Perhaps the death of the bears hastened his conversion, for a barber could not have a better advertisement in those times than a dead bear, it being then evident that his bear's grease was genuine.

There are plenty of other interesting natives in the neighbourhood. In a low dark room in a timber-framed wattle-and-daub house, sits an old cobbler on a shoemaker's bench that, he tells me, his grandfather bought from an old shoemaker named Patchit above a hundred years ago. His cobbling stump had been a cart leg in its younger days. His leather is "gradely," the best hide always coming off an old cow's belly or rib. He says there's "nowt" like leather, and that "cobbler" is not the correct term for his trade; it should be "shoemakker." "Bootmaker" refers to the makers of Wellington top-boots. Nevertheless he sits with his toes turned in in the orthodox fashion, uses cobbler's wax, and then licks his finger and thumb, fingers everything and licks alternately. His spectacles have rims about half an inch broad, and legs that wrap nearly round his head. They are alternately at the end of his nose or on the top of his forehead, as he wishes to see near to or far from him. Round about are a most extraordinary collection of tools—bellows and blowpipe and lathe; tools for gardening, for mending clocks and watches, chairs or cans, cameras and umbrellas. He says most of the old-fashioned clockmakers were "shoemakkers" also.

THE WISE MAN OF GALILEE.

Grandfathers' clock cases were best made out of old
coffins that had been dug up again. He makes his
own cameras and takes photographs. There is a large
collection of botanical curiosities, of butterflies, of prehistoric stone hammers and geological specimens. I
ask him if he has anything to take teeth out. "Oh
aye," he says, "this'll do; it tak's neals out o' shoes.
I can soon do that. 'An you got tick?" "Oh no,"
I replied, "I was merely asking out of curiosity. I
never had but one out." "Why, some folk are always
bothering wi' their teeth. I take lots out. Sixpence
each. It's chep."

I sit down on a chair that was evidently made in
the last century, admiring the curiosities of all sorts,
and ask how it is that cobblers are always Radicals.
"'Cos we think a lot," he replied. "If several of us
gets workin' together, we argue a bit; we're bun' to'
threeup 'bout politics or religion, but folk get so
plaguey hot 'bout religion. Ask a Catholic why he
prees to th' saints, an' he'll say, 'Cos it gets round
better. Then weer is th' saints, in th' sun an' moon
millions o' miles off? Then they'll wanten to thump
yo'. An' there's them thick-yedded Tories—O Lord!
some on 'em 'asner sense to go in th' 'ouse when it
reens; an' they talken,—O Lord! Can you mak' a
tatchin eend? That'll show whether you're a shoemakker. Get some hempen threead and rub it on
your leathern brat an' that uns, sithee. Then waxen
it well; then get a pig's bristle. There are no pigs'
bristles nowadays like as there'd used to was. They
kills th' pigs too young. A gradely owd sow that had
had six or seven litters, or an owd boar, used to have
some bristles. Now we 'an send to Rooshia for 'em."
Here he produces bristles like quills off the fretful
porcupine, and takes one about six inches long, splits

one end, twists it into the waxed hemp, and produces a first-rate "tatchin eend."

Then I heard a most interesting old proverb. If a young man had a very big foot, the shoemaker might say to him, "Why, thou'rt like a butterbump, thy foot's longer than thy leg." A butterbump turns out to be a bittern, and the saying shows those birds must once have been common at Gatley.

Then I heard of the Hellion Skellions coming at the time of the Luddite riots. I gradually made out that a troop of the Inniskillings was meant, but I preferred to talk of poachers and birds, and soon we had another "gradely threeup." "Did you ever hear of owd Pum? He wur the best cudgeller in these parts, an' he wur once sent for to t'other side o' Ottrincham to help some poachers agen Lord Leigh's lot. There wur boun' to be a gradely do, for Lord Leigh was out himsel' every neet wi' a lot o' keepers. When they met there was fourteen on each side. So they took man for man. Th' 'ed keeper fell to Pum's share, an' he wur a big strong man, and they'd a rare tussle ; but Pum bet him, and then 'is blood were up, an' he feart neither lord nor devil, for he made straight for Lord Leigh, who was directing his men, an' he tackled 'im. Now Lord Leigh wur a brave man and a skillt sworder, and they fenced and struck rarely ; but at last Pum's cudgel got in on his nob, an' he dropt like a bullock that's strucken wi' a pole-axe. What a hulloballoo there were. 'O Lord, O Lord! he's killt the Lord, he's killt the Lord ; what'll us do?' It ended the fight. All th' farmers i' the country were ordered out wi' their horses to catch th' poachers, but they wur never catched, an' it wus never known who'd welly killt Lord Leigh. But it wur our Pum. It matters nowt to no one now, for they're aw dead an' gone."

So you an' your cousin once took two poachers, did you? Was he much hurt, an' who kept th' men's families when they wur in th' lockups. I reckon they could do wi' th' rabbits as well as you. They seldom got cotched about Gatley. It wur allus a good hidin'-place. When they took any they often took th' wrong uns an' hanged them. They'd allus liefer a 'anged wrong uns than none at aw. That wur a shameful thing when they 'anged Henshall's lad from Hayhead.

GATLEY.

I've heerd that's in your book. Th' owd woman's curse told, though. Weer's yon Earl o' Stamford now, or ony on his breed? They're gone out."

"Were ony men ever listed from hereabouts, did yo' say? Why, lots. Yo' known that well enoo. What mi't ha' happened at Watterloo wi'out us? Why, Sergeant Ryle o' th' Guards wur born an' bred an' buried at Gatley. 'E's tode me scores o' times as Gatley wur just like Watterloo. It was aw corn-fields wi' two farm'ouses. Hug-em-on, which

P

they took six times, was just sich another as th' 'aw.
They fought barfoot, for their boots stuck i' th' mud.
Bloocher, him as they ca' th' boots arter, came from
Cat-o-brass, that's Sharson way.   Then there was
Garner ; 'e was wi' th' Duke i' Spain.   Three
Frenchies were for takking 'im prisoner once, but
'e shot one on 'em an' surrounded t'other two, an'
'stead of ums takking 'im, 'im tuk ums."

" Aye, Gatley folk is gradely uns, they is so."

HAYFIELD.

CHAPTER XV

CYCLING CROSS CHESHIRE

" Look forward on the journey you shall go."
—MEASURE FOR MEASURE.

N the summer of 1896 I bought a
bicycle, for I had gradually cared less
and less about riding on horseback,
and the last horse I really liked had
suddenly died. What a difficulty it
did seem to me to learn to ride a
bicycle! If I had never been accustomed to riding
a horse I should have managed better; but, in spite
of numerous falls, I persevered, and determined that
as soon as I could ride ten miles I would attempt the
journey of rather over forty miles, and go from Didsbury to Standon.

The way was well known to me, having walked it
once, and ridden it on horseback many times. It is
along the old coach road from Manchester to the
south, the first stage to Wilmslow being twelve miles,
the next to Congleton twelve, and the next to Newcastle twelve, all good roads excepting about Newcastle. As I was only a novice at cycling I started
early in the morning, when I could have the roads to
myself, and walked up and down all the hills. Five

227

o'clock on St. Swithin's Day found me going through Cheadle. At Wilmslow the workpeople were astir, and the clock at Fulshaw tolled six as I passed. Seven o'clock found me beyond Alderley in the open Cheshire country, with birds, rabbits, and young pheasants on the road, the air deliciously fresh, and the wind at my back, rolling quietly along a good road in the most beautiful manner possible.

MARTON CHURCH.

A short rest was made at the quaint timber-built church at Marton, and the clocks of Congleton struck eight as I passed through the ancient borough. Here a pint of new milk was taken on board, and shortly after the fine old church of Astbury came into view. It looks like a cathedral set on a country village green, and is a most imposing edifice; but all the

LITTLE MORETON HALL.

doors were fast locked, as if—like some sorts of religion—it was kept for Sundays only. Shortly after
the fine old hall of Moreton was reached. This is
well known to be one of the finest, if not the very
best specimen of the timber-built manor-houses. The
courtyard, the octagonal bay-windows, and the carved
and panelled oak were as beautiful as ever. I asked the
wife of the farmer (whose name is the same as that of
the master carpenter who worked on the house in 1559)
for a drink of milk, and was told all the milk was put
in the cheese tub. Then I asked for whey, and this
seemed to surprise the old lady, for Cheshire farmers
call supping curds or whey living at the best end of
the pig trough, and as she offered me a jug of whey
she said it did not agree with most folk. She evidently thought I looked delicate or desperate, but I
replied it always suited calves, and the beautiful calves
came to the bridge over the moat, and an old sow
waddled in, as if they all wanted their share. Regret-
ting I could not tarry longer, for it was then ten
o'clock and the difficult part of the journey was to
come, I again set off, having had five hours of bright
sunshine and fresh air at the time Manchester men
were getting to business.

Shortly after came the steep descent to the Red
Bull at Lawton, and the once-famous passage at Lawton Lydgate, where for so many years the passage
was farmed or the tolls were let at the junction
of the counties. Here I had my second little accident, and through no fault of my own, for I was
pushed into the hedge by a waggon-load of straw.
The Red Bull looked as if it had never been washed
or painted since I saw it twenty years before. Here
began the long, wearisome ascent of Talk-o'-th'-Hill,
six miles of bad roads into Newcastle. After passing

the summit I had two more accidents, apparently from
a foot slipping off the pedal when going down hill on
a rough and stony road.   I could ride a horse without
stirrups, but had not learnt the accomplishment of
riding a bicycle without pedalling.   Bicycles are queer
things that wobble about and run off down hill as if
they are bewitched, when they suddenly lie down.
The last time mine did it we parted company, and I
came a "proper cropper."   There was no friendly
hedge to hold me up with its thorns and let me down
gently ; there were only hard stones, and walls harder
even than a face or head hardened by long exposure
to business in Manchester.   However, not very much
harm was done.   The front wheel was out of place,
the near side pedal was bent askew, and there were
sundry dints about us, but nothing broken, and as
Newcastle was in sight two miles away, we journeyed
on, and found a good bicycle doctor, who worked at
the machine for an hour, and turned it out as good as
ever for eighteenpence.   Here I had some sponge-
cakes and another pint of new milk, which, with the
usual breakfast and the whey, made rather more than
half a gallon consumed before noon.   How the doctors
will shudder or sigh when they read this !   If they
really wish to cure any patient of a sluggish liver, let
them recommend bicycle exercise up and down Talk-
o'-th'-Hill.   The ways want mending, as they did in
the coaching days a century ago.

From Newcastle I pushed the machine along for
a full mile, always uphill, and making for the Shropshire road ; then came better country, with gradual
descent and good going.   A fox-hound puppy out at
walk, one of the last vestiges of the feudal system,
showed I was nearing Trentham and the vast possessions of the Duke.   Another walk down a steep

MAER CHURCH.

descent, past the old-world village of Whitmore,
or white moor, and the station is passed. This is
the highest station on the London and North-Western
Railway Company's line between Manchester and
London. The water supplies Crewe works, and
empties into the Weaver. A mile or so farther and
the Maer woods and hills are reached. Here the air
is sweet with the pine-trees and the bracken. The
rowan berries, bilberries, purple heather, and multi-
tudes of flowers bedeck the wayside, and through the
cuttings in the rocks the road winds below the quaint
old church, and under the gardens by the doors of
Maer Hall, where the beautiful mere is glistening in
the sun, and sending off its contribution to the waters
of the Severn. Here Darwin studied earthworms
and noted the quantity of black game. Black-cocks
are gone, but the woods are very beautiful still. In a
few yards farther the streams make for the river Sow,
which flows into the Trent. In about two miles,
therefore, I crossed the watersheds of the rivers
Mersey, Severn, and Trent, which empty themselves
into the sea at the very opposite corners of England.

Then comes the struggle for the last mile, which
must all be walked. A good rider could not ride a
bicycle up the Clay Aulers bank. The flies swarm;
they seem thirstier even than myself. The machine
is covered with them, my hands are full, and I "must
needs grin and abide." The flies literally feasted by
myriads, and seemed never to have tasted anything so
good before. But the long day's work is nearly done.
There is the wood from which, forty years ago, we
took the carrion crow's nest, when the eggs hatched
out on the way home. There are the fields where we
chased and fought the poachers when we took their
rabbits and ferrets and nets. There are the big pits

where the water-hens breed, and the big perch lie basking in the sun. A weasel runs away, and the wood queeee softly coo from the big oaks. Gradually I get up to the open fields, and the wind blows the flies away; and I think that if I were at the point of death and were placed on the green top at Standon, that glorious breeze would pump the blood through my veins again.

But what is the matter with the geese? They are running and tumbling over one another in the wildest fright. It is evident they have never seen a bicycle before, and imagine it to be a Gatling gun that is being wheeled into position against them, for geese are the wariest of all birds. When the Cheadle coach paid a visit to Standon Hall the geese flew away at the sound of the horn, for they thought it to be the archangel's trump and their last hour had come.

The last sixteen miles or thereabouts have been in Staffordshire, and I have walked more than half of them, as well as having had three spills, one of them having been a bad one, and in the last bit, while pushing the machine, the tyre has got punctured. But "all's well that ends well." Rest comes at last, and as the Promised Land was said to be with milk and honey flowing, so here fifty cows will soon be coming up for milking, and in the eventide there is the peaceful, placid, pastoral pursuit of picking mushrooms to have with the orthodox supper of toasted cheese. Then to bed, with the casement windows wide open, with no sound but the wind's lullaby or the yelp of the prowling fox, and we sleep the sleep of the innocent.

Another Route.

The next year, 1897, I waited for Whit-week to try another journey by another route to the same place, namely, Standon Hall. To avoid the bad roads and hilly country of Talk-o'-th'-Hill and Newcastle, I determined to cross Cheshire more to the west—that is, nearer to the sea, and consequently on flatter ground —trusting that better roads and easier gradients would compensate for greater distance.

Rising as the clock struck four, a cold bath was the first performance. Breakfast had been put ready the previous night. It consisted of a bowl of milk with a plate over it to keep the moths off the cream, the loaf turned upside down, and some fat ham. A thick nudge of the last named and the two last apples were put with some clothes in a handbag and hung in front of the machine where the lamp should be. At a few minutes to five I started on a cold grey morning, the chief feeling being the extreme coldness of the hands until exercise brought heat. Going westwards towards Altrincham, instead of southwards towards Congleton, I went down Stenner Lane, lifted the machine over the stiles across the Sandy ley, the once open field or sandy lea that is now wired into small enclosures, and went down Palatine Road over the Mersey.

The keen morning air was freshening and invigorating. A cock pheasant crew from Mr. Ashton's grounds, showing there was at least one pheasant left in Didsbury. A robin and its young one were perched on points of palings, trying to transfer a green caterpillar from one to the other without tumbling off their perch, and I nearly tumbled off mine with watching them. Rabbits and cats were plentiful beyond Nor- then, and as there had been heavy rain I turned down Gibb Lane and went through the wood to get on the better road between Stockport and Altrincham. At Timperley workmen were stirring and lazily calling to one another for lights, going to poison the beautiful morning air with their dirty pipes before they began work. At the level railway crossing a halt had to be made, and the little "Veeder" had registered six miles.

Walking up the town and off again, I had got past Bowdon when the clocks struck six. When seven was tolled I was passing Toft Hall, beyond Knutsford, and the register showed fifteen miles. Round by Toft I turned to the right for Middlewich, and shortly passed Lower Peover, with its quaint old black and white church. There is no time to notice it now, and I have purposely omitted all notice, topographical or his- torical, of the country between Didsbury and Knuts- ford, for lack of space. Middlewich was reached exactly at eight, the register showing twenty-three miles. The chief thing that struck me here was the enormous number of farmers' carts and waggons bring- ing milk from all directions. At that hour the streets were blocked with them, and the explanation of it is that there is a factory doing a large business in can- ning milk for export. I should have thought that canning might be done in other countries, leaving Cheshire farmers to make the cheese for which their county is famous, or to retail their milk about home. I notice the cows in this district smell differently to those at Didsbury, both of them being different to those at Standon, whither I am going. When I had some of the white-faced Hereford breed from their own country they had another very different odour, which mostly left them in a few days, showing it was mainly caused by a variation in the food.

At Middlewich there is little to see. There used to be a well under the churchyard famous for its good water. Perhaps some crank has objected to it. Outside the town there are miles of country which has been transformed since I was there. The fields are large and rectangular, with little hedges and wire fences; the houses all built in one style, staring red brick below, with black and white upper storeys, and on every house, cottage, inn, or farm is a big shield of arms with a Latin motto and huge letters " J. V." I wondered which of the Cheshire magnates owned all this, and why armorial bearings were put alongside initials. Any common beggar has initials, but they are not usually placed alongside the emblazoned badges of the aristocracy. When in these parts we see anything marked with the felon's head we know it is owned by the Davenports, the Sergeants of the Forest of Macclesfield, who had the regal power of hanging or beheading first, and trying after, and we had better beware of their power; or if the mark is the lion's gamb, we must ware the claws of the Crewes.

So I sat on one of " J. V.'s " new gates, trying to remember the arms of the Vernons, and there I ate my second breakfast or lunch. The fat ham or bacon naturally reminded me of the lad who was asked what he would do if he were made king, his prompt reply being that he would ride on a gate and eat fat bacon all day. An old servant of our family, in the country whither I am going, was a curiosity some eighty years ago. Several tales about her have already appeared in print, while others are kept for the Index Expurgatorius. Sally went religious, turned Methody, or "joined the Ranters," as conversion was then termed. There was a prayer-meeting in a barn, and Sally was asked to make prayer. She was a good worker and an original thinker, but her speech bewrayed her, being short and to the point. She was told, she must make prayer and show she had received grace; she had only to ask for her greatest need, and the Lord would shower it on her in showers of blessings. So Sally was sore troubled, and wrestled with her thoughts, but at last inspiration came upon her, and she cried aloud, "O Lord! O Lord! send me and my little Willy lots of fat bacon." As Sally was an unmarried lady, people might have wondered who little Willy was, but in that primitive district things were as they always had been.

> "Let not Ambition mock their useful toil,
> Their homely joys and destiny obscure;
> Nor Grandeur hear with a disdainful smile
> The short and simple annals of the poor."

I sat on the gate and enjoyed the morning air and the fat bacon, and thanked God for it, and from wayfarers I learnt that the big initials with the fancy coat of arms signify Joe Verdin, with the profits on salt.

Minshull Vernon is the next place, uninteresting enough, and yet here are memories of Milton. His third wife came from here, and it is possible Milton's ancestors came from here, for the name was common, and there are two places named Milton not very far away. Shortly after passing Minshull there was a longish descent, and my friends will be pleased to hear that I had a small accident. Coming up the hill was a flock of sheep, and going down was a farmer's gig, so I kept behind the gig and went very slowly;

but suddenly the farmer pulled up at a full stop, for the sheep were getting mixed with his horse, and I bumped the gig as one boat bumps another in college races. The farmeress screamed, though there was no harm done, and the sheep, having just been shorn of all their wool (like flutterers on the Stock Exchange), thought nothing worse could happen to them. This was my only accident, excepting little difficulties in learning to use toe-caps ; for having weighed the pros and cons as to their use, I decided, as I had done years ago in reference to docking a horse's tail, that as no one would dream of running a horse for the Derby or any important race with a docked tail, as long care and experience showed the shortened tail or vertebræ handicapped them immensely, so no experienced cyclist would race without toe-caps, and therefore, although I was not going to race, I should certainly be much better and safer with them.

Across Beam Heath I get to the quaint old town of Nantwich, the scene of some of the most prolonged and stubborn fighting in England all through the Civil Wars. In Malbon's diary may be found a most interesting account of the times, the firing of the old thatched houses, the prisoners in the church, the Irishwomen with the long knives, the order of Parliament to hang all Irishmen, the shooting in Tynker's croft of the betrayer of Beeston Castle, the prisoner with the church surplice in his breeches, the adulterers doing penance in the cage in the market-place, with many other quaint and curious records. Over vile old boulder pavement I get to Nantwich church at ten precisely, the register showing thirty-four miles run in five hours. In the church porch is a nice old lady with prayer-book, who tells me she expects the rector every minute. As all the doors are locked, I spend a quarter of an hour examining the outside of this interesting old church with its octagonal tower, and return to find the old lady patiently waiting. There are many notices in the porch as to offertories, and requests for prayers, even for the officials. Well, they certainly need them, for how parson-like it is, all begging and nothing in return, not even a look inside, and the grey-haired lady waiting twenty minutes while I was there, to say her prayers in her church. I asked her where I could get some good milk, and she replied, "Anywhere." She certainly had the great blessing of faith, both in milk and parsons.

Along the road to London's famous city I set off again, and after a few miles of beautiful country there appears on the left the glorious tower of Wybunbury. Here I ask before going up to it, if the church is open, and am told, "Oh yes, sir, the church is always open to any one." That sounds more Christian-like. And what a grand old tower it is! Who could have built it in this quiet, old-world village? It used to lean over like the more famous tower of Pisa, but it has been straightened, and a new church built up to it. Ormerod's history says very little about it. The wonderfully-carved oaken roof and the whole church of his day have vanished as though they ne'er had been, excepting one brass and a most elaborate monument of a stout old party with immense hair and his wife, under a canopy covered with heraldic shields.

The charwoman tells me the tower always leaned towards the Moss—for things do lean towards mosses, and that sounds funny to me—then she shows me the site of a former church that was probably a part only of one still older. Thinking of Hogarth's idle apprentice, I sat on an altar tomb and ate an apple. Round the tower towards the top there seems to be fretted work that may give a clue to the date of its building, for the fret was Lord Audley's badge at the battle of Poictiers, and Doddington is in the parish. On the western side are colossal statues of saints and martyrs, with a much-battered Virgin and Child above. I have seldom seen a finer tower on a finer site, and memory goes back to Ludlow and Boston Stump in Lincolnshire.

Forward again after a few moments' delicious rest in the balmy air of June. The roadsides by the splendid domain of Doddington are hung and carpeted with the mayflower and the speedwell, names that are now associated with the birth of a mighty nation. Between the road and the mere is a deeply-sunk fence that I incautiously dropped down to have a nearer look at a flock of Canadian geese by the side of the water. I was getting too tired to scramble out of a ditch over a six-foot wall; but across the mere was the hall, and I thought of Poictiers, where Lord Audley and his four esquires—Delves of Doddington being one—went to stay the advance of the armies of France, or sell their lives as the Spartans sold theirs at Thermopylæ. Hath not Froissart recorded that when Lord Audley was sore wounded (the French King having been taken prisoner), the Black Prince embraced him and promised him a pension of 500 marks a year out of the revenues of England. Audley gave that at once to his esquires, saying they were worthier than he, whereupon the Black Prince settled 600 more on him. Another of the Delves family fell on the field at Tewkesbury, and his son was dragged from the sanctuary of the Abbey to be beheaded. What a land of history, romance, and beauty this Cheshire is! Will some wizard ever write of it as Scott wrote of the Borderland?

Noontide found me toiling up the long, steep hill to Woore. Forty miles had taken me from end to end of Cheshire. Behind me lay the county of salt and cheese, with its waters running to the Mersey, and before me was the fair county of Shropshire, with the rivulets making for the Severn. This was the noted place for prize-fights, horse-races, cock-fighting, and other sports, for hereby, at a place with the suggestive name of Gravenhanger, three counties meet, and a man may touch all three at once and baffle the police. Like Gatley in our neighbourhood, it became a sanctuary for outlaws; though, like it, all is quiet now, save at the annual hunt races.

Over the crest of the hill I mount again, and bowl along through lovely country—Willoughbridge Wells, a haunt of foxes and wild-fowl; the lonely public-house at Blackbrook, the noted meet of the hounds; through the woods and hills of Maer, where I suddenly turn off the London road at what would appear to a stranger to be a private road cut in the rock between the lordly hall and the tiny ivy-grown church on the rock above. Here is an epitaph that may please the collector or the moraliser:—

> "'The little hero that lies here
> Was conquer'd by the diarrhœa."

Another mile of country lane and I have to dismount to walk the remaining one. Up the Clay Aulers bank the road is awful. The watershed changes again. I leave the Severn for the Trent, Shropshire for Staffordshire, and, 'mid the well-known fields, I reach home at last in time for a good old-fashioned dinner of rabbit pie.

The hour was one o'clock; the distance traversed, as shown by the register, fifty and three-eighths miles; the time taken was eight hours, perhaps one of which I had rested, and about three miles had been walked, leaving an average pace on the cycle of nearly eight miles an hour. This compares with six miles an hour last year on a shorter route, four accidents, and far more fatigue, but then I was only a learner of the art of bicycle riding. Thirty years ago, when in training and in the strength of manhood, I walked the distance, every foot of it, within twelve hours, or at an average rate of walking of almost exactly four miles an hour.

WYBUNBURY CHURCH.

Q

CHAPTER XVI

PILGRIMAGES

" God save you, pilgrim! whither are you bound? "
—ALL'S WELL THAT ENDS WELL.

A Pilgrimage to Hawarden.

S the Lancashire and Cheshire Anti-
quarian Society were visiting Hawarden
in the summer of 1896, and as I was
one who was disappointed at not being
able to see or hear "the Grand Old
Man," I determined to stay there for
the night, for it was said he would almost certainly
be at the church service in the morning. Hawarden
was crowded with tourists, and yet I was the only one
who stayed the night at the inn. The evening was
spent in the wilder part of the park, up among the
rabbits and the bracken, as was also the early morning
before breakfast. The corn harvest had begun, for
oats were being cut, although it was only the 18th,
or middle of July. The trees in Hawarden Park are
magnificent. There is as fine timber there of the
aboriginal old English trees as I ever saw, and the
church is beautifully situated, as are most of our old

parish churches. The manorial lords who originally built them for the repose of their souls, gave the best they had unto the Lord when they could keep it no longer, or when, by a vow in times of danger, they sought to influence or bribe the decrees of Providence. From Hawarden churchyard may be seen the famous city of Chester, with its cathedral towering over its quaint old streets; beyond it is the "castled crag" of Beeston, and Peckforton, with the ridge of the Forest stretching to Helsby, and the estuary of the Mersey. The whole of Wirral, with its villages, cornfields, and railways, lies spread out like a map. The sands of Dee, the hills of Wales, and the woods of Hawarden are all around. British, Roman, Saxon, Dane, Norman, and English place-names tell the nationalities of the bygone lords of the land, and the whole scene is very, very beautiful. What stirring times and deeds in the history of England have been watched from that old churchyard since Christianity came to the land! It is not five hundred years since all Welshmen when entering Chester had to leave their arms outside the city walls, and if any were caught within the city between sunset and sunrise their heads were cut off at once, without delay, without mercy. Before then the merchandise was chiefly horses, skins, and slaves; and centuries before, in almost prehistoric times, the Roman legions fought with the ancient British, and the pirates of the sea sailed up the river, under their black, raven flag, to seize or pillage the rich lands around. All have come and gone, leaving little or nothing but the names they gave to the places, and the language of the natives as heard to-day is English spoken by Welsh.

As soon as the doors of the church were opened I went in, but was confronted with an official, who

may have been a "parroter," or beadle, or even have
reached the sublime height of a full-blown churchwarden. He stopped me, saying parishioners only
were admitted then ; these were the rules. I replied
that I was a parishioner for the day, for I had slept
in the parish the previous night. That would not
qualify me, he said ; but I said it would, and advised
him to look up his Act and authorities. He said,
when strangers wished to be married in a parish they
qualified by three weeks' residence. "Slightly in-
accurate," I replied ; "one night a week for three
weeks would do ; and if I had been destitute, and died
here last night, I should have to be buried here. But
look it up, and I'll go in." Then I left him, and went
to the nearest free seat to where Mr. Gladstone sat,
having ascertained which that was when inspecting
the church on the previous afternoon. The gentleman seemed perplexed, and wanted to argue ; he
probably had a dash of lawyer in him, or perhaps he
had an uncle in the profession ; but he soon had to
look after others, for shortly before eleven the church
began to be filled rapidly.

There came swarthy foreigners and calculating
Yankees, who had doubtless driven from Chester.
There was the devout Dissenter, who seemed half-
scared, and looked with horror on the semi-papistical
service when the priest and choir turned to the east
and the whole congregation bowed down towards
Mecca. There was the stout party, who evidently
thought whatever was was right, and the size of
whose jaw proclaimed him to be a Tory. There
were cyclists staring about, and looking as wild as if
they had been brought up in a wood and were just
caught. Some of them may have ridden over from
Lancashire that morning, for there had been six hours

of sunshine. All sorts and conditions of men of many
nationalities were there gathered together for silent
hero-worship. As the bell ceased, there entered
slowly through the chancel door an old man upon
whom every eye was turned ; he walked without stick,
and was accompanied by two tall old ladies, one of
whom wore a sunshade to her bonnet, in the fashion
of forty years ago. He looked well preserved and
healthy, for I mentally compared him with relatives
of my own, some of whom are older and some not
quite his age ; and when service was over I timed
my exit to walk out with him. There is evidently the
usual slight deafness of old people, when they can
hear their friends and relations well, but cannot hear
strangers, for at the sermon he left his seat to sit
on a stool by the pulpit ; and on rising from a seat
there is also the usual steadying of the body before
walking. He never reads the lessons now, for we
were told that when he did so fifty or a hundred
people would leave the church as soon as he had
finished. It seems almost incredible, now that every
one calls themselves ladies or gentlemen, that so many
should be so ill-mannered. They might stop quietly,
and go to sleep in the good old-fashioned way. It
is very easy to go to sleep during the sermon, especially if one has been out for an hour before breakfast. Some of them say the Athanasian Creed might
be said or sung, and there could be no sleeping then,
for if that awful absurdity is alternately intoned by the
priest and gabbled by the congregation, they would
have to stand up to it, and then—"Oh for the wings
of a dove," and the fresh breeze on the hillside.

Adjoining the churchyard is the hostelry of St.
Deniol's, with its garden ablaze with poppies and
sweet peas. The fussy police say that part of the

churchyard is private, and that seems a new idea; but it's not worth arguing about, so, leaving the crowded village, I went trespassing in the park, and sat down by a pool, *recubans sub tegmine fagi*, as the schoolboys say, to meditate on things in general, and watch the birds and beasts. There were many fly-catchers about, and I had noticed the nest of one against the church. For the past few years these pretty little birds seem to have abandoned Didsbury. Presently some rats crawled along the wire fence, and were busy eating something that I found to be moles hung up by the mole-catcher. If the owner of the park knew of this there would be some indignant remonstrance against the killing of the harmless mole instead of the mischievous rat, and letting the latter feed on the former. I strolled through the park and on to Chester, a walk of seven miles altogether, three of them—from Broughton to Saltney—being along a perfectly straight road. At Chester Station I wanted tea, but could not get served at any of the refreshment bars. I had walked from Hawarden and taken a ticket to Crewe, thereby qualifying for a bona-fide traveller, and certainly I was very thirsty, for the day was hot; but their hearts were hardened, and they would serve nothing. When the Holyhead express was due I tried again, but without avail; it was only when the train arrived about twenty minutes late, and fifty people wanted serving at once, that we could get any tea. In the evening I had a conversation with a venerable and estimable old lady, whose opinions are somewhat strengthened by a very Conservative country newspaper. It was somewhat as follows :—

"I cannot imagine whatever you went to see that mischievous old humbug for. I wouldn't go across the yard to see him."

" Oh yes, you would ; you'd make quite a fuss of him if he came here."

" Would I ? I'd knock his old head off if he came here ; it ought to have been done long ago.   He's ruined us all : ruined the country.   How has he ruined the country?   Why, by his free trade.   Here's my beautiful fresh butter, with the strawberry roan cow and the buttercup print, only ·fetches ninepence a pound in the market, and it used to sell for two shillings a pound ; and you poor townsfolks are eating margarine or foreign rubbish, and cannot tell the difference, so they say.   I suppose it's because their mouths and nostrils are choked with soot or smoke.   That free trade, I tell you, has ruined the country."

" Why, you have yourself often told me that it was education that ruined the country."

" So it is.   Education has ruined it another way. I cannot get a servant nowadays who does not know how to read and write.   I want them to mind their work, not to read and write, but they won't work as they used to.   They write love-letters, or read rubbish where mouldy milkmaids turn out to be duchesses, or something of the sort.   Nice duchesses they'd be.   There's Begging Billy, the parson at the next parish, he actually teaches the children, now, that they must not notice the gentry or the better-class folk when they meet them.   The girls are not to curtsey, nor the boys to touch their caps.   And they've a servants' friendly society, the radicals, and sent me that Rebecca, who couldn't skin a rabbit, and wants £10 a year wages, double what we used to pay.   Why, in my poor mother's time, girls were glad to come for nothing but their meat and a few old clothes, with perhaps a guinea at Christmas.   But now they're as impudent; why, this is nothing but a danguessing doxey."

"Whatever's that? I know what an idle dossey is, but what sort of a lady is the other?"

"Why, a swaggering, brazen, impudent madam, that can give two words for one, and break more than she's worth. I tell you the country is ruined with them all. And as for those free-traders, they care for nothing in the world but themselves, and both they and that old beggar who led them on richly deserve a good flogging. And did he really go to church? Do you think he tried to pray? I should have thought the church would have fallen in on him and crushed him—though I don't wish any harm to any one, I don't. But, you'll see, old Scrat will have him."

A Pilgrimage to the Royal Oak.

The Royal Oak is not a public-house. It is a tree, a young one from, and the successor to, the original tree in which the young King, Charles the Second, was hidden after his defeat at Worcester. Most school-boys, and many old boys, "sport" oak on May 29, saying they do it to show their loyalty, and to com-memorate the miraculous escape of the King, who was saved by the shelter of the oak, which that year had providentially come into leaf earlier than usual. This popular belief shows a nice jumble of facts and fancies. Charles the Second was restored to the throne on May 29, but he was hidden in the oak on September 6. To wear oak in honour of the Stuarts is not to honour the present Queen, who is a supplanter of the Stuarts, and is not the rightful heir to the throne of England.

In the last century people were punished for wearing oak, for it showed they were rebels to the Queen's grandfather, or his predecessors, the German Georges. The following slight historical sketch will help the reader to understand the tale of the Royal Oak :—

When the armies of the Parliament and the King had their last desperate struggle in the streets of Worcester, the stern, dogged fighting of the Puritans gradually drove before them the fire and dash of the Cavaliers. Cromwell's "crowning mercy" had come, and the young King was hunted like a rat through the houses and streets of "the Faithful City." An upset ammunition waggon, with its team of oxen and a load of hay, blocked the gate while Charles doffed his armour and mounted a fresh horse, which was never returned or paid for. In the wild flight northwards for Scotland during the dark and wet night the army got fewer and fewer, though with hundreds the great cry was, "Save the King." Perhaps thirty to forty miles had been traversed, and the next day was dawning as the King, with about sixty lords and gentlemen, neared Boscobel, where the Earl of Derby had been hidden for a week on his flight from Wigan to Worcester. They were now among proved friends. The Giffards, or Giffords, of Chillington, the Fitz-Herberts of Swynnerton, and other landowners in the neighbourhood, were staunch Royalists. They owned the lands centuries before then, and they own them now, though Boscobel itself has slipped from them. To a secluded house, that had formerly been the Cistercian Monastery of Whiteladies, they were guided by Yates, a servant of the Giffords, who knew the country, being then on his master's land, and amid his own kindred, for he had married a sister of the Penderels, or Pendrills, the devoted band of brothers who, more than all others, saved the King. Five of the brothers were living as woodwards or feudal retainers on the estate, and a sixth had fallen at Edgehill. They did their part nobly and well, and lived to receive the reward of their labours ; but Yates, the guide, got hanged for his fidelity.

At Whiteladies the King and his horse were hurriedly taken into the hall, while Squire Gifford sent to Boscobel and elsewhere for others of the Pendrill family. On their arrival the Earl of Derby, who was known to them, said, "This is the King; thou must have a care of him, and preserve him as thou didst me." Then they stript him of his rich clothes and fine linen, his jewellery and orders he parted among them, and Lord Wilmot cut off his long hair with a knife or dagger, while they dressed him in a coarse patched hempen shirt (a hogging or noggen shirt), a greasy leathern doublet with pewter buttons, coarse green jump and breeches, green yarn stockings without feet, and heavy country shoes. Then the lords and their followers left him to God and the Pendrills, taking leave with heavy hearts as they again set off northwards. The Earl of Derby was shortly afterwards executed at Bolton. Gifford, who was with him, escaped from an inn at Bunbury. Some lords and gentlemen got off in disguise. The last remnants of Leslie's horse, with whom the King would not trust himself, were taken in their wild flight for Scotland at "a place called Diddesbury."

When they were gone the King was taken as a woodman into Boscobel woods, where it rained all day. As an old pamphlet says, "The heavens wept bitterly at the calamity." There he sat on a blanket and thought bitter thoughts. At nightfall one of the

brothers took him nine miles to a Mr. Woolf, near
Madeley, to try if they could get down the Severn to
Bristol. The King was left under a hedge in the wet
while "trusty Dick" went in to see if the Woolfs
would harbour a gentleman of quality. The old man
said his house had been searched already and his
secret chamber was known, his son was in prison, and
he would not venture his neck for any man but the
King himself. Pendrill said, "It is the King!" Then
Mr. Woolf at once cast to the winds his fears and
risked all to save him. The river was so guarded
that nothing could be done, and the King spent a day
and night in the Woolfs' barn amid the hay and straw,
where Mrs. Woolf dyed him with walnut juice to
darken his fair skin. She was probably pickling
walnuts at the time, just as I have seen the present
Mrs. Woolf, my father's sister, at that work in the
autumn; for I may as well say here, it was from Mrs.
Woolf's house that I started on this pilgrimage. In
the dark "trusty Dick" took the King back to
Boscobel.

Many times on this journey did the King throw
himself on the ground in despair and ask for death,
but his stout-hearted guide sustained him and struggled
on. At Boscobel they found Colonel Careless, afterwards named Carlos, a native of those parts, who
"had seen the last man killed in the Worcester fight,"
and then galloped homewards. Whiteladies had been
searched twice, and Humphrey Pendrill warned that
if he harboured the King it was "death without mercy,"
but that if he could tell where he was there was £1000
for him. "So vile a price they set upon so inesti-
mable a jewel." But the brothers were stout and true,
and, what the King feared far more, so were their
women also. They were plain men, "of honest parent-

age, but mean degree," of good courage, with all the craft of the woodmen, for again they took the King to the woods, and he and Careless got up a great oak, the famous Royal Oak. This was a polled or pollard tree, that had probably had its top blown off in a storm and then thickened out ; it was also overgrown with ivy, and formed a very thick shelter. Here the King slept, with his head on Careless's lap, while the Round-head soldiers went through the wood and Joan misled them. Thus was spent the whole of Saturday, Sep-tember 6, 1651, and at nightfall the King came down, and spent the night in the hole in the cheese-room of Boscobel, Careless probably having the other secret chamber (to which I must refer again), the brothers keeping watch and ward at all avenues to the house. Sunday was spent in the arbour on the mound in the garden, whence there is a good view of the country. The King was very footsore with his country boots, and food was scarce, for they durst not buy what they were not used to buy. In this dilemma the Pendrills caught a neighbour's sheep, which Careless stuck with his dagger. They fleyed it and cut it up, and the King cooked the cutlets.

At nightfall the King was mounted on a mill-horse, for he was too footsore to walk. He had wrapped paper round his blistered toes and made them worse, so he had to ride "the dullest jade" he ever rode, and was thus escorted to Moseley Hall by five of the brothers Pendrill, and Yates, their brother-in-law. The wonderful tale of his adventures and escapes should be known by all men. Truth is stranger than fiction, and it does one good to know how hundreds of men and women, far nobler than ever the King was, were ready to hazard their lives and all they had to serve him. "Greater love hath no man than this." Much better would it have been for his reputation if his life had ended then or at Worcester fight. He would then have been a hero and martyr. He did become, as I well remember one of the College lecturers telling us when remonstrating with us boys for "sporting" oak on May 29, "one of the worst kings that ever disgraced the English throne and prostituted the English nobility." For my lord the King came again in peace unto his own land, and the people clapt their hands and shouted, "God save the King!"

To find this Royal Oak and Boscobel I left Standon Hall early one fine morning in the gloriously fine July of 1897. For about two miles in any direction the country lanes are not fit for a bicycle, but I trundled mine with me in beautiful scenery and air that was heavy with the scent of honeysuckle. Striking a turnpike or county road a few miles from Eccleshall, a country town, whose chief inn is the Royal Oak, I set off for Stafford, and went through the town on macadam without dismounting. So far I had gone twelve miles in a country that was known to me. Then I made for Penkridge, on the Wolverhampton road, another six or seven miles of grand cycling. There I turned to the right into country lanes for Brewood, pronounced Brude, for the country people retain the old pronunciation of the letter " w " as if it still were "u u." Having got so far, I began to ask for Boscobel, and after many times dismounting and some little difficulty from the sparseness of population and the rough lanes, I gradually got over the few miles of country. The house called Boscobel was built by the Giffords in a remote and lonely part of Brewood forest as a hunting lodge. The name is derived from "bose" and "belle," meaning beautiful wood. Those who built it thought of sterner matters than sport, for it was built with two secret chambers and about the county border — the border-line between the two counties (unless it is a river) being often ill defined, and more or less waste even unto this day.

About a mile from Boscobel I came to several confusing lanes, some of them seeming to be merely cart tracks, and I had to go back to a cottage to ask again. I was told it was the first house on the left, down one steep hill and up another. This was all walking, the day was blazing hot, the lanes steep and stony. The country was beautiful—foxgloves, elder-berries, and honeysuckle were in flower; rabbits, pheasants, and water-hens on the pits were common; a hare came lobbing down the lane and nearly ran into me, for hares' eyes are made for looking back-wards over their shoulder, and they see but badly in front of them. As I went down bank on the cycle there was a terrible clamour, for I nearly ran over a covey of young partridges that were basking in the sand on the lane side. The old hen made a dreadful clatter, but I whirled away and left them. At last I came to some hay-ricks and hay-makers among grand trees, and as black and white buildings could be seen beyond I felt that was my destination. Going under a short avenue of these majestic trees I got into a very large farmyard or fold, and asking at what seemed to be a dairy door if this were Boscobel, and if I could see the place, I was told to go to a garden door, open it, go across the garden, and ask at the front door. I went to this garden door, a door in a lofty wall covered with masses of ivy, honeysuckle, and roses, opened it, and found myself in one of the most charm-ing gardens it was ever my lot to see. An ancient timber-framed, many-gabled house, the old-fashioned mound with the arbour on the top, the rolling hills

Lancaster Old Hall Farm.

THE ROYAL OAK AT BOSCOBEL.

(The successor to the original tree.)

and distant view, make an ideal place, and yet it is real and historical also.

The garden walks are very broad, formed of four big square red tiles in the middle, with an edging of boulder or kidney stones worked in patterns. The house, walls, and hedges are covered with climbing plants, and the flower-beds fairly blaze with the vivid colours of poppies, roses, escholtzias, campions, nasturtiums, and sweet peas. In the centre of the garden is one of those large mounds, with an arbour on the top, that are so delightful in hot weather, where there is plenty of air and scenery. This is evidently the place mentioned by the King where he spent his Sunday afternoon, and under other circumstances he could not have wished for a better. Perhaps a hundred yards from it on the adjoining field is an oak-tree, with huge iron palings round it, and pedantic inscriptions in Latin, saying, "This tree, under the blessing of the King of Kings, had the honour of sheltering His Sacred Majesty," and so on. It is obviously untrue, and the only thing about the place that is rather irritating and disappointing. The original, even in the time of its glory, was an old decrepit tree, overgrown with ivy and with its top off. It was cut up into souvenirs and trinkets at the restoration of the Monarchy, and it is even in print that the bole was used as a pig trough. The present tree is a successor to it, probably from one of its acorns or a sucker, and is on or about the same spot. In 1713 it was mentioned as being a young plant growing within the enclosure that had been built to protect the old one. A former inscription said this tree was the successor. The ladies who commemorated themselves in the new tablet probably wished the present tree had been the old one, and with them the wish was father to the thought, and faith only strengthened by contradiction.

Entering this most interesting old house by the front door under the flower-bedecked porch, I was courteously shown all the rooms used by the King. To one accustomed to old houses, and somewhat of an antiquary, the first glance showed the house to be real, like the garden and its mount, not like the tree. There are the almost inevitable modern alterations, the windows, fireplaces, and some furniture and pictures, but as a whole the house is exceedingly interesting. The Vandals have painted the oaken panelling a light colour to give more light. On the mantelpiece is a carved representation of the flight from Boscobel to Moseley, according to an old print in the Bodleian. The footsore King is on Humphrey Pendrill's mill-horse, "the dullest jade" he ever rode, when the peasant said, "It was used to carry six strike of corn, but now it had the weight of three kingdoms on its back." The five brothers and the brother-in-law are armed with clubs and pikels, for they were not allowed arms, but if need arose they evidently meant to sell their lives dearly. In one corner is a picture of the dissolute old King, taken in his prosperity and disgrace, and in the opposite corner is Oliver of the iron jaw, sternly keeping his eye on that man of blood, Charles Stuart.

> "The man of blood was there,
> With his long essenced hair."

Yes, here, in this very room, the King's hair was trimmed with the sheep-shears. The long perfumed cavalier's locks had been cut off by Lord Wilmot's dagger at Whiteladies, and here the toilet was completed, probably as I have seen it done in farmhouses

in that country. A basin or pie-dish is put over the
patient's head, and the sheep-shears soon cut off all
the hair outside the dish. With shepherds or men
who were much exposed to the weather, a tuft of hair
was sometimes left hanging over the ears to keep the
wet out of them, and it would appear the King had
his polled in that country mode. William Pendrill
kept the hair he cut off as a keepsake, unknown to
the King, who wished it burnt. A bloody handkerchief on which the royal nose had bled was long
kept as a cure for the King's Evil. It seems a pity
these old-fashioned remedies are now discarded for
drugs and doctors ; they were certainly cheaper, and
were about as efficacious. Nature and faith are the
great healers. There is the oaken table at which
they ate Dame Joan's chickens, with the posset of
thin milk and small beer ; and the mutton chops
cooked by the King, which were cut from the sheep
that was stuck by the Colonel. In after times the
Pendrills offered to pay Staunton for his sheep with
their bit of hard-earned money ; but when he knew
why it was killed he refused payment. Let it be
recorded of him. The table at which they feasted in
glee and yet in fear is now as worm-eaten as they
are. There is the tiny chapel or oratory, for they
who built the house and used it were of the old
faith. The sturdy Anglo-Saxon race that I know so
well in these parts, and from whom I am come, is
slow to choose and slow to change. Unconsciously
the unwritten lore of our fathers is inherited from
generation to generation, and in these days of super-
abundant book-learning there be some who do not
know what to believe.

    In the Squire's bedroom is a secret chamber in
the chimney-stack ; the window to it may be seen

in the photograph of the house, a little hole by itself in the side of the chimney ; and from the room there is a narrow flight of stairs leading to the garden below, the egress being hidden with climbing plants. The access to it from the room was formerly by a sliding panel in the wainscoting. These "priests' holes," as they were termed, were common in those days, and this one would have been discovered by any one used to search ; but there was another, a much more

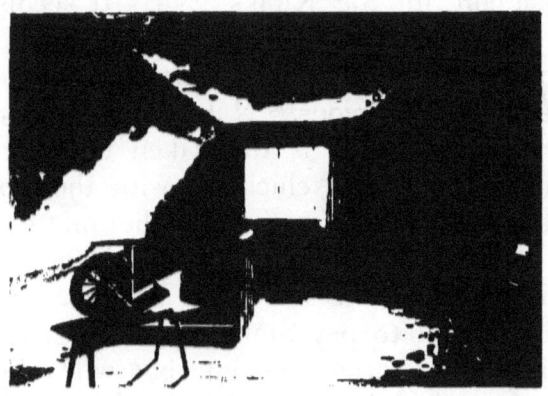

CHEESE-ROOM, SHOWING THE HOLE IN THE FLOOR
IN WHICH THE KING HID.

secret one, and that was allotted to the King. In the large cheese-room in the garret, which extends the entire length of the house, and which is crossed by massive oaken beams, is a little trap-door above what is literally only a hole built in the house. Here the King passed one night, a very uncomfortable one, but very safe ; for if the straw were spread on the floor, and the cheese placed on the straw, as is usual in those parts, the searchers might have had to move every cheese to find the trap-door, and at that time of the year the stock of cheese would be at its greatest. That useful article of food was of much greater importance in those days than it is now. In this hole, then, the King hid, for he spoke of looking from the window early on the Sunday morning ; that is the gable window at the top of the house as shown in the picture ; and it is probable, if the other hiding-place had been discovered, Colonel Careless would have passed himself off as the King, just as Lord Wilmot intended to do at the next house of refuge, namely, Moseley Hall.

Having seen through the place and being well satisfied, I asked for some milk, and was told there was none. Even a large dairy farm in a remote spot like that sends off all milk twice a day to some town — in this case to Bilston. However, they let me have a pint or so that had been reserved for family use, and that, with some bread and cheese, made me content. The day was blazing hot ; my cyclometer showed it had come twenty-seven odd miles, and there was the same distance to go back. Therefore, I went to rest in the arbour on the mount, where the poor, hunted, footsore King spent his Sunday afternoon ; a short peace, while his Puritan foes were singing psalms at their Sabbath's devotions. There was shade in the arbour, and a good breeze blowing through it, and there, thinking of many things, and lulled by the wind's lullaby, I fell fast asleep. No wonder at one's sleeping in a sermon, however full it might be of sound and fury, if I slept there with thoughts overcrowding one another. The view is boundless towards the south and "the Faithful City." The wearied King might fancy he was gazing over "the kingdoms of the earth and their glory," and feel they were slipping from his grasp for ever. This armed appeal of the Puritans to the Almighty God of Justice– if it were of men it would come to nought; but if it were of God? Charles and Cromwell, remote cousins to one another as they were, have passed away, and none of their seed sit on the throne of England or hold high place in her councils. Cromwell's work endures; for no King, Dread Sovereign, Sacred Majesty, Lord's Anointed, or Vicegerent of God dare again in England claim the power that they then claimed of Right Divine; and the land has peace and prospers still.

Boscobel seems as lonely and beautiful as ever. In the two hours I was there I saw no living thing larger than a butterfly, except the woman who showed me over the house. Everything seemed asleep in the blazing afternoon, and after a most delightful visit I reluctantly set off on the homeward journey. The rich pastoral country may be flowing with milk and honey, but they are hard to get, as everything seems sent off to the towns as soon as it can be fingered. At Eccleshall I bethought me of a relative, to whose house I went, and had five big cups of tea, my head and hands pumped on, and an hour's rest. The bicycle had then registered fifty miles, and there were still five to go, including Walford bank, which is half a mile of loose stones, as steep as the roof of a house. Having been proficient in most athletic pursuits, I have no hesitation in saying that cycling is the thirstiest of any, and yet it decidedly helps temperance. At supper I had seven glasses of new milk, and listened to instructions somewhat as follows: " Well, if you are thirsty, you have no need to make yourself into a swill tub with all those jugs of milk. If you would go into the garden and get yourself about a dozen nice young onions the size of pigeon or guinea eggs and eat them with a few inches of cucumber and bread and cheese and ale, you might grow into a strong man who wouldn't be tired if he had been a dozen hours in the sun, like one of those white-faced townsfolk that are reared on a bottle and fed on bread and butter and tea. Butter, indeed! Foreign grease; like so much foreign rubbish you free - traders and old Gladstone have ruined the country with. They may well look sickly. It serves those townsfolk right—reared on Gladstone's grease. Now, do get some onions and good home - made cheese and ale while you can, and get some strength in your bones." I listened to the old lady's advice, and promised to publish it for the benefit of others, though I contended that a cyclist could not be fed on anything cheaper and better than a gallon of new milk a day, for in that country it is only worth six-pence, and it should weigh ten pounds, one-eighth of which is good solids. It is also only fair to say that the onion mixture should be good, for the lady was eating at least a pound weight of raw onions and cucumber chopped up, with vinegar and cayenne, merely excusing the chopping as her teeth are failing her. As she is in her eighty-sixth year, and has given me leave to publish all this, I have pleasure in doing so; for although at that age the teeth may be expected to fail, the adjacent parts are as vigorous as ever.

Turning the conversation on to family history, I tried to learn more particulars and details as to the descent of the Woolfs from the rescuers of the King. In the old Tracts the names are spelt in many different ways. I have used the form Pendrill —not the modern Penderell—for it is so spelt in the Tract of 1660, which bears internal evidence of

having been dictated by some of the Pendrill family,
and "drill" is a common agricultural term. Woolf
is spelt in many ways. The diary of the King, as
dictated to Sam Pepys, gives Woolfe. Whitgreave,
of Moseley Hall, his neighbour, who must have
known him, spells it Woolf, so also does Blount
in his contemporary history of Boscobel, and that is
the way I have written my relatives' names hundreds
of times. It has been particularly interesting to me
to note how in all the old Tracts the character of
the Woolf who harboured the King a day and a
night agrees exactly with that of my late uncle,
whose portrait is facing page 209 : "An honest gentleman," very cautious, given to hospitality, shrewd, and
staunch. When others were clamouring for rewards
at the Restoration, Woolf never asked for anything,
and all he got was some plate with a silver tankard,
and the paltry royal gift of an augmentation of arms.
The crest is now a wolf, holding the royal crown in
its paws, and the motto "Fides in adversis." The
barn in which the King was hidden is, I understand, still preserved. The oldest form of the name
Wolf is probably in the Domesday Book, for it is
there recorded that Ulf, a Saxon Thane, was dispos-
sessed of a manor on the Cheshire border at the
great robbery called the Norman Conquest; and if
we consider that the country folk pronounce the
letter "l" broad and gutturally, as if it were "u,"
we have Uuf, which looks as like as possible to the
bark of the original animal.

A Pilgrimage to the Battlefield of Blore Heath.

Another pilgrimage, another quiet holiday in quest of historic sites, where men have lived and toiled and died, it may be to build themselves a home in which to live, or in which to lie in death, the monastery's calm retreat, or a sumptuous temple to their God, or the field of battle where the fierce love of fighting overcame their better nature, and where their blood dyed the earth and helped the harvest of another year. Our forefathers, whose nature we inherit (for we have made war upon every nation on the earth), often fought from a sheer love of fighting, for some shadow they knew little about, and which is still more shadowy now. We can go on pilgrimage to the scenes made historical by them, and thank God war is not in our time in our land.

On the second day after my journey to Boscobel I left Standon Hall to visit Blore Heath. It lies in the same romantic border-land of the counties. I went by the country lanes to Maer, then on the Nantwich and London road to where it crosses the Newcastle and Market Drayton highway. This last is one of the finest roads in England, a cyclist could not wish for a better ; it crosses the railway from London to Crewe at Whitmore Station. Shortly after Maer there is a long ascent of perhaps two miles, over the high table-land of Ashley Heath, and then comes the Loggerheads Inn, and a wonderful view over many counties. It is somewhere written that when Mahomet and his followers were spreading their new religion with fire and the sword they came to the hills whence they saw Damascus and its fair plain.

Then they said, "Surely this is Paradise! Here we may rest, and stay our hand." But the stern fanatic gazed for some time in silence, and then sadly turned away, saying, "There is but one Paradise, and mine is elsewhere."

In my childhood's days I have often gazed from Mucklestone Wood, by Ashley Heath, over the rich country that is spread below, and wondered whether Paradise were better than that. On the extreme left rises the dim bulk of the Wrekin; then come the hills of Hawkstone, crowned by the monument to Lord Hill. In the middle distance, five miles away, lies the sleepy old town of Market Drayton, with its quaint streets of overhanging timber-framed houses. There is the birthplace of the conqueror of India. If that adventurous youth from The Styche had fallen off Market Drayton tower when he would climb up it, the battle of Plassey would never have been fought, and hundreds of millions of men who came under England's sway might never have heard the name of England. Historic homes and churches dot the plain up to the castled crag of Beeston, on the extreme right, and beyond all are the blue mountains of Wales, that on clear evenings, when the setting sun is low, seem to rise in endless succession. Close at hand is the old grey tower of Mucklestone church, whence Queen Margaret saw her army melt away from the disastrous fight at Blore Heath, and there, not many years ago, was the forge where Skelhorn, the smith, reversed her horse's shoes to deceive pursuers. Skelhorn's direct descendant of the same name was smith and clerk of Mucklestone church when I knew it in the days of long ago.

From the Loggerheads the cyclist can roll down hill for two or three miles to the battlefield of Blore

MUCKLESTONE CHURCH TOWER.

From whence Queen Margaret watched the battle of Blore Heath.

Heath. I remembered a little of the locality, and
seeing a farmer bringing a load of hay out of a field,
I asked him if I could see Audley Cross, that is the
old stone cross that marks the place where Lord
Audley was slain. The man's answer surprised me,
for he said no one but an idiot would ask such a
question, and he soon became furious at the thought
of any bicyclist going on his land. I hesitated a
short time whether or not to go to his landlord,
Sir G. Chetwode, at Oakley, but finally I went a
little farther where there was a cottage and a woman
drawing water up from a well. I shut my eyes to
the fact of the cottages and pig-sties being within a
few feet of the top of the well, for the woman acted
the part of a good Samaritan, and gave me ice-cold
water to drink, and from her garden wall she showed
me the cross and the battlefield.

When the rival factions of York and Lancaster
(not Lancashire and Yorkshire) plunged England into
tumult and bloodshed in what were termed the Wars
of the Roses, the King, Henry the Sixth, was descended from John of Gaunt, time-honoured Lancaster, the fourth son of Edward the Third; and as the
King was a poor, weak thing, much henpecked by his
wife, the Duke of York, who was descended from the
fifth son, and on his mother's side from the third son,
of Edward the Third, claimed the throne. The Earl
of Salisbury, who had been gathering troops in north
Yorkshire, was marching through Cheshire to meet his
son (who was afterwards known as the King-maker),
and the Duke of York, at Ludlow, with their levies
from Wales. Queen Margaret, with her son Prince
Edward, who was afterwards murdered at Tewkesbury, were at Eccleshall, and she promptly marched
with Lord Audley to stop the Earl of Salisbury as

he passed south. The armies met at Blore Heath,
where there is a small stream called the Hemp Mill
Brook, that runs into the Tern, and thence to the
Severn. Its banks are very steep and were covered
with brushwood. Salisbury had the two wings of
his army in ambush on the banks, while his centre
attacked the Lancastrians and then feigned flight.
The Lancastrians hurried in pursuit down the steep
banks of this brook, and were then set upon and
completely routed. The majority of them fled down
the brook, as it would obviously be safer than re-
climbing the slope again ; but 2400 of them were
slain, and the traditions of the country-side say that
the brook ran red with their blood. Their strength
had been in their archers, the celebrated Cheshire
bowmen ; but they seem to have been badly generalled
or unfortunate, for their bowmen were never called
on. The battle was fought on Sunday, September 23,
1459. A stone cross, which was mentioned in 1686,
and repaired in 1765, marks the spot, that is about
the centre of the battle, probably where Lord Audley,
the Lancastrian leader, fell. The battle was particularly disastrous to the men of Cheshire, for as Salisbury had just come through that country, he had got
all he could on his side, and Lord Stanley had, like
others of his race, played with both sides.

> "There Dutton Dutton kills, a Done doth kill a Done,
> A Booth a Booth, and Leigh by Leigh is overthrown,
> A Venables against a Venables doth stand,
> A Troutbeck fighteth with a Troutbeck hand to hand,
> There Molineux doth make a Molineux to die,
> And Egerton the strength of Egerton doth try —
> Oh ! Cheshire, wert thou mad ? of thine own native gore
> So much until this day thou never shed'st before."

For one instance among many, Fitton of Gaws-

THE BATTLE CROSS, BLORE HEATH.

worth took sixty-six of his tenantry and retainers
into the fight at Blore Heath, and only half of them
returned again, so there must have been mourning
and lamentation and woe at Gawsworth.   They acted
up to their old motto of "Fyte on."   Sir Hugh Ven-
ables, fourteenth lord of Kinderton, fell with most of
his clan.   The Molineux were the ancestors of the
Earls of Sephton.   Any of us whose families have
lived long in these parts must have had ancestors in
the battle.   Over their commingled dust the earth
brings forth her harvests rich and rank from the
bones and other earths that are scattered there.   Amid
the golden corn the seasons bring the blood-red
poppies whose ancestors were dyed with the blood of
men.   The wild roses that were trampled under foot
and soaked with the blood of the dying, still wave
their blossoms, the badges of the contending armies,
and fickle as Fortune herself they seem to open red—
red as the rose of Lancaster—and gradually fade away
till they are as pale as the white rose of York.   Some
there be that favour both sides, and are both red and
white, for when the rival houses had nigh extermi-
nated each other they married; and in old-fashioned
gardens, where we carefully preserve them, there are
roses whose every petal is partly red and partly white,
lineal descendants of those from the field of battle,
and fit emblems of the union of the houses of York
and Lancaster.

The results of the battle were nothing—nothing
whatever but the loss of life, the wounds of the survivors, and the miseries and troubles of the thousands
of orphans of those who were slain; for the Yorkshire
army shortly afterwards dispersed, and its leaders got
across to France for a time.   In those days they
generally fought their battles when the harvest was

over and there was not much work for idle hands
to do.

> " ' But what they fought each other for
> I could not well make out ;
> But everybody said,' quoth he,
> 'That 'twas a famous victory.' "

A Pilgrimage to Beeston and Peckforton Castles.

This was another interesting pilgrimage on a
bicycle. The distance from Didsbury and back, being
sixty-five miles, was rather too far ; but the going
through Cheshire, especially through the forest, with
its miles of purple heather, beautiful scenery, and
well-kept roads, was very fine. The Lancashire and
Cheshire Antiquarian Society had gone to Beeston
by train, and as one of them I visited the castles, and
wrote the following short account :—

We went up the winding lanes by the model
cottages and farms of Lord Tollemache, through the
stately castellated entrance to the splendid modern
mansion called Peckforton Castle. With consummate
good taste the steep hill on which the castle is built
has been left in its primeval wildness. The gnarled
weather-beaten oaks and birches grow out of millions
of bilberry and blackberry bushes, while the purple
heather and golden gorse are infinitely handsomer
than any tulips or geraniums. After a stiff climb
another fortified gateway gives entrance to the castle
courtyard, a space big enough for a regiment of yeomanry. The immense buildings of dressed stone,
where everything had to be taken up a steep crag,
must have been enormously costly.

The lofty entrance hall, with vaulted stone roof, contains some genuine good armour, and large historical paintings and portraits are in the various rooms. The banqueting hall is very different from the ordinary conventional dining-room, for the room and table are round, being in one of the projecting round towers of the castle. What a place for a library! On the mountain-top, hundreds of feet above railway whistles, barrel organs, street cries, and all the nuisances of civilisation, with no sound but the music of the winds, and yet all that wealth can buy is there, with some it cannot buy, and all around stretches one of the finest scenes man ever saw—the rich plain of Cheshire from the base of the cliff to the blue distance over the Mersey, the Dee, and the mountains of Wales. The arid dry lands where gold and jewels are found are poor beyond compare with this land of milk and honey, of waving corn and fruitful orchards, of cattle in a thousand fields—a land studded with ruined castles and abbeys, stately churches, many-gabled halls, moated manors, and cosy cottages, all teeming with the traditions of an historic past. Time flies quickly on summer afternoons, and the descent had to be made through the woods and rocks, and up the corresponding ascent to the ruins of Beeston Castle. Here driving storms swept round and obscured parts of the landscape, and even parts of the old castle itself, while other parts were in golden sunlight.

The precipitous rock of Beeston was probably used as a stronghold when first the primeval savage thought of self-preservation. The Norman Earls of Chester fortified the rock scientifically from designs brought by the Crusaders from the Holy Land, for the double line of round towers and connecting walls are believed to be copied from the fortifications of Constantinople.

Tolls were levied from all passers-by towards the cost of the work. Of course the kings soon seized such a stronghold, and Richard the Second's treasure was here when he was done with and put away. In the Civil Wars the neighbouring towns of Nantwich and Bunbury were for the Parliament, and they held Beeston ; but a Captain Sandford, with eight firelocks or musketeers, surprised the castle and took possession of all its wealth and goods, letting the garrison depart in peace. Steel, the retiring captain, was accused of treachery, and of having had too much beer, for which he was shot at Tynker's croft, Nantwich. The Royalists held the castle for a year, when the siege ended again by the garrison marching out, but the Roundheads complained bitterly that there was nothing left in the place, not a drop of beer- and that was an item in politics then as now—and nothing to eat but a bit of turkey pie, and an old peacock and peahen that were all feathers. The castle was then demolished, and has never been rebuilt. Part of its strength lay in the fact of its having a well (in Webb's time two wells) from the top of the rock to water ; a depth variously stated at from 240 to 275 feet. In former times the Beestons of Beeston owned Peckforton and other manors. The Sir George Beeston to whom there is a monument in the fine church of Bunbury, is said to have fought bravely against the Armada at the age of eighty-eight, and died at one hundred and two. One would think he could not do much fighting at that age, but perhaps he found some money and flattered the Queen. Beeston Hall sheltered Prince Rupert in the Civil War time. It furnished another instance of this foreigner's freedom with English property, for he gave orders to burn the house as soon as he had finished his dinner, and had about a score of countrymen hanged who were not quick enough in obeying his commands.

The way back by the forest as the shades of evening were drawing in, and great storm clouds gathering round, was very fine. All speed must be used, for every moment was valuable. About Tabley the storm burst in darkness as black as the blackest night could be, and one pilgrim reached home literally wet to the skin, but very happy.

A Pilgrimage to Barthomley.

The autumn of 1897 may long be remembered, for the fine weather that often comes in the middle of October, known to the old folks as St. Luke's summer, extended on until it merged in St. Martin's summer, and on November 21 I counted over forty sorts of flowers blooming in this garden at Didsbury. All through the earlier and finer part of the time Manchester was in the turmoil of the most fiercely contested municipal election it has ever known, and every day I for one yearned to be off in the country, and wondered whether the fine weather could last. It did last, the day of election being satisfactory in every way. Then came a day of rest, of paying the bills, and picking up the pieces. The next day necessary work, and early on the following morning I was up with the lark and off on the bicycle across Cheshire.

I have already taken readers down the great south road from Didsbury to Newcastle and thence to Standon, also by the longer westerly route through Knutsford and Nantwich. This time let us take a middle course. The town of Crewe has sprung into

being since road-making became almost a lost art, and
the road to it is mainly by winding country lanes. The
old road is good to Congleton, and thence there is
an old turnpike by Sandbach to Nantwich. About a
mile before Crewe Station I branched to the left for
Barthomley, in which parish Crewe Station is, or was.
The town is mainly in the old village of Monks Cop-
penhall, an appendage of the Abbey of Combermere.
When the railways were projected between Liverpool
and London, and also between Manchester and Bir-
mingham, they were to have joined at Nantwich, but
short-sighted non-progressives forced them to have
the junction away from human habitations, and in
the memory of some who are living Crewe Station
was founded where there was only one house standing on clayey land in the midst of sour grass and
danksome rushes.

The ancient parish and village of Barthomley derived its name from Bettelin, Bertham, or Bertoline,
for the name is spelt in many ways, spelling not being
of much account with saints for the same reasons that
German emperors and American presidents are above
grammar. Bertoline was one of those holy men whom
we read about, but seldom see. Once upon a time
he was very righteous, but became ensnared with a
woman and fell. That part of the tale is applicable
to others, but this woman had a child, and when the
father went to get them food the wolves devoured
both mother and child. There must have been wolves
there some time, for the little river or brook is called
the Wulvarn. After that the father became piouser
than ever, and would have nothing to do with any
one. Another account says he was a hermit who
was driven from Stafford and went to Bertham's ley,
the church being the only one in the world which is

dedicated to St. Bertoline. It is a most interesting
church, built, like so many other old churches, on a
steep hill, called the .Barrow Hill, the tower probably
having been as much a fortress as a church. There is
a beautifully ornamented Norman doorway now walled
up, and the tomb and effigy of one of the four squires
of Lord Audley who won the battle of Poictiers.
This one was Robert Fulleshurst or Fowleshurst.
Another one lately mentioned was Delves of Doddington. Fifth in descent from this Robert Fulleshurst was another of the same name, who, with
hundreds of other Cheshire men, left his bones on
the lone hills of Flodden.

In the next century the warfare came home, and
almost every house in this part of Cheshire was
plundered and burnt. On Christmas Eve, 1643, a
party of the Royalists, under Major Connaught, an
Irishman, came to Barthomley, where the people had
mostly sided with the Parliament, and the villagers
took refuge in the church. The Royalists broke open
the church, and the natives retreated up the tower.
The son of the rector is said to have fired from the
top of the tower, and everything in the church was
made into a heap and set on fire, the savage Royalists
trying to set the church on fire and burn it up with
all who were therein. The villagers and Puritans
were probably safe as long as they held the tower ;
but they yielded, and when the King's men had them
in their power they stripped them stark naked and cut
their throats in the cause of God and the King.

Here are the names of those who were butchered
on this merry Christmas in the olden time : Mr. John
ffowler, minister (probably curate and son of the rector), Henry ffowler (perhaps another son), Mr. Thomas
Elcocke (the previous rector was named Elcocke),

s

James Boughey, Randall Hassall, Richard Steele, William Steele, George Burrowes, Thomas Hollins, James Butler, Richard Cowill, and John Buttress who left a widow and seven children. Others were wounded and left for dead. Left naked and hungry in the winter, they had no sleep day or night. They dared not go home, for the savage band of Royalists quartered themselves on the neighbours and in the houses of the slain, confiscating everything they could wear, or carry, or eat.

The descendants of these victims are still in the land, and about the old place you may find the old names. It is two hundred and fifty-four years since the deed was done in one of our beautiful Cheshire villages, and the generation seventh or eighth in descent from them may here read for the first time of the murder of their forefathers. Details of the massacre have seldom or never been given, for historians lean too much to the side of their patrons, and it is fashionable, though untrue, to lay all the blame of the spoiling of the churches on Cromwell and the Puritans. In this case the Royalists burnt everything they could burn in the church, and the historians dismiss the massacre of Barthomley with one or two lines, leaving it almost an open question as to which side did it. I have heard even venerable-looking clergy confess that they did not like speaking of it, "for it was done by the wrong side." Sir Thomas Byron, the Royalist commander at the time, justified it, writing : "They put them all to the sword—the best way to proceed with their kind of people, for mercy to them is cruelty." The church registers should give details of the burials, if nothing else were given, but the leaves for that time have been cut out, doubtless by some fanatical Royalist.

Nowadays the church is beautiful once more. The carved oaken roofs are very fine, as is the screen of Jacobean work round the organ. Aloft on it is very appropriately placed one of the oldest texts from one of the oldest records, " Let there be no strife, for we are brethren." In the centre of the Crewe chapel, 'mid the time-worn effigies of mail-clad warrior and robed priest, there is a beautiful pale marble recumbent statue of Sibyl, the wife of the second Lord Houghton. It looked so life-like that, in a silence as deep as the grave—for in the still November air there was no sound of bird or wind—I crept softly away, fearful of disturbing that last sweet sleep.

From Barthomley I cycled a little farther round to see Audley church. It used to be said that one of the clerks of Barthomley, who was also schoolmaster and host of the White Lion, got very drunk at times. In those days, as at Didsbury, the clerk of the church often kept the village alehouse. Nowadays not even a churchwarden would be allowed to keep one. The parsons look upon the publicans as the Pharisees of old looked upon them. The alehouse is abandoned to the brewer, and the last state is worse than the first, for the brewer and his man are only welcomed when money is to be begged, or there is an election at hand. This clerk went with some farmers to draw the rector's coals from the pits at Audley (a small survival of the feudal tenures), and they took a barrel of beer in the cart and had a spree. The clerk got so sleepy drunk that they took him down a coalpit and left him. When the naked colliers roused him and asked who he was, he said. "Oh, please good master devils, I was clerk of Barthomley when I was on earth, but now I'm what you please."

Journeying the few miles to Audley I found the

country gradually getting more like that of the Staffordshire potteries, so I made a hurried visit to the church and came away. Over the west door of the church is a painting of the Crucifixion in a vesica, over the pulpit is a large crucifix, another on the altar with banners and finery. Another altar and crucifix, with coloured statue of the Madonna and child, caused me to think that I had got into the wrong church, so I took a book off the altar to read what it said, and there I saw something about Sarum on the title-page, when I thought spectators might be shocked at my presumption, and I had better be minding my work and getting home, for there were twelve miles of country lanes before me. A cyclist told me that as I was cycling I had better go a few miles round to get to Madeley, and strike into the Nantwich and Newcastle road at Betley. That village I knew with its quaint old houses, some of them built in the original manner with roughly adzed oak-trees meeting at the ridge of the roof—solid black oak, half a yard thick, worth more than all the house and garden. In Betley Hall is the famous window with coloured pictures of the Morris dancers. It is thought to be about the date of Henry the Eighth and Katherine of Arragon, and shows the costumes of Morris dancers and the Queen of the May at the Maypole. Betley Pool, which is to be seen from the railway beyond Crewe, is in two parishes, two dioceses, and under the jurisdiction of two Archbishops, Canterbury and York. In some parts of the pool a little fish when being swallowed by a big fish might object, " This is not your diocese, you have no right here, I shall complain to my Archbishop."

At Madeley we come to more pools and memories of Izaak Walton. His famous work, " The Compleat

Angler," was dedicated to John Offley of Madeley Manor. It is said to have gone through more editions than any other book excepting " Pilgrim's Progress." The latest edition is about the one hundred and thirtieth, and is dedicated to the Earl of Crewe, John Offley's far-descended son—

> " Lord of the Madeley peace, the quiet grass,
> The lilied pond, and muffled sleepy mill ;
> Lord of each legendary fish that swims
> Deep down and swift beneath that emerald glass ;
> While, soft as shadows, round its grassy rims
> The patient anglers move from east to west.
> Patient at morn, at evening patient still—
> Peace, if not fish, is theirs, and peace is best."

Yes, peace is best, I keep repeating to myself as I bowl through the charming village alongside the placid pool and patient anglers. There is the old black and white house with its inscription in the oak, " Walk, knave, what look'st at ? " The clipped yew-trees, the quaint church, the alms-houses, the allotment gardens with their handsome fountain, which the traveller may see near to the railway station, and the charities, remind me of that clause in the will of Sir John Offley, the son of the Lord Mayor of London : " Item, I will and devise one Jewell done all in Gold and Enamelled wherein there is a Caul that covered my face and shoulders when I first came into the world . . . to my own right Heirs Males for ever, and so from Heir to Heir so long as it shall please God in goodness to continue any Heir Male of my name, to be never concealed or sold by any of them." The heirs male have failed, but the line exists in the Earl of Crewe, and so long as that jewelled caul is cherished as a precious heirloom the luck shall never leave the Crewes, and they and the charities shall flourish.

Soon after leaving Madeley I have to dismount to trundle the bicycle over the Maer hills and through the woods, that is, over the watershed of England down to the tiny church and palatial hall at Maer, which I have mentioned before, for here the three different routes join, and another short ascent brings me, as the shades of evening close round the calm November day, to the hospitable old house in which I sleep for probably the last time.

STANDON POST-OFFICE

CHAPTER XVII

VOTERS

" For thy favours done to us in our election, I give thee thanks."—TITUS ANDRONICUS.

N the autumn of 1893 I conceived the idea of personally canvassing the voters of that ward of the city of Manchester in which myself and family had for many years been in business. I had no expectations of winning the seat at the City Council at the first trial, especially as no one whatever was supporting me ; but I thought I should win some day, and the experience of canvassing every one would certainly be valuable, although it was hard work.

As events happened, I had four contests in four years. The first I lost by 140 votes ; the second I lost by 36 ; the third I won by 50 ; the fourth I won by 206.

The reader should imagine himself starting on a canvass, that is, literally asking for votes from door to door. The only guide he has is a list of the voters in the ward, which list can be obtained at the town hall, and after issuing an address, which is sent to each elector, he calls and asks them if they will vote for him. I started at one corner of the ward where Market Street and High Street join, and from there I worked steadily street by street. It took my spare hours in the daytime for about two months. The voters are nearly all business men occupying offices or shops of all degrees. There are scarcely any of the ordinary small householders. If any one wishes for a cure for ennui or a sluggish liver, let him canvass all the free and independent electors in a city ward where there are hundreds of thousands of stairs ; it will open his mind and his bowels, and give him an interesting reminiscence for the rest of his life. The experience is decidedly useful. The "cheek" may be hardened, but the mind must be broadened through the interviews with all sorts and conditions of men.

Mr. Voter A says, "I'm a Conservative, and if you are one I'll vote for you. If you're not, I won't, so that's straight."

B says, " I am a strict Liberal, and always vote with my party." These answers are repeated *ad nauseam*. They remind me of the days in Rome when each was for his party and none were for the State.

C says, "I come to town to do business, and will vote for any man who will give me a good order." This answer also is repeated many times, though it is generally better wrapped up.

D says, "I vote by ballot. What right have you to come here asking me how I vote? What business is it of yours? What's the Ballot Act for? What's——" "A soft answer turneth away wrath," and some answers are very soft.

E says, "Vote for you, old fellow ; if I'd ten votes you should have them all. What's it all about? Come and sit down." Doth not a meeting like this make amends?

F wants to know my opinion of the coal strike,
and advocates the agitators being shot; seems rather
grieved that I am not thoroughgoing enough to have
somebody shot.

G informs me that shopkeepers should never vote,
as it interferes with business, and therefore he has not
voted for twenty years. " Letting ' I dare not ' wait
upon ' I would,' like the poor cat in th' adage."

H asks if I own the Green Dragon ; says he has
been done out of it. If his great-grandfather had not
married a drunken old besom when he was in his
dotage, they would have had all that property. Interesting information for an antiquarian, and of course it
carries the vote.

I is a well-dressed, prosperous-looking gentleman,
who thinks our Town Council are a low lot on the
whole. Says there are too many outsiders among
them and the magistrates. He wants local men, and
his first and chief question would be, " Have you been
long in the city ? " My reply is blunt, but scarcely
diplomatic : " I have been here since I was born. I
could not be here much sooner, you know." It is
satisfactory, and the vote is pledged, although a man
hath no honour where he is born and bred.

J is greatly surprised, and asks, " But are you
really the candidate himself ? Why, I have been here
thirty years and never saw one before. Well, this is
just as things should be. Of course, I will vote for
you."

K says he wants a candidate who has nothing
whatever to do with politics. He detests politics in
municipal affairs. He will certainly vote for me, and
get me all the votes he can.

L is a seedy, haggard-looking individual, who says
his chief concern is to combat the demon drink, with

its body and soul destroying traffic. The reader will
feel we are now getting nearer heaven—up in the
attics, in fact.

M avows himself to be a Socialist, and has advanced ideas on the brotherhood of man. Finally he
pays me the greatest compliment I receive, for he says
he is also a phrenologist, and will vote for me.

N wants to argue. That's all right if he won't
be too long about it. He who argues is hooked—old
proverb slightly altered.

O, an Owdham chap: "What's tha getten for th'
job. Tha mun get summat. Nay, nay, I'll ne'er believe tha traypses up them steears but tha kops summat
some road." We are getting down to earth again.

P, an intelligent foreigner: "Vat do you vant—
somesin' scheap? Vote—oh yaas, Mr. ——, I vill
vote for you." But he names my opponent's name,
and I explain that I want him to vote for me, not for
my opponent. "Of course I vote for you, no feear.
Zee ow awfly scheap goods." "Breed is stronger
than pasture"—good old proverb.

Q, a stout, eupeptic party, with a red face and a
big blue tie spotted with white: "Why, t'other beggars
have just been cadgin' for my vote." The words are
not written as they were uttered, for he spoke in the
vulgar tongue, and used archaisms.

R, a female, who persistently giggles. Rather
embarrassing.

S, a handsome, well-dressed young swell, with
slightly curled moustache and well-polished tanned
boots. He says he is a Tory, and would never vote
for those low Radicals, who try to upset everything.
Then he promises to vote for me, as I am the first
who has asked him. An eminent judge said it was a
mistake to give reasons for your decision.

T, an irritable old party, evidently very rich and
very miserable, says, "Why should I vote for you?
I don't know you; I never saw you before." I explain that is the very reason why I came to show
myself to him. But this explanation vexes him still
more, and he gets worse, and might have a fit. The
poor man's riches make him suspicious, and he is
better left alone.

U, in answer to my inquiry if Mr. U is in, says,
" Why, don't you know me? Bless me, I've known
you since you were in petticoats. Oh, I shall be only
too pleased to vote for some one I have seen. We
generally have ragged lads asking us to vote for some
one we never did see and are never likely to see."

V says, "Aye, aye, if you get in you'll guzzle and
booze like the rest of them, and let the officials do as
they like. One is as bad as another, and if he isn't
they soon make him so." This man is all lamentations
and woe. Perhaps his trade or his liver is bad, or he
may be henpecked.

W wishes to know if I would vote for the suppression of barrel-organs? Most certainly. And for
the suppression of all hideous noises and the shouting
of papers? Certainly; most happy. Don't know that
I ever should be asked, but that is a trifle.

X has the garrulity of a parson, with the reserva-
tions and circumlocutions of a lawyer. He will not
promise anything to anybody, but he will give my
case his favourable consideration, and will even go
further, and say—what he will not say to the other
side that after due deliberation with his partner he
will endeavour to decide between two good men, and
do his best to meet my views. Good morning, Mr.
Facing Bothways.

Y says bluntly, "Oh, you are the man who won't

let the police have all their own way, and also objects
to our Council paying a female more than a pound a
day to teach girls to make skirts and flounces. I
shall vote for you if I'm alive—no mistake about
that."

Z says, "Now, old friend, what's the good of
running your head again' a wall by trying to get in
independently? You canner do it; no man can.
These wirepullers and political clubs and committees
won't let you. Take one side or the other—there's
six o' one an' half-a-dozen o' t'other. I've had a deal
of experience, and worked for both sides, and I tell
you the Liberals can beat the Tories into fits at lying.
They'll promise anything and everything. But th'
Tories can beat them at boozing, and that goes for a
great deal if there's cheap drink to be got. You say
you don't want to lie or to drink, but you mun do one
or t'other to get in, and you mun knuckle under to
these committees. That's what keeps so many good
men out of our councils. There are some good uns
in, of course, but there's a vast of t'other sort, and
you may as well oss to fly to heaven as go in
independently." A very impartial summary.

After having exhausted the letters of the alphabet,
the public clamoured for more "answers," and seemed
anxious to identify themselves or their friends.

1. An old man in a dark cellar. Says he was one
of the old Chartists, and is still a thorough Radical.
He always sticks to his party in the ward, for they
have always had the very best men to represent them,
and if they put up a stump he should vote for it.
What a sublime faith! And yet the parsons are con-
stantly asking for more faith—or more money.

2. Says he "shanner vote for no one. What's th'
odds? It's all same to us. We get nowt by it. Things

is awtered so. We'd usedened to get a bit. Maybe if a load o' coal were dumped down my cellar I'd vote an' not ax questions neither. But them as has a bit wunner part."

3. A man in a bad temper. Asks if I am a free-trader. Yes. A free-trader in work? I don't understand. Then he broke out, "Corporation officials come here asking what wages I pay my workmen before they'll give me orders for work, but I'll dress 'em down. Now, what would you do?" I prefer not to meddle with strife that belongeth not to me.

4. A struggling young man, who has grudges against the police. Asks me to tell him some of my experiences of them. I give him some blood-curdling ones, and am even mentioning names and rank, when we are suddenly startled by a gruff voice close to us that comes from under a helmet, and says, "If yer don't take yer dust-bin in I'll get yer fined five bob and costs; so look sharp." "Talk of the devil"—the proverb's somewhat musty. Let us leave for a while these common folk, and get among the big men in the chief streets.

5. A magistrate for the city. It behoves one to be circumspect and to walk delicately; but the J.P. promises like any ordinary man, and seems very nice and middling honest, yet he turns out to be a little given to lying, for he never voted at all, although on the day of election he said he had voted. Our catechism teaches us "to honour and obey, to order ourselves lowly and reverently to all our betters and those who are set in authority over us."

6. A shopkeeper in the literary line. Says he has promised the other side, but he'll vote for me all the same, for shopkeepers have to promise both sides to keep their customers together.

7. Tailors. Promised all right, but never polled. Perhaps they also promised both sides and tried to act impartially. The public think that under the sweet simplicity of the Ballot Act, if they promise their votes no one will know anything more about them, but they are mistaken. "Where ignorance is bliss, 'tis folly to be wise."

8. Another tailor. What scores of them there are, and how they look at one's old clothes! This one pledges faithfully, and is so agreeable, but he never polled. We have heard of Israelites in whom there was no guile, but that was long ago, and in another country.

9. A ladies' tailor or dressmaker. The master was out, but the missus was in. She asks if it was I who mentioned about the Council paying more than a pound a day for girls to be taught to stitch on trimmings and cut out flounces. She thinks it monstrous, and her husband shall certainly vote for me; and then she follows me to the stairs for further conversation, and calls out to me over the banisters as I slowly descend, "I'll take good care he votes for you." "Like music o'er the waters came her sweet voice unto me."

10. A consequential individual, with abundance of jewellery, who says he shall not vote at all, for he comes of a good old Whig family, and "I can assure you, sir, that since that lunatic Gladstone went for Home Rule it has ruined trade. The very day he took office the receipts of this shop fell off, and they have fallen away ever since, and what will be done I don't know. But I'll vote for nothing or nobody but to turn out that old villain."

11. A man wise in his own conceit—and we know what hope there is of them. Says that he could not support any one who had ever been engaged in the demoralising traffic in drink or tobacco. He exhibits

a grand illuminated card about half a yard square,
showing he is a member of the Anti-Narcotic League.
He is also an Anti-Vaccinationist, and preaches on a
Sunday. *Miserere Domine!* I have had some horrible
sermons inflicted on me before now—sermons that
have made men swear, and done more harm than
"taking money tarnished with the blood of my fellow-
creatures." So the best thing to do is to quietly leave
this local saint, and wish the other side joy of him. I
wonder if he is on their committee.

12. A dentist. I feel rather nervous, but things
might be worse. "There was never yet philosopher
who could endure toothache patiently."

13. A chiropodist, and in the same building a
female one under another name. I wonder whether
they are man and wife. They try to be pleasant, and
promise ; but one, at least, does not perform.

14. I was shown into a drawing-room full of ladies,
and got frightened. I rushed out again, and asked
the footman for explanations. Then I learnt that his
master was the great ladies' doctor, and I fled.

15. A showy, handsome swell asks me questions
to test me. I soon infer that he is a Tory, whose
chief ideas are for big men and little rates. He is
hard to hook ; but at last he says, "I shall only vote
for some one who has some property, something at
stake in the city." I reply that I own the Spread
Eagle Hotel property, and he says at once, "Oh, that
is quite sufficient, I will vote for you with pleasure."

16. Another crank. He knows me, and says,
"Are not you the owner of the Spread Eagle Hotel?
Then I would not vote for you on any account whatever. I will have no excuses or explanations. If I
had a public-house given to me to-day, I would not
go to bed before I got rid of any connection with it."

This man actually voted, and spoilt his ballot-paper by writing across it that neither candidate was good enough for him.

17. A licensed house kept by a widow. Licensed houses are generally kept by widows; their poor husbands are gone to heaven long ago. Widows don't like putting on their best things and going out in the wet to vote.

18. Photographers. They all get in the attics, as near heaven as they can, whilst plumbers gravitate in the opposite direction. From a photographer's point of view, the first duty of every candidate is to have his likeness taken. I explain that I dabble in the art myself. They say that is merely amateur's work, and they smile in pity.

19. Estate agents. They are always out on Mondays, but some of them ask plenty of questions on other days. Here are two questions: Whose duty is it to clean a dirty house, the owner's, the tenant's, or the Corporation's? What is the difference between a road and a street? When Shakspere wrote about lawyers that would circumvent heaven, estate agents had not been discovered, or it would have been interesting to have had his remarks about them.

20. A vegetarian restaurant, where you can dine off Eccles cakes and pop. The poor old cat sits with tears in its eyes, wondering if it will ever get a bit of fish or fowl again. A paper states that a pound of beans contains more nutriment than a pound of beef, and yet the beef costs ten times the price. So it ought to do; it's worth it. It might have added that the seller of the beans gets more profit and the eater of them more flatulency, but they don't give the whole truth, and no doubt they will "vote by ballot."

21. An eating-house with a strong smell of beef-

steak and onions, and what a gorgeous smell it is! The poor lads in the street stop and sniff, and their eyes gleam like the eyes of wolves, or as hungry dogs when they are fed. Their eyes would not shine like that at the smell of beans or boiled cabbage, not if all the doctors in Manchester swore that a vegetarian diet would be better for them.

22. A fine, old-fashioned, double-chinned Tory. Wants to know if my stomach and digestion can stand the Corporation feeding. Also if I ever heard what old Cobbett said about getting on with the big folks : I must either kick their body or kiss it. He thought I should prefer kicking it. He should vote for me "chus how," for he knew my father, and liked a good Tory, or a good Radical either, but he "hated them Liberal Conservatives, milk-and-water psalm-singing devils."

23. A rabid bimetallist. Says he will vote for me, of course, for he has known me all my life ; but he wishes I would read and try to improve my mind, for on the subjects of bimetallism or protection my ideas, he says, are simply chaotic and idiotic ; we are all being slowly ruined, and trade is worse than ever was known. That, I say, is variously attributed to the coal dispute, to drink, to Gladstone, to the decay of faith, and various other causes, bimetallism being considered gibberish. Then he swears, and says, "You never think. You think you think without thinking; but if you would only try to think, you would soon find that all the ruin in the country is being caused by obstinate stupid folks like yourself, who will not believe in bimetallism, and people are getting depressed and falling victims to influenza. They cannot even buy boots and clothes, and rheumatism is increasing through it." So, after an hour's

T

argument on a dual standard, we gradually think we
thought we thunk, but we feel sure the glad time
spoken of by the prophet Cade is now near at hand,
when "there shall be in England seven halfpenny
loaves sold for one penny, and it shall be felony to
drink small beer."

24. A mysterious place with several doors, and
people hurrying to and fro, who seem to make money
out of nothing. An old tale comes to my memory of
a city man telling a country man that he would show
him hell with all the devils at work. The man from
the country came to town to see the dreadful sight,
and through a peep-hole he was shown the members
of the Stock Exchange shrieking and gesticulating.
This is something like a Stock Exchange, for it turns
out to be a betting club in a large way of business.
There are two detectives coming slowly up, who are
evidently coming to obtain information or to put a bit
on. I wonder if it will be their own money they put
on, or the money of the ratepayers provided by the
Watch Committee. Perhaps that is left an open
question until after the event. I wonder if the Watch
Committee ever win, and if so, what they do with the
winnings. Do they give them to a chapel, or do they
have a jollification? When it is my turn, a smart-
looking swell asks me if I am going to the post, and
how many entries there are. Then he irreverently
remarks, " If the other bloke gets scratched you'll
have a walk over. Good biz that. But I'll lay short
odds again' you, just to be doing a bit. What odds
do you want?" I reply that I want no odds, I want
his vote ; but he wants business.

25. Asks me what religion I am. I should like to
ask him what he means by religion, but that might
offend his religious feelings. I tell him that I had

determined to contest the election without any reference to religion or politics. I had been continually
asked about the latter, but never about the former,
and therefore I hoped he would not ask me. He
promised to vote for me, or gave me to understand he
promised, but he never polled.

26. A rational teetotaller this time. Offers me a
seat on a sofa, and says he has known me since I
wore a pinafore; asks a lot of questions, and very
practical ones too, for a wonder. Wants to know,
first of all, if I advocate the Council building model
houses and letting the rooms at a loss. Did I know
how many licensed houses they now own? Did I
ever hear of the chairman and vice-chairman of an
important committee formerly selling their beer to any
of these houses? Did I know anything of wash-out
closets, of gully traps, of socketed pipes? I replied
that I knew I had a deal to learn, and finally the vote
got promised and polled.

27. A man from the Land o' Cakes, with a book
full of blank forms for any one to sign and "take the
pledge." Is it a popular error about Scotch being
fond of "Scotch"?

28. A pug-nosed man. Asks if I will vote for
rents being reduced. I reply that the very thing I
am trying to do is to reduce rates, and that is practically the same thing. "Bedad, sorr, ye're the very
mon I'm saking afther. Shake hands," and we shook.

29. Members of the oldest, the largest, and the
most respectable, and therefore the poorest trade in
the world, who, with great care and very little profit,
supply the daily food of this great city and its suburbs,
and yet have no representative in the City Council!
"Poor and content is rich and rich enough."

30. A lady-like man in the tea trade. These tea-

dealers have a good innocent trade, with plenty of profit and little expense, but they are hard to please, and wriggle a deal before they promise. Perhaps the liquoring up makes them dyspeptic.

31. Says he shall certainly not vote for me, and will tell me why, as I ask. It is because he has known me for about thirty years and yet I never speak to him. I assure him that I was not aware of ever having seen him before; but he does not believe me, and says, "Why, I have seen you thousands of times, and you never speak or move to me; and now, as soon as you want something out of me, you can come bothering fast enough. No, I will not vote for you. I'm not going to be humbugged."

32. Says he would have voted for me with pleasure if he had been asked sooner, but a customer persuaded him to promise the other side, and as a man of honour he must keep his word. Then on the day of election he went to vote as a man of honour, but his ballot-paper was refused him, as he had already voted in another ward.

33. Asks, if he votes for me, will I vote for him getting the contracts for his goods that he offers to the Council? He says he always makes that bargain, and other candidates have agreed. It seems a case to be left to canvassers. I merely promise to remember him.

34. Says he had meant to vote for me, but my wife had been bothering him, and he did not know what to do now. I say I never had a wife; I daren't, and I couldn't afford. But he sticks to his text, and says, "A woman has been here, saying she was your wife, th' candidate's own wife, and she talked enough to moyther a growing tree. I was minding this machine, and had to keep one eye on it and one on her, and she talked such rubbitch and such a lot on it, I

thought, Why canner 'er mind th' babby, or get
someut cooked? But if you say you know nowt about
her, I'll vote for you as I said; but I'd send th' police
after yon woman." "Not I," I replied; "the police
are fond enough of going after the women without
being set on."

35. A good young man, with pale freckled face
and red hair. He turns his toes in, holds one shoulder
up and his head on one side. He seems great on
Sunday observance, and asks me if I would vote for
keeping the Sabbath day holy. "Certainly," I reply.
"What do you mean by 'holy'?" Slowly and pain-
fully his ideas evolve out of chaos, and then he asks,
"Do you ride a bicycle on Sunday?" I never did in
my life, for I never had one (this was in 1893). I
ride a horse, but not on Sundays. That pleases him,
and he partly promises; but he will probably fall a
prey to the lady canvassers. How they will enjoy
themselves with him!

The reader may see from these cross-questions
and crooked answers, that if a man be desirous of
serving an ungrateful public, he may do a deal of
really hard work in showing himself to and learning
the views of those he hopes to benefit and serve. He
will also find that a college education will not enable
him to answer their puzzling questions, or even to
understand their various dialects. An important
thing for the candidate to do is to get an influential
committee, and if he does not wish to go as a political
delegate he must get men of good repute, tolerably
honest, and as truthful as a prospectus. They should
be gifted with an infinite capacity for making promises
and giving orders, "shipping" orders sometimes, and
of course more or less unauthorised. Then when they
are in the fight they will go on for fighting's sake, and

if the election be not won it is the fault of the electors, and all parties must abide by it.

The canvasser, if he be an old resident in the district, will find many strange men and strange manners in the increased foreign element. The only church in the ward has lately vanished, not one stone remains upon another, and round the site of it there swarm the Greek, the Jew, the Vandal, and the Goth. For centuries past our National Church has regularly used a special prayer for "Jews, Turks, Infidels, and Hereticks," and yet they are gaining on her, as may be seen by the names on the doorposts round the vacant site of the church. In other parts of the ward the natives are also being crowded out, literally driven from their business and from their place, steadily, unceasingly, and unrelentingly, by tribes of men who are not of our speech, or manners, or religion, or race. The natives themselves are sometimes curiosities, rude in speech, and peculiar in manner, yet fairly "jannock." If we are to have the blessings of free government, and there are queer folk among the electors, we must not be surprised if there are queer folk among the elected.

CHAPTER XVIII

THE LOCAL BOARD OF DIDDLETON

(An Imaginary Farce)

*" Dost thou not suspect my place ? Dost thou not
suspect my years ? Oh that he were here to
write me down an ass ! but, masters, remember
that I am an ass ; though it be not written down,
yet forget not that I am an ass.—Oh, thou villain,
thou art full of piety, as shall be proved upon thee
by good witness.—I am a wise fellow, and one
that knows the law, go to : and a rich fellow,
go to : and a fellow that hath had losses : and,
which is more, an official : and, which is more, a
ratepayer."*—DOGBERRY.

SCENE.—*The Local Board Offices. The Sanitary Committee sitting.* JEREMIAH BILDER, Esq., J.P., *in the
chair. Members Present*—Messrs. JONES, BROWN, and
ROBINSON, *retired gentlemen, interested in building ;*
Mr. BLACK, *a Scotchman, who also builds a bit at
times ;* Mr. WHITE, *a reformer ;* and Mr. GREY, *of
no particular colour ;* the Clerk, the Medical Officer,
and the Surveyor.

The MEDICAL OFFICER reports : " In accordance
with instructions given, I beg to report that I have
visited the house called Laburnum Villa in the
Celestial Road, and I find the whole of the premises

in a very insanitary condition. The drains are defective and insufficiently trapped, and the smell is abominable. There is an old pan-closet upstairs, with a deficient supply of water, and the soil-pipe leaks into the meat cellar. The downspouts have defective joints, and the ventilating shafts open below the bedroom windows. There have been three cases of sickness and one death in the house.

Mr. GREY. Why is not the name of the owner given?

Mr. WHITE. The premises should be closed at once ; they are unfit for human habitation.

Mr. BLACK. What does the Medical Officer suggest?

The M. O. It would be rather exceeding my duty to make suggestions. I merely report.

Mr. BLACK. Then what does the Clerk say, or the Surveyor—has he nothing to say ?

The SURVEYOR. Structural alterations to remedy some of the defects might be made ; but, to be of permanent value, they would have to be very extensive and costly.

The CLERK read an extract from an Act of Parliament bearing on the subject of insanitary dwellings, which he soon contradicted and confused by a section of another Act.

The CHAIRMAN suggested that the whole matter be left in the hands of Messrs. Jones, Brown, and Robinson, with power to settle.

Mr. GREY. That would be leaving the matter with three builders, whose interest it is to evade the law. I demand to know who is the owner of the premises.

Mr. WHITE. I second the demand for the owner's name, and would close such jerry premises at once.

Thereupon the scene became stormy, all the members storming at once at Messrs. Grey and White, and Mr. Black remonstrated with them, saying, "Why should they be always against the builders? People must have cheap houses to live in. I have been begged to build more cheap houses, for the public know I'm honest ; and why should I make the walls nine inches thick when four and a half is plenty, and the poor people can have the extra space inside the room? If I am a Scotchman, I am honest, any one knows that, and I don't build nearly as many houses as Mr. Jones does. It's a shame for people like Mr. Grey or Mr. White to be setting every one against the poor builders, who work for next to nothing, doing all they can for the public, and are as honest as they are."

Gradually the information was given that the house was owned and built by Mr. Brown, whereupon Mr. White remarked, "Yes, I thought it would be one of the old gang." Then Mr. Brown lost his temper, and spake in the dialect to which he was born. " I wunner 'low ony on yo' to ca' me one o' th' owd gang, an' say as 'ow I builds jerry. I wur born an' bred i' th' parish, an' bin buildin' a' my life, an' never once built a bit o' jerry—not me. Nor I wunner a' thi talkin' to me an' that uns. I can o'erdraw my 'count at my banker's seven hoondert pounds, an' that's more than mony on yo' can. An' I drives my own carriage, an' that's wot mony on yo' don't. Yo' munner talk to me, for I wunner 'ave it. I know what dreens is, an' I tells yo' them dreens is a' good, bricks on eend an' mortared. If folk fillen them wi' rubbitch, an' it chokes 'em, whose fau't is it?—not mine. They ne'er 'ad closets when I wur a lad, nor eddication, nor pleegrounds. I ne'er pleed, nor 'ad eddication neither, but I con buy most on yo' up, an' I wunner be talked to by yo', an', wot's more, I wunner do naught; so theer."

The CHAIRMAN. I'll not allow these cowardly and blackguardly attacks to be made on respectable men like Mr. Brown. If Mr. Brown has no other claims to respectability, he's a relation of mine ; and as to the houses he builds, any one can see them, and they speak for themselves. It's like the low, mean, dirty work of these meddling reformers to be always making mischief, but I'll not let the blackguards do it as long as I'm in the chair. Poor folk must have cheap houses ; how can they afford big rents? It's very good of builders to build for those poor people who cannot help themselves. As Mr. Brown is interested in the houses, I would suggest Mr. Black's name instead of his, and let the sub-committee settle the matter.

The resolution was then put to the meeting, and carried by five votes to two, and the drains remained choked, and the soil-pipe leaked into the meat cellar, until further orders.

CHAPTER XIX

RELICS OF THE TUDORS

*" Life's but a walking shadow ; a poor player,
That struts and frets his hour upon the stage,
And then is heard no more."*—MACBETH.

HIS chapter is composed of two articles
that were written at the request of the
Art Gallery Committee of the Corporation of Manchester, to draw the attention of the public to the very interesting
collection of pictures, armour, books,
and other relics of the times of the Tudor kings and
queens, that were gathered together in the City Art
Gallery in the summer of 1897.

If the proper study of mankind be man, there is a
good opportunity of making that study through history
and art, socially and politically, by noting how the
makers of history in one of its most stirring times
looked in life in the clothes they wore, and with the
passions on their faces, as shown by the likenesses of
the Tudors, kings and queens, and their contemporaries,
with the weapons they used and the books they had,
that are now being exhibited at the Manchester City
Art Gallery.

The first of the Tudors, the first man with any
Welsh breed in him to get the throne of England, was

Henry the Seventh, and does not his likeness in the picture by Jan de Mabuse, where he meets his bride at the church door for the union of the houses of Lancaster and York, agree with his reputed character—a sad, sour, mean miser, clutching at everything he could get.   His bride, "the white rose of York," looks much too good for him, though she has the red hair that is not liked in folk-lore.   Their three children, what greedy, self-willed brats they look!   How they would cam and squabble and stuff!   One of them fortunately "took good ways," while another rose to be one of the most famous, or infamous, of England's kings.   He and his victims are plentiful enough in the next room. Let us note here his grandmother, Margaret Beaufort, who wore out three husbands and then became a nun. It was time she did, for writing books, founding colleges, and beautifying churches absorbed the rest of her energies, and her work, marked with the portcullis, the badge of the Beauforts, still exists in stone and glass and oak in many of our beautiful old buildings. Another woman of the same type, but not so desperately pious, we shall see further on in Bess of Hardwick.   Grammar-school boys should note the picture of the founder of the Manchester Grammar School.   He was a native of the town, and the picture is from Corpus Christi College, which he also helped to found.   Other portraits in this room are from Knowsley, of the first Earls of Derby, who got their vast estates in this neighbourhood by their great treachery on the battlefield of Bosworth.   Their family motto is, " Sans changer," but they have changed oftener than most families ; and here is young George, who had so near a shave of his head on that troubled day.   " Off goes young George's head."

In the next room is a copy of the effigy of Henry

the Seventh, by Torrigiano, the man who broke the
nose of Michael Angelo, and all round are the great
Harry, his wives and victims.   It was said the Reformation first saw light in Anne Boleyn's eyes, and
without doubt the King quarrelled with the Church
of Rome because it would not sanction his divorce
and second marriage to one whose family was not
friendly to the pretensions of the priests.   Here are
several portraits of Anne Boleyn, or Bullen, and some
articles of her dress.   She appears a fairly good-looking,
pleasant young lady, probably of easy manners and
virtue, who was pitched up and cast down by fortune
in an extraordinary way.   She was married in a hurry,
before her husband's divorce, for there was no time to
lose if the expected heir to the throne was to have
any pretensions to legitimacy.   They made her queen,
and anointed that young head with the sacred oil, and
crowned it with the crown of the Confessor, and shortly
after chopped it off and rolled it in the sawdust, for
the expected heir was a wench, a red-haired one.
Jane Seymour, one of her maids of honour, being
publicly married to the King the day after Anne was
beheaded, was put in her place, and was made to
understand she must bring forth a son, like unto the
King, or look out for squalls and the scaffold.   She is
here also, a good-looking, pleasant woman, who brought
the son, and, taking good ways, left them all to it.
The son took after his mother, as you may see by his
portraits in the next room, a good-looking English
lad, delicate, with a wistful, sad expression.

The next to have the offer of being Queen of
England was Christina, Duchess of Milan.   Look
well at her picture by Holbein.   It is said that in old
houses, where the family portraits hang on the walls
for generations, the spirits at times return as the church

clock tolls midnight, and the pictured ones descend from their frames to glide around their old haunts. If the crowd round this Christina would only keep quiet, she looks as if she might descend even here in broad daylight. I saw one of our wealthy citizens, whom I know to be very hard of belief, feeling at the glass that enclosed her as if he really were doubtful as to her being alive and warm. She was very much alive at one time, for to the offer of being Queen of England she replied, " She had but one head ; if she had two, one should be at his Highness's service."

The immense picture from Hampton Court of the Field of the Cloth of Gold is well worth study in its numerous details. The old houses and dresses, the stone figures on the battlements as if they were casting down stones, the ovens for baking bread, the feasting, and the effects of free drinks when the "fountains ran with wine," were similar to what they would be to-day. The head of the King is said to have been cut out of the picture by Charles the Second, who perhaps was a little envious of him. There are many other portraits of the King in many wonderful costumes, but be he dressed ever so grand he looks a bloated brute. See the lecherous, overfed dog dancing with Anne Boleyn, and then look at the fine head of another victim, Sir Thomas More, the author of " Utopia," Speaker of the House, Lord Chancellor, saint, and martyr, with many other portraits of the best and noblest in England, who one after the other died under the headsman's axe. Henry the Eighth certainly broke every one of the Ten Commandments, regularly and systematically, although he was the first Defender of the Faith, and the first Supreme Head on earth under Christ of the Church of England. In another room is a drawing of the head of Thomas,

Lord Cromwell, his minister, the *malleus monachorum*, or hammer of the monks. He is often confounded with the great Oliver who flourished a hundred years after. This one acted on the saying of "Down with the nests and the rooks will fly, while we get the eggs." He overthrew the religious houses, spoiled the churches, and hanged their custodians, as suited himself in that terrible time of terror. Look at the great heavy jaw of that brute also, and think what a blessing death often is. Here, too, is the Lord High Cardinal, the famous Wolsey, the builder of Hampton Court and founder of Christ Church College, Oxford. He it was who set his King before his God, and in his "Ego et rex meus" set himself before his King—

> "Had I but served my God with half the zeal
> I served my King, He would not in mine age
> Have left me naked to mine enemies."

Wolsey, "who sounded all the depths and shoals of honour," the Archbishop, the Cardinal, Prince of the Church, who spent the wealth of England in furthering his claims to the chair of St. Peter, to the triple crown of Rome, to be the Vicar of Christ on earth—can these coarse fat chops and swollen paunch be his? They look more like those of the butcher's pup from Ipswich. How the breed shows through all the priestly pomp and churchman's pride. Something more substantial than "arrogance, spleen, and pride" swelled that bloated figure. In the later portrait the back of his neck is shrinking away, while his nose becomes more swollen and polished at the end, like that of an ordinary police-court official. Even a dog-fancier does not like a cherry-nosed fox-terrier. When in the hour of his fall he kept his eye on the double event of both worlds, and gave most excellent advice ;

when his robe and his integrity to heaven were all
that he dared call his own, he could sincerely say—

"Vain pomp and glory of this world, I hate ye!"

In the third or King Edward's room the principal
picture is one from Bridewell Hospital of the young
King granting a charter to the Lord Mayor and
Aldermen of London, and if we are to continue the
customs of our ancestors we should be prepared to
go on our knees in the mud when royalty comes to
open our great show. But some of us are afflicted
with old age, gout, and rheumatics; others are afflicted
with dreadful Radical notions; and others seldom go
on their knees except to say their prayers, and not
always then. Another large picture is of the Earl
of Surrey, who was sent with his father to the Tower
to be beheaded. The son was operated on one day;
the father was to be on the day following, but luckily
the great fat King died in the night, and the father
got off. Shakspere quotes the son as quarrelling
with Cardinal Wolsey and saying he would sheath
his sword in him but for his priest's cloak, and the
Cardinal's reply, "If I do blush, it is to see a noble-
man want manners."

What a model of a subtle, scheming plotter is
the dark Duke of Somerset, the Protector. Here is
the original deed in which Sir Nicholas Moseley buys
from Lacye "the mannor, lordshipp, and seignory of
Manchester for £3500, with all fayres, marketts, tolls,
liberties, customes, priviledjes, free warren," and so on.
The Corporation of Manchester gave £200,000 for
those manorial rights, and their value to-day is considerably greater. In another case is a hat of
Henry's, with slippers of Anne Boleyn. They are
part of the title-deeds of an estate in Hertfordshire

which the King gave to a courtier in right royal
fashion. Giving like a king is giving some one
else's property. It does not suit everybody. The
hat is a peculiar one, with a big green feather. The
King's brains do not appear to have been about the
top of his head. There are many relics of Queen
Katherine Parr, from the place of her death and
burial, that storehouse of antiquities, Sudeley Castle,
near Cheltenham, and a curious love token that
Henry gave to Anne Boleyn, and she gave to the
captain of the guard at her execution, saying, " It
was the first token the King had given her. A
serpent was on it, and a serpent the giver had
proved to her."

The next room is the chamber of horrors. Look
at the wonderful picture of Queen Mary, the stiff
dress, stiffer figure, and stiffest face. How fervently
she would thank God every night that she had
been permitted to do His will and burn a few more
heretics. How like an infuriated cat she looks!
In another picture she is trying to smile. What
a smile! She said the word Calais was engraved
on her heart, but that was probably another slight
mistake.

The next room is for the great and glorious
Queen Elizabeth, of whom the poet wrote

"'The saints must have her — yet a virgin,
    A most unspotted lily."

A nice old blossom she looks. Let us say nothing
about the spots, but think of a besom in a fit, and
wonder at the dress in the large picture lent by the
Duke of Devonshire. What toil and misery and
heartburnings there must have been to many before
she could be got into that dress ; and then, how

U

could she eat her dinner? there is nowhere for it. The elaborate ornamentation on the dress is meant to show that she is the incarnation of everything that is wonderful. School-girls say she left 300 dresses when she died, and said she would give all the wealth of England for another day of life. She had a wonderful show of pearls; the heirs or the priests or some one would look after them, no doubt. And there are two purses that she worked herself when she was a girl; they would hold about a quart each, so she must have had grand expectations even then. They are long blue silk ones that were fashionable when I was a child, for I had one given me with a crooked sixpence in it; but hers would have done for stockings, with a little alteration. See her in the picture by Zucchero, where she certainly looks as if she could not tell the truth by accident, and think of the intricate double-dealing she had to practise all her life—the suspicions of all men, the cruelties to many, the ingratitude to faithful servants, especially those who then and there laid the foundations of England's power at sea, the poor, starving, unfed, unpaid sailors in the greatest sea-fight of all time. Here are the likenesses of the only men she ever loved, if she could love anything but herself — the Earl of Essex, who, in his last hours, sent the ring she had given to him to remind her of her promise to him, but which ring was kept from her until after he was beheaded; and Robert Dudley, Earl of Leicester, her "sweet Robin," who was believed to have died of poison. His first wife, Amy Robsart, is not forgotten. What intrigues, jealousies, hatreds, and murders there were, and what terrible times they seem to have been if we look below the gilt on the gingerbread!

Here also is

"Sidney's sister, Pembroke's mother;
Death, ere thou hast slain another,
Learned, fair, and good as she,
Time shall cast a dart at thee."

Sir Walter Raleigh, author, traveller, soldier, courtier, famed in many ways, yet miserably unsuccessful. His portrait represents him as a plausible-looking man who would probably fail. I should have expected a keener and more resolute look ; here he looks more likely to be the hero of the old tale of the cloak and the mud. Sir Philip Sidney, of Arcadian fame, who sent the cup of water which was brought to him when he was dying to another soldier whose necessity, he said, was greater than his. Cecil, Lord Burghley, the great statesman, who did one thing at a time, and guided the policy of England for forty years. Lord Chancellor Bacon, sometimes called "streaky," from his reputation. Archbishop Parker, whom the old Catholics would not consecrate. He is said to be the missing link in the Apostolical succession of the prelates of the English Church. Drake, the hero of England's Salamis, who singed the Spaniard's beard when he sank a hundred of their ships in the harbour of Cadiz; who sailed round the world, bringing home the *Pelican* literally ballasted with bars of pure gold and precious stones, wealth beyond the dreams of avarice, the spoil the treasure-ships of Spain were taking in fancied security from the pillage of America. The picture fails to give any idea of the man, and his letters and signature in one of the cases are almost illegible to most of us.

A speaking portrait is that of Bess of Hardwick, surrounded by her husbands ; not that she had more than one at once, but she wore them out quickly ; married them for wealth and power, got it, then got without them, and went in again. She looks like a woman who balanced her cash — and very few women can do that, even when they do not like parting with it. This one looks like having the last penny, shrewd and sensible. She built Hardwick, Chatsworth, Bolsover, and other stately halls. In fact, it had been prophesied to her, and she believed it, that she would never die as long as she went on building. Unfortunately there came a severe winter when building could not possibly be done, and the old lady died, or she might have been going on still and showing our rubbishy builders how to do it.

Judging by their portraits, the deaths of the four husbands must have been brought about by various causes. Sir William Cavendish, who, like so many others at that time, got his wealth from the spoils of the religious houses, and adapted his religion to that of his King or Queen, evidently drank too much, and the captain of the guard, who was the third husband, lost all his hair. Her step-son, Talbot, the seventh Earl of Shrewsbury, was married to her daughter, and a punishing time of it the poor fellow seems to have had, for, with such a daughter, who is evidently triumphing over her meek, tame cat of a husband, and such a mother-in-law, his hair has not only come off, but his face looks smacked and scratched all over. I looked in vain for a good picture of Katherine of Aragon, for she was said to have been

> "A constant wife to her husband,
> One that never dreamed a joy beyond his pleasure."

And perhaps that sort is scarce even in these days of "the higher education of women."

There is in a corner a bust that must not be forgotten. It is a cast of the famous one in Stratford-on-Avon church, from a cast taken after death of the greatest man who ever lived, the greatest of all time. As the kings and queens and lords and ladies who were his puppets, and to many exist only in his pages, pass further and further into oblivion, his fame increases. He must increase while they must decrease. They were terrible powers in their day. Where are they now? and who cares for them in comparison with him?

In the chapter on ghosts is an account of Combermere Abbey and the curse that rests on it. Norton Priory in Cheshire was also given in "pure alms" for the poor and sick, and the founder prayed in his deed of gift that whoever should diminish that charity should be punished with Judas and Pilate in hell. There are letters of Henry VIII. ordering his soldiers to hang the abbot and canons without any delay if they refused to give everything up to him. The place is wasted and the charity is gone. Whether Henry is with the aforesaid gentlemen I do not know, but since the times of the Tudors, that is in the last 300 years, we have advanced distinctly nearer to the time spoken of by the prophet, when kings and soldiers and priests would cease to be, and the people would not be burdened by them any more.

CHAPTER XX

COUNTRY SPORTS

" Though we are justices, and doctors, and church-
men, we have some salt of our youth in us ; we
are the sons of women."—JUSTICE SHALLOW.

HEN spending my holidays in July 1897
at the old place, I returned one Saturday
evening from some pilgrimage on the
bicycle to find the youngest grandson
of the house had come to spend the
week-end with his grandmother. This
boy had inherited the sporting instincts of his forefathers in an unusual degree, and he had caught a
stoat and two big rats before he had been as many
hours about the place. As soon as supper was over
he produced a coil of copper wire and began to make
hangs, so I helped at the interesting occupation, and
enjoyed some unconventional conversation, free from
politics, and savouring of sport.

Asking him how he caught the stoat, he said he
was going quietly alongside the wood when he heard
a rabbit squeal, and saw the stoat kill it, then he ran
up to the house for a trap. I remarked it was a
wonder the stoat and rabbit were not both gone when
he got back, but the boy's reply raised him very much
in my estimation : "Oh, I thought of that. I cut a

peg out of the hedge, and pegged the rabbit down by the hind-leg. Then when the stoat pulled at its head he could not move it, and he could not see the peg. He was angry when I got back, and just ran into a hole a bit off and spit at me; so I set the trap by the rabbit's head and went quietly off, and in about two minutes he was in fast enough. What did I cover the trap with? Nothing; why should I? The stoat never saw a trap before; he did not know what it was. If he had got out once he would have been bad to catch again, but I didn't let him get out alive." Then I asked if he had ever caught a weasel asleep, and the answer came pat: ": No, did you?" Discussing the merits of various modes of trapping vermin, we sat on the old oak settle that would have many a curious tale to tell if it could speak, and there we made hangs. Perhaps there is no harm in giving the *modus operandi*, as not many poachers will read this. Put two large nails loosely in a board, about half a yard apart. Then fasten the end of the wire to one nail, twist it to the other and back again several times, then break it off and fasten the other end. Take the nails with the wire on them from the board, twist them round several times, and remove them. Then pass the loop at one end of the wire through the other loop, and there is a running noose which, if set on the ground and made fast by a peg, will catch and hang anything that gets into it and struggles.

Then I was told that Pandy had learned to set trout, and that the trout would then go under the bank of the brook, and could be tickled easily, some beauties having been taken. Who was Pandy? "Why, the dog, of course." Where did he get his name from? "Why, we gave it him, of course."

What about the bull? "Oh, he wanner stout, we feart him;" and the boy lapsed into the dialect of the country in his excitement about the bull. Stout, in that district, means of good pluck or determination, and bulls often object to lads or dogs prowling about the fields. His tale about the bull was somewhat as follows : "Oh, it was fun, fighting the bull. He used to run us off from fishing, so we made up to try if he were stout. There were three of us, and we'd two good catapults and a sling. We went higher up the brook and filled our pockets with smooth stones. Then, when we got in the field, Billy came for us, roaring and hiking the ground, so we spread us-selves out, one a one side, and one a one, and one i' th' middle, then when he come for us we let fly ; by Jove, didn't the stones bounce off him. It's no use 'ittin' a bull on the 'ed ; 'it 'im on th' legs, and aim low ; a good crack on the knee does fetch a bellow. When he rushed at one of us, 'e ran, and t'others closed round his flank, and, by Jove, didn't we sling 'em in. We feart him at last, but, oh, how we did sweat! Oh, it was fun!"

What says the old song? "David and Goliah they went out to fight a battle," but here were three Davids ; was not that rather hard on the bull ? It seemed so until the explanation was given, that if the real Goliath had been a bull that stone of David's would not have sunk in his forehead ; it would have bounced off again.

Then the talk gets on to other branches of sport, and the boy innocently tells us that he had taken home a young gamecock from his grandmother's, but this cockerel was bashful, and would not fight, so he kept it in a barn with some "littler" cocks that it could master, and sharpened its spurs with a bit of glass. Then, when it got its pluck up, he took it to where a neighbour's cock came through the hedge. When both cocks crew he set his down, and it soon killed the other cock; so he repeated the performance with another neighbour's. Then it killed two of their own cocks, and the boy said his mother got angry, and would not let him keep a gamecock that had sharp spurs; so he looked very sorrowful, not on account of what he had done, but for the forbidden sport he had missed, and I gave him sixpence to comfort him and get another tale—

"For the thoughts of my youth come back to me
With a joy that is almost pain."

The dog came in to say there was a rat under the turkey pen, and the meeting was adjourned for another small hunt. Mr. Rat was killed, and the boy looked very thoughtful as he set his lips tight and considered the placing of various traps for cats, rats, stoats, or foxes; and then to bed for the sleep of the innocent and the hunter.

Next morning at church time that boy was missing. No one knew what had become of him. He seemed very well and hearty at breakfast, and if temporary illness had seized him it was all gone by dinner-time. Boys seldom forget the time then. In the evening came the happy, peaceful occupation locally known as "looking the things." That means a walk round the fields, inspecting anything or everything, judging the crops, noting the cattle, and prognosticating the weather. We soon came across a rabbit in a hang, and then another. No one seemed to know when these hangs had been set. They were only made the previous evening, and it is not always good to ask too many questions. When Isaac told Esau, "Take thy weapons, thy quiver, and thy bow, and go out to the field and take me venison, and make me savoury meat such as I love," it may be remembered that Jacob brought it; and when his father asked that paragon of patriarchs, "How is it that thou hast found it so quickly, my son?" the ready lie came, "Because the Lord thy God brought it to me." These hangs, or the setting of them, certainly seemed to have been blessed, for there were soon more rabbits than the boy's orthodox poacher's cudgel of a holly plant could carry. The orthodox cudgel is somewhat less and not so murderous-looking as an Irishman's shillelagh, though it is rather knobby. This one was thrown at a rabbit, in a form not quite as an Australian throws his boomerang, but quite as effectively. Then there was a commotion with an old buck rabbit that had dragged away the hang and peg, but the dog followed it to the hedge and caught it. Finally, there were thirteen rabbits taken, all of them being legged or hocked and squozen. Those skilled in venery use the rabbit's teeth to cut the skin of the leg above the hock, and everything seemed to be done in proper and orthodox fashion. Then came a sort of wardance, or Indian's dance of triumph, over the prey. Here was food enough and to spare: young rabbits for pies, half-grown ones for roasting, old bucks and does to be sold to the higgler to take to those ignorant townsfolks who don't know old from young. A couple of old ones might do for the schoolmaster or parson, and then the boy may be let off some of his impositions. Always remember the doctrine of absolution.

My thoughts go back on the many enigmas of life. Here we are, on a lovely summer's evening, in a most beautiful country, with the setting sun lighting up miles and miles of fertile fields and woods, killing rabbits and thinking of them as food. As we get older and more civilised, we cannot kill and eat things as we did when we were young. The instincts bred in me from generations of forefathers who, from the time that man first appeared on the earth, have more or less lived by the chase and from pastoral pursuits, struggle with a higher civilisation. If we did not eat the rabbits, something else would eat them. That is certain, and it is not my fault that I am not adapted for a vegetarian. I live mainly on the produce of our own cows, poultry, and garden. In my father's time we lived largely on game and rabbits in the shooting season. In his father's time they lived almost entirely on the produce of their own fields and flocks and herds. A sweet pastoral simplicity. Perhaps one of the few things my grandfather may have bought a hundred years ago would have been a pound of tea with the price of a sheep. We cannot, if we wished, put our inherited instincts away all at once; and finally our higher thoughts succumb, and we enjoy a rabbit pie.

The boy is in his glory, in bliss unalloyed and triumphant. Thirteen rabbits and one cat from eighteen 'hangs! He has no qualms of conscience about the day or the deed. He says the rabbits want eating, for they eat the crops; and as for the old cat, it was only after poaching, and got served "jolly well right." He could not catch them any other day, for he must go back to school early in the morning. The Rev. Mr. Spankem may say a lot, but he won't do anything if he gets a couple, and old bucks are good enough for him. Then, as we wend our way homewards, this boy asks if there is any game, or sport, or anything to do at Didsbury, and says, "By Jove, if I brought old Pandy and the ferrets we would give them Didsbury rats snuff. But I must go back to school in the morning, for they say I'm very back'ard in my learning, though I am in decimals now; but I don't like decimals, I'd liefer cotch rots."

The above appeared as a newspaper article on the eve of a contested municipal election, and it brought forth many replies and inquiries, both public and private, some of which I remarked upon as follows :—

I write a little more about the rabbit-catching, for some correspondents seem to have a genuine wish for more information.

One woman wrote me a most angry, scolding letter for my "shameful cruelty," but she did not specify what was to be done with the rabbits. One of the City Fathers spoke to me about it even in the august Council-chamber when the concentrated wisdom of the city was solemnly inaugurating the Lord Mayor, and said, "Yu'v bin writin' about stowuts. What is stowuts?" Then, without waiting for a reply, for I was trying to collect my wandering thoughts, he added, as he turned a peppermint over in his mouth, and pointed to a newly-elected member who was coming in, "I'm afeart we shan 'ave some trouble wi' them common beggars." This was said as the object of his scorn looked pale and intellectual, being a member of the progressive party and a B.A. of an university.

There was a proverb we wrote out in the copy-books when we were boys, "*Poeta nascitur, non fit*," which means, a poet, orator, rat-catcher, or man of genius in any capacity is born, not made; or, in

THE FAMILY RAT-CATCHER.

other words, that for a man to excel in any pursuit he must have great natural aptitude for it; or, again, in other words, it should be born and bred in him. My interest was aroused in the boy who caught so many rabbits when he told me how he caught the stoat. He said he was going quietly along. There is a very great deal in that word "quietly" for all lovers of nature. Then he had the forethought, which was much beyond his years, to peg the rabbit down by the hind-leg before he left it, not otherwise to meddle with it, and on his return to set the trap by its head. The weasel tribe always fly at the head of their prey, and the fore-part of the rabbit had not been touched. Hence success. The hangs or snares for the rabbits were set with the same knowledge and forethought, or they would not have had the same success. They were set in the likeliest places, and without disturbing the game by much trampling of the grass, or noise, or smell. Some gamekeepers, with their tobacco and gin and various other odours, smell worse than any old dog-fox. The best place to set a hang is where the rabbit's path in the grass narrows and the long grass grows over and round it. Then set the peg in the long herbage where it is not seen, and without disturbing anything, and take your luck.

The success lay in the skill of the trapper, just as one angler may catch fish while another cannot, one man may shoot game while another cannot. The man who is simply a good shot may not be good at finding the game. The boy knew "the lie of the land." That was worth a deal. He was also lucky, for time and chance happen to us all. If I understand Darwin's doctrine of Pangenesis aright, this is another instance where the accumulated heritages from an endless line of sporting forefathers gave this lad a

double dose of the sporting instinct. It does not
follow that all his kindred are the same, but some of
us are in a greater or lesser degree. I always wanted
to be a farmer, and lead the life of a country gentleman, but I was long since taught and made to see that
I must earn my own living in a town, and have the
other for a recreation. I still have to circumvent the
wily rat even in Manchester, for in Hanging Ditch
they are as hard-faced as the merchants themselves.

Though I have written above of the sporting forefathers, I do not wish to be misunderstood or to go
into genealogies. This boy is of the sixth generation
that I know has been bred in another of the old
country halls, that is Walford (probably derived from
Well ford) Hall, in the parish of Standon. In that
house my father's mother was born and married and
died. The further back we go for her ancestors, the
more primitive would they be. My antiquarian studies
and hardness of belief, engendered by much bargaining, make me distrust the emblazoned pedigrees with
descents from kings and saints ; but the men who in
unbroken descent lived on the land from prehistoric
times until now, from the time when the primeval savage
caught his own game and fish, must have endowed
their progeny with sporting instincts, and generally
with sound, hardy bodies also. Two good old country
proverbs say, " Breed is stronger than pasture," and
" What's bred in the bone will never come out of the
flesh."

Here is another little sporting reminiscence. Thirty-
five years ago the uncle of this boy and myself went
shooting. The former's keen eye detected a hole in
marly ground made by a peg, with signs of nets. He
said poachers must have been there very recently, and
we found two. There was a chase, a scuffle, a fight,

and we took home sundry bags and nets, two ferrets, and six rabbits as the spoil of the spoilers, otherwise the poachers, who ultimately got "three months" as their share of the day's work. When his son's arm was being dressed—for he had been hardly mauled— my late uncle, who stood six feet three, and was well known all over that country, gave us the following advice, which, though he knew it not, corresponded almost exactly with that given by Napoleon Bona- parte to his generals : " If ever you do have to hit a man, hit him with all the strength you've got in your body, for you cannot hurt him too much."

The bit of cock-fighting the lad spoke about in his artless manner was very old-fashioned.   He kept a gamecock with "littler" cocks, and sharpened its spurs with a bit of glass.   These game fowls have been bred pure in unbroken continuity of descent for above a hundred years.   Men may come and men may go, and they breed new varieties with wonderful names and wonderful reputations, but none of them would do for a patch on the old fighting game for use and beauty, and none are fit to compare with them.

A Steeplechase.

Once only has any horse that I have bred and ridden about home appeared in a public steeplechase where the fences have been in accordance with the National Hunt rules.   When my favourite mare Blink Bonny was three years old she employed her time with having a foal, which I called Macaroni, after its grandsire, a winner of the Derby.   As the foal grew up, I rode him a little ; but having no use for him, I bartered him away to my cousins at Buerton

Hall. As we had very little money, the bartering was done in a primitive fashion, and took up the greater part of a day. Eventually I had "swopped" the horse for a newly-calved cow, ten big cheese, and a brace of partridges, which were thrown in for luck. The cow we kept for her milk, the cheese we sold,

TWO GOOD SERVANTS.

and the partridges we ate. The new owner of the horse, Mr. John Nunnerley, rode him hunting a little, and then entered him for the steeplechase at the local hunt meeting at Woore. He was sent to be trained, but, much to our surprise, the trainer said he was unsafe and dangerous, and returned him shortly before the

time of the races. A professional jockey was then
got from Keele, but a few minutes before the race
came off he refused to mount, as he had been told
the horse would kill any man. We became suspicious
of foul play, but in the dilemma the only thing to do
was to let his stable lad ride him. This lad was
only a country "gorby," who had scarcely seen a
race, much less ridden in one ; but he jumped at
the thought, and rode well. He was rigged up and
mounted, and in a hurricane of wind and rain I got
to the top of the grand stand to see what I could of
what was to me the most interesting horse-race that
I ever did see. I did not make a single bet, but, all
the same, I was most interested in the betting, for, as
a business man, I knew that was the barometer of
public opinion, and although sharpers might "sharp"
their sharpest, there were others as sharp as they.
After a long delay in a downpour of rain, which
was much against Macaroni, the race began, odds of
ten to one being laid against him. The course was
three times past the stand, with a brook about a hundred yards before the straight run in, and the double
fence, known as "the grave," shortly after it. First
over the water jump came Mac, and past the stand
fully fifty yards ahead of all the other horses ; the odds
against him dropped to seven to one. Over "the
grave" he flew like a bird, two others came down, and
one was galloping about riderless. "Four to one
Macaroni!" went up from the ring. "Four to one!
four to one! three to one Macaroni!" The odds were
dropping fast as through the wood and the hollow he
came with a long lead of four or five others. A second
time he skimmed the water like a swallow on a summer's eve, and "Evens Macaroni!" was yelled by the
ring. As he came past the grand stand above a hundred

yards ahead there went up a hoarse roar from the betting
men, " Macaroni agen the field!" and I saw more than
one bookmaker refuse to lay against him. Then came
another roar, "'The grave' has him!" for the good
horse stumbled at the broken fence at "the grave," and
the lad, who was worse done than he was, tumbled off;
so good-bye, Macaroni. But some one helped him up
and sent them off again after the others. At least
three hundred yards had been lost, but a grand finish
had to be fought out. The two leaders had a long
start, a third disappeared at the next water jump, a
fourth Mac passed, and he finished third, with good
hopes of having won if the race or the time had been
a little more. The jockey's face was streaming with
blood from his fall. He and the horse received quite
an ovation, for an unknown horse and rider won the
stakes for the third, and would certainly have been first
but for one of the chances that happen to us all.

EXERCISE.

CHAPTER XXI

CRITICS AND QUERISTS

*" Let me have no lying, it becomes
none but tradesmen."*—AUTOLYCUS.

OME of the criticisms that I have re-
ceived of the articles on the folk-lore
beliefs and old customs of our neighbourhood are amusing and instructive
from their originality, and as showing
the widely-diverse minds they reflect.
I have letters from all sorts and conditions of men
(and women too sometimes) with extraordinary remarks and requests. Five came in one week, one
being from a Romish priest, one from the chairman
of the County Council, one from a learned antiquary,
and one from the chairman of the county magistrates,
and they were all addressed to the Rev. Fletcher
Moss, some of them beginning " Reverend Sir."

One day I was abruptly asked what I meant by
insulting the Pope. I meekly replied that I was not
aware I had insulted him, and certainly had no wish
to do so. " Then what do you mean by writing such
nonsense about the Pope granting a patron saint to
the lawyers? It is an insult to the Pope, and an
insult to the Catholic faith, and we'll not stand it,"

said my inquisitor, waxing wrath. Again I meekly submitted that there was no insult to the Pope. On the contrary, if he got out of a difficult position with what have been termed necessary evils, it was evidence of his sagacity, and if the lawyer's natural instinct took him to the devil, why should others complain? The lawyer would probably argue that he wished to help the poor oppressed devil, whom the great archangel was ill-treating, thereby qualifying to be a saint himself, or securing a good patron saint. But my inquisitor only became more excited and angry, finally assuring me that if I insulted the Catholic religion in that way some of the boys would break my head; so I thought it better to leave him to his own countrymen.

Another party complained that I had written disrespectfully of a chief constable, thereby casting a slur on all who inherited his wealth, for any remarks on perquisites, "pecks of watches," or ill-gotten gains, were disagreeable to relatives. I certainly was sorry to hurt the feelings of any one whom I had never seen, but it was refreshing to find there were some people, even elderly men, who regard the police as little inferior to the parsons, and who look upon any chief constable with as much awe as they would on a dean or a bishop. This one seemed to assume that they were all immaculate, and to write disparagingly of any was like railing on the Lord's anointed, and in itself was evidence of bad character. Finally I was assured by my newly-found inquisitor in the strongest possible language that I was everything that was bad, and that even my thoughts showed me to be nothing but a—low Radical!

One day I was riding on the box-seat of a 'bus, and was considerably surprised at the 'bus-driver abruptly telling me that I had never written an article upon something or other that he had expected. He was a sympathetic and friendly critic, who seemed much interested in me and the articles.

A lawyer came with smooth, hard questions—what a numerous and subtle breed these sons of Zeruiah are! They want all the law and the profits, while I have no profits and but little folk-lore. This one says: "Why, Moss, you've been writing about ghosts. You must be going dotty; I thought you had some sense." He wanted to argue the matter at the Old Parsonage some night, but I preferred the ghosts. Even in the august Council-chamber I was asked one day three separate times by those "potent, grave, and reverend signiors," the City Fathers, if there were really those ghosts I wrote about, and could I show them one. As if I kept ghosts in my pocket like spirits in a flask. I explained there should be a fitting frame of mind, and the Council-chamber was not a likely place for a ghost unless it were deaf or had lost its way.

A neighbour who was travelling happened to say he lived at Didsbury, and some one said to him, "You live at Didsbury, do you? Then probably you know the Rev. Fletcher Moss, do you? Ever hear him preach?" My friend, who is not always as polite as he might be, merely replied, "Yes, rather." "Then may I ask you how he does preach?" was the second query; and the answer to it, "Oh, awful rot."

There are ministers of religion who complain of anything being written slightingly of the devil or other religious subject. They send tracts to show that it would be a very false hope for any sinner to hope to escape the devil by not believing in him, therefore he should always be treated with proper respect.

The pedigree hunters are much more numerous than is commonly supposed. Few of them can
give any particulars beyond their grandfathers, and
yet they write to me for pedigrees, with interesting
accounts of family history. One of them never had a
father or knew anything about him, so his pedigree
was very short. It seemed he had written because
there was a man of the same name whom I had mentioned as being hanged in chains on Stockport moor
about a century ago.

Then there was a well-known literary gent who
had taken to cycling about the time that I wrote the
account of my day's journey into Staffordshire. He
met me in the street, and said, " I saw your article on
bicycling, and before beginning it I said to myself,
' Now, if he does not own to a tumble or two, I won't
believe him ;' but when I saw you had had four tumbles,
and smashed your machine at Talk-o'-th'-Hill, I felt it
was all true, and was delighted."

One day an old man called with a present for me,
a piece of a quaint silken kerchief. An old woman
had sent it, saying her uncle (I think his name was
Dan Collier) had fought at Waterloo, and brought
back that piece of figured silk from the body of some
officer who was killed there. She had no friends or
relatives who would treasure it when she was gone,
and therefore she asked me to keep it. So the
woman's mite is labelled, and this is the acknowledgment for it.

One evening I was much amused with a young
artist who called to ask if he could make sketches of
the church and of my house. We were entire strangers
to one another ; and he showed me some of his work,
amongst it being a most gorgeous coat of arms, "gleam-
ing in purple and gold," which, he said, he had to

paint on the backs of chairs to earn a living, and as it was his family shield of arms it was rather hard on him. Therefore I asked him his name, which we will call Barrister; and on hearing it, I asked which branch of the family he was from. He told me they were an old county family from Cumberland, who had come over with William the Conqueror, and for some time had been settled in Ireland. Pressing him for particulars, as I was getting interested in the case, he said his grandfather had come from Cumberland, where he was born, and had inherited large estates, with the family arms. I said, "Oh no! the man you are speaking about was born in Redbank, Manchester, and never had any arms but what he bought." Then he replied, "It must have been his father;" and again I said, "Oh no! his father was from Hale Barns, the little house near the chapel; and his father, again, came from Lindow Moss, near the Quakers' meeting-house. None of them had any arms." That seemed to take his breath, for he said, "Mr. Moss, you seem to know more of my family than I do myself." "Very likely," I replied. "If old John Barrister was your grandfather, you are the son of —— ——." Then he said he would have a plain shield of his own, with a hammer, and hammer his own way, and asked if I could say what was the derivation of the family name. The answer was simple, but not pleasing, "A man fond of going to law." After that we discussed art and churches, and from some remarks he made I hazarded a guess, and said, "If you are so fond of sketching old churches, and are, as you say, a strong Tory, you will probably some day turn Roman Catholic." It was then my turn to be surprised, for he answered, "I am one;" and his great-great-grandfather, whose portrait I have, was a Quaker. Altogether it was an interesting interview.

The strangest querist I have had was a somewhat ill-nurtured and desponding-looking man who called at the Old Parsonage six times before he found me. In a strong American accent he asked after the ancestry of the Brundretts, a family who have been long resident in the neighbourhood; and, in reply to my inquiries, I learnt that he was descended from them, though he came from Idaho. In my history of Didsbury he had seen that Widow Ann Brundrett, from Hardy, was "the first corpse drawn in Didsbury hearse," and he was anxious in his inquiries about his ancestors. Gradually I learnt that he was anxious as to their baptism, and would not be satisfied with the validity of the baptism according to the Church, even if it were recorded in the parish registers. Becoming more pointed in my inquiries, I learnt that he wanted to have all his ancestors baptized; and when I asked, "How can you baptize any one who has been dead a hundred years, and whose dust is probably dispersed?" he quietly answered, "By proxy. Yes, by proxy. I would be immersed for them. Total immersion. I am a Latter-Day Saint, from Salt Lake City. We do not believe in your baptism, but we believe that Jesus said unto Nicodemus, 'Ye must be born again of water and the spirit.' I am come from America to search for all my family and kindred, and when I go back I shall be baptized for all of them that I can find. Yes, friend, total immersion for each one of them separately." Then he proceeded to give me tracts to convert me, and appeared to have many pockets, each containing different tracts, all of which I read or tried to read; but as so many people ask me about their

pedigrees and ancestry, and some trace their descent
up to Charlemagne and Wodin and the semi-mythical
gods of antiquity, I thought what a dreadful thing it
would be if they got converted into being Latter-Day
Saints, and had to suffer total immersion for each one
of the ancestors of which they were so proud.

LONG-EARED OWLS AT THE OLD PARSONAGE.

Index

Printed by BALLANTYNE, HANSON & CO.
Edinburgh & London

A History of
The Old Parish of Cheadle in Cheshire

And the Hamlet of Gatley in Etchells

Profusely Illustrated. Price 7s. 6d. Nett. Postage 4½d.

The Times.

" A popular history of an interesting parish, well illustrated, and dealing, as all such histories should, not merely with church and buildings, with personal and historical associations, but with local folk and folk-lore, and with local natural history."

The Athenæum.

" It is difficult to know exactly what to say of 'A History of Cheadle in Cheshire,' by Mr. Fletcher Moss. . . . As a son of the soil he has had means of accumulating information on diverse subjects which would never have come to the ears of one who, in many other respects, might have been far better fitted for the work. . . . We gather from various good stories which Mr. Moss tells . . . a pathetic story about a witch named Bella, told in very good dialect. . . . We can speak with unmixed praise of the series of photographs of the old half-timber houses by which the book is illustrated."

The Manchester Courier.

" . . . The whole of the volume is a proof of the large amount of valuable material waiting for conversion into such fascinating literary chapters as are given in 'The Chronicles of Cheadle.' But the author must not lack the keen observation, sense of humour, above all, the vigorous and inherently picturesque style of the writer who has done so much for the southern suburbs of Manchester."

The Manchester City News.

" . . . Excellent accounts, admirably illustrated, follow of the church and halls, with a mass of curious and interesting information concerning them. The concluding chapters deal with the folk of the district and its natural history, the last most excellent. Mr. Moss's book will probably remain the standard authority on the subject, . . . and the illustrations, varied and well chosen, are an attractive representation of an interesting neighbourhood."

The Cheshire County News.

" . . Simply invaluable to all who care to know the history of the village. The book is well got up with the highest workmanship, full of humour wherever humour is possible ; there are witty raps at abuses and evils, trenchant criticism, and good temper pervades the whole volume."

A History of Didsbury

Also

Didisburye in the '45

Price 6s. each Nett.

The Manchester Guardian.

"There are few places whose history will not be found interesting, if only you are lucky enough to meet with some one who knows all about them and is willing to impart his knowledge. These qualifications Mr. Moss undoubtedly possesses as regards Didsbury. . . . If there be such a thing as the genius of the place, he is probably better entitled than any one else to be considered its incarnation. . . . The book is, moreover, full of salt – touches of homely and sometimes rather pungent humour expressed in racy vernacular. We rather like the flavouring."

The Manchester Courier.

". . . Pleasant, chatty, and entertaining, and cannot fail to be interesting to Lancashire men generally, . . . brightened by the numerous anecdotes, wise sayings, and old rustic phrases of the people."

The Manchester Examiner.

". . . Pleasant books of one of Lancashire's oldest villages, free from personal bias, free from misstatements, and free from tediousness. . . . A vivid picture of life in Didsbury in the times which are rapidly passing away."

The Manchester City News.

". . . More delightful he could not possibly have been, nor could he have produced anything more racy or more genuinely characteristic in the description of the old-fashioned natives. Whilst the record is delightfully chatty and free and unconventional, there is no lack of the solid information which goes to the making of a trustworthy history. . . . He brightens his narrative with abundance of anecdotes, particularly the odd sayings of the ancient natives. Almost every page tempts to a quotation. . . . We take leave of a charming book with reluctance, . . . and higher praise we could not give."

The Cheshire County News.

". . . Intensely attractive. Who has not longed for a real history that would tell us how the people talked and felt and lived. . . . Full of interest to the lover of local lore and to the England of years ago."

Any of these books may be bought from the Author. The Set of three, sent carriage paid, for £1.

AUTHOR AND PUBLISHER—

FLETCHER MOSS, THE OLD PARSONAGE, DIDSBURY.